Wedding of the Year

Saying 'I do' in the spotlight!

Eloise Miller and Laurel Sommers have
their lives turned upside down by
Melissa Sommers's celebrity wedding.

With Eloise promoted to maid of honour,
and Laurel's wedding planning skills
pushed to their very limits, the last thing
these two need is for the best man and
the groom's brother to intervene…

But as the media descends the headlines
get more scandalous. Can Eloise and Laurel
pull off the wedding of the year without a hitch?

Find out in…

Slow Dance with the Best Man
Proposal for the Wedding Planner

You won't want to miss this sparkling
duet from Sophie Pembroke!

D0496164

PROPOSAL FOR THE WEDDING PLANNER

BY
SOPHIE PEMBROKE

MILLS & BOON

First Published in Great Britain 2017
By Mills & Boon, an imprint of HarperCollins*Publishers*
1 London Bridge Street, London, SE1 9GF

© 2017 Sophie Pembroke

ISBN: 978-0-263-92279-0

23-0317

Our policy is to use papers that are natural, renewable and recyclable produc... ...g and
manuf... ...s of
the co...

Printe...
by CPI...

Sophie Pembroke has been reading and writing romance ever since she read her first Mills & Boon at university, so getting to write them for a living is a dream come true! Sophie lives in a little Hertfordshire market town in the UK with her scientist husband and her incredibly imaginative six-year-old daughter. She writes stories about friends, family and falling in love—usually while drinking too much tea and eating homemade cakes. She also keeps a blog at www.sophiepembroke.com.

For Ali, Ally and Ann Marie

CHAPTER ONE

Laurel Sommers stepped back from the road as a London taxi sped past through the puddle at the edge of the kerb, splashing icy water over her feet, and decided this was all her father's fault, really.

Well, the fact that she was stuck in London, waiting in the freezing cold for a car to take her back to where she *should* be—Morwen Hall, the gothic stately home turned five-star hotel in the countryside an hour and a half's drive out of the city—was clearly Melissa's fault. But if their father hadn't wanted to have his cake and eat it for their entire childhoods then her half-sister probably wouldn't hate her enough to make her life this miserable.

Sighing, Laurel clasped the bag holding the last-minute replacement wedding favours that Melissa had insisted she collect that afternoon closer to her body as a stream of cars continued to rush past. It was three days after Christmas and the sales were in full swing. London was caught in that strange sense of anticipation that filled the space between December the twenty-fifth and New Year's Eve—full of possibilities for the year ahead and the lives that might be lived in it.

Any other year Laurel would be as caught up in that

sense of opportunity as anyone. She usually used these last few days of the year to reflect on the year just gone and plan her year ahead. Plan how to be better, to achieve more, how to succeed at last. To be *enough*.

Just last year she'd plotted out her schedule for starting her own business organising weddings. She'd been a wedding planner at a popular company for five years, and had felt with quiet optimism that it was time to go it alone—especially since she'd been expecting to be organising her *own* wedding, and Benjamin had always said he liked a woman with ambition.

So she'd planned, she'd organised, and she'd done it—she had the business cards to prove it. Laurel's Weddings was up and running. And, even if she wasn't planning her own wedding, she *did* have her first celebrity client on the books…which was why this year that optimism would have to wait until January the first.

All she had to do was make it through her half-sister's New Year's Eve wedding without anything going terribly wrong and she would be golden. Melissa was big news in Hollywood right now—presumably because she was a lot nicer to directors than she was to wedding planners—and her wedding was being covered in one of those glossy magazines Laurel only ever had time to read at the hairdresser's. If this went well her business would boom and she could stop worrying about exactly *how* she was going to earn enough to pay back the small business loan she'd only just qualified for.

She might not have the husband she'd planned on, and she might not be a Hollywood star like Melissa, but once her business went global no one would be able to say she wasn't good enough.

But of course that meant rushing around, catering

to Melissa's every whim—even when that whim meant a last-minute trip back to the capital to replace the favours they'd spent two weeks deciding on because they were 'an embarrassment' all of a sudden.

And, as much as she'd been avoiding thinking about it, a peaceful wedding also meant dealing with seeing Benjamin again. Which was just the cherry on top of the icing on top of the wedding cake—wasn't it?

Another car—big and black and shiny—slowed as it reached the kerb beside her. Lauren felt hope rising. She'd asked the last of the cars ferrying wedding guests from Heathrow to swing into the city and pick her up on its way to Morwen Hall, rather than going around the M25. It would mean the passenger inside would have a rather longer journey, but she was sort of hoping he wouldn't notice. Or mind having company for it.

Since the last guest was the groom Riley's brother—Dan Black, her soon to be half-brother-in-law, or something—she really hoped he didn't object. It would be nice at least to start out on good terms with her new family—especially since her existing family was generally on anything but. Her mother still hadn't forgiven her for agreeing to organise Melissa's wedding. Or, as she called her, 'That illegitimate trollop daughter of your father's mistress.'

Unsurprisingly, her mother wasn't on the guest list.

Dan Black wasn't a high-maintenance Hollywood star, at least—as far as Laurel could tell. In fact Melissa hadn't told her anything about him at all. Probably because if he couldn't further her career then Melissa wasn't interested. All Laurel had to go on was the brief couple of lines Melissa and Riley had scribbled next to every name on the guest list, so Laurel would understand why they were important and why they'd been invited, and the address she had sent the invitation to.

Black Ops Stunts. Even the follow-up emails she'd sent to Dan when arranging the journey and his accommodation had been answered by the minimum possible number of words and no extraneous detail.

The man was a mystery. But one Laurel really didn't have time to solve this week.

The car came to a smooth stop, and the driver hopped out before Laurel could even reach for the door handle.

'Miss,' he said with a brief nod, and opened the door to the back seat for her. She slid gratefully into her seat, smiling at the other occupant of the car as she did so.

'I *do* hope you don't mind sharing your car with me, Mr Black,' she said, trying to sound professional and grateful and like family all at the same time. She was pretty sure the combination didn't work, but until she had any better ideas she was sticking with it.

'Dan,' he said, holding out a hand.

Laurel reached out to take it, and as she looked up into his eyes the words she'd been about to speak caught in her throat.

She'd seen this man's brother Riley a hundred times—on the screen at the cinema, on movie posters, on her telly, in magazines, on the internet, and even over Skype when they'd been planning the wedding. Melissa hadn't *actually* brought him home to meet the family yet, but Laurel couldn't honestly blame her for that. Still, she knew his face, and his ridiculously handsome, all-American good looks.

Why hadn't it occurred to her that his older brother might be just as gorgeous?

Dan didn't have the same clean, wholesome appeal

that Riley did, Laurel would admit. But what he *did* have was a whole lot hotter.

His hair was closer cropped, with a touch of grey at the temples, and his jaw was covered in dark stubble, but his bright blue eyes were just like his brother's. No, she decided, looking more closely, they weren't. Riley's were kind and warm and affable. Dan's were sharp and piercing, and currently looking a bit amused...

Probably because she still hadn't said anything.

'I'm Laurel,' she said quickly as the driver started the engine again and pulled out. 'Your half-sister-in-law-to-be.'

'My...*what*, now?' His voice was deeper too, his words slower, more drawling.

'I'm Melissa's half-sister.'

'Ah,' Dan said, and from that one syllable Laurel was sure he already knew her whole story. Or at least her part in *Melissa's* story.

Most people did, she'd found.

Either they'd watched one of Melissa's many tearful interviews on the subject of her hardships growing up without a father at home, or they'd read the story online on one of her many fan sites. Everybody knew how Melissa had been brought up almost entirely by her single mother until the age of sixteen, while her father had spent most of his time with his other family in the next town over, only visiting when he could get away from his wife and daughter.

People rarely asked any questions about that other family, though. Or what had happened to them when her father had decided he'd had enough and walked out at last, to start his 'real' life with Melissa and her mother.

Laurel figured that at least that meant no one cared

about her—least of all Melissa—so there were no photos of *her* on the internet, and no one could pick her out of a line-up. It was bad enough that her friends knew she was related to the beautiful, famous, talented Melissa Sommers. She didn't think she could bear strangers stopping her in the street to ask about her sister. Wondering why Laurel, with all the family advantages she'd had, couldn't be as beautiful, successful or brilliant as Melissa.

'So you're also the wedding planner, right?' Dan asked, and Laurel gave him a grateful smile for the easy out.

'That's right. In fact, that's why I'm up in town today. Melissa…uh…changed her mind about the wedding favours she wanted.' That sounded better than her real suspicions—that Melissa was just coming up with new ways to torment her—right?

It wasn't just the table favours, of course. When Melissa had first asked her to organise her wedding Laurel had felt pride swelling in her chest. She'd truly believed—for about five minutes—that her sister not only trusted in her talent, but also wanted to use her wedding to reach out an olive branch between the two of them at last.

Obviously that had been wishful thinking. Or possibly a delusion worthy of those of Melissa's fans who wrote to her asking for her hand in marriage, never knowing that she tore up the letters and laughed.

'She's not making it easy, huh?' Dan asked.

Laurel pasted on a smile. 'You know brides! I wouldn't have gone into this business if I didn't know how to handle them.'

'Right.'

He looked her over again and she wondered what he saw. A competent wedding planner, she hoped. She hadn't had as much contact with Dan over the last few months as she had with the best man or the bridesmaids. But still, there'd been the invitation and the hotel bookings, and the flights and the car transfer—albeit she'd gatecrashed that. She'd been pleasant and efficient the whole way, even in the face of his one-word responses, and she really hoped he recognised that.

Because she knew what else he had to be thinking—what everyone thought when they looked at her through the lens of 'being Melissa Sommers's sister.' That Laurel had definitely got the short straw in the genetic lottery.

Melissa, as seen on billboards and movie screens across the world, was tall, willowy, blonde and beautiful. She'd even been called the twenty-first-century Grace Kelly.

Laurel, on the other hand—well, she wasn't.

Oh, she was cute enough, she knew—petite and curvy, with dark hair and dark eyes—but 'cute' wasn't beautiful. It wasn't striking. She had the kind of looks that just disappeared when she stood beside Melissa—not least because she was almost a whole head shorter.

No, Laurel had resigned herself to being the opposite of everything Melissa was. Which also made her a less awful person, she liked to hope.

Dan was still watching her in silence, and words bubbled up in her throat just to fill the empty air.

'But you know this isn't just *any* wedding. I mean, Melissa and Riley wanted a celebrity wedding extravaganza, so that's what I've tried to give them.'

'I see,' Dan replied, still watching.

Laurel babbled on. 'Obviously she wanted it at Morwen Hall—she has a strong connection to the place, you see. And Eloise—she's the manager there...well, the interim manager, I think... Anyway, you'll meet her soon... What was I saying?'

'I have no idea.'

'Sorry. I'm babbling.'

'That's okay.'

'Oh!' Laurel bounced in the car seat a little as she remembered where she'd been going with the conversation. 'Anyway. I was just about to say that there's lots planned for the next few days—with the welcome drinks tonight, the Frost Fair, and then the stag and hen dos tomorrow, local tours for the guests on Friday before the rehearsal dinner...'

'And the actual wedding at some point, I assume?' Dan added, eyebrows raised.

'Well, of course.' Laurel felt her skin flush hot for a moment. 'I was working chronologically. From my Action List.'

'I understand. Sounds like you have plenty to keep you busy this week.'

Laurel nodded, her head bobbing up and down at speed. 'Absolutely. But that's good! I mean, if this wedding goes well... It's the first one I've arranged since I started my own business, you see, so it's kind of a big deal. And it's not like I'm in the wedding party at all—'

Neither was he, she realised suddenly. Wasn't that a little odd? I mean, she knew why her sister wouldn't want *her* trailing down the aisle in front of her with a bouquet, but why didn't Riley want his brother standing up beside him for the ceremony?

Dan's face had darkened at her words, so she hurried

on, not really paying attention to what she was saying. 'Which is just as well, since there's so much to focus on! And besides, being behind the scenes means that it should be easier for me to avoid Benjamin—which is an advantage not to be overlooked.'

Oh. She hadn't meant to mention Benjamin.

Maybe he wouldn't notice.

'Benjamin?' Dan asked, and Laurel bit back a sigh. Too much to hope for, clearly.

'My ex-fiancé,' she said succinctly, wondering if there was a way to tell this story that didn't make her sound like a miserable, weak, doormat of a person.

Probably not.

'He's attending the wedding?' Dan sounded surprised. She supposed that normal sisters wouldn't invite their sibling's ex-partner to their wedding. But the relationship between her and Melissa had never even pretended to be 'normal'.

'With his *new* fiancée,' she confirmed.

Because it wasn't humiliating enough *just* to have to face the man she'd thought was The One again, after he'd made it abundantly clear she wasn't his anything, in front of her family, celebrities and the world's media. She also had to do it with her replacement in attendance.

'His parents are old friends of my father's. We practically grew up together. Unlike me and my sister.' She was only making things worse. 'So, yeah, he'll be there—just to maximise the awkward. And I'm not exactly looking forward to it, I'll admit—especially since I haven't seen him since… Anyway, it'll all be fine, and I'll mostly be organising wedding things anyway, like I said, so…'

There had to be a way out of this conversation that

left her just a *little* dignity, surely? If she kept digging long enough maybe she'd find it—before her pride and self-confidence hitched a ride back to London in a passing cab.

'The Wedding March' rang out from the phone in her hand, and Laurel gave a silent prayer of thanks for the interruption—until she saw the name on the screen.

Melissa. Of course.

Sighing, she flashed a brief smile at Dan. 'If you'll excuse me?'

He leant back against the leather seats and nodded. 'Of course.'

Laurel pressed 'answer'. Time to see how her half-sister intended to make her day a little worse.

Considering that the hot little brunette who'd gatecrashed his ride to the hotel had done nothing but talk since they met, she was doing surprisingly little talking on her phone call.

'Yes, but—' Another sigh. 'Of course, Melissa. You're the bride, after all.'

Melissa. The blonde bombshell who'd exploded into his little brother's world a year ago and taken it over. Dan and Riley had never been exactly what he'd call close—the six-year age-gap meant that they'd done their growing up at different times, and their parents' blatant favouritism towards their younger son hadn't made bonding any easier.

But the distance between them didn't change the fact that Riley was his little brother and Dan loved him regardless. He'd loved him all through his Golden Boy childhood, through their parents cutting Dan off when he'd moved to LA and become a stuntman without their approval, and even through their outstanding hypocrisy when Riley had followed him nine years later.

Their parents were both world-renowned in their fields—cardiac surgery for their mother and ortho-paedics for his father. That would have been enough to try and live up to under normal circumstances. But Dan had given up competing with anybody long before his younger brother had moved to Hollywood and become a star.

It wasn't as if he was doing so shabbily by anyone's terms—even his own. He owned his own business and his turnover doubled every year. He probably earned nearly as much as his hotshot brother, and even if the public would never know his name, the people who mattered in Hollywood did. He—or rather his company, Black Ops Stunts—was the first port of call for any major studio making an action movie these days. He'd made a success of the career his parents had been sure would kill him or ruin him.

Not that they cared all that much either way.

Dan shifted in his seat as he contemplated the week ahead of him. Five days in a luxury hotel—not so bad. Five days with the rich and obnoxious—less good. Five days dealing with his parents—nightmare.

When the invitation had first fallen onto his doormat he'd honestly considered skipping the whole thing. Formal events weren't really his style, and he spent enough time with Hollywood actors to know that some of them had surprisingly little respect for the people who saved them from risking their lives doing their own stunts. And from what he'd heard about Melissa Sommers she was definitely one of them.

In fact it was all the industry gossip about Melissa

that had persuaded him that he needed to be at Morwen Hall that week. Or rather the conflicting reports.

As far as Dan could tell every director and co-star who had ever worked with Melissa thought she was an angel. Anyone who ranked lower than a named credit in the titles, however, told a rather different story.

He sighed, running through his mind once more the series of off-the-record conversations he'd had recently. It wasn't an unfamiliar story—he'd met enough stars who played the part of benevolent, caring, charitable celebrity to the hilt when anyone who mattered was looking, then turned into a spoilt brat the moment the cameras switched off. He'd even been married to one of them. The only difference was that this time it was *Riley* marrying the witch—and he needed to be sure his baby brother knew exactly what he was getting in to.

Riley didn't *do* personas, Dan thought. In fact it was a mystery how he'd ever got into acting in the first place. It probably said something that he always got cast to play the nice guy, though. The 'aw, shucks, good old country boy' who found true love after ninety minutes, or the clean-cut superhero who could do no wrong.

That certainly fitted with the way their parents saw him, anyway.

But this week Dan was far more concerned with how *Melissa* saw him. Was it true love? Or was he her ticket to something bigger? Her career was doing well, as far as he could tell, but Riley was a step up. Stars had married for a lot less—and he didn't want to see his brother heartbroken and alone six months after he said, 'I do.'

'Melissa...'

Laurel sighed again, and Dan tuned back in to the phone conversation she was enduring. Seemed as if

Melissa didn't count her half-sister as someone who mattered. Hardly unexpected, given their history, he supposed. Everyone knew that story—inside and outside the industry.

He wondered why Melissa had hired her famously estranged half-sister to organise the celebrity wedding of the year. Was it an attempt at reconciliation? Or a way to make Laurel's life miserable? Judging by the phone call he was eavesdropping on, it definitely felt like the latter. Or maybe it was all about the way it would play in the media—that sounded like the Melissa he'd heard stories about from Jasmine, his best stunt woman, who'd doubled for Melissa once or twice.

This wedding would be his chance to find out for sure. Ideally *before* she and Riley walked down the aisle.

At least he had a plan. It was good to have something to focus on. Otherwise he might have found himself distracted—maybe even by the brunette on the phone…

'I'll be back at Morwen Hall in less than an hour,' Laurel said finally, after a long pause during which she'd nodded silently with her eyes closed, despite the fact her sister obviously couldn't see the gesture. 'We can talk about it some more then, if you like.'

She opened her mouth to speak again, then shut it, lowering the phone from her ear and flashing him a tight smile.

'She hung up,' she explained.

'Problems?' he asked, raising an eyebrow.

Laurel, he'd already learned, talked to fill the silence—something that seemed to be absent when she was speaking with her half-sister. If he let her ramble on maybe she'd be able to give him all the information about Melissa he needed to talk his brother out of this wedding. They could all be on their way home by dinner time, and he could get back to business as usual. Perfect.

'Oh, not really,' Laurel said lightly, waving a hand as if to brush away his concerns. 'Just the usual. Last-minute nerves about everything.'

Dan sat up a little straighter. 'About marrying Riley?'

'Goodness, no!'

Laurel's eyes widened to an unbelievable size—dark pools of chocolate-brown that a man could lose himself in, if he believed in that sort of thing.

'Sorry, that wasn't what I meant at all! I just meant… there are so many arrangements in place for this week and, even though I really *do* have them all in hand, Melissa just likes to…well, double check. And sometimes she has some new ideas that she'd like to fit in to the plans. Or changes she'd like to make.'

'Such as the wedding favours?' Dan said, nodding at the glossy bag by her feet.

'Exactly!' Laurel looked relieved at his understanding. 'I'm so sorry if I worried you. My mouth tends to run a little faster than my brain sometimes. And there's just so much to think about this week…'

'Like your ex-fiancé,' Dan guessed, leaning back against the seat as he studied her.

An informant who talked too much was exactly what he was looking for—even if he hadn't really thought about her as such until now. Fate had tossed him a bone on this one.

Laurel's face fell, her misery clear. Had the woman ever had a thought that wasn't instantly telegraphed through her expression? Not that he was complaining— anything that made reading women easier was a plus in his book. But after spending years learning to school his responses, to keep his expressions bland and boring, he found it interesting that Laurel gave so much away for free.

In Hollywood, he assumed people were acting all the time. In the case of people who had to deal with the over-expressive actors, directors and so on, they learned to lock down their response, to nod politely and move on without ever showing annoyance, disagreement or even disgust.

Laurel wasn't acting—he could tell. And she certainly wasn't locking anything down. Especially not her feelings about her ex-fiancé.

'Like Benjamin,' she agreed, wincing. 'Not that I'm planning on thinking about him much. Or that I've been pining away after him ever since…well, since everything happened.'

Yeah, that sounded like a lie. Maybe she hadn't been pining, but she'd certainly been thinking about him— that much was obvious.

'What *did* happen? If you don't mind me asking.'

Dan shifted in his seat to turn towards her. He was surprised to find himself honestly interested in the answer. Partly because he was sympathetic to her plight— it was never fun to run into an ex, which was one of the reasons he avoided celebrity parties these days unless he could be sure Cassie wouldn't be there—and partly because he couldn't understand why Melissa would invite her half-sister's ex-fiancé to her wedding. Old family friends or not, that was a level of harsh not usually seen in normal people.

Which only made him more concerned for Riley.

Laurel sighed, and there was a world of feeling in the sound as her shoulders slumped.

'Oh, the usual, I suppose. I thought everything was perfect. We were going to get married, live happily ever after—you know, get the fairytale ending and everything.' She looked up and met his gaze, as if checking that he did understand what a fairytale was.

'Oh, I understand,' he said, with feeling. Hadn't that been what he'd thought would be his by rights when he said 'I do' to Cassie? Look how wrong he'd been about that.

'But then it turned out that he wanted the fairytale with someone else instead.' She shrugged, her mouth twisting up into a half-smile. 'I guess sometimes these things just don't work out.'

'You seem surprisingly sanguine about it.'

'Well, it's been six months,' Laurel answered. 'Melissa says I should be well over it by now. I mean, *he* obviously is, right?'

Six months? Six months after Cassie had left him Dan had still been drinking his way through most of LA's less salubrious bars. He probably still would be if his business partner hadn't hauled him out and pointed out that revenge was sweeter than moping.

Making a huge financial and professional success of Black Ops Stunts wasn't just a personal win. It was revenge against the ex-wife who'd always said he'd never be worth anything.

'People get over things in their own way and their own time,' Dan said, trying to focus on the week in front of him, not the life he'd left behind.

'The hardest part was telling my family,' Laurel admitted, looking miserable all over again. 'I mean, getting

engaged to Benjamin was the first thing I'd done right in
my father's eyes since I was about fifteen. Even my stepmother was pleased. Benjamin was—*is*, I suppose—quite
the catch in her book. Rich, well-known, charming…'
She gave a self-deprecating smile. 'I suppose I should
have known it was too good to be true.'

'So, what are you going to do now?' Dan asked.

Laurel took a deep breath and put on a brave smile
that didn't convince him for a moment.

'I've sworn off men for the time being. I'm going
to focus on my business and on myself for a while.
And then, when I'm ready, maybe I'll consider dating
again. But this time, I want to be a hundred per cent
sure it's the real thing—the whole fairytale—before I
let myself fall.'

Well, that was rather more information than he'd
been looking for. Dan smiled back, awkwardly. 'Actually, I meant…how do you plan to get through spending a week in the same hotel as him?'

Laurel turned pale. 'Oh, I'm sorry. Of course you
don't want to hear about that! Melissa always says I
talk about myself *far* too much. Anyway… This week…
Well, like I said, I've got a lot of work to do. I'm hoping that will keep me so busy I don't even have to think
about him.'

If Melissa had her way Dan suspected Laurel would
be plenty busy. And probably only talking about Melissa, too.

'What you really need is a new boyfriend to flaunt
in his face,' he joked, and Laurel laughed.

'That would be good,' she agreed, grinning at him.
'But even if I hadn't sworn off men I've barely had time

to sleep since I started organising this wedding, so I *definitely* haven't had time to date.'

That was a shame, Dan decided. Laurel, with her warm brown eyes and curvy figure, should definitely be dating. She shouldn't be locking herself away, even if it wasn't for ever. She should be out in the world, making it a brighter place. Less than an hour together and he already knew that Laurel was one of the good ones—and the complete opposite of everything he suspected about her half-sister. Laurel should be smiling up at a guy who treated her right for a change. A guy who wanted to spend the rest of his life making her smile that way. The prince she was waiting for.

Dan knew he was definitely *not* that guy. Treating women right wasn't the problem—he had utter respect for any woman who hadn't previously been married to him. But he didn't do 'for ever' any more. Not after Cassie.

Besides, he knew from experience that 'for ever' wasn't what women wanted from him, anyway. They wanted a stand-in—just like the directors did when they hired him or one of his people. Someone to come in, do good work, take the fall, and be ready to get out of the way when the real star of the show came along.

But maybe, he realised suddenly, that was exactly what Laurel needed this week.

A stand-in.

That, Dan knew, he could absolutely do. And it might just help him out in his mission to save his baby brother from a whole load of heartbreak, too, by getting him closer to the centre of the action.

'What if he just *thought* you had a boyfriend?' Dan asked, and Laurel's nose wrinkled in confusion.

'Like, lie to him?' She shook her head. 'I'm a terrible liar. He'd never believe me. Besides, if I had a boyfriend why wouldn't he be at the wedding?'

'He would be,' Dan said, and the confusion in Laurel's eyes grew.

He almost laughed—except that wouldn't get him any closer to what he wanted: a ringside seat to find out what the bride was *really* like.

'I don't understand,' Laurel said.

Dan smiled. Of course she didn't. That was one of the things he was growing to like about her, after their limited acquaintance—her lack of subterfuge.

'Me. Let me be your pretend boyfriend for the week.'

CHAPTER TWO

LAUREL BLINKED AT HIM. Then she blinked a few more times for good measure.

'Are you…?' *Pretend*. He'd said *pretend* boyfriend. 'Are you fake asking me out?'

Dan laughed. 'If you like.'

'Why?'

Because he felt sorry for her—that much was clear. How pathetic must she look to elicit the promise of a fake relationship? Really, there was pity dating and then there was *this*. How low had she sunk? Not this low, that was for sure.

'Because it feels wrong to let your ex wander around the wedding of the year like he won,' Dan replied with a shrug. 'Besides, I'm here on my own—and, to be honest, it would be nice to have a friend at my side when I have to deal with my family, too.'

His words were casual enough, but Laurel couldn't shake the feeling that there was something else under them. Something she was missing. But what?

'So it's not just a "Poor, sad Laurel, can't even get a date to the celebrity wedding of the year" thing?' she asked, cautiously.

Dan gave her a quick grin. 'I'm not even sure I know

what one of those would look like. No, I just figured…
we're both dateless, we both have to spend the week
with some of our less than favourite people, we're both
non-Hollywood stars in the middle of a celebrity extravaganza…why not team up?'

Who were his 'less than favourite' people? she wondered. Who was he avoiding, and why?

Suddenly the whole suggestion sounded a little bit
dodgy. Especially since…

'Aren't you a stuntman?' Laurel narrowed her eyes.
'Doesn't that count as a Hollywood star?'

'Definitely not,' Dan said firmly. 'In fact it probably
makes me the exact opposite. Put it this way: if I wasn't
related to the groom by blood there's not a chance I'd
have been invited to this wedding.'

'Same here,' Laurel admitted.

One thing they had in common. That, plus the whole
far-more-famous-sibling thing they both had going for
them. Maybe—just maybe—this was a genuine offer.

Leaning back against the car seat, she considered
his proposition. On the one hand, the idea of having
someone there to back her up, to be on *her* side for
once…well, that sounded pretty good. Especially when
she had to face down Benjamin for the first time since
that really awkward morning in the coffee shop, half
an hour after she'd walked in on him in bed with her
replacement.

*'You understand, don't you, Laurel? When it's true
love…you just can't deny that kind of feeling.'*

She hadn't thrown her coffee cup at his head. She
still felt vaguely proud of that level of restraint. And just
a little bit regretful… Breaking china on his skull would
have been a reassuring memory to get her through the

weeks that had followed—breaking the news to her family, cancelling the save-the-date card order, dealing with all the pitying looks from friends... And Melissa's amusement as she'd said, *'Really, Laurel, couldn't you even satisfy old Benjy? I thought he'd have done* anything *to marry into this family.'*

Her mouth tightened at the memory, and she fought to dispel it from her brain. Back to the problem at hand. A fake relationship? *Really?*

As nice as it would be not to have to face this week alone, who was she kidding? *She* wasn't the actress in the family. She couldn't pull this off. Even if Dan played the part to perfection she'd screw it up somehow—and that was only if they got past the initial hurdle. The one that she was almost certain she'd fall at.

They'd have to convince Melissa that they were in love.

Melissa and Laurel might not have spent much time together for half-sisters—they hadn't grown up in the same house, hadn't spent holidays together, celebrated Christmas together, fought over toys or any of that other stuff siblings were supposed to do. Laurel hadn't even known Melissa existed until she was sixteen. But none of that changed the fact that Melissa had known about Laurel's existence her whole life—and as far as she was concerned that meant she knew everything there was to know about her half-sister.

And Melissa would never believe a guy like Dan would fall for Laurel.

Fair enough—she was right. But it still didn't make Laurel feel any more kindly towards her sister.

Laurel shook her head. 'They'll never fall for it. Trust me—I'm an awful actress. They'll see right through it.'

'Why?' Dan asked, eyebrows raised. 'Do you only date A-List celebs like your sister?'

Laurel snorted. 'Hardly. It's the other way round. Melissa would never believe that you'd fall for me. Besides, when are we supposed to have got together? We've never even met before today!'

'They don't know that,' Dan pointed out. 'It's not like my family keeps a particularly tight check on my calendar, and Melissa and Riley have been in LA the whole time. I could have been over in London for work some time in the last six months. Obviously we'd been emailing about the wedding arrangements, so I suggested we meet up while I was in town. One thing led to another...' He shrugged. 'Easy.'

'Is that my virtue or the lie?' Laurel asked drily.

He made it sound so simple, so obvious. Did everyone else live their lives this way? Telling the story that made them look better or stopped them feeling guilty? Her dad certainly had. So had Benjamin. Could she do the same? Did she even want to?

'The story,' Dan answered. 'And as for no one believing it...'

He reached out and took her hand in his, the rough pad of his thumb rubbing across the back of her hand, making the skin there tingle. His gaze met hers and held it, blue eyes bright under his close-cropped hair.

'Trust me. No one is going to have *any* trouble at all believing that I want you.'

His words were low and rough, and her eyes widened as she saw the truth of them in his gaze. They might have only just met, but the pull of attraction she'd felt at the first sight of him apparently hadn't only been one-sided. But attraction…attraction was easy. A relationship—even a fake one—was not.

Laurel had far too much experience of her world being tipped upside down by men—from the day her father had declared that he'd been keeping another family across town for most of her life and was leaving to live with them to the most recent upheaval of finding Benjamin naked on top of Coral.

But maybe that was the advantage of a pretend boyfriend. She got to set the rules in advance and, because she had no expectations of for ever or fidelity, or anything at all beyond a kind of friendship, she couldn't be let down. Her world would remain resolutely the right way up.

Something that, after a week filled with Melissa's last-minute mind-changes and the vagaries of celebrities, sounded reassuringly certain. She eyed Dan's broad shoulders, strong stubbled jaw and wide chest. Solid, safe and secure. He looked like the human embodiment of his company brochure—which she'd studied when she'd been memorising the guest list. Black Ops Stunts promised safety, professionalism and reliability. Just what she needed to help her get through the week ahead.

Maybe—just maybe—this wasn't a completely crazy idea after all.

'Basically, it comes down to this,' Dan said, breaking eye contact at last as he let go of her hand. 'I have a feeling this is going to be the week from hell for both of us. Wedding of the year or not, I can think of a million places I'd rather be—and I'm sure you can too. But we're both stuck at Morwen Hall until New Year's Day, along with our families and all their friends.'

Laurel pulled a face. She'd been trying very hard not

to think too much about how much she wasn't looking forward to that. But when Dan laid it out flat like that she knew he was right. It really *was* going to be the week from hell.

'So I guess you need to decide something before we get there,' Dan went on. 'Do you want to go through that alone, or do you want a friend on your side? Someone you can rant to when people are awful and who understands *exactly* what you're going through?'

He was pushing it, she realised. This wasn't just for her, or just to make the week less awful. There was some other reason he wanted this—and it wasn't because he was attracted to her. The minute he'd dropped her hand she'd seen his control slide back into place, noted the way his expression settled into that same blankness she'd seen when she'd first got into the car.

Dan Black was after something, and Laurel wasn't sure she wanted to know what it was.

She shook her head. 'No. Sorry. It just won't work.'

'Your choice,' Dan said, with a no-skin-off-my-nose shrug.

Laurel frowned. Maybe she'd been wrong after all. It wasn't as if she was the best at reading people.

'I mean, we can still help each other through this week as friends,' she added quickly. 'Just… I'm no good at faking it—sorry. I'd mess it up.'

Not to mention the fact that Melissa would have an absolute fit if Laurel showed up with a new boyfriend at the last moment—especially Riley's brother. That was the sort of thing that might draw their father's attention away from Melissa, after all. And Melissa did *not* like people stealing her thunder.

Frankly, it wasn't worth the risk.

Besides, she could handle Benjamin. It had been six months. She was over it. Over men. And far too busy focussing on her career to let him get to her at all.

It would all be fine.

'Friends would be good,' Dan said with a small smile. 'And if you change your mind…'

'I'll know where to find you,' Laurel said, relieved. 'After all, I'm organising this party. Remember?'

Well, there went the easy option. Still, friends was good, Dan decided. He'd just have to make sure to stick close enough to Laurel to get the information he needed on her sister. Maybe he might even manage to get Melissa alone, for a little brotherly chat. The sort that started, *If you hurt my brother I'll destroy your career.*

See? He could do friendly.

Besides, Dan had been the rebound guy far too often to believe that it ever ended well. Laurel was looking for a prince, and he was anything but. A fake relationship was one thing, but a woman with a broken heart could be unpredictable—and Dan didn't have space in his life for that kind of drama.

One thing his marriage to Cassie had taught him was that giving up control was a bad idea. He'd never concede control of a stunt to anyone else, so why give up control of his heart, or his day-to-day life? Love was off the table, and so were complicated relationships. His was a simple, easy life. Complicated only by his family and by potential heart-breaking film stars who wanted to marry his brother.

'So, tell me more about this wedding, then,' he said, figuring he might as well ease Laurel into talking about her sister now, while he had her undivided attention.

'What's the plan? I mean, who takes a whole *week* to get married?'

'Celebrities, apparently,' Laurel said drily, and he knew without asking that she was quoting Melissa there.

'And you said something about a…?' He tried to remember the term she'd used. 'A Frost Fair? What on earth is one of those?'

Laurel grinned. 'Only my favourite part of the whole week! They used to hold them on the Thames when it froze over, back in the seventeenth and eighteenth centuries. It's like a country fair, I guess, with food stalls and entertainment and all sorts. It's going to be brilliant!'

'It sounds like a health and safety nightmare waiting to happen,' Dan replied, wondering when he'd become the sort of person who noticed those things. Probably when he starting risking life and limb for a living.

'We're not actually holding it *on* the river. It's probably not frozen over, for a start. We'll just be on the banks. But I've got an acting troupe lined up to perform, and a lute player, and a hog roast…'

Her enthusiasm was infectious, and Dan couldn't help but smile. 'It sounds great. I bet Melissa was really pleased when you came up with that one.'

Laurel's smile faltered, just a little. 'Well, I think she'll like it when she sees it,' she said diplomatically, but Dan got the subtext.

Melissa, he suspected, hadn't been actively *pleased* with anything Laurel had done.

He decided to play a hunch. 'Oh, well. A job's a job, right? And this one must be paying pretty well, at least?'

It was crass to talk about money, his mother had always told him that, but if her answer was the one he expected then it would be a clear indication that Melissa was the user he suspected her to be.

The answer was clear on Laurel's face as her smile disappeared altogether. 'It's great experience. And an opportunity to get my company name in the world's media.'

Translation: Melissa wasn't paying her anything, and Dan knew for sure that she and Riley could afford it.

'Right,' he said, ignoring the burning sense of unfairness in his chest. Laurel didn't deserve this—any of this. Not her ex at the wedding, not her sister taking advantage—not even him, using her to suss out the truth of his brother's relationship with Melissa.

It was a good job he'd decided that Laurel was off limits, because Dan had always had a soft spot for a damsel in distress, and a habit of rooting for the underdog. As a friend, he could help her out. But he couldn't let himself even consider anything more.

Which was where that iron-clad control he'd spent so long developing came in.

The car took a sharp turn and Dan turned away to peer out of the window. As they broke through the tree cover—when had they left the city? How had he missed that?—a large, Gothic-looking building loomed into sight, all high-peaked arches and cold, forbidding stone.

That just had to be Morwen Hall. It looked as if Dracula wouldn't feel out of place there, and as far as Dan could tell Melissa was the nearest thing the modern world had to a vampire, so that was about right.

'I think we're here,' he said.

Laurel leant across the empty seat between them, stretching her seatbelt tight as she tried to look out of his window. 'You're right. I'm sorry, I've spent the whole journey talking about me! We're supposed to be being friends, and I still don't know anything about you!'

Dan shrugged. 'I'm a simple guy. There's not much to know.'

She sighed. 'I was hoping I could pick your brains about your family. Get a feel for who everyone is before tonight's welcome drinks.'

Thinking back to all the highly detailed emails she'd sent him during the wedding planning process, Dan laughed. 'Come on—don't try and tell me you haven't got the guest list memorised, alphabetically and backwards probably, along with pertinent details on everyone attending. You probably know my family better than I do at this point.'

It wasn't even a lie. He hadn't stayed in close touch with any of them these last few years. When it came to their jobs, their hobbies, their movements, Laurel probably *did* know more than him.

She smiled down at her hands. 'Well, maybe. I like to do a thorough job.'

There was no hint of innuendo in the words, but something about them shot straight to Dan's libido as she looked up at him through her lashes. Laurel, with her attention to detail, her perfectionism…everything he'd seen through her emails as she'd been planning the wedding…maybe he knew her better than she thought, too. And he couldn't help but imagine what all that detail orientated focus would feel like when turned to their mutual pleasure.

Not that he would have a chance to find out. Seducing Laurel Sommers was not an option—not when she might still be harbouring feelings for her ex, and not when she was holding out for a prince. Which was a pity...

He shook the thought away as the car came to a stop directly outside the Gothic monstrosity that was Morwen Hall.

'We're here,' Laurel said, and bit her lip.

He flashed Laurel a smile. 'Time to face the mob.'

The mob. Her family, his family, her ex...most of the Hollywood elite and a delegation from *Star!* magazine.

All the people she'd least like to see. *Hooray.*

Laurel's knees wobbled as she stepped out of the car, but in an instant Dan was there, offering her his hand as she descended. A friendly hand, she reminded herself as he smiled at her. She wasn't going to waste time pretending that there could be anything more between them. Apart from anything else, if there was a chance of that he wouldn't have offered to be her *fake* boyfriend, would he?

Besides, she was waiting for the real thing—the right person, the right time, the right place. And Dan, at Melissa's wedding, surrounded by their families, while Laurel was working every second to make the week perfect and magazine-worthy, was definitely not any of those things.

She looked up to thank Dan for his assistance when something else caught her eye. A too-flashy car, pulling up beside theirs on the driveway. A shiny silver convertible, the sort that Benjamin had liked to drive...

Oh. Perfect. There he was, her cheating rat of an ex, all ready to make her miserable week just a little bit more unbearable.

Her feelings must have shown in her face, because as

Benjamin shut off the engine Dan bent his head so his mouth was by her ear and whispered, 'This is the ex?'

Laurel nodded, unable to keep her eyes off the car. She couldn't look at Benjamin, of course. And she couldn't look at Dan or he'd know how truly pathetic she was. And she *definitely* couldn't stare at the tall, leggy blonde that Benjamin was helping out of the car, even if she *did* look a bit like Melissa. The car seemed by far the safest bet.

Cars didn't betray a person, or break her heart. Cars were safe.

Far safer than love.

Love, in Laurel's experience, went hand in hand with trust and hope. None of which had ever worked out all that well for her.

Every time she'd had hope for the future that relied on another person, and every time she'd trusted a person she loved, she'd been let down. More than that—she'd been left abandoned, feeling worthless and hopeless.

Which was why, these days, she was putting all her faith, hope and trust in herself and in her business. That way at least if she got hurt it was her own stupid fault. One day her prince would come—and he'd be the kind of equal opportunities prince who loved it that she had a successful career, and thought she was brilliant just the way she was. In the meantime, she would never, *ever* feel that worthless again.

'Laurel!' Benjamin called out, a wide smile on his face as the blonde stepped out of the car, high heels sinking in the gravel of the driveway. 'How lovely to see you! Quite the venue you've picked here.' He shot a glance over at Morwen Hall and winced. 'It doesn't exactly scream romance, I have to say, but I'm sure you know what you're doing.'

Always that slight dig—that slight suggestion that she was doing something wrong. Never enough for her to call him on it—he'd just put his hands up and laugh, saying she was being over-sensitive. But just enough to leave her in no doubt that he knew better than she did. She wasn't *quite* good enough.

Well, the biggest advantage of not being in love with him any more was that she didn't have to care what he thought.

'Giving my sister the wedding of her dreams!' she said, smiling as sweetly as she could as she held a hand out to the blonde, for all the world as if she was meeting her for the first time and *hadn't* found her naked in her own bed six months previously. Because she was a professional, dammit, and she would prove it. 'Hi, I'm Laurel Sommers. The wedding planner.'

The blonde's smile barely reached her cheeks, let alone her eyes. 'Coral. Ben's fiancée,' she added, obviously wanting to make her status absolutely clear. As if Laurel didn't already know the whole sordid history of their relationship.

'Lovely to meet you, Coral,' Laurel lied. She glanced down at Coral's left hand, unable to help herself. There it was: a beautiful diamond, oversized and ostentatious and… *Hang on.*

That was *her* engagement ring. The one she'd given him back that morning in the coffee shop because she couldn't bear to look at the damn thing a moment longer and, besides, it was an expensive ring and she hadn't felt right keeping it.

She'd expected Benjamin to return it or sell it or something.

Not to give it to the woman he'd cheated on her with.

A strange, shaky feeling rose up in her—something between fury and confusion. How *could* he? Wasn't it humiliating enough that he was here at all? And now *this woman* was wearing *her* ring? How much embarrassment was she supposed to take? How little had she mattered—to Benjamin, to Melissa, to her own father—that she found herself in this position? Alone and humiliated and…

Wait. Not alone. Not quite.

Laurel took a deep breath. And then she made a decision.

Reaching behind her, she grabbed Dan's hand and pulled him forward, keeping a tight grip on his fingers as he stood beside her. 'Benjamin, this is Dan. My date for the wedding.'

Until that moment Dan had stayed quiet and still just behind her, not drawing any attention to himself, and it seemed that Benjamin and Coral had barely even registered his presence. Which, now she thought about it, was quite a trick. Maybe that was what you had to do as a stuntman—be mostly invisible or at least easily mistaken for the person you were standing in for. But since Dan had to be over six foot, and solid with it, disappearing in the pale sunlight of an English winter day was a real achievement.

Now he squeezed her fingers back, as if asking, *Are you sure?*

She wasn't. Not at all. But it seemed she was doing it anyway.

'Dan…' Benjamin echoed, holding out a hand, suspicion already in his gaze.

Laurel resisted the urge to roll her eyes as Dan dropped her fingers to grip Benjamin's hand hard enough that he winced slightly.

'That's right. I'm Laurel's *new* boyfriend,' Dan explained, with a sharp smile.

Laurel bit back her own grin as Benjamin's expression froze. Yeah, *that* was why she'd changed her mind about this crazy scheme. That look, right there. That look that said, *Really? Are you sure?*

Because of course Benjamin wouldn't expect her to have a new man already, given how crushed she'd been by their break-up. And even if she had he wouldn't expect it to be someone like Dan—someone big and muscly and gorgeous and just a little bit rough compared to Benjamin's urbane polish.

Sometimes it was nice to surprise a person. Besides, knowing that Dan was clearly not her type—and that she was almost certainly not his either—helped to keep it clear to both of them that this was just a game. A game that they'd need to discuss the rules of, she supposed, but how hard could that be? The charade would be over the minute the wedding guests departed anyway.

But until then…it would be kind of fun.

Coral was looking at Dan with far more interest than her fiancé, and Benjamin retrieved his hand and quickly took Coral's instead. Staking his claim, Laurel realised, just as he'd always done with her—holding her hand, or placing a proprietorial hand at her waist whenever she spoke to another man. Something else she really didn't miss.

Benjamin's gaze flipped from Dan back to Laurel,

and she stopped reflecting on the past in order to concentrate on fooling her ex in the present. Dan slipped a hand around her waist, which helped. Somehow it felt totally different from the way Benjamin had used to touch her there. Less possessive, more a gentle reminder that she wasn't alone.

She liked that, too.

'Actually, Laurel, it's handy we've bumped into you. Could you spare a moment? I have something I want to talk to you about…'

Laurel ran down her mental checklist of any outstanding Benjamin issues and came up with nothing. She'd already given back his ring—as evidenced by the fact that it was sparkling on Coral's left hand right now. He had no stuff left at her flat—mostly because he'd never left anything there longer than overnight if he could help it anyway. He'd kept all their mutual friends in the break-up, since they'd all been his to start with, and she was sort of relieved to have more time for her old uni friends instead of having to hang out with his society people.

What else could there possibly be for them to talk about?

'I should really get back to work,' she said, wishing she could sound more definite, more confident in her denial. Why couldn't she just say, *There is nothing left I want you to say to me*?

'It'll only take a moment,' Benjamin pressed, moving a step towards her.

Laurel stepped back and found herself pressed up against Dan's side. He really was very solid. Warm and solid and reassuring.

She could get used to having that sort of certainty at her back.

'Sorry, but the lady has a prior engagement,' Dan said.

Laurel knew she should be cross with him for speaking for her, but given that she couldn't say the words herself she was finding it hard to care. Besides, he *was* supposed to be her boyfriend. It was all just part of the act.

'I've had a very long journey, and Laurel promised to show me to my room the moment we arrived. Didn't you, honey?'

The warm look he gave her, the innuendo clear in his gaze, made her feel as if her blood was heating her up from the inside.

Just an act, she reminded herself. But, given the way Benjamin stepped back again, and Coral pulled him close, it was an act that was working.

'Sorry,' she lied, flashing the other couple a short, sharp smile. 'Maybe later.' Then she gave Dan a longer, warmer, more loving smile. 'Come on, then, you. I can't wait to give you a *thorough* tour of your room.'

Turning away, she led Dan up the stone steps and through the front door of Morwen Hall, victory humming through her body.

Maybe Melissa wasn't the only actress in the family after all.

'What an idiot,' Dan whispered as they moved out of earshot, leaving Benjamin supervising the retrieval of his bags and handing his keys over to the valet. 'What did you see in him?'

'I have no idea,' Laurel said, honestly.

'So—we're doing this, then? I thought it was a terrible idea.'

But he'd gone along with her lies the minute she'd told them, she realised. Even though she'd insisted not half an hour ago that they couldn't do it. A person who could keep up with her whims was a very useful friend to have, she decided.

'It probably still is.' Laurel flashed him a smile. 'But…it could be fun, don't you think?'

'Oh, definitely,' Dan replied, and the secret half-smile he gave her felt even warmer than the victory over Benjamin.

CHAPTER THREE

LAUREL LAUGHED SOFTLY as they entered Morwen Hall, and Dan congratulated himself on handling the situation with the ex well—*and* getting to play the game he'd wanted all along. It was hard enough judging how a woman wanted him to behave in such a situation when they really *were* dating, but trying to guess it on an hour or two's acquaintance with no notice… Well, he was just glad he hadn't got it wrong. If he had, he wouldn't have got to hear Laurel's giggle—and Laurel had a fantastic giggle. Low and dark and dirty, with just a hint of mischief. Totally at odds with her perfectionist organisational tendencies—and not what he'd expected.

If that giggle told the true story of who Laurel really was, underneath everything—well, then she was definitely someone he was looking forward to getting to know better.

She'd surprised him, though. When she'd dismissed his idea of a fake relationship in the car she'd seemed very certain. He hadn't expected her sudden change of heart—and he couldn't help but wonder what had caused it. Surely it couldn't just have been seeing Benjamin in the flesh again, since she'd been expecting that. Unless she really *was* still hung up on him, and this was all an act to make her ex jealous. Dan hoped not. Revenge games weren't the sort he liked to play at all.

He'd have to remember to ask her, later, he realised. Even if it was too late now to back out, having all the facts would make deciding how to play things a lot easier.

'Hey. You're back!'

A tall redhead strode towards them across the lobby, a clipboard in hand, looking every bit as professional and efficient as Laurel did when she wasn't giggling.

He glanced down at Laurel, keeping his hand at her waist as she gave a forced smile. Dan applied just a little pressure to let her know he was still there while he tried to read the situation. Was this one of the people destined to make his week miserable? Or might she be on their side?

'I am,' Laurel said, sounding uncomfortable.

Was she changing her mind again? Dan hadn't taken her for a fickle woman, but under the circumstances he might have to re-evaluate.

'And you brought company.'

The redhead's gaze flicked up to meet his, and Dan gave a non-committal half-smile. No point encouraging her until he knew which way Laurel was going to jump.

'Eloise, this is Dan. Riley's brother,' Laurel explained. The redhead didn't look particularly reassured by the information. 'Dan, this is Eloise. She's the manager of Morwen Hall.'

'Pleased to meet you,' Dan said, placing the shopping bag full of wedding favours that he'd lugged in from the car on the ground and holding out his hand.

'Acting Manager,' Eloise corrected, as if unable to stop herself, as she took it and shook. She had a good handshake, Dan decided. Firm and friendly. Much better than that idiot outside, who'd tried to crush the bones in his hands before realising, after a moment, that Dan hadn't even begun to squeeze.

'Not for long,' Laurel said, and this time when Dan glanced down her smile seemed real. Friend, then. *Good*. They needed some of those.

He upgraded his expression from noncommittal to cautiously friendly. 'So, what's been happening here?'

'Cassidy, the maid of honour, has taken a fall while skiing and broken her leg, so her husband is bringing his mistress to the wedding instead.'

Eloise's words came out in a rush, and Dan had to run them through his brain twice to process them. Maid of honour. Broken leg. Mistress. None of that sounded good.

Laurel's mouth fell open in an O shape, and her eyes were almost as wide. Apparently she'd reached the same conclusion. 'So Melissa doesn't have a maid of honour?'

Eloise winced. 'Not exactly. She's making me do it.'

Laurel's eyes widened even further, into dark pools of amazement. 'You poor, poor thing,' she said, sounding genuinely sympathetic.

Under other circumstances Dan might have been surprised that Laurel wasn't offended that she wasn't even her sister's *second* choice as maid of honour. But, given the phone call he'd heard in the car, he suspected she viewed it as a lucky escape.

'Yeah. I'm thrilled, as you can imagine. And it means I'll have to call in my deputy to cover for me at the hotel this week. He will *not* be thrilled. I can probably keep on top of the wedding events at least, so he only has to deal with the guests.' Eloise sighed. 'What about you? How did the favours go?'

She eyed Dan again, her gaze slipping down to where his hand rested at Laurel's waist. They might have passed the ex test, but now their unexpected fake relationship faced an even tougher challenge—convincing a friend. Still, it would be good practice for facing his family later, he supposed. *Oh, no, his family.* Maybe he hadn't thought this through properly either…

He reached down to pick up the bag of wedding favours again, just in case Laurel decided they should make a run for it.

'Fine, they're all sorted.' Laurel waved her hand towards the large glossy shopping bag in his hand. 'Then I got Dan's car to pick me up on the way back.'

'That was…convenient.' Eloise's stare intensified.

Dan glanced down at his fake girlfriend in time to watch her cheeks take on a rather rosy hue. Women didn't usually blush over him. It was kind of cute.

'Um, yes. Actually, I meant to tell you… Dan and I…'

Laurel stumbled over the lies and sympathy welled up inside him. She was right—she really wasn't good at this. Maybe he'd have to give her lying lessons. Except that sounded *really* wrong.

'So I see,' Eloise said, when Laurel's words trailed away.

Time for him to step in, Dan decided.

'We had sort of been keeping it under wraps,' he said, pulling Laurel closer against his side.

Laurel stiffened for a moment, then relaxed against him, warm and pliant. He could get used to that. Wait…

what had he been saying? Oh, yeah, making up an entire relationship history on the fly.

'What with the wedding and everything. Didn't want to steal Melissa's thunder, you know? But now the secret's out anyway…' Secret relationship…fake relationship. It was kind of the same thing. Right?

'This is brilliant!' Eloise burst out, and Dan blinked at her.

Either they'd been a lot more convincing than he'd thought, or there was something else going on here. Something that meant Eloise didn't want to examine their lies any more deeply than she had to.

'Melissa has insisted on Riley staying in a separate room until their wedding night, so I had to give him Dan's—sorry, Dan.' She gave him a quick smile. Dan didn't return it. 'But if you two are together, then that's fine because you'll be sharing anyway!'

There it was. That other shoe dropping.

He really, *really* hadn't thought this through. But, in fairness, he hadn't thought it would actually be happening. It had just been an idle suggestion—a possibility that Laurel had quashed almost instantly. If she'd said yes in the car, they'd probably have talked it through and realised how impossible it was. Instead here they were, stuck with a fake relationship Dan was rapidly realising was clearly destined for disaster.

'Sharing…right.'

Laurel's smile had frozen into that rictus grin again. He didn't blame her. How had things escalated this quickly?

Eloise frowned. 'As long as that's okay…?'

'Of course!' Laurel said, too brightly. 'I mean, why wouldn't we?'

'Exactly,' Dan said, trying not to imagine how his week had just got worse. 'Why wouldn't we?'

Because we're not a couple. Because it's all just an act. Because I was really looking forward to a quiet room and a mini-bar all to myself.

Because I'm not sure I can keep my hands off her for a full week.

No. *That* he could do. Laurel was cute—gorgeous, even. But Dan prided himself on his control—and this situation definitely required it. Especially considering all the people who would be watching.

He'd offered to be her fake boyfriend for the week, promised to be a friend—nothing more. And she needed that. This was going to be a hellish week for both of them, and they each needed someone to lean on—Laurel most of all. He couldn't take advantage of that just because she was hot and they only had one bed between them.

Besides, she was waiting for her prince, and he was all out of crowns and white chargers.

'Well, I'm glad that's all sorted,' Eloise said, clapping her hands together with glee. 'See you both later, then.'

And with that, the new maid of honour disappeared, leaving them to figure out how, exactly, they were supposed to share a room.

Dan looked down at Laurel. 'Honey, I think we need to talk.'

Laurel couldn't blame Eloise for this ridiculous situation, she realised as she led Dan towards the lifts. Melissa had obviously decided to be a cow—again—and who could blame Eloise for finding the best way out that she could? And, as an added bonus, Melissa would be really annoyed not to have caused Eloise trouble. So, really, this was all win-win for her.

Except for the part where Laurel now had to spend the next four nights sharing a room with the gorgeous guy who was pretending to be her boyfriend for the week.

Pretending. As in fake. As in a hilarious prank that had seemed a *lot* funnier before they'd realised they were sharing a room. A room with only one bed.

The worst part was she couldn't even blame *Melissa*. No, this was a full *mea culpa* Laurel mess. *She* was the one who had stupidly seized Dan's offer at the last minute and dragged him into this charade. He probably hadn't even been serious when he'd suggested it in the car. It had probably been a joke that she'd taken way too seriously and jumped on because she'd felt worthless in the face of Coral wearing *her* engagement ring.

One moment of ring-based madness, and now here they were.

'I'm really sorry about this,' she said as the lift doors shut and the lobby of Morwen Hall disappeared from view. At least here, in the privacy of the lift, they both knew the whole situation was a sham.

Dan stepped away from her, his hand dropping from her waist for almost the first time since they'd arrived. Her middle felt cold without it there.

'It's not your fault,' he said, not looking at her, obviously knowing that it totally was.

Instead, he seemed to be staring at their wobbly, muted reflections in the brushed steel of the doors. They looked hazy—indistinct blobs of colour on the metal. Which wasn't far off how she felt right now—as if she wasn't as sharp or as focused as the rest of the guests arriving for the wedding.

They all knew exactly who they were, what they were portraying. All Laurel knew was that she'd let herself get carried away with a pretence that was about to come back and bite her.

'Eloise means well,' she tried, not wanting Dan to spend the week blaming her friend, either. 'I suspect Melissa was just trying to make things difficult....'

'Seems to me that's what Melissa does best,' Dan said.

'Well, sometimes,' Laurel agreed. 'Most of the time. Possibly all of it.'

'And she's going to be my sister-in-law.' He sighed.

'You don't sound thrilled about that.'

Or was it just sharing a room with her he wasn't looking forward to? How was she supposed to know? She'd only known the man a couple of hours. Hardly enough to get a good mind-reading trick going.

'I just don't want Riley to make a big mistake.'

'Marrying Melissa, you mean?'

A cold feeling snaked down through Laurel's body. Was Dan planning on persuading Riley to call off the wedding? Because that kind of thing really *didn't* tend to get the wedding planner any repeat business, even if it wasn't her fault.

Dan flashed her a smile. 'Don't worry, I'm sure everything will be fine. I'm just…interested to meet her, that's all.'

'Right…' Laurel said, unconvinced.

Was this why he'd suggested the whole fake relationship thing in the first place? She'd *known* he had an ulterior motive—that was one of many reasons she'd turned him down. And then she'd panicked and forgotten all those reasons.

This was why she didn't do impulsive. It always ended badly.

Well, if Dan thought that Melissa was a bad choice for Riley, Laurel would just have to prove otherwise. Hard as it was to imagine trying to persuade someone that Melissa was a good person, apparently that was now the latest task on her wedding planner to-do list. Great—because that wasn't long enough already.

'So, tell me about your room.' Dan turned towards her, sharp blue eyes watching her face instead of their reflections now. 'For instance is it a suite, with multiple bedrooms and a stuffed mini-bar?'

'It has a mini-bar.'

'And bedrooms?'

'Bedroom. Singular.'

'Two beds?'

Laurel winced, and Dan turned away with a sigh just as the lift doors parted again, opening onto Laurel's floor.

'Sorry,' she said, leading him out into the corridor. 'I'll cope.'

'I'm sure you will.' Big, strong stuntman like him—he'd be fine anywhere. It wasn't him she was worried about.

What was the protocol for this? Laurel wondered as she slipped her key card into the door and pushed it open. He *was* the guest—did that mean she had to give him the bed? In fairness, she'd probably fit better on the tiny sofa than he would. But on the other hand it was *her* room… No. He was the one doing her a favour, pretending to find her attractive and worthwhile in front of her family. He probably deserved the bed.

It was just that it was a really *comfy* bed.

Dropping her key card on the tiny dressing table, Laurel moved across the room to the window, staring back at Dan, looming in the doorway. He was too big for her room—that was all there was to it. It had been the perfect room for just her—queen-sized bed with a soothing sage-coloured satin quilt, white dressing table with carved legs, a small but perfectly formed bathroom with rolltop bath…even the dove-grey wing-back chair by the window was perfect for one.

One her. Not her plus one oversized, muscular stunt-man.

Dan looked out of place in Morwen Hall to start with: his leather jacket was too rough, his boots too scuffed, his jeans…well, his jeans fitted *him* pretty much perfectly but, much as she liked them, they didn't exactly fit the refined Gothic elegance of the wedding venue. But if he was too…too much for Morwen Hall, he overwhelmed her little room entirely.

Who was she kidding? He overwhelmed *her*.

'So…um…how are we going to do this?' she asked, watching as he took in the room. *Their* bedroom. There was no end to the weirdness of that. 'The sharing a room thing, I mean. As opposed to the faking a relationship thing. Which, now that I come to mention it, is next on my how-to list, actually. But first… You know… We should probably figure out the room thing.'

'The room thing…' Dan echoed, still looking around him. 'Right.' Then, dropping the bag of wedding fa-vours onto the dressing table, he moved through the bedroom, exploring the bathroom, pressing down on the bed to test the mattress, then yanking open the mini-bar door and pulling out a bottle of beer.

'So the plan is drink until we don't care which one of us sleeps on the sofa?' Laurel asked cautiously.

Maybe she should have found out a few more things about her supposed boyfriend before she'd started this charade. Like whether or not he tended to solve *all* his problems with alcohol. That would have been useful information about someone she now had to share a room with.

'We're sharing the bed,' Dan said, dropping to sit on the edge of the satin quilt.

Laurel's heart stuttered in her chest.

'Sharing. Like…both of us in it at the same time?'

Her horror must have shown on her face, because he rolled his eyes.

'Nothing to worry about, Princess. I'm not going to besmirch your honour, or whatever it is you're imagining right now.'

'I wasn't…' She tailed off before she had to explain that it wasn't his besmirching she was worried about. It was how she was going to keep her hands from exploring those muscles…

'We'll share the bed because it's big enough and it's stupid not to,' Dan went on, oblivious to her inner muscle dilemma. 'This week is going to be deadly enough without a chronic backache from sleeping on that thing.' He nodded towards the chaise longue, shoehorned in under the second window at the side of the bed. 'Apart from that…the bathroom has a door that locks, and we're going to be out doing wedding stuff most of the time we're here anyway. Especially you—you're organising the whole thing, remember? How much time did you really expect to spend in this room before I came along?'

'I figured if I was lucky I might get four or five hours here to sleep at night,' Laurel admitted.

He was right. They'd probably barely see each other all week, given how much she had to do. And the chances of her passing out from exhaustion the moment her head hit the pillow, regardless of who was snoring away beside her, were high. It would all be fine.

'There you go, then. Not a problem.'

'Exactly,' Laurel agreed, wondering why it still felt like one.

For a long moment they stared at each other, as if still figuring out what they'd let themselves in for. Then Laurel glimpsed the clock on the dressing table and gasped.

'The welcome drinks! I need to get ready.'

Dan waved a hand towards the bathroom. 'Be my guest. I'll just be out here.'

He leant back and stretched out on the bed, his black T-shirt riding up just enough to give her a glimpse of the tanned skin and a smattering of dark hair underneath. She swallowed, and looked away.

'Don't give me another thought,' he said.

'I won't.' She grabbed her dress from where it hung on the outside of the wardrobe, gathered up her make-up bag from the dressing table, and retreated to the relative calm and peace of the bathroom.

Where she promptly realised, upon stepping into the shower, that she still knew next to nothing about her pretend boyfriend and she had to go and meet his parents within the hour.

Clunking her head against the tiles of the shower

wall, Laurel wondered exactly how she'd managed to make this week even more unbearable than Melissa had managed.

Dan heard the click of the bathroom door opening and put down the magazine he'd found on the coffee table, which extolled the wonders of the British countryside. Laurel stepped through the door and he realised that the British countryside had nothing on the woman he was sharing a room and apparently a fake relationship with.

'Think I'll do?' Laurel asked, giving him a lopsided smile as she turned slowly in the doorway.

The movement revealed that the long, slim black dress she'd chosen—a dress that clung to her ample curves in a way that made his brain go a little mushy—draped down from her shoulders to leave her back almost entirely bare.

'I mean, we need this charade to be believable, right? Do you think your family will believe you'd date someone like me?'

'I think they'll wonder why you're slumming it with a guy like me,' he replied honestly, still staring at the honey-coloured skin of her back. Did she know what that sort of dress could do to a man? 'You look better than any of those actresses that'll be out there tonight.'

Laurel pulled a face. 'I appreciate the lie, but—'

'Who's lying?' Dan interrupted. 'Trust me, I've met most of them. And none of them could wear that dress like you do.'

She still looked unconvinced, so Dan got up from the bed and crossed over to her. 'This,' he said, laying a hand at the base of her back, 'is a very nice touch.'

'You don't think it's too much? Or…well, too little?'

She looked up at him with wide, dark eyes, all vulnerability and openness, and Dan thought, *Damn*.

This was where he got into trouble. Every time. A woman looked at him that way—as if he could answer all her questions, give her what she needed, make her world a better place—and he fell for it. He believed he *could* make a difference.

And then she walked off with the first *real* movie star to look at her twice. Every time.

Well, not this one. Laurel wasn't his girlfriend, his crush, or his lover. She was his partner in this little game they were playing. Maybe she'd even become a friend. But that was it. She was looking for a prince, not a stand-in.

Which meant he should probably stop staring into her eyes around now.

'It's perfect,' he said, stepping away. 'Come on. We'd better get down to the bar, right? I figure you probably have work to do tonight.'

Laurel nodded, and grabbed her clutch bag from the dressing table. Then she turned back to frown at him. 'Wait—you're going like that?'

Arms spread wide, Dan looked down at his dark jeans, the black shirt open at the collar, and his usual boots. Admittedly, they were somewhat more casual than the suits and ties he imagined the other guys in attendance would be wearing.

'You don't like it?'

'I love it.' A smile spread across her face as she opened the door for him. 'And not *just* because Melissa will hate it.'

Dan grinned back. 'All the more reason, then.'

* * *

The bar where they were holding the welcome drinks had been decked out with decorations in cool shades of icy blue and green. Not streamers and bunting and stuff—the sort of decorations Dan remembered from other kids' parties when he was younger. These decorations were…classy. Expensive. Yet somehow slightly over the top, as if they were trying too hard. But then, he was starting to get the feeling that that was just Melissa all over.

'It looks like the seaside threw up in here,' he said to a passing waiter as he grabbed a champagne flute from the tray he was carrying.

'Very good, sir,' the waiter said, as if his words had made sense.

Dan sighed. Laurel might have understood. Except Laurel had probably decorated the room herself, so maybe he wouldn't mention it. Just in case.

Besides, every time he caught a glimpse of Laurel through the crowd all he saw was that honey-gold back, taunting him. It was as if her very dress was screaming, *See this? You have to look at it, lie next to it all night, and never touch it. Ha!*

Perhaps the dress was punishment for something—except he hadn't even known Laurel long enough to do anything worth punishing. Unless it was more of an existential punishment. A general torture inflicted on him by the universe for past sins.

Even then, it seemed a little over the top. He hadn't been *that* bad. Had he?

As if to answer the question, he caught a glimpse of a balding head through the crowd, accompanied by a shrill voice, and realised that his parents had arrived. Apparently his day was about to get worse.

Steeling himself, Dan drained his champagne as his father spotted him and beckoned him over. Of course they couldn't *possibly* come to him. He had to go and report in with them. They'd travel all the way to England for Riley's wedding—just as they'd visited him on set across the States and the rest of the world. But they'd never once visited Dan's offices, or any film he was working on, even while they were staying with Riley in LA.

He supposed it was fair. He'd never visited their workplaces either—never made it to a lecture they'd given. Never even shown up and been the respectable son they wanted at any of their fancy events. In fact from the moment he'd realised that he'd always be second-best to Riley in their eyes he'd given up trying all together.

Why bother trying to live up to expectations he could never match, or trying to be good enough for people who not only expected more, but wanted someone completely different? He wasn't the son they wanted, so he didn't try to pretend otherwise. In fact, for most of his teenage years he'd gone out of his way to be the exact opposite. And during his twenties, actually.

Even marrying Cassie had been a big middle finger to his parents, who'd hated every inch of the trailer-trash-made-average actress. Of course that little act of rebellion had come back to bite him when he'd fallen in love with her, against his own better judgement. Love made you *want* to be good enough, something he'd spent his whole life avoiding.

When she'd left him he'd known he'd never try to be

good enough for anybody else again. He was his own man and that was enough.

Even if it meant dealing with his parents' disappointment every now and again.

He snagged another glass of champagne as he crossed the room towards them, but refrained from drinking it just yet. If the conversation went at all the way he expected he'd need it later.

'Quite the venue our Riley has managed to get for this shindig, huh, son?'

Wendell Black smacked Dan between the shoulder blades, too hard to be casual, not hard enough to actually hurt—even if Dan wasn't sure that hadn't been the intention.

'Oh, Wendell, I'm sure *Melissa* had the final say on the venue.' His mother's nose wrinkled ever so slightly. 'Didn't she work here once, or something?'

'Nothing wrong with working your way all the way up,' Wendell said. 'It's working your way down that's the problem!' He laughed—too loudly—and Dan clenched his jaw.

'Hello, Mother, Father,' he said, after the laughter had subsided. Just because *they'd* forgone basic greetings—as if it hadn't been two years since they'd last seen each other—it didn't mean he had to.

'Daniel.' His mother eyed him critically. 'Do you really think that's an appropriate outfit for tonight?'

'I'm hoping that Riley will be so pleased to see me he won't care what I'm wearing.' It was partly true; Riley generally cared far less than his parents about appropriate attire. Probably because he just let Melissa or his stylist dress him for all events.

Dan shuddered at the very idea. The last thing he

needed was someone telling him what to wear. In his experience next came what to say, then what to do, then who to be.

He was very happy being himself, thank you.

Letting his gaze roam around the room, he tried to pretend he was just taking in the occasion, even though he knew there was really only one person he was looking for. One long black dress, and dark brown hair pinned up at the nape of her neck above that bare back. How had she captivated him so quickly? Dan couldn't help but think he wouldn't mind taking directions from Laurel, under certain circumstances. Especially if she was telling him what clothing to take *off* rather than put on.

But that line of thinking was dangerous. If anyone had expectations it was Laurel. And he had no intention of trying to live up to them.

'So, I suppose I should ask how the business is doing,' his mother said, ignoring his comment about Riley, just as she always ignored anything she didn't agree with.

'It would be polite,' Dan agreed. He'd scanned the whole bar and not spotted her—and she was hard to miss in that dress. Where was she?

'Daniel,' his mother said, warning clear in her voice.

He shouldn't make her actually ask. That would be showing far too much interest in his disreputable industry.

How his parents managed to live with the hypocritical distinction they made between cheerleading Riley's A-List celebrity career and looking down on his own lucrative and respected film-related business, Dan had no idea. He suspected it had something to do with column inches in the celebrity magazines his mother pretended she didn't read.

There. There she was. Laurel stood at the bar, her posture stiff and awkward as she talked to an older couple. He squinted at them. Nobody he recognised, so probably family. In fact, probably *her* family. And she looked about as excited to be talking to them as he was to be stuck alone with his.

Well, now. Wasn't that just a win-win situation for everyone in the making? He could swoop in, save Laurel from her family, then drag her over to meet his and she could at least keep him company and give him something pretty to look at while his parents put him down.

'Sorry, Mother. If you'll excuse me a moment, there's someone I'd really like you to meet. I'll be right back.'

Not waiting for an answer, Dan pushed his way through the crowd towards the bar—and Laurel. Spotting Benjamin watching him as he crossed the room, he gave Laurel's ex a flash of smile and a small wave, just to remind him that *he* was Laurel's boyfriend now. Fake or otherwise.

Then he got back to the task in hand—rescuing Laurel. He paused just a metre or two away from where she stood, hands twisting round each other in front of her belly, and took stock of her companions.

The man who Dan assumed was her father was short and stocky, with a thatch of grey hair above deep-set eyes. His suit looked expensive, but he fiddled with the cufflinks as if they were still a little unfamiliar. Dan guessed that Melissa had dressed her parents up for the occasion, the way she wanted them to be seen. See? It wasn't even just wives who did that. Perhaps all women were just as culpable.

Except Laurel. She'd thought his outfit was perfect—if only because it would annoy her sister. Which was a good enough reason for him to keep wearing it.

Melissa's mother—Laurel's stepmother, he supposed—wore a peacock-bright gown that looked too flashy next to her faded blonde hair. Her make-up was heavy, as if trying to hide the lines of her age, but somehow making them all the more obvious.

Then Laurel turned slightly, glancing over her shoulder—maybe looking for him? Dan stepped forward, ready to play knight in shining armour for his pretend girlfriend even if he couldn't manage to be a real prince.

'Laurel.' He smiled, resting his fingertips against her shoulder as he moved behind her. 'There you are. Do you have a moment, honey? I know you're busy working, but there are some people I'd like you to meet.'

Or rescue him from. It was practically the same thing, right?

The relieved smile she sent up at him told him he'd done the right thing, even if her parents were looking rather less impressed at the interruption.

'Dad, Angela, this is Dan. He's my...' She faltered for a moment, then started again. 'We're together.'

'Dan?' Angela's eyes narrowed. 'You didn't say you were bringing a date to the wedding, Laurel. I know we talked about the exclusivity of the guest list, under the circumstances. It's not like this is any old wedding.'

'And I'm not any old date,' Dan said cheerfully as he held out his hand to Laurel's father. 'Dan Black, sir,' he said as they shook. Then he turned to offer his hand to Angela. 'Riley's older brother.'

Angela's face tightened as her handshake turned weak and she tugged her fingers from his. 'Riley's brother.' She turned to glare at Laurel. 'Well. This *is* unexpected. Does Melissa know that you two are…?' She waved a hand vaguely between them, as if articulating the relationship was too disgusting even to contemplate.

'Not yet.'

Laurel's words came out small, subdued, and Dan reached out to touch her again, to remind her that she wasn't alone. Wasn't that the whole point of this charade, anyway?

'We thought we'd share our good news with her this evening,' Dan said, trying to keep his tone bright and his expression oblivious to the glares Angela was spreading around their little group. 'I'm sure she and Riley will be very happy for us.'

'I'm sure they will,' Laurel's father said, apparently also immune to the glares. At least until Angela elbowed him in his soft middle. 'Oh, but…perhaps tonight isn't the night to tell them, darling,' he added, having finally got a clue. 'It's a very big night for Melissa.'

'It's a very big week all round,' Dan agreed. 'But, really, I do always think that keeping love a secret sends the wrong message, don't you? And I wouldn't ever want Laurel to doubt my feelings about her.'

Maybe that was going a little far, judging by the way Angela's face paled and Laurel's father's cheeks turned a rosy shade of red at the reminder of how she'd been his mistress for almost two decades. Dan tested his conscience and discovered he didn't care. If they couldn't take it, he decided, they really shouldn't spread such poisonous looks and comments around in the first place.

'Now, if you'll excuse us a moment?'

He reached an arm around Laurel's shoulders, trying hard only to touch the dress and not her bare skin—which, given the design, wasn't easy. But he knew that if he placed his hands on that long, lean back he'd be done for. And he needed all his wits about him if they both wanted to make it through the evening intact.

'You shouldn't have said that,' she whispered to him as they turned away.

'Probably not,' he agreed. 'But you have to admit it *was* fun.'

The secret smile she gave him was reward enough.

'Where are we going?' she asked as he steered her across the room.

'Ah.' As much as he wished he could just lead her out of the bar, back through the endless hotel corridors to their room, he had promised his parents he was coming back. With her. 'Well, if you consider your parents the frying pan…let's just say our next stop could be thought of as the fire.'

Laurel groaned. 'I'm going to need more champagne for this, aren't I?'

'Definitely,' Dan said, and flagged down a passing waiter.

CHAPTER FOUR

LAUREL'S MIND WAS still replaying the moment Dan had managed to insult and embarrass her father and stepmother all in the same moment, with just one passing comment, as he handed her a glass of champagne and they continued their journey across the huge hotel bar. She had a feeling she'd be reliving it all week, as an antidote to whatever repercussions Angela deemed appropriate for the injury. The thing was, of course, she couldn't *actually* disagree with anything Dan had said. Just the implications, and the suggestion that he had every intention of sharing the news of their relationship with the bride that evening.

Melissa, Laurel knew, would be livid. The thing she hated most in the world was people stealing her thunder. And while at her own wedding that might be moderately understandable, the fact was it wouldn't matter what the circumstances: Melissa hated anyone else getting any attention at all—especially if she felt it had been taken away from her.

Perhaps it was a hold-over from her childhood when, ignored by her own father for sixteen years, she'd had to try and win attention in other ways. Maybe that explained why she'd become not just an actress, but a celebrity, whose every move and look was pored over by the press and the public.

As far as Laurel was concerned it certainly explained why she'd become a stone-cold witch.

'Brace yourself,' Dan muttered as they approached another older couple—far more polished and professional-looking than her own father and stepmother, despite Melissa's insistence on stylists for them both for the week.

'This is the worst Meet the Parents evening ever,' she murmured back, and Dan flashed her a quick smile.

'And we're only halfway there.'

Halfway. That was something. She'd survived her own parents—with Dan at her side had done more than just survive. She'd left on her own terms and with the upper hand—something she wasn't sure had ever happened before in the history of her relationship with them.

Now she owed Dan the same.

'Mother. Father.' Dan gave Laurel the slightest push so she stood half in front of him. 'I'd like you to meet my girlfriend—Laurel.'

There was no hesitation in his speech, no hitching of his voice over the lie. He seemed perfectly comfortable introducing an almost total stranger to his parents as his one and only love. Maybe she should be a little more concerned about sharing a bedroom—and a fake relationship—with such a consummate liar.

But Dan's parents' attention was entirely on her, and there was no more time to worry about it. It was time to put on the show.

'Laurel, these are my parents—Wendell and Linda Black.'

'It's a pleasure to meet you both at last,' Laurel said, pasting on her prettiest smile. 'Dan's told me so much about you, and of course we've been in touch over the wedding planning.' She just hoped they didn't ask exactly *what* he'd said about them, since the sum total of her knowledge of them was their names and what she'd scribbled down in her notebook when Melissa had been running through the guest list.

'You're the organiser woman,' Wendell said, clicking his fingers. 'Of course! All those detailed schedules and flight plan options. Well, Dan, I have to say, she's not your usual type!'

'Which can only be an advantage, I suppose,' Linda added drily.

She scrutinised Laurel so closely that she felt almost as if she were on a doctor's examination table.

'So. You're a wedding planner.'

'She owns the business organising Riley and Melissa's wedding,' Dan corrected her, before Laurel could answer. 'The biggest celebrity wedding of the year. Quite the coup, I'm sure you'll agree.'

'Unless your sister is the bride,' Linda said, and Laurel gritted her teeth.

Melissa being her sister had only made this job harder, not easier, and the truth was she'd done an amazing job in difficult circumstances. Somehow, she didn't think Dan's parents were the sort of people to appreciate that.

'So, you purposely set out to build a business that… organises people's weddings for them?' Wendell was frowning, as if he couldn't quite make sense of the idea. 'Why? I mean, you're obviously a bright young woman. You'd have to be good with details and planning to pull

off this sort of affair. Why not use your talents somewhere they could really matter?'

'Maybe you were wrong, Wendell,' Linda put it.
'Seems like she's just like Dan after all.'

Beside her Laurel felt Dan stiffen, and wondered how
many times they'd said the same thing to him. That he
was wasting his time doing what he loved, running the
company he'd built from the ground up all by himself.
That his success didn't matter because he wasn't doing
something they approved of. That he was wasting his
time on something unimportant.

Did they feel the same way about Riley? Or was
his celebrity status enough of an achievement to avoid
their censure?

Dan hadn't spoken, and when she glanced up at him
his expression was stone-like, flat and hard and unyield-
ing. She hoped the glass stem of his champagne flute
was strong, given the tight grip he seemed to have on it.

Time for her to return the parental put-down for him.

'You're both doctors, aren't you?' she asked, still
smiling sweetly. 'Very successful and famous ones,
by all accounts.'

'That's right,' Wendell said, puffed up with his own
pride.

Linda nodded a little more cautiously.

'I think that's marvellous,' Laurel said honestly. 'I
think it's wonderful that your natural talents have led
you to a field where you can make such a difference in
the world. I think it's so important for *everyone* to follow their natural talents, wherever they lead, don't you?'

'I suppose so,' Wendell agreed, but he was frowning as he spoke.

'Some talents are obviously more valuable than others, though,' Linda added.

Laurel tilted her head to the side. 'Do you really think so? I've always believed that *every* talent is equally valid and valuable. I mean, imagine if everyone in the world only possessed the same sort of talent! If we were all doctors there'd be no one left to do anything else. You'd suddenly find yourselves spending your whole days learning how to design a car, or having to clean your own home, or write your own books to read—and have no time left for medicine at all.'

'Well, I hardly think that's going to happen.'

Linda folded her arms over her chest, and for a moment Laurel wondered if she was simply going to walk away from her. But she didn't. Whether it was politeness or morbid curiosity, she was going to wait and see where Laurel was going with this.

Good.

'Of course not,' Laurel agreed. 'Not everyone is going to be a doctor. Or a wedding planner, for that matter. But the thing is, the people I organise weddings for…quite often they're not good at the same things as me. They're not good at the details, or the inspiration, or the planning. I can take that off their shoulders so they can get on with what they *are* good at—whether that's saving lives, educating children, or starring in movies. And at the same time I get to do what I love—and make a decent living out of it, thank you. So it works for everyone.'

'Not to mention the fact that a wedding can be the most important, memorable day in a person's life,' Dan put in. 'Laurel makes sure that it is perfect for them.

She literally makes their memories. I think that's pretty important, don't you?'

He reached out to rest a hand at the small of her back and Laurel froze at the contact, feeling the warmth of his touch snake all the way up her spine. Why on earth had she chosen this dress? Couldn't she have picked something with a little more fabric? Something that didn't make her feel as if she was naked in front of his parents?

Of course when she'd packed it she hadn't expected to be spending the evening as someone's girlfriend.

'And the same goes for Dan's business, of course,' Laurel added, smiling dotingly up at him. 'He's made a hugely successful career out of doing what other people can't—what they wouldn't dare to try. I imagine Riley's career in blockbuster action movies would have been a lot less successful without people like Dan stepping in to do the really wild stuff. Don't you agree?'

Even if they did, Laurel was sure Wendell and Linda wouldn't say so. But sometimes, as she'd found with her parents, just letting them know that their opinion wasn't the only one was enough. Enough to make her feel a little better about never being *quite* good enough for them.

And, from the way Dan's fingers caressed her spine, she suspected he felt the same.

Leaning in against his side, she let herself imagine for a moment that this wasn't an act. That he really was there to support her.

Wait. That part *was* true. They might not be a couple, might not be in love, but they were both there to help the other through the week from hell. And suddenly Laurel realised that that might be all she needed after all.

'Linda! Wendell!'

Laurel stiffened again at the sound of her stepmother's voice. Yes, that was what this situation needed—more awful parents.

'Angela.' Linda's voice was tight, her smile barely reaching her lips. 'And Duncan. So lovely to see you both again.'

'Well, we should probably—' Dan started, but Angela interrupted him.

'Oh, no, Dan, do stay. I mean, now we're all going to be family I'm sure we're all just *dying* to hear exactly how you met our Laurel and how you came to be together. *Such* a surprise—don't you agree, Linda?'

'A total shock,' Linda said flatly. 'But then, we're rather used to those from Dan.'

'So, how *did* you two meet?'

Laurel glanced up at Dan at her father's words, hoping he might have a suitable story prepared. Why had she wasted so much time hiding from him in the bathroom when they could have been preparing for this exact question?

'Well…' Dan said.

Laurel held her breath, waiting for the lie.

But before he could start to tell it the main door to the bar flew open and there stood Melissa, resplendent in the forest-green gown her stylist had finally got her to agree to, after twenty-two other dresses had been deemed unsuitable. Riley was half hidden behind her, his tux making far less of an impact even with his all-American good looks.

'Friends! My fiancé and I are just so delighted to welcome you all here to celebrate our wedding.' Melissa beamed around the room and Riley stepped out of her shadow, looking awkward in his dinner jacket, and gave

a little wave. 'I hope you all have just the best time—'
She cut off abruptly, her sideways smile replaced by a
sudden scowl as her gaze fell on Laurel and Dan.

Oh, dear.

Laurel made to move away from Dan's side—just
enough to give them plausible deniability until Melissa
had finished her public announcements. But Dan's arm
tightened around her waist, holding her close, and when
she looked up at him his eyes were locked with Melissa's.

He wanted this. Wanted the conflict and the declaration and Melissa's wrath. But why? Just to see her
reaction?

Laurel couldn't help but feel she was missing half
the story, here, and she really didn't like it.

'What the *hell* is going on here?' Melissa demanded,
still staring at them, her hands on her hips.

'We...' Laurel started to speak, but her mouth was
too dry and the word came out as little more than a
whisper. Her whole body felt too hot, flushed with panic
and the sort of intense guilt and fear that only Melissa
could make her feel. Only the half-sister whose life
she'd stolen, whose happiness she'd lived, even when
she hadn't known Melissa even existed.

She could never make that up to Melissa, no matter
how hard she tried. But Laurel knew she had to keep
trying, regardless. That was only fair.

And now she was ruining Melissa's big night. She
was a horrible person.

From nowhere, Eloise appeared, looking slightly
flustered and flushed, her cheeks a shade of pink that
clashed horribly with her red hair. She swooped in and
put an arm around Melissa's shoulders, whispering fast

and low into the bride's ear. Slowly Melissa's thunderous expression retreated, to be replaced with the sweetness-and-light smile that she usually displayed for the crowds and her public.

'Anyway, I do hope you are all enjoying your evening,' she went on, as if her previous outburst had never happened.

Whatever Eloise had said, it seemed to have worked. The tightness in Laurel's chest started to ease just enough to let her breathe properly again. Dan stroked the base of her back once more, and she relaxed into his touch. She wasn't alone. She wasn't the only one Melissa was furious with right now. Whatever happened next, she had back-up.

And that meant a lot today.

'I'm looking forward to talking with every one of you, and welcoming you personally to Melissa and Riley's Wedding Extravaganza!' Melissa finished, with a flourish, holding out her skirt and giving a slight curtsey.

As sponsored by Star! *magazine*, Laurel added mentally. It was still all a show to Melissa. She wondered if the actual marriage part—the bit that came next and theoretically for the rest of their lives—had even really registered with her half-sister. She hoped so. Because otherwise she had a feeling that Dan would be having words with his brother, and she really didn't want this whole thing called off at the last moment.

The crowd applauded, as if on command, and then turned back to their own conversations. The moment the attention was off her Melissa's face dropped back into a disapproving scowl once more. She strode across to where Dan and Laurel were standing with their parents, Riley tailing behind.

'Something you'd like to tell me, *sister*?' Melissa asked, her voice dripping with sarcasm.

Laurel felt her chest start to tighten again. 'Um… Well…'

Dan's fingers splayed out across her bare back—a reassuring presence. 'Melissa. It's so lovely to finally meet you,' he said, all politeness. 'Obviously I've heard plenty about you already, but it's nice to actually meet my sister-in-law-to-be in the flesh, so to speak.'

Melissa blinked up at him, wrong-footed by the polite tone. 'Of course. It's lovely to meet you too. Dan. I just wasn't aware that you were so well acquainted with my sister.'

Half-sister, Laurel's brain filled in. Melissa always referred to her as her half-sister, unless there was something to gain by claiming the full connection. In this case, she guessed, that would be guilt. Laurel's guilt, particularly. She wanted Laurel thinking, *How could I possibly do this to my sister at her wedding?*

And, of course, that was exactly what she *was* thinking.

'Dan and Laurel were just about to tell us how they met, darling,' Angela said, leaning over to kiss her daughter on the cheek. 'You look stunning, by the way.'

'Thank you,' Melissa replied, accepting the compliment automatically, as her due. 'That's a story I'd be very interested to hear. It's really quite difficult to imagine *how* or *when* you two might have been able to meet and start a relationship. Or what on earth you've found in common.'

You mean, what on earth does he see in me? Laurel

translated. She'd been interpreting Melissa's put-downs and comments for enough years now to figure out exactly what their underlying message was. It helped to know that whenever Melissa next got her alone, Laurel could be sure to hear the unfiltered version—the cutting words she wouldn't say in front of other people. Laurel had taken to treating it as a game, a way to distract herself from the hurt Melissa's comments caused, scoring herself on how accurate her translations were rather than dwelling on what truth there might be in her half-sister's words.

'Oh, we got chatting over email to start with,' Dan said lightly, answering the question Melissa had actually asked rather than the implied one. 'All that wedding planning, organising flights and such. I had some scheduling issues, and Laurel helped me sort them out. Went above and beyond, really.'

All true, so far, Laurel observed. Obviously he was banking on the fact that the truth was easier to remember than a lie.

But next came the part where he started making things up.

'Then I got a call inviting me over to London for some meetings with a couple of people in the industry here,' Dan said, shrugging. 'At that point—well, it seemed natural that I suggest we meet up for a drink while I was over here. One thing led to another...'

'I don't think we need to hear about that, Daniel,' Linda said sharply, and Laurel hid her grin.

'You never said, man!' Riley beamed at his brother and held out both hands, clasping Dan's between them. 'This is so great! We'll be like, brothers, but we'll also be, like, brothers-in-law!'

'It's all still fairly new,' Laurel cautioned, sensing that Riley was about to get carried away.

The last thing she needed, after the humiliation of one broken engagement, was for her family to start believing she'd be the next one up the aisle, when in truth they hadn't even made it to a first date. Which was kind of a shame, really. Under normal circumstances maybe she and Dan *could* have gone out on a date like normal people. That was one thing this charade had taken firmly off the table, though.

Not the right place, not the right time, and not the right prince. She had to remember that.

'But it's serious,' Melissa said, looking at them both thoughtfully.

Apparently she'd bought the lie, Laurel realised. Which only made her more nervous about what Melissa planned to do with the knowledge.

'Very,' Dan lied, pulling Laurel closer.

Laurel tried to smile in agreement.

'Because obviously you wouldn't want to steal my thunder like this for a casual fling, would you?'

There it was.

'Of course not,' Laurel said, knowing that there was no way out now. This mock relationship had to make it all the way through to the wedding or all hell would break loose. The only thing Melissa would consider worse than Dan and Laurel getting together at her wedding, distracting attention from her, was them splitting up in any kind of public way between now and the wedding.

Which meant they were stuck with each other for good. Or at least for the next five days. Which kind of felt like the same thing. Laurel had found it impossible to see past New Year's Day for months now…the idea of a world in which she wasn't organising Melissa's wedding was just a strange, faraway dream.

'I'm afraid that true love just doesn't work to order, Melissa.'

Dan kissed the top of her head, and Laurel tried not to feel the walls closing in on her.

'Let's get some more champagne,' Eloise said, clapping her hands together and drawing the attention of a passing waiter.

'What a marvellous idea,' Laurel agreed.

It was a couple of hours before Dan finally managed to drag Laurel away from the welcome drinks. As the wedding planner, she'd insisted on staying until the bitter end, making sure that everything went according to her schedule. At least their parents had all toddled off to bed around midnight, shortly after Melissa's precisely timed and highly orchestrated departure. And, despite Dan's best efforts to get his brother alone for a chat—thwarted mostly by the endless stream of friends wanting to buy the groom a drink—Riley had sloped off shortly after Melissa, with far less fanfare, presumably to the room that was supposed to be Dan's.

So when all that was left was a few of the hardcore drinkers, doing shots at the bar, Dan steered Laurel towards the door.

'Come on. There's nothing left for you to do here. I'm shattered, and you must be too. Let's go get some sleep. It's going to be another long day tomorrow.'

Laurel smiled up at him wearily. 'You're right, I know. I just hate leaving before everything is finished and tidied away.'

Dan glanced back towards the bar. 'You could be here all night with this lot. Better save your energy for a more important battle.'

Which, in Dan's case, he suspected would be trying to sleep in the same bed as Laurel without touching her. It was one thing to decide that a woman was off-limits, employing that famous control he was so proud of. It was another thing entirely to *like* it. Resisting temptation was always harder when temptation was lying right next to him.

'Like managing Melissa,' Laurel said, and sighed. 'Yeah, okay.'

They made their way up to their room in companionable silence, but Dan couldn't help but wonder if she was doing the same thing he was—mentally reliving their evening together.

The strangest thing, he decided, was the difference in Laurel when she spoke to her sister. With her father and stepmother she'd been reticent, as if she was holding back from saying what she really felt. She'd had no such compunction with his parents, he realised. She'd been polite, charming, but forthright with it—and left them in no doubts about her views.

A warm feeling filled his chest when he remembered the things she'd said about him and the importance of living according to your *own* talents, dreams and values, not someone else's. For the first time in years he had honestly felt as if someone understood what he was doing, what he wanted. Understood *him*.

It was almost a shame it was all an act, really.

Besides, that confidence and conviction had disappeared the moment Melissa had entered the room. He'd watched it drain away from her, as if Melissa had sucked it out, leaving her half-sister empty.

He hadn't liked seeing Laurel like that. Since the moment they'd met she'd been so bright and vivacious—except when Melissa was there, in person or on the phone, commanding her complete attention and energy.

'Here we go,' Laurel said, rubbing her eye with one hand while the other fumbled with the key.

Dan took it from her and opened the door, letting her through first. As it swung shut behind him he headed straight to the mini-bar. 'Want anything?' he asked, staring at the contents as he tried to decide if one more drink would make things better or worse. Alcohol wasn't always the best thing for retaining his control.

Of course his control would be a lot easier to hold on to if he knew that Laurel wasn't at all interested. Maybe he should just ask her—get it out of the way. She'd tell him once again that she was holding out for a hero, or whatever, and that all they could ever have was a fake relationship. Then he could move on, safe in the knowledge that there was no risk of anything more at all.

Except…there were hints. Tiny ones. Hints Laurel might not even be aware of but he couldn't help but catalogue and add to his list of things he knew about Laurel.

The way she leant into his touch. The warmth in her eyes when she looked at him. The shiver he'd felt go through her when he'd first touched the base of her back…

Laurel had told him herself that she was a terrible actress. So why was she acting as if she was as attracted to him as he was to her?

Dan stared balefully at the tiny bottles of spirits

in front of him, knowing that the chances were they wouldn't help at all.

Laurel shook her head. 'I'm done.'

'Me too.' He let the fridge door close. 'Want to use the bathroom first?'

It was a gentlemanly offer, and had the added advantage that Laurel looked so exhausted that if she got into bed first Dan was pretty sure she'd be passed out before he even managed to slip between the covers.

At least that way she wouldn't notice if he couldn't sleep at all.

As she locked the bathroom door behind her Dan took the opportunity to strip down to his boxers and a T-shirt. That was acceptable nightwear, right? Usually he didn't bother, but he figured even sleepy Laurel would object to complete nudity when she woke up in the morning.

Sitting on the edge of the bed to wait his turn, Dan tried not to imagine what Laurel might be doing in there. Whether she was naked, most specifically. What she wore to bed. How she looked sleep-tousled, her hair loose around her shoulders…

It didn't matter. She was *off-limits*.

As much as he might fantasise otherwise.

Finally she was done. She waved a hand to motion him towards the bathroom as she passed him, and before he could stand she'd already slipped under the covers— on the side of the bed *he* usually slept on. Fantastic.

Still, she looked so tired he couldn't even object.

In the harsh light of the bathroom he stared into the mirror at his familiar old face and tried to convince himself that this wasn't a big deal. So he was sharing a bed with a beautiful woman? So what? It wasn't as if it hadn't happened before. And he sure hoped it would happen again. Often.

So why was his heart hammering just a little too fast in his chest? And why did his hands shake as he reached for his toothbrush?

Okay, fine. He knew exactly why, and he couldn't even claim it was all down to Laurel.

It was the Cassie thing.

But Laurel didn't know that he hadn't spent a full night in bed with another woman since his divorce—and she didn't need to know. Yeah, it might feel a bit strange, but so what? This wasn't romance, and it wasn't love—they'd been clear about that, if nothing else. He wasn't going to get his heart trampled on when Laurel looked around and found someone better.

This was platonic. All he had to do was keep his hands to himself for the night and it would all be fine.

Pep-talk over, he switched off the light and headed back into the bedroom, trying to be as silent as he could to avoid waking Laurel.

But to his surprise, when he settled under the covers, she murmured, 'Goodnight,' and he realised she wasn't asleep at all.

'Night, Laurel,' he whispered back.

And then he lay there, staring at the ceiling and listening to her breathe.

She wasn't a heavy breather, at least. Her shallow breaths were barely audible, even in the stillness of the night. He waited almost without realising he was doing so for them to deepen, for her breathing to grow slow and steady, the way it did when a woman was sleeping. Usually it would be a signal that it was time for him to leave. Tonight…tonight maybe it would mean that he could sleep.

Except her breathing *didn't* even out. It didn't grow deeper.

Because she wasn't sleeping.

Dan held in a sigh. One of them was going to have to cave and fall asleep first—and it wasn't going to be him.

In which case… Well, since they weren't sleeping anyway, they might as well get to know one another properly, at last.

CHAPTER FIVE

LAUREL STIFLED A sigh as Dan remained resolutely awake beside her in the darkness. He lay motionless under the covers, but even with her back turned to him she could tell that he hadn't relaxed a single muscle. How was she supposed to sleep with the world's tensest man in bed with her?

And why on earth was *he* so tense anyway? He was probably used to sharing a bed—a guy who looked as good as Dan did couldn't be short of partners when he wanted them. She, on the other hand, hadn't shared anything with anyone since she'd broken up with Benjamin—and even before that, he hadn't stayed over for months. Well, not with her, anyway.

She was used to her own space. Used to spreading out starfish-style, in the bed. Used to not having to worry if she snored, or if her hair looked like bats had been living in it, or if she'd missed a bit of last night's mascara which was now smeared across her cheek.

She was *not* used to having a big, gorgeous, untouchable man taking over her space.

'Why are you scared of Melissa?'

And asking her difficult questions in the middle of the night.

Laurel's body tensed at Dan's words, and she forced herself to try and relax. 'I'm not scared of her.'

'Really?'

The covers rustled as Dan turned on his side, and Laurel could feel the movement of the mattress, of his body, even if she couldn't see it. She stayed facing away from him, her eyes tightly closed, and hoped he'd give up. Quickly.

'Really,' she said firmly. 'Now, if you don't mind, I'm trying to get to sleep.'

'No, you're not. You're lying there wide awake, same as me.' Dan shifted again, and the warmth of his body radiated out towards her as he grew closer.

Her eyes flew open. 'What are you doing?' Dan's face loomed over her as she flipped onto her back.

'Proving my point.' He pulled back. 'I'm not asleep… you're not asleep. We should take advantage of this time to have that getting-to-know-you conversation we should have had before we decided to stage a fake relationship this week.'

'You mean the primer we needed *before* we had to meet each other's families?' Laurel asked, eyebrows raised. Talk about shutting the barn door once the horse had stood around, drunk too much champagne and been vaguely insulting to everyone. Wait…that probably hadn't been the horse…

'So it's a little late?' Dan shrugged, pulling himself up to a seated position, his back against the headboard. 'Doesn't mean it's not still worthwhile. I mean, we have to spend the whole week with these people.'

'Fooling them,' Laurel agreed reluctantly. They really did need to talk. And if they didn't do it now, goodness only knew when they'd get the time.

Dan obviously sensed her agreement. He patted the pillow beside him and she dragged herself up, tugging the slippery satin of her pyjama top with her to make sure she was still decently covered. The problem with curves like hers, she'd always found, was that they liked to try to escape, and normal clothes weren't always built to stop them.

'But you definitely get to start,' she said as she settled herself down. It felt oddly intimate, talking in the darkness with Dan. 'Everyone in the world already knows everything there is to know about my family and Melissa.'

'Not everything,' Dan said quietly.

His earlier question echoed through her brain again. *'Why are you scared of Melissa?'*

'Enough to be going on with,' she countered. 'So, your turn. What's the deal with your parents? Can't cope with their sons not going into the family medical business?'

Dan shook his head slowly. 'Not exactly, I don't think. Partly, I'm sure. As you probably noticed, they don't have all that much respect for what I do.'

'Or what *anyone* does if it isn't saving lives?' Laurel guessed. 'Except they're not like that with Riley. Or are they?'

'Riley's always been different.'

His voice sounded rough, as if it carried the weight of a thousand slights, of a hundred times he'd not been as good. Laurel wondered for a moment if that was how Melissa had felt those first sixteen years.

She waited, silent in the dark, until he was ready to fill the void with his story.

'Riley was always the golden boy, from the moment

he was born. I was…eight, I guess, so old enough to re-member life without him. Before him everything just seemed normal. Probably because I didn't know anything else. But when Riley was born…' He sighed. 'He was their miracle boy. The baby they never thought they'd be able to have. The doctors had warned them, after they had me, that my mother might struggle. But you've met my parents. They don't give up without a fight. And they love to celebrate their victories.'

'So Riley was a victory to them?' Laurel shifted a little closer, tugging the duvet up to her shoulders to keep warm.

'Riley was *everything* to them. It was like I ceased to exist.'

'I know that feeling,' Laurel said, and the image of her father's face when he'd seen her in Angela and Melissa's house for the first time filled her mind. That was the moment when she'd realised that her father had a new life, a new daughter. That he didn't need her any more.

Dan's arm snaked around her shoulder, pulling her against his side, and the warmth of his body took the chill from her thoughts.

'I suppose you do,' he said. 'I guess we're more alike than I would ever have thought.'

'Both older siblings of a more famous brother or sister?' Laurel guessed. 'Or both the least favoured child?'

'Either or,' Dan said easily. 'You and me…we're the ones in the shadows, aren't we? The ones who just get on with the business of living.'

The business of living. She liked that. She liked the idea that her life could just carry on going, regardless of what Melissa chose to do. That she still had her own life, her own value, when the spotlight of Melissa's fame moved on again, as it always would.

'I guess we are,' she said. 'It's nice to have someone who understands for a change.'

And strange to think that if it hadn't been for Melissa's last-minute change of heart about the wedding favours they might never have been in a position to discover that about each other.

Suddenly the idea of making it through the week without Dan by her side felt…impossible.

'So, what did you do?' she asked. 'When you realised you could never live up to Riley in their eyes?'

It was something she often wondered about herself. Whether, if she'd known about Melissa earlier, if her father had left when she was a baby rather than a teenager, her life would have been different. Would she still have spent her whole adult life trying to be good enough? She certainly wouldn't have spent the last sixteen years trying to make amends to Melissa for something she knew in her heart wasn't even her fault.

Maybe Melissa would have tried to make amends to her, impossible as that sounded.

'Do? Nothing,' Dan said. 'Well. Not really. I mean, I knew I couldn't be what my parents, what everybody wanted me to be. I couldn't be Riley. So I decided to do the opposite. I rebelled in basically every possible direction for years. Then I joined the army straight out of school, more as a way to escape than anything else.'

'The army? How did that work out for you?'

Dan gave her a rueful smile. 'Turned out I didn't like them telling me what to do any more than I liked my parents doing it. I served my time, got out the minute I could and moved to LA.'

'And became a stuntman?'

Dan shrugged. 'It was a job, and I was good at it. I had the training, and the control, and I knew how to make sure people didn't get hurt. Soon enough I had more work than I could handle, which is why I set up Black Ops Stunts.'

'You'd think that would be enough to make your parents proud.'

'Any parents but mine,' Dan joked, but Laurel could hear the pain under the flippant words. 'At least in the army I was doing something of value, even if it wasn't what they wanted. But in LA no one even knows it's me. I think that's what drives them crazy. They're all about the recognition, the fame.'

'And you're not.'

'It's the ultimate rebellion, I guess.'

How crazy. And she'd thought *her* family were dysfunctional. At least no one expected her to be famous— that was Melissa's job. In fact she wasn't sure what they wanted from her at all.

And all she wanted was to be good enough for them at last. To earn her place back in her family.

Melissa's wedding was her chance to do that.

'So. Your turn,' Dan said. 'I've heard how Melissa tells your story. How do *you* tell it?'

'Pretty much the same, I guess,' Laurel said with a small shrug. The facts were the horrible, horrible facts, and nothing she said could change that.

'Tell me anyway,' he said.

Laurel shifted under the covers, sitting cross-legged as she twisted to face him. Her side of the story… She didn't think she'd ever told that before.

'Okay… Well, until I was sixteen everything was

perfectly normal. Normal parents, normal house, normal school, normal teenage angst. Then one day my dad came home from work and said he was leaving.'

She took a deep breath and for a horrible moment she could feel tears burning behind her eyes. She hoped Dan wouldn't be able to see in the darkness.

'My mum followed him upstairs, and I could hear her sobbing and shouting while he packed his bags. Then he came downstairs, kissed me on the forehead, said he'd see me very soon and left.'

The pain didn't fade. It stung all over again as she remembered it.

'And did you?' he asked. 'See him soon, I mean?'

Laurel nodded. 'I didn't figure out what was really going on until a few days later. I was busy taking care of Mum, so I didn't leave the house much. But eventually I had to go out for some shopping. I kept my head down at the supermarket, but it didn't take long for me to realise that people were whispering and pointing at me. I started listening to those whispers…and that's how I found out that my dad had another daughter. Another family—another wife, to all intents and purposes. And he'd chosen them over me.'

Okay, never mind the other stuff. *That*, right there, was the killer. That was the part that burned every day.

'Anyway, for a while I tried to ignore it. I had Mum to look after and she…she just fell apart when I told her I knew what had happened. Maybe she could deny it if no one else knew. But once I confirmed what Dad had told her…it was like she gave up completely.'

Laurel shuddered at the memory. All those horrible days coming home from school to find her mum in the exact same position she'd left her at eight-twenty that morning. She'd tried so hard to be enough for her mother, to be reason enough for her to come back to the land of the living, to give her the love she'd lost when her dad had left.

But she'd never been able to fill the hole in her mother's heart that her father's walking out had left. And her mother had never been able to forgive her for being her father's daughter.

It was horrible to think it, but Laurel couldn't help but believe that her mum moving away to Spain eight years ago to live with an old schoolfriend was the best thing that could have happened to their relationship. Postcards and the odd phone call were much easier than dealing with each other in person.

'Eventually, once it was really clear he wasn't ever coming back, I confronted him.' Laurel continued her story, twisting her hands around each other. 'It was easy enough to find out where he was living with…*them*. People were falling over themselves to tell me.'

'Probably wanted to follow and watch,' Dan muttered.

'Probably,' Laurel agreed. 'He looked shocked to see me. Like his two worlds were colliding and he didn't like it—even though it was all his fault. Eventually he invited me in…introduced me to Melissa and her mother. We had the world's most awkward cup of tea, and then… I left.'

'That was it?' Dan asked, sounding confused. 'You didn't yell, scream at him? Anything?'

Laurel shook her head, smiling faintly. 'Melissa's mother, Angela, explained it to me. I'd had my fair share—I'd had sixteen years of a loving, doting father that Melissa had missed out on. And now it was her turn.'

Dan frowned. 'And you bought that?'

'It was the truth,' Laurel said with a small shrug. 'What else was there to say? He didn't want us any more—he wanted them. And Melissa *had* missed out.'

And she'd been making Laurel pay for it ever since.

'But that can't be your whole life,' Dan said. 'Everything didn't stop when you turned sixteen.'

'Sometimes it feels like it did,' Laurel admitted. Then she sighed. 'What happened next? Um… I went away to university, studied subjects that were utterly useless in the real world. Got a job at a small events company and worked my way up. Met up with Benjamin again in London and started dating—you already know how that ended. Then last year I decided it was time to go out on my own and start my own wedding planning business.'

'And Melissa hired you for her wedding.'

Laurel nodded. 'See? It pretty much always comes back to her in the end.'

'I know the feeling,' Dan said wryly. 'Trust me, when you're Riley Black's brother you spend a lot of time in the shadows, too. It's like you said—we understand each other. Which is why I'm going to ask you again. Why are you scared of Melissa?'

Sighing, Laurel stretched out her legs in front of her, and on impulse rested her head against his shoulder. Why couldn't constant support and understanding somehow magically come without having to actually *talk* about things? She wasn't used to having to talk about herself instead of Melissa. She didn't like it.

'I'm not scared of her. Not exactly…' she began.

Dan snorted. 'That's not how it looked to me.'

'Oh, really? Perhaps that was because you were egging her on.' Laurel bristled. 'Don't think I didn't notice how you suddenly started playing up the close body contact and the kisses on the top of the head the moment she arrived.'

Dan's laugh was utterly unrepentant. 'Can you blame me? I mean, what's the point of doing this if we can't enjoy it.'

'And you enjoyed upsetting my sister?'

'No,' he said slowly. 'But I'm not going to deny that reminding her that she's not the only thing that exists in the universe—let alone the only thing that actually matters—felt kind of good.'

Laurel sighed. 'I know what you mean. Melissa…she gets a little self-focussed. I don't know if it's a celebrity thing, or a no-father-until-she-was-sixteen thing—'

'I think it's a Melissa thing,' Dan interrupted. 'Yeah, she had some issues growing up. And, yeah, now she's a big star. But that doesn't mean she should be able to get away with treating everyone else like they don't matter.'

Laurel looked at him, trying to make out his features in the darkness. The same fears she'd felt earlier rose up inside her and she knew she had to ask. 'Are you planning on trying to stop the wedding? I mean, if you think so little of Melissa…are you really going to let her marry your brother?'

Dan sighed. 'The thing is—and this is one of those things Melissa doesn't understand—it's not up to me. I don't get to say who my brother falls in love with, or when. Do I want to make sure that he understands who he's marrying, make sure she's not lying to him about anything? Sure. But stop the wedding…' He shook his head. 'Like I told Melissa. True love doesn't work to order.'

'You meant that? I figured you were just winding her up.'

She felt him shrug, his T-shirt rubbing against her bare arms under the blanket. 'In my experience love is the most unpredictable—and inconvenient—thing in the world.'

He sounded more resigned than bitter, which Laurel took as a good sign. But his comments still left her with more questions than answers.

'You've been in love before?'

The way he'd said it, she knew he meant real love. The for ever, all-encompassing kind. Not whatever she'd shared with Benjamin. She wondered what that felt like—and how it must tear a person apart once it was gone.

'Once,' he said shortly. 'I don't recommend it.'

They sat in silence again, until Laurel felt a yawn creeping up her throat and covered her mouth as it stretched wide.

'You need to get some sleep.' Dan slid down, back into a lying position, taking her and the covers with him. 'Big day tomorrow.'

'I know.'

But going to sleep would mean breaking this fragile connection between them—and moving away from the comfort of his embrace. His arm around her, his body at her side…they were physical reminders that she wasn't alone in this. And here in the darkness, with Melissa's barbs and meanings twisting in her brain, she needed that.

But needy was never a good look on a person. For

all she knew he was starting to regret ever suggesting this thing. Maybe if he'd known how damaged she really was he wouldn't have bothered.

She wouldn't have blamed him.

With a breath so deep it was nearly a sigh, she shuffled back down into the bed and rolled away from him, turning her back as she tried to get comfortable enough on her side to sleep.

'Goodnight, Dan,' she whispered.

In response a hand brushed over her side, finding her fingers under the duvet and holding on. She clung to them, relief flooding through her.

'Goodnight, Laurel.' He squeezed her hand, then let go again. 'I'm glad we have each other this week.'

He wouldn't have said it in the daylight, Laurel realised. Even though it was the premise of their whole agreement, he wouldn't have admitted that need when she could see him.

But in the darkness…there was no need for secrets.

Laurel smiled into the night. 'Me too.'

Laurel was already gone when Dan woke up the next morning, and for a brief, stupid moment he felt his heart clench at her absence. Another woman gone—except he wasn't trying to keep this one, was he?

Keep it together, Black.

Rolling over, he squinted at his watch on the bedside table. Eleven-thirty. No wonder he was waking alone. Laurel must have been up early and working, while he slept off his jet lag and too much champagne.

He'd feel guiltier if it hadn't been the best night's sleep he'd had in years.

Not that he was putting that down to Laurel being

in the bed with him. But maybe it was those shared confidences in the darkness, the reassurance that he wasn't alone in dealing with his family for once. Even the memory of his mother's face as Laurel went on about the importance of following a dream. All of it had added up to let him feel…what, exactly? Safe? Secure? He'd been those things for years, except when he was making a movie. Except it wasn't *physical* safety he'd felt. More a feeling of…*home*.

Which was crazy—and clearly the jet lag talking, because he was three thousand miles away from home, and stuck there all week.

But at least he was stuck there with Laurel.

And that really wasn't a thought he wanted to examine too closely.

He showered and dressed quickly, whistling as he ran a towel over his damp hair. It was bitterly cold outside, but his hair was short enough to dry fast, hopefully without freezing. Dan pulled his leather jacket on over his jeans and jumper and headed out to find his fake girlfriend.

'All the other guests are already down at the Frost Fair, sir.'

The man behind the reception desk eyed him with suspicion. Dan wasn't a hundred per cent sure if he was concerned about what Dan might have been up to all morning, or if he felt that he wasn't suitably attired or recognisable enough to be attending the wedding in the first place. Either way, Dan was satisfied with the outcome. He didn't *want* to look the same as all those overpaid mannequins, and making people worry about what he might have planned was always fun. So he flashed the receptionist a smile, and headed out in the direction of the river.

He heard the Frost Fair before he smelt it, and smelt it long before he saw it. The scent of cinnamon and apple and winter hung in the air, all the way up to Morwen Hall, and the sound of laughter, conversation and strange music hit him as he turned the corner down to the water.

Dan smiled at the sounds, grinning even more widely as a veritable village of wooden stalls and rustic huts came into view along the riverbank. It looked like fun—and utterly unlike the showbiz parties the women he dated from time to time were always trying to drag him along to or use him to get into.

This, he knew, had to be all Laurel—not Melissa. Yes, it was a spectacle, and impressive. But it was also something new, something different, and relaxed in a way Melissa wouldn't even have begun to imagine when she'd been planning her wedding. But more than anything it was *fun*. Not a statement, not the latest trend, just pure, wintry fun.

And fun this week was always down to Laurel, he was learning.

Dan made his way through the rows of stalls and entertainment booths, helping himself to some spiced apple cider and admiring the wood carvings and painted pottery on the way. Local craftspeople, apparently, showcasing their wares.

He nodded to himself. Yep, definitely all Laurel. Except his wedding planner was nowhere to be seen.

Sipping his cider, he continued his search, nodding at acquaintances as he passed and ducking behind a stall providing a hog roast for the guests when he spotted his parents across the way.

He finally found Laurel at the far end of the Frost Fair, looking completely out of place in her smart coat and holding her clipboard. The whole day felt so relaxed—like a holiday—but Laurel was still all work, keeping everything running smoothly for Melissa. Where *was* the bride, anyway? Had she even come down to see the festival Laurel had put on for her? Somehow Dan doubted it.

Seemed to him that Laurel spent far too much of her life trying to satisfy her half-sister, to make up for a past that wasn't even her fault. And in return Melissa spent *her* time making life even more difficult for Laurel.

And probably, in the future, for Riley. Dan's gaze darted around the crowd. He should find his brother—try to have that conversation they needed to have. Hopefully while Melissa was distracted with something—anything—else.

Except… Laurel looked harried. Not that she'd admit it, but there was a tiny line between her eyebrows that he only remembered seeing before when she was talking to Melissa.

Dan was learning that Melissa wasn't so hard to read, or to understand. Making sure Riley understood what he was getting into might be another matter, but it was one that could wait until the stag do tonight, he decided. Dan stopped looking for Riley and stepped forward to see what he could do to make Laurel's day better. After all, wasn't that what fake boyfriends were for?

'I'm sure that can be arranged,' she was saying to a discontented wedding guest, ignoring the phone buzzing in her hand.

She kept a permanent smile on her face, nodding

politely as the guest launched into another diatribe—something about the brand of bottled water in the mini-bar, from what Dan could overhear.

Definitely not something that mattered.

'You'll excuse me.' He flashed his most charming smile at the complaining guest, then yanked Laurel towards him by her elbow. 'But I'm afraid I have to borrow my girlfriend for a moment. Wedding emergency.'

The guest looked displeased, but didn't argue, so Dan took advantage and dragged Laurel out of view, behind an apple cider stall.

'Was he seriously complaining about water?' he asked as Laurel's phone started to ring again.

'Yes.' She lifted the phone, but paused before pressing answer. 'Wait—what's the emergency?'

Dan shrugged. 'I need a tour guide for this Frost Fair of yours.'

Raising one eyebrow, Laurel pressed 'answer', but the phone stopped ringing seconds before her finger connected with the screen. 'Sorry. I'd better—'

Dan reached out and took the phone from her. 'What about my emergency?'

'That's not an emergency. That was Eloise calling. She might have an *actual* wedding emergency that really needs my help.'

'Like?'

'Like… I don't know. They were having final dress fittings this morning. Maybe something went wrong. Maybe the maid of honour's dress can't be refitted for Eloise and she's going to make me do it. Maybe Melissa now hates her dress. Maybe—'

Her face was turning red, and Dan wasn't sure they

could blame the cold for it. Plus, that line between her eyebrows had returned and brought a friend.

He handed her back the phone. 'Fine. Call. But only because I'm scared you might hyperventilate with all those "maybes" otherwise.'

Laurel redialled quickly, and Dan waited as the phone rang. And rang. And rang.

'Obviously not that much of an emergency, then,' he said as it clicked through to voicemail. 'Looks like you have time to show me around this place after all.'

Laurel glared at him, and he laughed. 'Oh, come on! Won't it be more fun than listening to people complain about water?'

'I suppose…'

'I'll buy you an apple cider,' he offered.

'All the drinks are free,' Laurel pointed out.

Dan shrugged. 'Then you can have two.'

She rolled her eyes, but put her phone away in her pocket, her forehead clear and uncreased again. He had her now—he knew it. 'Come on, then. Let's go.'

CHAPTER SIX

IT FELT STRANGE, wandering around the Frost Fair with Dan, pointing out the different stalls, introducing him to the various local craftspeople she'd researched and persuaded to come along for the day and showcase their work. Strange because it didn't feel like work, but also because she wasn't used to having someone so interested in what she was doing. Even Melissa had routinely zoned out when it had come to talking about the parts of the Wedding Extravaganza that didn't exclusively star the bride.

It should have felt odder still when, somewhere between the hog roast and the dreamcatcher stall, Dan reached out and took her hand, holding it warm and tight within his own. Benjamin had never really been one for public displays of affection, unless he was trying to prove a point—usually to keep her in line.

Really, she should have got a clue that he didn't think she was good enough for him long before she'd caught him with Coral.

When she glanced up at Dan he shrugged. 'People might be watching,' he said, his eyes already on the next food stand.

But he didn't let go of her fingers.

The weird thing was, people really *weren't* watching. Nobody cared about them. She'd expected this week to be five days of people staring and pointing, knowing that she was Melissa's half-sister and the reason the bride hadn't had a father for her whole childhood. But as it turned out no one much cared about the wedding planner—the sister who wasn't even a bridesmaid. Not even when she was supposedly dating the groom's brother.

Nobody cared. Nobody expected anything from her. Not even that she try and live up to Melissa. It was amazingly freeing.

For about thirty seconds, until Dan said, 'So, I hear people have been talking about us. After last night.'

'What?' Laurel looked up, startled, from the dream-catcher in her hand. 'When? I haven't heard anything.'

Dan shrugged. 'I caught a few whispers on the wind today, that's all. Let's just say Melissa's outburst at the drinks thing last night didn't go unnoticed.'

Oh, well that made more sense. It wasn't her and Dan they were interested in. It was only the reaction they'd provoked in Melissa.

It was all always about Melissa in the end. And Laurel found she preferred it that way.

'Do you mind?' Dan asked.

'That they're talking about us?' Laurel shook her head. 'They're not really. They're talking about Melissa, and we just happen to be nearby. That's all.'

'What about Eloise? Do you mind that Melissa made her maid of honour instead of you?'

For a man who looked the stoic and silent type, he certainly asked a lot of questions. And, while she expected him to ask them about Melissa, she couldn't quite get used to him asking about *her*. About her feelings, her thoughts—not just how she related to her sister.

Maybe it was because he was in the same situation as her in lots of ways. How had he put it? They were the ones in the shadows. And Melissa and Riley cast very long ones.

'What about you?' she returned, twisting the question back on him. 'Are you bitter that Riley chose Noah as best man rather than you?'

Dan laughed, shaking his head. Under the bright and icy winter sky his eyes looked bluer than ever. She almost wished she'd been able to see him like this when they'd talked the night before—except then maybe neither one of them would have said so much.

'I've never been the best man—or even the better man—before,' he said, but despite his denial there was just a hint of bitterness behind his words. 'Why would I want to start now?'

She wanted to ask him what he meant, but before she could find the words a cheer went up from where a crowd was forming, just around the bend in the river.

'Come on,' Dan said, tugging her along behind him. 'I want to see what's going on over there.'

'It'll be the troupe of actors I hired,' she explained as they wove their way through the crowd. 'They're performing some Shakespeare scenes and such.'

'No one cheers like that for Shakespeare.'

Laurel was about to argue the point when they finally reached the front of the crowd. She blinked up at the small wooden stage she'd seen being assembled that morning. On it stood a beautiful redhead in a gorgeous green and gold gown, and a man she was more used to seeing on the movie screen than wearing a doublet and hose a mere metre or two away.

'Is that—?'

'Eloise and Noah,' Dan confirmed. 'Guess we know what she was calling about before.'

'And why she didn't answer.'

As they watched, Noah and Eloise launched into a segment from *Much Ado About Nothing*, bickering as only Benedick and Beatrice could.

'They're good,' Dan observed, clapping as the section came to an end. 'Some of these Hollywood actors can't act to save their lives. Would have figured Noah for one of them, but actually…he's not half bad.'

He said it easily, as if it didn't hurt him at all to compliment the guy his brother had chosen to be his best man over him. But his earlier words still rang in Laurel's brain, and as Noah and Eloise started in on their next scene she couldn't help but ask the question she'd been thinking about ever since.

'What did you mean? When you said you weren't ever the best man before?' Because to her mind he'd been pretty perfect since the moment his car had picked her up in London the day before.

'It doesn't matter.' Dan didn't look down at her as he spoke, keeping his eyes focussed on the stage.

Laurel scowled with frustration. 'It matters to me. Is it because of your parents?'

'No.' Dan sighed, and scrubbed a hand over his hair. 'You're not going to give this up, are you?'

He sounded resigned. *Good.*

'Unlikely.' She gave him an encouraging smile.

'Fine. I wasn't talking about my parents. I could have

been, I suppose. But, no. I was thinking about my wife, actually.'

The cold winter air chilled her blood as his words sank in. 'Your wife? You're married?'

Of all the possibilities that had floated through her mind since they'd started their fake relationship that really hadn't been one of them. How could he pretend to be dating her if he already had a wife back in California? No wonder his parents had been so disapproving.

'Ex-wife,' Dan clarified, and the world shifted back to something approaching normality. 'Sorry. It's been… two years now, since she left.'

Well, that made more sense, at least. Apart from the bit where she'd apparently left him. Who would leave Dan? From what Laurel knew of him, on one day's acquaintance, tying a man like Dan down to marriage must have been a feat and a half in the first place. What sort of idiot would go through all that and then just *leave*?

It didn't make sense.

'She left? Why?'

Dan's smirk was lopsided, almost sad. 'She found someone better. Why else? I was just a stuntman, remember. Even if I *did* own my own company, even if I *was* on my way to being a success. She was an actress—and an ambitious one, too. I couldn't match up to a Hollywood star, now, could I? I was just the stand-in, same as always, until something better came along.'

The sad part was that it made sense, in a twisted sort of way. As much as Laurel hoped that Riley and Melissa truly were in love, she knew that part of the attraction for her sister was Riley's A-List status. Even Benjamin… If she was honest with herself, Laurel had to admit that a small part of the attraction she'd felt for him came from knowing that he'd be seen as a good match for her. Why should Dan's ex-wife be any different? But for someone like Dan, who'd already spent his life since the age of eight knowing he'd been replaced in his parents' affections by his brother, knowing that he could never match up…

'Ouch, that must have hurt. I'm so sorry.'

He shrugged. 'Don't know why I was surprised, really. It wasn't like Cassie was the first woman to want me just until she got a shot at the real thing—a proper star. She was just the only one I was stupid enough to marry.'

The way he said it—without emotion, calm and even—made her heart ache. She knew how it felt to be cast aside for a better option—first by her father, then by Benjamin. But Dan… He seemed to have made a profession out of it. Of being the one they called on set only to do the dangerous work, never to get the credit. To be replaced by the actor with top billing. And it wasn't only his work. Apparently his relationships had followed the exact same pattern.

And that was just crazy.

'Why?' she asked. 'Why just…accept that? Why always be the stand-in?'

'What else is there?'

He hadn't known anything else, she realised. Not since he was eight and his brother came along and usurped him. It had been bad enough for her at sixteen, but at least she'd still had her mum…in a way. Dan hadn't had anyone left at all.

Were they both just doomed to repeat the same old patterns? Not if she could help it.

'You know, Melissa might be the big star in our family, but I like to think I can at least be the heroine of my *own* story,' Laurel said. 'You don't even seem to believe you can be that.'

'The heroine of your own story?'

Dan raised his eyebrows, and Laurel felt the heat rising to her cheeks.

'What kind of heroine scampers around after her half-sister, giving up everything to make her day perfect?'

'Cinderella,' Laurel snapped back, without thinking, and Dan tipped his head back as he laughed, long and loud.

'Waiting for your prince. Of course. I'm sure he'll be along soon enough.' Dan flashed her a sharp smile. 'And until then maybe I'll do.'

'Maybe you will.'

They were standing too close, Laurel realised suddenly. As the conversation had turned more private, more intimate, they'd each leaned in. Talking quietly under the laughter and cheers of the crowd, they'd needed to be close to hear one other. Dan had moved his hand from hers and rested it at her waist instead. His arm was around her back, holding her close to him as they spoke.

Laurel stared up into his bright blue eyes and swallowed hard at what she saw there.

'Kiss her again!'

The cry went up through the crowd and broke the spell between them. Laurel jerked her gaze away, turning her attention back to the stage, where Noah was kissing Eloise very enthusiastically.

'That looks like fun,' Dan commented, and Laurel's face turned warm. Too warm.

Because it *did* look like fun. But she didn't want to be kissing Noah Cross, film star extraordinaire, no matter how good-looking he was.

She wanted to be kissing Dan.

Wrong place, wrong time, and categorically not her prince.

'It really does,' she breathed, and grabbed Dan's hand as he started to pull away.

She knew what he was thinking now. And she couldn't let him think it a moment longer. Turning her body towards his, until she was practically pressed up against him, she decided to take a chance.

If she was the heroine of her own story, then it was high time she got kissed. Even if it *was* only pretend. She might have given up on relationships until she found the right one, but that didn't mean she couldn't keep in practice in the meantime. And what better way than with a fake boyfriend? In a relationship that couldn't go anywhere because it had never existed to start with?

'You know, if we really want this charade of ours to be believable it's not just our backstories we need to get right.'

'No?' Dan asked, eyebrows raised. 'What else were you thinking?'

'It needs to *look* real, too,' Laurel said, her mouth dry. 'It needs to look every bit as real as Noah and Eloise do up there.'

'You're right.' Dan tilted his head, ducking it slightly until his lips were only a couple of centimetres from hers. 'So...what? Are you asking me to kiss you?'

'Well, if you want to be convincing...'

'I'd hate to fall down on the fake boyfriend job,' Dan murmured.

And then his lips were against hers, strong and sure, and Laurel's whole body woke up at last.

The only problem was it didn't feel fake at all.

The crowd cheered, and just for a moment Dan thought they might actually be cheering for him. For him and Laurel and a kiss that would have broken records, if such things existed.

If their relationship was fake—and it was, he mustn't forget that—they were both rather good actors. *They* should be the ones up there on the silver screen, convincing the audience they were in love. Heaven knew, if he hadn't known better, that kiss might even have convinced him.

But he always knew better. He knew exactly who he was, and how much he could expect. And it was never everything.

Except for one moment…with Laurel in his arms… he'd wanted to believe there was a chance. A possibility of something more.

And then, of course, she'd pulled away.

Her cheeks were pink, her eyes bright, and the smile on her lips couldn't all be pretend. But he'd kissed enough women to know it wasn't sufficient for him to be a great kisser. They wanted something more—something he didn't have. A kiss was only a kiss.

'I need to get back to the hall,' Laurel said.

On stage, Noah and Eloise took their bows and the crowd began to disperse.

'I need to get things ready for the hen night.'

'Sure,' Dan said, letting her go easily. At least he

hoped it looked easy. It didn't feel it. 'Don't let me keep you from your work.'

She hesitated before leaving, though. 'I'll see you later?'

'We're sharing a room, remember.'

Not just a room. A bed.

If last night had been difficult…trying to sleep beside her, knowing he couldn't touch her…how much more impossible would it be tonight, now he knew how it felt to have her in his arms, to kiss her like that?

He was doomed.

'Better make sure you don't drink so much at the stag night that you don't make it back there, then.'

'The stag night. Right.'

Where he would try to corner his brother alone, make sure he really knew what he was letting himself in for with this marriage. He mustn't forget that. *That* was why he was here, after all. Not to play make-believe love affairs with Laurel.

Except after he spoke to Riley he'd have to go back to his room and sleep with Laurel. No, *next* to Laurel. An important distinction. Unless…

'I'll see you later, then. Although I might be in bed by the time you get there.'

And with that Laurel stretched up onto her tiptoes and pressed another kiss against his mouth. Almost swift enough to be a goodbye, but just long enough to hint at a possibility. A promise, maybe, for later.

Suddenly Dan knew that, no matter how badly his conversation with his brother went, he would *not* be getting drunk with Riley and his friends that night.

Just in case.

* * *

Up in the hotel bar, Laurel tied pink and purple balloons to ribbons and hung them from the wooden beams that rose from the bar and along the ceiling. Each balloon had a piece of paper in it—a question for the bride, the maid of honour, or one of the bridesmaids. Laurel had tried to get a look at them, but Melissa had written them herself, then folded them up tight and watched as Laurel blew up the balloons and put the notes inside. Once she was satisfied that Laurel hadn't read them, she'd departed, leaving Laurel to finish organising the rest of the hen party.

The balloon game was only one of many Laurel had planned. The way she figured it, the busier she kept all the guests with silly party games, the less time there was for anything to go desperately wrong. There were a lot of famous people in attendance, and a lot of egos. The last thing Laurel wanted was a row at the hen night.

All she wanted was for everything to go smoothly, no one to get too drunk, and for everyone to go to bed nice and early so she could go back to her room and…

Well…

What exactly was she going to do? Wasn't that the question of the day?

In the moments after that kiss she'd known exactly what she wanted to do that night—seduce Dan. But after twenty minutes of Melissa and balloons, and then another twenty of checklists and setting up, and worrying about everything that still needed to be done, her resolve was failing.

Maybe she was the heroine of her own life, but this week she was also a wedding planner—and that had to come first. Once she'd done her job—and done it well—she could get back to thinking about her own love life. That was the plan. Wait for the right time, the right place, then let herself think about finding the right man.

Except by then Dan would be on his way back to LA and she'd have missed her chance. He might not be her prince, but he was an excellent fake boyfriend, and it seemed silly not to take advantage of that. After all, heaven only knew how long it would take her prince to come riding up. And a girl had needs.

Which led her back to the seduction idea.

Laurel sighed, and decided just to get on with work for now. Maybe the 'Make a Male Body Part out of modelling clay' game would inspire her. Or put her off for life. It really could go either way.

She'd just finished setting up the tequila shots on the bar when the door opened. She turned, smiling, expecting it to be Melissa, or maybe even Dan…

'Oh. It's you.' Smile fading, Laurel glared at her ex-boyfriend. 'What do you want?'

Benjamin put up his hands in a sign of surrender. 'I come in peace. No need for the death glare. I thought we decided we could still be friends?'

'*You* decided,' Laurel replied.

She hadn't had a say in the matter. Benjamin had said, 'We'll still be friends, of course,' and that had been the end of the discussion.

'I thought about it some more, and decided that my friends wouldn't treat me the way you did.'

Funny how once you decided you were the heroine in your own story it became a lot easier to speak the truth to people who didn't respect that. Just yesterday, when she'd seen him again for the first time, she'd dived for cover behind a pretend relationship. Today, after talking with Dan, she'd realised a few things. And one of those was that she had no place in her life for people like Benjamin.

'Oh, Laurel.' Benjamin shook his head sadly. 'You always were so naive. You really are going to need to toughen up if you want to survive in this world, you know.'

Was that really what she needed to do? Develop a tough outer shell that would help her ignore all the awful things that people did? It might at least help her to deal with Melissa. But on the other hand…

'Is that why you love Coral? Because she's tough?'

'I love Coral because she's driven. Ambitious.'

I'm ambitious. Just not the way you wanted.

Gratitude flooded her as she realised how lucky she was to have escaped her romance with Benjamin when she had. She might not have enjoyed the circumstances at the time, but with some distance between them she now knew it was the best thing that could have happened to her. Imagine if she'd gone on believing that he truly was her prince… She might not even have recognised the real thing when it *did* come along. And that would have been a very sorry state of affairs.

'She's a journalist—did you know?' Benjamin went on, looking stupidly proud of his new fiancée.

'Really? I thought she was a gossip columnist.'

It was petty, perhaps, but since Laurel had been responsible for getting every guest to sign a non-disclosure agreement about the wedding, banning them from speaking to the media, publishing photos online, or doing anything else that would jeopardise the exclusive agreement Melissa and Riley had signed with *Star!* magazine, she felt it was relevant.

She'd actually argued against her being invited to the wedding at all—something that Melissa had decided was sour grapes.

'Really, Laurel, you have to grow up. We're all adults and professionals here. We know how the industry works—well, everyone except you, anyway. Just because she won Benjamin, you can't be petty about it.'

Petty. If Benjamin and Coral had betrayed Melissa the way they had Laurel, she was sure they'd have been blacklisted from every celebrity event involving Melissa for all time. But Laurel was being petty for being concerned that a gossip columnist might take a chance and ruin the exclusive with *Star!* magazine, so that Melissa and Riley would have to forfeit the obscenely large fee they were being paid.

Benjamin scowled. 'She's very talented.'

'I'm sure she is.' Suspicion prickled at the back of her neck. This wasn't about being friends—that was rapidly becoming obvious. So what *was* it about?

'What exactly do you want from me, Benjamin? Because, in case you hadn't noticed, I have got a wedding to organise here.'

'Of course. For your sister—sorry, half-sister.'

Benjamin's expression formed into a perfect facsimile of concern, but somehow Laurel was sure it was fake.

'How *are* things between the two of you? I know your relationship has always been difficult, and I can't imagine that the stresses of organising her wedding have helped.'

Laurel's eyes narrowed. 'What do you want, Benjamin?'

'I'm sure you weren't always this blunt.' He sighed, and dropped the fake concern. 'The magazine Coral works for—they've ordered her to get details of the wedding, and the dress, so that they can get them up on the website *before* the *Star!* exclusive goes to print.'

'She can't.' Laurel shook her head. 'She's signed a non-disclosure agreement. If she gives them *anything* she'll be sued.'

'I know. But someone else could.'

'Everyone attending the wedding signed the agreement. It was to be sent back with the RSVPs.' Which made it one of the more absurd aspects of her job, Laurel conceded, but she'd done it.

'What about you?' Benjamin asked.

Laurel froze. She hadn't RSVP'd because she hadn't needed an invitation. She'd signed a contract for the job, sure, but that had been *her* newly developed standard contract, and Melissa had barely looked at it.

She hadn't signed a non-disclosure agreement. She could tell anyone she liked about the details of this wedding and there was nothing Melissa could do about it.

'You didn't sign one, did you?' A Cheshire cat-like grin spread across Benjamin's face. 'I told Coral you wouldn't have. Melissa is too sure of you—too certain that you're under her thumb—to even think that she needed to get you to sign. This is perfect!'

'No. No, it's not.' Laurel gripped the back of the chair in front of her, knuckles whitening. 'I'm a professional. I still have an obligation to my client.'

'Really?' Benjamin raised his eyebrows. 'After the way she's always treated you? Just imagine her face when her *Star!* deal goes down the pan. Wouldn't that be glorious? And…if revenge isn't enough for you… Coral's employers are willing to pay good money for the information. Especially if you can get a snap of the wedding dress before the big day. Serious money, Laurel. The sort of money any new business needs.'

'My business is fine.'

'Sure—for now. But be honest. How much is Melissa paying you? Is it a fair rate? Or did she insist on a family discount?'

Her face was too hot, her mind reeling as she remembered Dan asking almost the same question, and the pitying look in his eye when he realised she wasn't being paid at all.

'The exposure of such a big wedding is great for my business.'

Benjamin barked out a laugh. 'Good grief. Is she paying you at *all*? Beyond expenses, I mean? This wedding must have been all of your billable hours for months now. Whatever she's paying you, I can tell it isn't enough.'

He leant forward, into her personal space, and Laurel recoiled.

'She *owes* you, Laurel. And we'd like to help make her pay up—one way or another. Help us out and Melissa gets everything she deserves. So do you. It's winwin.'

'She's my sister,' Laurel whispered.

Benjamin shook his head. 'She really isn't.' Straightening up, he turned and headed for the door. 'Just think about it, Laurel. But remember—you haven't got long to decide. We need whatever you can get *before* she walks down the aisle on Saturday.'

And then he was gone, leaving Laurel with a lot of very uncomfortable thoughts.

CHAPTER SEVEN

WHERE ON EARTH was the best man? Dan scanned the room, trying to find Noah, but he was nowhere to be seen. Not that Dan could blame him; if he'd been able to find an excuse to get out of the stupid stag night he'd have left hours ago. Noah was probably cosied up in bed with the maid of honour—and more power to him.

If Laurel hadn't been stuck throwing the hen do Dan might well have dragged her off to bed himself.

It was all he'd been able to think about ever since that kiss. That knockout, blindsiding kiss.

Or at least it had been until the stag party had got out of hand.

Riley had insisted on throwing the stag party himself, with no help from Laurel. Dan assumed that Noah and his other mates had had a hand in it, though, because everyone knew Riley couldn't organise his way out of a paper bag.

The groom, in his infinite wisdom, had decided that his stag party would be an homage to frat movies past—complete with beer keg, red cups and some dubious-looking cigarettes over on the other side of the room that Dan wasn't investigating too closely.

Of course frat parties only ever ended one way—

with the good old frat boys drunk out of their minds and often getting into a brawl.

Riley had always liked his roles to look authentic, and by the time Dan had arrived—not late, but not exactly early either—it had been clear from his brother's slurred greeting that the conversation he'd hoped to have about Melissa, and love, and marriage, was firmly off the cards. So he'd settled down with a bottle of proper beer from the bar, and winced as he watched Riley tackling a yard of beer.

And things had only got worse from there.

Dan yanked his brother out of the way of his mate's flying fists and tossed him back into the chair behind him. Then he turned to the fighter, sighing when he saw that the drunken idiot intended to try and take *him* on next.

'No,' Dan said, with finality in his voice. 'We are *not* doing this.'

'Scared to fight me?'

The man could barely look in one direction, he was so out of it, but Dan couldn't fault his courage.

'Yeah, sure. That's exactly it.'

In one swift movement he'd caught the guy's fists, wrapping his hands behind his back and holding them there. Then he marched him across to the other side of the room, deposited him in the corner behind the pool table Riley had had brought in, and placed one foot lightly on his chest to hold him in place. Then he turned to address the room.

'Okay—here's what is going to happen next. I'm going to go take my brother back to his room and put him to bed. I'm also going to send some hotel staff up here to finish this party. I suggest that all of you go drink about a gallon of water, take a couple of aspirin, and get some sleep—so you can function well enough for whatever our beautiful bride has planned for you tomorrow.'

'Hey, why do *you* get to call time? We're having fun! It's a stag party, man.'

Dan rolled his eyes at the man who'd spoken. 'Yes, it is. But the stag has practically passed out already, there's no stripper coming, and honestly…? We're all a little old to be playing at frat boys.'

And he'd never felt quite as old as he did tonight. He was almost a decade older than a lot of these guys, but not all of them. And even they should be old enough to know better.

'Feel free to ignore my advice, boys. But I wouldn't want to be in your shoes tomorrow.'

With that, and feeling about a hundred years old, he went and retrieved Riley from where he was still slumped in his chair. Wrapping his brother's arm around his shoulders and hoisting him up onto his feet with an arm around his waist, he half led, half carried him out towards the elevators.

Fate, or just blind luck, meant he had to walk past the bar where the hen party was happening to get there. And just as they approached he saw Laurel step out into the corridor and stand there, her head tipped back to rest against the wall, her palms flat against it at her side, eyes closed.

'Long night?' he called out, and she turned her head, smiling as she opened her eyes to look at him.

'No longer than yours, by the look of things.'

Riley gave an incoherent mumble, and Dan rolled his eyes.

'I can't believe you let him organise his own frat-movie-themed stag do.'

Laurel shrugged. 'Melissa said as long as there weren't any strippers she didn't care what they got up to. And, quite frankly, I'm not being paid enough to worry about idiot boys.'

'Join the club.' He hefted Riley up again, to keep him from sliding out of his grasp and onto the carpet.

'Want a hand?' Laurel offered.

'I thought you weren't being paid enough?'

'This one's a freebie.' She met his eyes. 'Or you can pay me back later. Personally.'

Heat flared between them again, just as it had when they'd kissed that afternoon, and Dan mentally cursed his brother for being a lightweight.

'Help me get him to his room?' he asked, flashing her a grin. 'I promise I'll make it worth your while later.'

Laurel slipped under Riley's other arm, helping bear his weight as they lugged him towards the elevators. 'I'll hold you to that.'

'Please do.'

It took longer than Dan would have liked to get Riley settled. He was all for tossing him onto the bed and leaving him there, but Laurel insisted on removing his shoes and belt at least, and trying to get him to swallow some water before they lay him down in the recovery position.

Laurel left painkillers and a large glass of water on his bedside table, dimmed the lights, and placed a call down to Reception for someone to sneak in and check on him throughout the night.

'Well, it's not like Melissa's going to do it,' she

pointed out. 'I doubt he'll be with it enough to even notice, but I won't sleep if I'm worrying about him.'

If Dan had his way she might not be sleeping anyway, but he didn't mention that.

Laurel shut the door behind them, and suddenly it was just them again, heading back to their room like an old married couple at the end of the night.

'Are you…?' Laurel started, then trailed off. 'Did you enjoy the stag party? I mean, apart from the last part.'

'Not really.' Dan gave her a one-shoulder shrug. 'Not my kind of thing any more.'

'Frat parties? No, I guess not. So, what is?'

His kind of thing? *You. Naked. With me.* Yeah, that probably wasn't what she meant.

Laurel punched the button to call the elevator, and Dan felt his body tensing, getting warmer the closer they got to being alone with a bed. How had he ever imagined he'd be able to survive another celibate night after that kiss? He really hoped he didn't have to…

'My kind of thing?' he echoed as the elevator arrived and they both stepped in. The enclosed space felt airless, and Dan struggled to concentrate on the conversation. 'Uh… I don't know. Not Hollywood parties either, I guess. I just like…quiet nights. A few good friends, good food, quality drinks. Conversation.'

The sort of night he found almost impossible to have in Hollywood, even with his oldest friends. There was always someone new tagging along. Dan wasn't against new people in principle, but when they were only there to get a foot in the door of the industry…it got old pretty fast.

Laurel smiled up at him, her eyes warm and her lips

inviting. 'Same here. In fact…' She bit her lip. 'It kind of felt like that last night. With us.'

'Once we got rid of our families…yeah. It did.' Amazement flowed through him at the realisation. He'd known that last night had been something new, something meaningful. He just hadn't realised how close it had been to everything he wanted.

Except it was only pretend. And he wasn't anything close to what *she* wanted.

Laurel wanted everything—but all they could have was tonight.

He'd just have to hope it would be enough.

But he couldn't assume. Couldn't be sure that it was what she wanted unless he asked.

The doors opened and Laurel stepped out first, leading him towards their room. Dan paused at the door as she slid the key home.

'Wait.' He grabbed the door handle to hold it closed.

Laurel looked up at him in confusion. 'What's the matter?'

'Nothing. Just…' Dan shook his head, trying to rid himself of the confusion that came more from her presence—the scent of her, the feel of her—than the couple of beers he'd had at the stag party. He took a breath and tried again. 'Once we go in there… I liked last night. I liked spending it with you. And if that's what you want again I'm fine with that. But…'

'But…?'

Was that hope in her eyes? He couldn't be sure. But he had to take a chance that it was.

'When you kissed me today I realised…it could be more. *We* could be more. I know this isn't real—that this whole wedding is like a week out of time. But while we're here, pretending to be together...'

'Why not *really* pretend?'

She was closer now, suddenly, her curves pressing against his chest, one hand on his arm. And he knew from her smile, from her eyes, that she wanted this every bit as much as him.

Oh, thank goodness for that.

'Exactly.' He lowered his lips to hers, sinking into her embrace, letting her kiss overwhelm every one of his senses.

This. This was exactly where he was meant to be.

He wrapped his arms around her waist, pressing her up against the door, moaning against her mouth as she responded by twining her arms around his neck and holding him closer. He reached lower, boosting her up until her legs were around his middle and he could feel every inch of her against him...

'Inside,' she murmured against his mouth. 'Oh. The...the room. Not me. Yet.'

The room. The bedroom.

Geez, they were still in the hallway. What was she doing to him that he'd lost all track of space and time?

'Inside,' he agreed, reaching for the door handle behind her. 'One and then the other.'

It looked as if it was going to be a good night after all.

Later—much later, Laurel suspected, although she was too boneless with pleasure to check the time—they lay together in the darkness of the room, much as they had the night before, except with fewer clothes.

'You know, this fake relationship plan was a really good idea,' she said, her words coming out breathless.

Dan laughed. 'I do have them. Sometimes.'

'You do.' Even this—even knowing it was just for the week, just pretend—Laurel couldn't see it as a mistake. Even if the relationship was fake, the passion between them was real. So why shouldn't they indulge it…make the most of their time together? Everyone thought they were together anyway. This could only make the charade more realistic.

And a hell of a lot more fun.

There was time for 'perfect' later. Her prince would show up eventually. And in the meantime… She pressed a kiss against Dan's bare shoulder and his arm tightened around her.

'So,' he asked after a moment. 'How was your night?'

'Are you fishing for compliments? I'd have thought my enjoyment of the night was pretty obvious.'

She hadn't held anything back with him, she realised. With Benjamin, and the one serious boyfriend she'd had before him, she'd always been too concerned about how she looked or sounded, or what they were thinking about her, to really let go. To let herself fall into the pleasure.

With Dan, it hadn't mattered. He wasn't staying, so he couldn't leave her—not really. Leaving and leaving *her* were very different things, and Dan was already committed to the first. So what did it matter how she looked or sounded? As far as she could tell he was enjoying himself too much to notice anyway.

'I meant before we met up again,' he said, chuckling. 'But it's good to have confirmation all the same.'

The hen party. She'd almost forgotten about it—and

the conversation with Benjamin that had taken place before.

Laurel shifted, resting her head on Dan's chest as she spoke. His fingers tangled in her hair, teasing out strands as he smoothed it down. It felt strangely comforting…as if it might lull her into sleep if she stopped talking.

'The hen party was fine, I guess. By the time I left we'd done all the games—stupid party games Melissa found on the internet, mostly. Eloise disappeared ages ago, and the rest of them were settling in for tequila shots, so I figured no one would miss me.'

'Noah left early on, too. Reckon they're together.'

'Probably,' Laurel said. 'Although they'd almost certainly deny it if you asked them.'

'How was Melissa?' Dan asked.

'Oh, you know. Melissa-ish.'

In truth, she'd ordered everyone around, tried to humiliate Eloise, and made pointed comments about each of her bridesmaids. Laurel had been glad to escape when she had. She was under no illusions that she wouldn't have been the bride's next target.

'Fun.'

'Yeah.'

Benjamin's words from earlier came back to her, unbidden. *She owes you, Laurel. Help us out and Melissa gets everything she deserves.*

She tensed at the memory, and Dan's hand stopped moving through her hair in response.

'What? What did she do?'

'It wasn't her, for once.'

Sighing, Laurel sat up, tugging the duvet over her as she crossed her legs and looked down at him. She needed someone to talk to about Benjamin's offer, and who better than her fake boyfriend?

'I had a conversation with Benjamin. Before the party.'

This time it was Dan who tensed, his muscles suddenly hard and his jaw set. 'What did he say?'

Laurel took a breath. There was no way to make Benjamin's offer sound good. 'His fiancée, Coral, is a gossip columnist. Her magazine is offering big money to anyone who can get them a photo of Melissa's dress, or any details of the wedding ceremony, before the big day—before the *Star!* exclusive goes to print.'

'Except all the guests have had to sign a non-disclosure agreement, right? No exceptions.'

'No exceptions,' Laurel agreed. 'Except…one.'

'You,' Dan guessed. 'Melissa didn't make you sign one?'

'I guess she thought she didn't need to.' Laurel sighed. 'Benjamin said I was so under her thumb she knew I'd never do anything to betray her like that.'

'Is he right?' Dan looked up at her, his gaze steady but with no judgement. 'Or rather, is Melissa?'

She looked away. 'Probably. She's still my client. My sister.'

'Yeah, she is.'

'Even if she isn't paying me properly or treating me like one.'

'He knew just what buttons to press, huh?' Dan shifted to rest against the headboard, pulling her against his bare chest.

'He really, really did.' She sighed. 'I can't do it. I mean, I *could*—but I won't. But the way he said it… the way he knew that I'd be tempted…'

'Who wouldn't? The way she treats you…her over-whelming sense of entitlement…it's natural to want to bring her down a peg or two. It's what you decide to do next that matters.'

'Yeah. I guess.'

He gave a low chuckle. 'Funny to think you're the only person in the whole hotel who couldn't be sued for leaking those details and she put you in charge of planning the whole thing. She must really trust you.'

'I don't think it's trust,' Laurel said thoughtfully. 'I just don't think she sees me as a real person at all—a person with her own thoughts and feelings beyond the ones that matter to her. Do you know what I mean? Maybe that's why she was so angry about us being to-gether.'

Dan nodded and held her closer. 'You're real to me,' he said. 'I don't know if that helps, but you are.'

Real. Despite everything that was between them being fake, right then—in the moment—Laurel felt more real than she ever had before. More herself.

And it was all thanks to Dan.

'It does.' Laurel stretched up to kiss him again. 'It really, really does.'

This time when Dan woke up Laurel was still in bed be-side him, her legs tangled with his and her hair stream-ing out across the pillow. He breathed in the scent of her shampoo and marvelled at how right it felt, being there with her.

He hadn't expected this. Hadn't thought anything like this was even remotely possible for him any more.

How could it only have been two days? Two days since he'd been suggesting a stupid prank to the hot brunette in his car. Two days since he'd stepped up, taken her hand and shouldered the role of Laurel's fake boyfriend.

Two days since he'd started something he suddenly didn't want to finish.

But he would—he knew that. It was Friday morning. In another two days the wedding from hell would be over and he'd be on the flight Laurel had booked him back to LA. Back to his real life.

And that was exactly how he wanted it. And how Laurel wanted it too—she'd made that clear. He wasn't the prince she was waiting for, and she wasn't miraculously going to be the first woman who thought he was enough. Life didn't work that way.

This week was a space out of time, and it was wonderful. But it couldn't last. It never did—not for him.

He'd rather take these five days and enjoy every moment of them without worrying about when things would change. When Laurel would realise she needed something more. Something else. Some*body* else.

Laurel wanted to be the heroine of her own story. She needed a leading man for that—not a stand-in. And that was all he could ever be.

No, he'd have his five days and be grateful for them. And then he'd get back to reality.

Laurel stirred in his arms, and he kissed the top of her head. 'Morning. I thought you were channelling Cinderella, not Sleeping Beauty.'

Even the joke stung—just a little. After this week she would always be a princess, just out of reach. And the chances were he'd never even see her again.

'Someone wore me out.'

She stretched up and kissed him, long and easy and

sweet. But before he could deepen it, roll her over on top of him and relive some of the highlights from the night before, she slipped out of his arms and padded naked across the room to the bathroom.

'Come on. I've got work to do, and you've got a tour of the local sights to go on with the other guests. Might as well save time and shower together…'

She looked back over her shoulder from the doorway and Dan grinned, throwing off his doubts with the covers and hurrying to follow her.

He was *definitely* making the most of the time he had left with Laurel.

Which was why, once they were showered and dressed and heading down to the lobby, he set about convincing her to come on the tour instead of staying at Morwen Hall with the wedding party.

'They're doing the wedding party photo shoots and the interviews for *Star!* magazine,' Laurel said, shaking her head. 'I need to be here for that.'

'Why?' Dan asked. 'It's for the wedding party, right? And you're not in that.'

'No, but—'

'And in fact your job is organising the entertainment for the guests. Which, today, is this stupid tour of the local area.'

'You don't have to go if you don't want to,' Laurel said, rolling her eyes as they reached the lobby.

Dan caught her waist and spun her up against the wall, pressing a light kiss to her lips. 'Maybe I *do* want to go. But only if you're there with me.'

He saw the hesitation in her eyes and kissed her again, hoping to convince her.

'Let me talk to Eloise,' she said, coming up for air. 'As long as she's okay with it…'

Dan grinned at the victory and kissed her a third time—just because he could.

Eloise raised no objections, so Laurel and Dan boarded the coach, together with all the other guests, and headed out into the surrounding countryside.

Dan was only slightly disappointed to see that the parents of the bride and groom had also been deemed surplus to requirements for the photoshoot—presumably because they weren't famous enough. He resolved to try and avoid all four of them. He had a feeling that family bonding wouldn't help him enjoy his last couple of days with Laurel.

'So, where are we going?' he asked as he settled into the luxurious coach seat beside her. Where Laurel had found a coach fancy enough to make it suitable for Hollywood royalty he had no idea, but he was starting to believe that Laurel could do anything she set her mind to. It even had a mini-bar and a top-end coffee machine, with its own barista to operate it.

'The seaside,' Laurel replied, grinning like a small child on her way to see the ocean for the first time. 'It's going to be brilliant!'

'Not exactly beach weather,' Dan pointed out, looking out of the coach window at the frost still lingering on the trees.

'We're not going to sunbathe.' Laurel rolled her eyes. 'Have you ever been to the British seaside before?'

He shook his head.

'It's the best. There'll be tea shops and amusement

arcades—oh, and there's a castle up on the cliff above the beach that we can walk to, if you like?'

Dan didn't care what they did, as long as it kept that smile on Laurel's face. But he said, 'That sounds great,' anyway, and it was worth it when she kissed him.

'Okay, so this isn't exactly what I was imagining when you said the beach,' Dan said, looking down at the pebbles under his feet. 'Don't beaches normally involve sand?'

'Not this one.' Laurel skipped ahead, following the water line along the beach as the waves lapped against the stones.

The crisp winter air whooshed through her chest, making her whole body feel fresh and new. She was miles away from Morwen Hall, and the stone walls and Gothic architecture were fading away, freeing her from the wedding, from Melissa, from all that responsibility. Today it was just her and Dan.

'Come on! I want to climb up to the castle.'

Probably she should be supervising the other guests, or at least making herself available for questions. But since they'd mostly scattered, to explore the little shops that peppered the side streets of the seaside town, or to indulge in cream teas in the cafés, Laurel figured she was allowed some fun too. If it hadn't been for Dan she wouldn't even be there—she'd be back at Morwen Hall, watching Melissa play sweetness and light for the cameras.

She was really glad she was at the seaside instead.

'So, tell me about this castle,' Dan said, catching her up. He had a smooth round pebble in one hand, and was turning it over and over between his fingers. 'Is it a real one? Any princesses living there I should know about? Are we visiting your royal brethren?'

Laurel laughed. 'Yes, it's a real castle. But, no—no one has lived there for hundreds of years. It's probably missing half its walls, and definitely its roof, for a start.'

'Probably no princesses, then,' he said seriously. 'The way I hear it, those royal women are kind of demanding. They like walls, and real beds, and walk-in showers for two…'

Laurel blushed at the reminder of their early-morning activities. Yes, if she were a princess she would be a big fan of showers for two.

'No princesses,' she agreed, smiling up at him. 'Now, come on.'

The cliff path was a steep one, but Laurel scampered up it easily, knowing Dan was right behind her. The icy winter air had moved from bracing to become stinging, filling her lungs as she breathed it in, deep and invigorating. Her face felt wind-burned and scratchy, and her hair whipped around in her eyes. She didn't care. She was free and happy and *alive*.

'You look beautiful,' Dan said as they reached the top at last, and she turned to him, trying to catch her breath.

She gave up at the sight of him—his short hair tousled beyond repair, his blue eyes as bright as the winter sky. He looked every inch a film star—only *better*. He looked real in a way none of them ever seemed to.

And he looked at her as if she mattered. As if she was real too.

'I wish you didn't have to leave so soon,' she said without thinking—and he turned away, a rueful smile on his face.

'Yeah, well… Don't want the novelty to wear off, now, do we?'

But it wouldn't, Laurel knew suddenly. It couldn't. Not for her, anyway. But for him… He had to be used to a new woman every week, didn't he? The way he told it they all moved on quickly enough, but she wondered suddenly if that was the whole story. If they left him or if he kept them at such a distance that there was nothing for them to stay for.

He'd given up trying to be good enough for anyone the minute his brother had come along, while she'd kept on striving to prove her worth to a family that she was starting to realise might never see it. But if he rebelled against being what others wanted how would he ever know what it was like to be someone's everything?

Laurel wanted to find her prince. But part of her heart ached for Dan, who might never find his princess.

'Come on,' he said, striding ahead. 'I want to see this castle.'

Frowning, and still lost in her thoughts, Laurel followed.

She caught up to him as he crossed the moat into the keep, standing in the centre of the square of grass inside the walls. Hands on his hips, he turned around, taking in the crumbling stone of the battlements and the sky stretching out beyond it.

'It's pretty impressive, huh?' Laurel asked, leaning against the stone of the gatehouse.

'It is,' Dan said. 'It's strange. I thought it would feel like a movie set. Or something of another time. But it doesn't. It's here—now. It's survived.'

'Well, some of it has.' She pushed off the wall and crossed the grass towards him, leaning her back against his chest as she tried to see what he saw. He wrapped his arms around her waist and kissed the top of her head. 'I love it here,' she said.

'I can tell.'

'I'm glad I got to bring you.' Glad they could have this moment, this perfect time together. Even if they both knew it could never last.

'Me too,' Dan said, and spun her round to kiss her again.

After the castle, Laurel took him down into the small seaside town and introduced him to the wonders of gift shops that sold small boxes covered in shells, and pebbles with googly eyes stuck on them. Dan smiled as she darted from shelf to shelf, fascinated by all the wonders, like a child looking to spend her first allowance.

'What's that?' he asked, pointing to the flashing bright lights of a storefront across the way. It looked like a mini-casino, but there were kids walking in so he figured it couldn't be.

'The amusement arcade!' Laurel's eyes lit up as she grabbed his hand and dragged him across the road towards the lights.

Inside, the darkness of the room was punctuated by the glow of slot machines, and the air was filled with beeps and tinny music and the sound of coins falling.

'Feeling rich?' he asked as she stepped towards a change machine.

She shook her head as she popped a single pound coin into the slot and a cascade of coppers tumbled into the pot she was holding. 'I'm not a gambler,' she said, turning back to him. 'I don't risk more than I can afford. So...' She held up the pot. 'Tuppenny Falls!'

Feeding the machine full of two-pence pieces, being pushed by moving bars with coins kept them entertained for a full fifteen minutes, as coins dropped off the edge of the ledge and into their pot every time they thought they were about to run out. Dan spent more time enjoying the childlike glee on Laurel's face than he did watching the coins, loving the way she brought so much life and appreciation to everything she did.

He knew she felt she could never live up to her sister, or be good enough to win back her father's affection—knew it deep down in the same place *he* knew that he could never be Riley for his parents. He didn't need her to say it.

But he also knew that she was wrong. She was worth a million Melissas, and her family were fools if they couldn't see it. He just wished that before he left he could make Laurel see that the only person she needed to be good enough for was herself.

Eventually their coins ran out, and Laurel shook her head when he offered to fetch more change. They headed for the exit, with the lights and sounds of the amusement arcade still buzzing in Dan's brain.

'So, what's next?' he asked as they stepped back into the brisk winter air. 'We have—what? Another hour before the coach comes back?'

An hour didn't seem long enough. Already it felt as if his time with her was ebbing away, like the tide going out on the pebble beach.

'Something like that,' Laurel agreed. 'Ready for tea and cake?'

'Definitely.'

The café she chose had tiny delicate tables in the window, draped with lace. Dan took a seat on a slender-legged white chair and hoped it wouldn't collapse under him. He was under no illusion as to how out of place he looked here, even without the old women at the next table glaring at him.

Laurel sat down opposite him, her cheeks still flushed. 'I've ordered us two cream teas.'

'Sounds great.'

They sat in silence for a moment, while a million questions flooded Dan's brain. Everything he wanted to ask her if only they had time. He wanted to know everything, but what was the point when he was leaving so soon?

In the end he settled for the questions he might get to see the outcome of.

'So, did you decide what to tell Benjamin?'

Laurel pulled a face. 'I'm hoping he won't ask again. But if he does… I can't do it. Not even to Melissa.'

Dan smiled faintly. 'I never thought you would. Not for a moment.'

'Because I'm too scared of Melissa?' Laurel asked, eyebrows raised.

'Because you're the heroine in your own story,' he corrected her. 'And *she* wouldn't do that. Would she?'

'No,' Laurel admitted. 'She wouldn't.'

Dan leant back in his chair gingerly, trying not to put too much pressure on the flimsy wood. 'So, what would she do?'

'Hmm?' Laurel asked, distracted as the waitress, dressed all in black with a frilly white apron and mob cap, brought pots of tea and two giant scones with jam and cream on the side. 'Look at the size of those things! We'll never eat at the rehearsal dinner tonight.'

'No offence to the chef, but I doubt whatever Melissa

has ordered could live up to these,' Dan said, smearing jam over half a scone. 'What is for dinner, anyway?'

'Seven-course tasting menu.'

'Of course.' Pretentious, and not enough of anything to really enjoy it. Just like Melissa's latest movie.

Laurel took a bite of her scone and a blissful smile broke out across her face as she chewed. 'Mmm…that's good.' She swallowed. 'Sorry, you asked me something. Before I got distracted by food.'

'I was asking what she would do next. After the wedding. Your heroine, I mean.'

Laurel gave a low laugh and looked down at her plate, tearing a bit of scone off and crumbling it between her fingers.

'Do you know, I have no idea?' she said after a moment. 'For months, whenever I've tried to think beyond this wedding, it's like the whole world has gone blank. Like everything ends the moment Melissa and Riley say, "I do".'

'The end of the movie,' Dan said. 'Credits roll.'

'Exactly. They get their happily-ever-after, and I… cease to matter.'

'Except you're not living in Melissa's movie, remember? You're living in your own.'

'I know.'

However much she said it, Dan couldn't help but think she didn't believe it yet. Maybe it wouldn't be real to her until after the wedding, when the credits *didn't* roll. When life went on, away from Melissa's influence.

He almost wished he'd still be around to see it.

'So, if you could do anything what would it be?' he asked. 'Would you be a film star, like Melissa? Own a castle? Marry actual royalty? Take over the world?'

Laurel laughed. 'None of those things. I think…' She crumbled another piece of scone, chewing on her lip as she did so. 'I think I'd like to make my business a success. I'd like to make people's dream weddings come true. And I'd like… I'd like my own, one day. Maybe a family. Like I said before, I want my prince—the man who is perfect for me, who comes riding up just when I need him.'

'The right guy, right place, right time. Right?' His chest ached. He knew that he could never be that for Laurel, even if he wanted to. He wasn't anyone's prince, but more than that he couldn't even risk trying to be. Laurel deserved every happy ending she dreamt of, and he knew from past experience that he couldn't live up to that sort of expectation.

'Yeah. But really all I want is… I guess mostly I'd just like to be happy. Fulfilled and content and *happy*.'

Dan smiled, even though it hurt, and raised his tea cup to her. 'That sounds like a pretty damn fine ambition to me.'

And she'd fulfil it—he had no doubt. That, right there, was the future he wanted for Laurel…even if it was a future he couldn't be part of.

She clinked her china cup against his. 'So, what about you? You already have the successful business, by all accounts. What's next for you? True love?'

Love. Thoughts of Cassie and the day she'd left rolled through him again, turning his tea bitter in his mouth.

'I already tried that, remember? It's not for me.'

Something to be grateful for, he supposed—whatever was between him and Laurel, it wasn't love. Couldn't be after just a few days of knowing each other. No, their pretend relationship had grown into something less fake, he'd admit. But that didn't make it *real*. Not in the way that hurt.

'Then what?'

Laurel's eyes were sad as she asked, and he realised he had no answer for her. She had all her dreams laid out before her, and he had…

'Maybe I'm happy just as I am,' he said.

'Maybe…' Laurel echoed. But she didn't look as if she believed him.

And Dan wasn't even sure he blamed her.

CHAPTER EIGHT

BY THE TIME they made it back to Morwen Hall Laurel was ready for a nap. But instead she had to prepare for the rehearsal dinner.

The staff at the hall had been busy setting up most of the decorations, table settings and so on, but Laurel knew she wouldn't be able to relax if she didn't check on them. Leaving Dan to find his own way to their room to prepare, she headed to the restaurant—only to find she wasn't the only person checking up on the arrangements.

'Hey!' Laurel called as she crossed the restaurant to where Eloise was slumped at a table. 'Everything ready here? We just got back. Everyone's gone to get changed for the rehearsal dinner. Which I'm guessing you will be too…?'

She left it hanging, not entirely sure Eloise didn't plan on attending in her suit. Eloise didn't like dressing up, she'd learned, and after a day of being poked and prodded by stylists for the photoshoot she wouldn't blame her for being done.

'Yeah.' Eloise glanced at her watch. 'Oh, yes, I'd better get moving. Did the tour go okay? Nice romantic day out with Dan?'

'Yes, thank you,' Laurel said simply.

There weren't words to explain how perfect her day had been—or how bittersweet. Not without explaining the whole fake relationship and her feelings about the fact he was leaving in two days. And nobody had time for that this week.

'What about you? How were the interviews?'

'All fine,' Eloise said, and Laurel relaxed a little.

She was incredibly grateful she hadn't been thrust into the role of maid of honour, and so didn't have to deal with photoshoots and interviews, but she had been a little nervous about how Eloise would cope with it. She wasn't used to the spotlight any more than Laurel was. She was glad it seemed to have gone off without incident.

'And how is the very gorgeous Noah?'

Laurel raised her eyebrows expectantly. Because, really, wasn't that what everyone in the hotel wanted to know? After their kiss at the Frost Fair the day before *everyone* had an opinion on the possible relationship between the best man and the maid of honour. She'd heard at least three theories on the bus back from the seaside, but there was definitely a prevailing one.

Eloise groaned. 'Don't ask.'

'So there *is* something going on with you two!' Laurel cried triumphantly. 'I knew the gossip was wrong.'

'Gossip?' Eloise jerked her head up. 'What gossip? What are they saying?'

'Nothing bad, I promise.' Laurel pulled out the chair next to Eloise and sat down. 'Nobody's laughing or anything. In fact everyone seems to think that you're keeping Noah at arm's length. I take it that's not entirely the case?'

'It's a secret,' Eloise blurted out. 'I don't want anyone to know.'

'Well, so far, they don't. In fact, from what I heard people are pretty amazed. They've seen him hanging around, chasing after you—apparently that's not his usual *modus operandi*.' She didn't mention the more outlandish theories—that Eloise was actually his estranged wife and he was trying to win her back, or that everything that seemed to be going on was actually an audition for a new film, or something.

Eloise sat back in her chair and stared at her. 'Really? How do you mean?'

Laurel shrugged. 'Seems he usually lets people come to him. He's the chase-ee, not the chaser, if you see what I mean.'

When it came to her and Dan, which one of them had chased the other? Laurel wondered. Dan had suggested the fake relationship plan, but *she'd* put it into action. And she would be hard pressed to say exactly which of them had kissed the other first. And as for last night… There hadn't been any chasing at all, she realised. Just two people coming together as if it were simply too much effort to stay apart. As if gravity had been dragging them in.

Until Sunday—when all forces would be reversed and they'd be thrown apart again.

She shook her head, hoping to dispel the depressing thought. But when she turned her attention to Eloise she realised that her friend's expression echoed exactly the way she was feeling. She hadn't been able to put a name to it herself, but seeing it on Eloise's face it was suddenly so, so obvious.

'Are you okay?' Laurel asked, trying to ignore the lump in her throat. 'You look…scared.'

As terrified as I feel. Like you don't know what happens next, and you can't see your way clear to the happy-ever-after.

There *had* to be a happy-ever-after. That was the only thing keeping her going through all the wedding prep—knowing that once it was over she got to chase her own dream.

So why was she suddenly so reluctant for Sunday to come?

Laurel's heart tightened. *I don't want him to go. Not even if it means I don't get to go searching for my happy ending.*

'I'll be fine.'

Eloise pasted on a smile that Laurel was sure was only for her benefit. Underneath it, she looked utterly miserable.

'I need to go get ready for tonight.'

With a groan, she pushed her chair away from the table and stood, walking away without a goodbye, leaving Laurel alone at the table, wondering how the two of them had ended up in such a mess. And whether they could legitimately blame Melissa for the whole thing.

Dan had showered, changed and headed down to the bar before Laurel came back to the room. He figured he might as well give her the time and space to get ready for the rehearsal dinner in peace.

He wasn't avoiding her. Really he wasn't.

Well, maybe a bit. But only because if he was there and he knew she was in the shower…naked…there wasn't a chance of them making it to the rehearsal dinner on time. Or at all.

Besides, he still needed to find his brother. Theirs was a long overdue conversation that couldn't wait much longer.

He knocked on Riley's door on his way down, but there was no answer. Still, when he saw how many guests were already congregating in the bar he figured it was only a matter of time before Riley appeared too, so he might as well have a drink while he waited.

He signalled the barman over and ordered a beer, trying not to think how much more fun he'd be having if he'd stayed in the room and waited for Laurel.

Despite his decision to enjoy every second of the time he had left with her, somehow that seemed to be getting harder as the hours ticked by. Already he was counting down to Sunday, and he couldn't shake the feeling that everything would change then.

Laurel had said she couldn't see beyond the wedding itself, except for some fantasy happy-ever-after. He'd never had that problem—he'd known exactly what he was going back to, what was waiting for him, what his life would be.

The only problem was for the first time in a long time his life didn't seem like enough.

It was crazy—he knew that. He'd known Laurel all of sixty hours. That wasn't enough time to make any sort of decision on their acquaintance. And even if he wanted to, he couldn't.

Because however good it felt, being with her, he knew the truth: that it was all an act. He wasn't her prince, her happy-ever-after, or anything except her fake boyfriend. Yes, they had chemistry. Yes, they had fun.

But he'd had that before, with plenty of women who'd seemed perfect—and they'd all left him when something better came along. Someone more famous, someone who could help their career more. Or just someone who was willing to marry them.

He couldn't do that again. Not after Cassie. And Laurel deserved that fairy tale she wanted—which meant she couldn't have it with him.

End of story. Credits roll.

'Starting early, are we, son?' His dad's voice echoed across the mostly empty bar. 'Your brother seems rather less inclined to indulge after last night.'

'Have you seen him?' Dan asked quickly. With the wedding less than twenty-four hours away his time to talk to his brother about Melissa was running out. He should have done it sooner, he knew, but he'd been... distracted.

Wendell nodded. 'He was just heading to Melissa's rooms—that honeymoon suite out in the gatehouse.'

Dan cursed silently. If Riley was with his fiancée, then he had no hope of getting him alone. Why had he waited so long to do this?

Because I didn't want to, he realised. It wasn't just that he'd been busy with Laurel. He hadn't wanted to potentially ruin all Riley's hopes and dreams for the future.

Happy-ever-after might not be waiting for Dan, but that didn't stop him hoping that others might find it.

'I did invite him to join me for a drink, but he turned green around the edges at the very suggestion,' Wendell went on. 'What on earth did you do to him?'

Put him to bed and saved him from his friends, Dan thought. But there was no point saying it. His father expected *him* to be the bad influence, and no amount of facts or logic would change that.

'It was his stag night,' Dan said, shrugging. 'You were invited. You didn't want to come.'

'It was. And I didn't. But when I stopped by to see how it was going around midnight—your mother was still up reading and I couldn't sleep, so I thought I might as well—Riley wasn't there. And neither were you or his best man.'

'It had been a long day.'

'One of Riley's friends told me you'd taken Riley off to put him to bed. Is that right?' Wendell asked, one eyebrow raised.

'He'd had enough.' Where was his father going with this?

Wendell nodded. 'Probably for the best, then. So, where's that girlfriend of yours this evening? Working?'

'Getting ready, I think,' Dan said, frowning at the sudden change of subject. 'But she will be working, yes. It takes a lot of hard work to put on an event like this.'

'I'm sure it does,' his dad said, without even a glimmer of understanding. 'So, is this one serious? Are you considering settling down again? Your mother wants to know if she needs to clear some time in her schedule next summer.'

Dan blinked. His parents hadn't asked about a girlfriend since Cassie had left. And they hadn't even made it to that wedding—mostly because he and Cassie hadn't planned on getting married until they'd arrived in Vegas and suddenly it had seemed like the obvious idea.

Wendell rolled his eyes. 'Come on, Daniel. She might not be changing the world with her career, but it's obvious to anyone with eyes that she's changing *your* world.

I wasn't sure when we met her that first night—she seemed a little mouthy, I thought. But then I watched you today, walking with her on the beach, and later I spotted you in that café. And I saw that this is real for you.'

'It's not...' *Real*. The one thing his relationship with Laurel couldn't be. Even if it felt like it—felt more real than his *actual* life, in fact. 'It's still quite new,' he said in the end, knowing that at least it wasn't a lie. 'I don't know where it's going to go.'

That part was a lie, of course. He knew exactly what happened next for them.

His dad clapped a hand on his shoulder and Dan tried to remember the last time he'd done that. If ever. 'When it's love you know, son.'

Love. Was that really what this was? It hadn't felt this way with Cassie—that much was for sure. Cassie had been all high adrenaline and passion and never knowing what happened next—and then later their marriage had been bitter arguments and fear and pain. None of which he wanted to relive.

But with Laurel it was...peaceful. There was still passion, of course, but knowing he had nothing to lose—that he couldn't let her down because he'd never promised her anything beyond the weekend, that she couldn't leave him and break him because he'd be leaving first—had taken the fear out of it. He'd been able to relax, enjoy her company, to feel...at home, somehow.

Until now. Until his father had said 'love' and he'd realised that it didn't matter that he'd only met her three days ago, or that their whole relationship was fake.

Laurel *mattered* to him. And that changed everything.

'But what if you're wrong? What if you don't know?'

He didn't know what had made him ask the question, or where the desperate tone in his voice had come from. His dad looked at him in surprise, but he didn't seem to have an answer. His hand fell away from Dan's shoulder and they stood in awkward silence for a moment—until the best man, Noah Cross, came barrelling across the room looking for a drink and Dan was able to put down his glass and slip out unnoticed.

He stood in the hallway, resting his head against the wall, and tried to get a grip. He had to, he knew. He had to get control of his body, of his mind, of his emotions, before he saw Laurel again.

Usually he was good at this. Control was what he was famous for. The ability to control a fall or a dive or a stunt so perfectly that no one got hurt every time. The control to keep his face expressionless as directors waxed lyrical about the risks their stars took without even mentioning him or his team, and the fact that *they* did all the stuff the more famous actors couldn't. The control to keep his heart safe as another person walked away from him.

His mind drifted back to the strange conversation with his father. What had that been, exactly? An attempt to find a way back? To give some fatherly advice twenty years too late? Dan didn't know. But whatever it was…it had felt like the start of something. He just wasn't sure he was willing to risk it ending as abruptly as it had begun.

Just like him and Laurel.

As her name floated across his mind he heard her voice, not far away, and focussed in on it.

'Benjamin, I don't want to talk about this again.'

Benjamin. Her good-for-nothing ex. Well, Dan might not be her prince in shining armour, but he could save her from that idiot, at least.

He followed the sound of their voices around the corner in the corridor, finding them just outside the restaurant where the rehearsal dinner was being held. He hung back for a second, taking in the annoyance on Laurel's face—and the stunning dark red dress she was wearing.

'All I'm saying is you're running out of time to take advantage of this offer, Laurel.'

Even his voice sounded smarmy and weaselly.

'The wedding is tomorrow.'

'I had noticed, thanks. And I have quite a lot of work to do before then. So, if you'll excuse me…' She made to brush past him, but Benjamin reached out and grabbed her arm, holding her in place.

And that was it for Dan.

Striding forward, he wrapped strong fingers around Benjamin's forearm and levered it away from Laurel.

'The lady said she was leaving.'

'I haven't finished talking.' Benjamin looked up, annoyance in his face as he shook his arm out. He turned back to Laurel. 'I don't think you realise how important this is. Coral's job is depending on it.'

'And what about mine?' Laurel asked. 'If word gets around that I leaked confidential details of a client's wedding, who will hire me after that?'

'We can help with that!' Benjamin sounded excited, as if he thought he had her now.

Dan knew better.

Laurel sighed. 'Benjamin, no. I won't do it. Please stop asking me.'

'That sounds pretty clear to me.' Dan yanked Benjamin back a few feet and stood between him and Laurel, arms folded across his chest. 'I think we're done here. Don't you?'

Benjamin glared at him, then peered around to try and catch Laurel's eye again. 'It's not too late, Laurel. Even tomorrow morning a sneak preview of the dress could be worth serious money. Don't forget—she deserves it. Right?'

Dan took a step closer and Benjamin finally backed away. 'Fine, fine. I'm going.'

He waited until Benjamin had disappeared around the corner, presumably back to the bar, before he turned to check on Laurel. 'You okay?'

'Fine,' she said, nodding. 'I just... I really didn't need him tonight, you know? And he wouldn't listen. So, thank you.'

'You'd have got through to him eventually,' Dan said. He reached out to take her hand. 'I just speeded things up a little.'

'Well, I appreciate it.' She smiled up at him then, raising herself onto her tiptoes and pressing a kiss to the corner of his mouth. 'Thank you.'

'Any time,' he said, without thinking.

Because he wouldn't be there any time. He only had until Sunday morning. He had to remember that.

'I might take you up on that. Now, come on—we've got a rehearsal dinner to attend.'

She sashayed off down the corridor, her curves looking so irresistibly tempting in that dress that Dan couldn't help but follow.

Even if he *was* starting to fear exactly what he was following her into and how far he'd go.

CHAPTER NINE

SATURDAY MORNING—New Year's Eve—Laurel woke early, kissed Dan's cheek while he slept, then slipped out from between the sheets and into the shower. As much as she'd have liked to stay in bed with him it was Melissa's wedding day, and she had far too much to be getting on with.

The rehearsal dinner had gone off without a hitch— well, the dinner part anyway. Laurel closed her eyes as the water sluiced over her and tried to forget the way that Noah and Eloise had disappeared halfway through, only for a furious-looking Noah to return alone, behind a triumphant Melissa. Laurel didn't know what had happened, but she could only imagine that whatever it was would be back to cause trouble for her today.

As she rubbed shampoo into her hair she mentally ran through her list of things to do that morning. As she smoothed on conditioner she ticked off everything she needed to double-check on. When she switched off the water she was ready to start her day.

She grabbed her notebook and pen at the same time as her wedding outfit, making notes as she slipped into her dress and hoping the hairdryer in the bathroom wouldn't wake Dan. She smiled to herself. After last night she figured he probably needed the sleep to re-cuperate.

She didn't know what had changed, but he'd been frantic the night before—desperate to touch every inch of her, to make love to her for hours. Even as they'd slept he'd kept his arms wrapped tight around her.

Maybe he was feeling the pressure of their time limit as much as she was. Sunday was creeping ever closer—but first they had to make it through the wedding.

By the time she'd finished dressing, and her hair was pinned back neatly from her face, Laurel's checklist was complete—along with some extra notes for things she'd thought of in the shower. With one last glance back at the man sleeping in her bed she let herself out of the bedroom and headed down, out through the front door of the hotel to the honeymoon suite to wake Melissa.

The honeymoon suite was housed in the old gate-house, just a short walk away from the hotel proper, and the crisp winter air blew away the last of the cobwebs from not enough sleep and one more glass of wine than she'd normally allow herself at the rehearsal dinner.

It was still early, and when she'd left her room the hotel had seemed asleep. But as she approached the bridal suite she heard laughter—Melissa's laughter—echoed by two more voices that Laurel assumed belonged to her bridesmaids. For a moment she was just grateful she didn't have to wake her up—her half-sister was notoriously grumpy first thing. But then her phone pinged in her pocket, and when Laurel checked it she knew exactly what Melissa must be laughing about.

She scanned the text as she waited for Melissa to open the door. It was one of the alerts she'd set up to notify her whenever a new article was posted about Melissa, Riley, or one of the wedding party. In this case she had a whole page of articles about Noah scrolling over her screen.

· But not just Noah. Front and centre was a photo of Eloise, holding her dress up to her chest as she and Noah stumbled out of a closet she recognised from the same floor as the restaurant, obviously caught in the act.

Noah Cross says, 'A fling always makes a wedding more fun, right?'

Laurel closed down the image, but the horror and shame on Eloise's face stayed with her. *Poor Eloise.* Laurel wanted to run back up to the hotel and check on her friend, to try and find the words to make everything less awful.

But as she turned to go Melissa opened the door, beaming, and Laurel knew that somehow her half-sister was behind this.

'Did you hear?' Melissa asked, gleefully chivvying Laurel into the gatehouse. 'Noah and Eloise—who would have thought it? I mean, obviously he was just fooling around with her—but the poor girl looked thoroughly besotted with him. I imagine he must have broken her heart completely, saying what he did.'

'I saw,' Laurel said, trying to keep all emotion out of her voice. 'I do wonder how the photographer found them, though.'

A flash of something spread across Melissa's face. Not guilt. Laurel was sure of that. But perhaps...fear? Of being found out? Laurel couldn't tell.

'Well, they did go missing from the rehearsal dinner at the same time,' Melissa said, busying herself with straightening the perfectly hung wedding dress that was suspended from the spiral staircase leading to the upper floor.

That was the only place with the height to hang the dress without risking wrinkles to the train, Laurel remembered.

'I mean, it was only natural that someone would go to find them.'

'That someone being you?' Laurel guessed. 'And you just happened to take a reporter and a photographer with you?'

Because of course Melissa wouldn't be able to stand that people were talking about Noah and Eloise instead of *her*. That Eloise, whom she'd tormented through all their teenage years by all accounts, might end up with a bigger Hollywood star on her arm than Melissa had.

Laurel could almost see Melissa's thought processes working. This was her wedding, and no one should be talking about anyone except her. Not Laurel and Dan, not Eloise and Noah. And God forbid any of them try to step out of the roles Melissa had assigned them in the movie of her life.

They were all there as bit players—extras to her leading lady. And, as such, they didn't really matter to Melissa at all. Not even if she destroyed them.

Laurel felt the heat of anger flooding through her, and tried to keep it down. Anger wouldn't help her today. What she needed was cold, dispassionate rational thinking. She needed to get through this wedding and get on with her own life—not Melissa's. That was what Dan had been trying to tell her all week.

Just saying that she was the heroine in her own story

wasn't enough. She needed to live it. She needed to *believe* it.

Starting the moment this stupid wedding was over and done with.

Or maybe even sooner.

'It's funny how these things work out sometimes, isn't it?' Melissa said airily, dropping her hand from the wedding dress.

But she didn't turn to meet Laurel's eyes. And Laurel couldn't look away from the dress. Couldn't forget Benjamin's words. *She deserves it.*

'Anyway, Caitlin and Iona are already upstairs, checking through their responsibilities lists. I'm going to go and get showered, and then we can all run through the details for the day. Yes?'

Melissa didn't wait for Laurel's agreement. Instead she disappeared up the stairs to the bathroom, leaving Laurel alone in the main room.

With the wedding dress.

Biting her lip, Laurel raised her phone and snapped a quick photo of the dress.

Just in case.

Dan woke alone again, and felt that same sudden spike of panic before he remembered what day it was. New Year's Eve. Melissa and Riley's wedding day. Laurel would be rushing around the hotel somewhere, getting everything ready for the wedding, or out at the gatehouse with Melissa.

But tonight, once it was all over, she'd be done—and they could just enjoy their last night together.

Maybe not even their last night. Maybe he could change his flight—stay an extra day or two. A week at the most. By then surely they'd both be ready to move on. Really, they hadn't had enough time for this fling to run its course—not with all the wedding stuff Laurel had had to do. It only made sense to make the most of their passion before it ran cold.

But, no. He couldn't risk it. Dan knew that. One day would stretch to two. Which would become a week. Or a month. And before he knew it he'd be trapped. Drawn in. Attached.

He wouldn't be able to leave until he'd stayed long enough for Laurel to leave him.

And *he* had to be the one to leave this time. Whatever the truth about his feelings—and, really, what good would it do to examine them too closely at this point?—Dan knew he couldn't give Laurel the happy-ever-after she wanted. Couldn't live up to her fairy tale expectations.

And so tonight would be their last night. However much that hurt. Better to take the sharp sting of the controlled fall now than risk the much greater injuries that came from being unprepared for the blow when it came. Because that blow always came eventually.

Decision made, he rolled out of bed and went to get ready for the wedding of the year.

Half an hour later, dressed in his tux and as prepared as he could be for the day ahead, Dan headed down to the large hall where the ceremony would be held, looking for Laurel.

He spotted her adjusting the flowers at the ends of the rows of chairs either side of the aisle, and found himself grinning just at the sight of her. She was wearing a dark blue dress, cut low in a cowl at the back, but higher in the front, and falling just past her knees. Her shoes were high and strappy—far higher than he'd seen her wear before—and he wondered if it would change how they kissed if she was so much taller.

Maybe it was time to find out.

'I think that flower arrangement is lopsided,' he called—unhelpfully—then laughed when she looked up and glared at him. 'Kidding. Everything looks perfect.'

'It should. I've been up for hours getting everything just right. Including the bride.' She crossed the aisle towards him, slotting so easily into his arms he might almost believe she was meant to be there.

'How is she?'

'Gloating,' Laurel said, with bitterness in the word. 'Did you hear about Noah and Eloise?'

Dan nodded. 'It was all everyone was talking about at breakfast.'

'Poor Eloise.' She shook her head. 'I'm going back out to the gatehouse now, to try to protect her from Melissa's gleeful barbs.'

'I can't believe she's going through with being maid of honour. I'm assuming the whole photo thing was a Melissa set-up?'

'Of course.' She looked up at him, her expression serious. 'Are you *sure* you don't want to try to talk your brother out of marrying her?'

Dan pulled a face. 'I've been trying to get him alone all week, but somehow I keep getting distracted… Not to talk him out of it, exactly, but to check he's sure about this. That he knows what he's letting himself in for.'

'If he knew that I can't believe he'd really marry her,' Laurel said bluntly. 'I always thought… I knew she wasn't always a nice person to *me*, but I always figured that she had her reasons. That our relationship would always have to bear that strain. But to do this to Eloise…' She shook her head, as if the magnitude of Melissa's cruelty rendered her speechless.

'I might be able to manage a quiet word with Riley this morning,' he said. 'Won't that ruin all your hard work, though? If he decides not to go through with it?'

'At this point I'm not sure I even care.' She checked her watch and gave him an apologetic smile. 'I've got to get back out there. Sorry.'

'I'll walk you,' Dan said easily.

They were into their last hours now. He couldn't waste a moment of them.

'Great.' Her phone started to ring. 'Sorry—I just need to take this…'

Her call—something to do with the exact placement of various table centrepieces, as far as he could tell—lasted long enough for them to leave the hotel and walk across the gravel drive to the honeymoon suite in the former gatehouse. They were almost at the front door of the suite before Dan had a chance to talk to Laurel alone again. But somehow, he found himself just enjoying the sensation of being near her.

'I'm sorry,' she said, one hand on the door handle as the winter wind ruffled her hair. 'I wasn't much company for that walk, was I?'

'Never mind. We'll still have tonight. Once this is all over.'

'Before your flight tomorrow.' Laurel's smile faded as she spoke. 'Unless… I could always look at changing your flight. Put it back a couple of days. If you don't have anything to rush back for…? We could maybe enjoy ourselves a little longer—without the whole wedding party thing going on.'

He could hear the nerves in her voice as she suggested it, and he wanted nothing more than to pull her into his arms and tell her it was a great idea.

Except it wasn't. He'd already made his decision. He couldn't go back on that now. Couldn't give her expectations that he couldn't live up to.

His silence made her smile wobble even more as she chatted on, obviously trying to fill the gap where he hadn't responded.

'I know we said that this was just for the week. But I wondered if maybe that might change? I mean, it's been kind of wonderful, these last couple of days. It seems a shame to limit it, don't you think? Perhaps we could just…see where things go?'

She was trying to keep it casual, he could tell. Trying not to spook him. But she didn't get it—how could she? He'd thought she might understand—she of all people. But apparently even Laurel couldn't see that it was always better to get out before things went bad.

'That's not…' Letting his arms drop, he stepped back from her, trying to harden himself against the disappointment in her eyes. 'I don't think it would be a good idea.'

'But *why*?' Frustration leaked out of Laurel's voice. 'Why not try? We've got a good thing going on here.'

The worst thing was, she was *right*. And it still didn't change anything.

Because a good thing could go bad in a heartbeat, the moment her prince came riding by. He couldn't take that. Not from her.

'We have a *fake* thing going on here. A pretend relationship, Laurel—that was the deal. And, yes, it's been fun. And, sure, I'd like a couple more nights in your bed before I go. But that's all. This isn't love, it isn't for ever, and it isn't happy-ever-after. That's not what we agreed. You're waiting for your prince, remember? All I said was that I'd pretend to be your boyfriend for the week to give you some sort of moral support against your ex. That's it. The rest was just…fringe benefits.'

It was all the truth—every word of it. They'd never promised anything more—never expected it either.

So why did it hurt so much to say it out loud? Why did the pain in Laurel's eyes burn through him?

'I know what we agreed,' Laurel said slowly, her face pale and determined. 'But I thought… I hoped that things might have changed.'

Dan shook his head sadly. 'I'm not your leading man, Laurel. And I definitely can't be the prince you're waiting for. I'm only here until your ex isn't. I'm just a stand-in. The pretend boyfriend. That's it.'

He was so focussed on her face, on making her understand why he *couldn't* risk this, that he barely noticed the door behind her opening.

Until Melissa's incredulous laugh echoed through the air.

'Oh, my God! I was just coming to find out what all the shouting was about, but *really*! This is like the best wedding present ever!'

Laurel spun round to face her, and Dan took a step closer before he realised he shouldn't. Melissa stood there, dressed from head to toe in white lace, her silk gloved hands on her hips.

'This is none of your business, Melissa,' Laurel said, more calmly than Dan though he could have managed. 'Now, if you'll just give me a moment—'

But Melissa shook her head. 'Oh, no. This is far too

good. So let me get this straight. You were so scared about being at this wedding dateless—especially since your ex was bringing the new fiancée he cheated on you with, right?—that you persuaded poor Dan, here, to pretend to be your boyfriend!'

She laughed again.

'Well, that is just *precious*, honey. I mean, I can see why you'd be a tiny little bit intimidated, surrounded by all these wildly successful people, when all you've ever really done is arrange a few flowers and some cake. But, really, Laurel—*lying* to everybody? Trying to steal my thunder?'

'That's not what this is—' Dan started to say, but Melissa just gave a low chuckle.

'Oh, but it is. I heard the truth from your own mouth, Dan. There's no point trying to protect her any more, you know.'

Melissa turned her attention back to her half-sister, and Dan braced himself for whatever vitriol she came out with next.

'I should have known you couldn't score a *real* date for the wedding. I mean, even for a fake boyfriend you could only manage to snare the lesser brother—the stand-in stunt man. Really, Laurel. You're an embarrassment.'

Fury flooded through him at Melissa's words, hot and all-encompassing, burning through his self-control. 'You don't speak to her like that—'

'Dan.' Laurel's sharp tone pulled him up short. 'This has nothing to do with you any more—you've made that perfectly clear. I'll arrange for you to have Riley's room tonight, once he moves down here to the honeymoon suite, and the hotel staff will move your stuff. Now, if you'll excuse us, we have a wedding to prepare for.'

With that she walked past Melissa, into the honeymoon suite, not looking back at him for a moment.

Melissa flashed him a satisfied grin and slammed the door in his face.

And Dan felt his whole world crumbling around him as he tried to tell himself it was for the best…tried to find his famous control again.

'Honestly, Laurel, I can't *believe* you!'

Melissa gave Laurel what she imagined was supposed to look like a friendly pat on the back, but actually made her shoulder blade ache.

'You lot won't believe what this one has been up to! It's almost as outrageous as Eloise's fling with Noah!'

Laurel glanced around the room, looking for Eloise, but her friend seemed to have escaped the wedding prep somehow. Laurel was almost grateful; Eloise was having a bad enough day without having to deal with Laurel's disastrous love-life.

Given the choice, even *Laurel* would opt out of this one, thanks.

Iona and Caitlin, however—the other two bridesmaids—were listening to Melissa with rapt attention.

'Ooh, tell us!' Iona cried. 'You know how we love a bit of wedding gossip!'

'Can you believe Laurel actually guilt-tripped Dan into pretending to be her boyfriend for the week? I mean, how *funny*!'

'How desperate,' Caitlin said, giving Laurel a look.

Melissa tutted, and wrapped an arm around Laurel's shoulder. 'Now, Caitlin, don't be catty. Not everyone is as lucky as me, you know, to find such a perfect true love so easily.'

Laurel's shoulders stiffened under her half-sister's touch. Why was she doing this? Why bother pretending she was still sweetness and light? Surely everyone had to have at least glimpsed the real Melissa by now.

But from the way Iona was smiling at Melissa she knew they hadn't. They still believed that Melissa was on everyone else's side. That she wasn't a stone-cold witch who'd do whatever it took to take down anyone she perceived as a rival for her attention.

Of course, they were very, *very* wrong.

'Really, Laurel, what *were* you thinking?' Iona asked. 'Everyone knows that fake relationship plot device never works out well in the movies.'

Except it hadn't been a plot device, or a movie. It had been her life. Her heart on the line in the end.

She'd offered him a chance at a future, a shot at a happy-ever-after when the credits had rolled on Melissa's wedding. Their own story—together—without worrying about anyone else.

And he'd turned her down. He'd made it abundantly clear that all he was interested in was a few days of fun before he got back to his real life.

Which either meant he was an idiot, or he really didn't feel the same connection she did. Or possibly both.

Melissa and Caitlin had turned to look at her now, waiting for her to answer Iona's question.

Laurel took a breath and realised that her next words were in some way her first line. The first sentence of her new story—after Melissa, after Dan, after everything. Just her.

'Honestly?' she said. 'I was thinking that this was going to be the week from hell, and it would be nice to have some friendly company while I endured it. Now, if you two don't mind, I need to speak to my sister. In private.'

Iona and Caitlin both looked to Melissa, whose expression had turned flinty.

'Why don't you two head up to the hotel and wait for us in the lobby with the ushers? See if you can find my maid of honour, too,' she said. 'Dad will be here to walk me down the aisle at any moment, anyway.'

The bridesmaids didn't look happy about it, but they gathered up their bouquets and headed out to find their opposite numbers amongst the groomsmen. As the door shut behind them Melissa smoothed down her wedding dress once more and turned to Laurel.

'Well? What on earth do you have to say to me?'

'First off, you made a mistake inviting my ex-boyfriend to your wedding.'

Melissa rolled her eyes. '*That's* what all this is about? Really, Laurel, when are you going to grow up and understand that it can't be all about you all the time?'

The hypocrisy was almost enough to make her choke, but Laurel managed to go on. 'Not because of me—although, actually, any sister with a hint of empathy wouldn't do that to a person—but because he's engaged to a gossip columnist. One whose magazine has offered anyone who can get a shot of your wedding dress in advance a really hefty fee.'

Melissa sniffed. 'No one here would do that to me. They love me too much. Besides, they've all signed non-disclosure agreements. I'd sue them.'

Laurel restrained herself from pointing out that if she

was so sure they all loved her that much then surely they wouldn't have *needed* the non-disclosure agreements.

'Not everyone signed one.'

'Well, they should have done!' Melissa sprang to her feet. 'That was your job. If you let a guest RSVP without signing, or a member of the hotel staff—'

'Not a guest,' Laurel said calmly. 'And not the hotel staff. Me. You never asked *me* to sign a non-disclosure agreement.'

'Well, of course not! You're my *sister*. You wouldn't...' Uncertainty blossomed in Melissa's eyes. 'What have you done?'

'Nothing. Yet.'

Laurel moved to sit in the armchair at the centre of the room and motioned for Melissa to take the sofa opposite.

'Sit. I have a number of things I want to say to you.'

Frowning, Melissa did as she was told, and a brief surge of satisfaction bloomed in Laurel's chest.

'I *am* getting married in ten minutes. In case you've forgotten.'

'This won't take long,' Laurel promised. 'Besides, it's the bride's prerogative to be late.'

'So? What do you need to say to me so desperately?'

Laurel thought about it for a moment. She'd never expected even to get this far. Now that she had Melissa there...listening to her...she didn't think there was enough time in the world to make her understand everything she needed to.

So she decided to focus on what mattered most.

'I want you to know that I could have sent this photo to Coral's magazine and made a fortune—but I didn't.' She flashed the screen of her phone at her, showing the shot of the wedding dress hanging from the staircase. 'Not because you're my sister, or because you'd sue me, or anything like that. But because that's not the sort of person I want to be. Okay? But there was a part of me…not a small part of me, either…that thought you'd deserve it. For not paying me a decent wage for organising this wedding. For being so awful to people when the people who matter to you aren't looking. For what you did to Eloise. And for what you just did to me.'

'What did I do to you?' Melissa cried, indignant. 'You're the one who lied to us all.'

'I did—to start with,' Laurel admitted. 'But after that it was more than the lie, even if Dan can't admit that. But you know what? I was putting my heart out there. I was having a moment with the man I…'

Laurel swallowed, feeling as if there was a Christmas tree bauble stuck in her throat. But it wasn't a decoration—it was the truth, bubbling up inconveniently when she couldn't do a thing about it.

'The man I love. And you made it all about you. About your wedding, and your thunder.'

'You're in love with him?' Melissa looked incredulous. 'Why? He's just a stand-in. A stuntman.'

'He's more than you'll ever see,' Laurel said. 'He's real in a way you'll never be. In a way that I want to be.'

Dan wasn't a prince, wasn't a fairy tale. This wasn't the right time, or the right place. But he was the right man. And she knew in an instant, even after he'd turned her down, that she'd rather have him here, now, always, than some mythical prince who might never arrive.

It was just a shame she wasn't enough for him to take the chance.

She got to her feet, almost done. It was time to walk

out there, watch Melissa get married, and get on with her life—with or without Dan. And apparently it was to be without.

'So, here's what I want you to know most of all,' she said. 'It's not all about you. Life isn't the Melissa Sommers show. We all get our own starring roles, and we don't just have to play supporting actress to you. You can't treat people like they don't matter just because they can't give you something, or do something for you. And that means that I don't have to pay for your childhood any longer. I'm not responsible for what our father did, and it's not up to me to make you feel better about that. From now on I'm only taking responsibility for my own actions. And the only things I've done this week are try to give you a perfect wedding and fall in love. Okay?'

Melissa's eyes were wide, astonishment clear in them. But she nodded.

'Great. Then let's go get you married.' She held out a hand to her sister and helped her up.

At least then she'd be officially Riley's problem and not Laurel's.

CHAPTER TEN

DAN MADE HIS way along the frosted drive, back to the main hotel. His head was still spinning from everything Laurel had said, and that was all tied up with Melissa's laughter, echoing through his brain. *A chance. A future.* Everything she'd offered him he'd wanted to take. But he'd known he couldn't.

He wasn't good enough. He couldn't live up to the sort of expectations Laurel had for her future. She wanted everything—love, forever, happiness. And for the first time since Cassie had left he wanted to give that to someone. He *wanted* to be what someone else needed him to be.

But he couldn't. How could he promise Laurel everything she wanted when he already knew he wouldn't be able to deliver? He'd never been enough for anyone before—and he had no faith that he'd suddenly be able to be now.

Dan fought the urge to go and get lost in the woods—to escape, to run. His little brother was getting married. So he couldn't.

He couldn't do anything, it seemed, except what he'd always done. Rebel against expectations. Go the opposite way to the one people wanted him to. Carry on being who he was, with the little he knew he was allowed. Financial success, business success, friends, an estranged family and a series of women for whom he would never be 'the one'.

If he could have been anyone's 'the one' it would have been Laurel's, he realised. But he didn't have that kind of faith in himself.

His father was waiting at the door, and he frowned at Dan as he climbed the steps to Morwen Hall. Suddenly, the Gothic exterior seemed all the more appropriate for the week Dan was having, and he spared a glance up at the architecture rather than meeting his father's gaze.

'Where have you been? Melissa will be here any second and Riley has been asking for you.' Wendell grabbed him by the shoulder and led him off to a side room, near the hall where the ceremony was taking place.

'Asking for me?' Dan frowned. 'For *me*? Why?'

He'd been trying to get his brother alone all week, and now he had him he didn't have a clue what to say.

Don't marry her...she's the devil incarnate. But if you love her...if you think you can be what she needs and that she can be who you need...then take that chance. Jump and forget the safety net. Be a braver man than I am.

'Damned if I know. He's in here.'

And with that, Dan was cast into the side room, where his brother stood by a window, looking very much as if he'd like to climb through it and make a run for it.

'Riley?' Dan said, closing the door quietly behind him. He had a feeling this conversation would be best unobserved. 'Everything okay?'

Riley spun to stare at him, eyes wide with panic. 'Am I doing the right thing? Marrying Melissa?'

Dan closed his eyes. Everything he'd wanted to say to Riley had flown out of his head, pushed aside by the memory of Laurel's face when he told her no.

'How should I know?' he said eventually.

It wasn't as if he was the expert on all things romantic. Look at the mess he'd made with Laurel.

'Because you're my big brother!' Riley ran a hand through his hair in despair. 'Look, I've never asked you for anything before. I know you resented me coming along and ruining your only child status—'

'I didn't—' Dan cut himself off. *Had* he? He'd always thought it was the other way—that Riley had stolen everything from him. But what if that wasn't the whole story?

'Yes, you did. But that doesn't matter now. Because you're my brother, and I need you, so you have to help me. Okay?'

'Okay,' Dan said, settling down into an armchair in the corner of the room. 'What do you need?'

'Thank you.' Riley sank into the chair opposite him. 'So, how do I know if I'm doing the right thing? Marrying Melissa?'

'You remember that my only experience of marriage ended in divorce, right?' *Bitter, painful divorce.*

'Then I'll learn from your mistakes,' Riley said desperately. 'Why was it a mistake to marry Cassie?'

'Because I wasn't enough for her.' The words were automatic, the feeling ingrained. 'She wanted more than just a stuntman. She wanted a star.'

Riley frowned. 'That can't be all of it. She wouldn't have married you in the first place if that was all there was.'

'I…' Dan stalled. Was he right? What else had there been? He'd spent so long not thinking about Cassie, not wanting to examine what he'd lost. Had he missed something?

'She said… Right before she left she said that I wouldn't let her in. Wouldn't let her be what I needed.'

He hadn't known what she meant then, and he wasn't sure he did now. But he knew what he needed, at last. He needed Laurel. And yet he couldn't risk having her.

'Well, that's no help at all.' Riley sighed. 'Okay, well, what about Laurel? You two seem pretty close. How did you know that she was the one?'

'Riley, you and Melissa were engaged before I even *met* Laurel. Besides…it's not what it seems.'

'What it seems?' Riley raised his eyebrows. 'What is it, then?'

'We were…' Now Melissa knew it meant Riley would also know soon enough—along with the rest of the world. He might as well tell his brother himself. 'It was a prank, I guess. We're not really together. We just thought we'd pretend this week, so neither of us had to come to the wedding alone.'

It sounded pathetic, put like that. And more like a lie than telling everyone they were together had, somehow.

Riley's eyebrows were higher than ever now. 'A fake relationship? Really?' He shook his head. 'Man, you're a better actor than I gave you credit for. Because you two sure looked like the real thing to me.'

The real thing. Not an act…not a stand-in.

Could he have that? For real? He'd run when she'd suggested it, knowing he couldn't live up to expectations and not wanting to disappoint her—or risk the pain when she realised the universal truth that Dan Black was Not Enough.

But what if he *could* be? What if he could have been for Cassie? For Riley? For his parents, even?

What if he could change his story? What if it wasn't too late?

He shook his head. One epiphany at a time.

'Yeah, well. Today's not about me and Laurel. It's about you and Melissa,' Dan said, bringing the conversation back to the more urgent matter at hand.

The wedding was supposed to start… He checked his watch. Now. The wedding was supposed to be happening right now. He needed to sort out Riley's head—and then maybe he could start on his own heart.

'So…why did you ask her to marry you in the first place?' he asked.

'I didn't really, I don't think.' Riley's forehead was scrunched up a little, as if he was trying to remember. 'It was more like we'd been dating for a while, you know, and it seemed like the logical next step. Well, that's what Melissa said in her interview afterwards, anyway.'

'Of course.' Dan rubbed a hand over his forehead. 'Okay, tell me this. What's got you thinking all these second thoughts anyway?'

Riley sighed. 'It's this thing with Noah and Eloise. Melissa seems kind of…worked up about it. I think she might even have had something to do with it hitting the internet.'

'I'm certain she did,' Dan said evenly. 'So? How does that make you feel?'

He was starting to sound like that therapist Cassie had wanted him to see. He'd gone once and refused ever to go back. Even in LA, not *everyone* needed to see a therapist.

'A little uncomfortable, I guess. But…it's kind of part of the job, right? The publicity and everything. I mean, we take it when we want it, so we have to put up with it when we don't too.'

'I suppose so.' Another reason to be glad he was merely a very successful businessman and stuntman, rather than a star. He didn't want anyone prying into his private business, thanks. 'Okay, so, next question. Why do you want to marry Melissa?'

'Have you *seen* her? She's gorgeous. And she's a rising star. Together, we can be a proper Hollywood power couple.'

'And do you *like* her?'

Never mind love, Dan decided. That could be fickle as anything. But liking was important. Liking was what got you through the long days and the bad times. Having a friend at your side.

As he'd had Laurel this week.

Not thinking about Laurel.

'You know, I really do,' Riley said, smiling soppily. 'I mean, I know she can be a bit of a pain sometimes, but when it's just us…she's funny, you know? Like, when she's not being "Melissa Sommers, film goddess" she can just be Mel. And that's nice.'

'Sounds like you have your answer right there, then,' Dan said.

'Yeah. I guess I do.' Riley looked over at him and frowned. 'But what about you? There's seriously nothing going on between you and Laurel? Because, honestly, I thought the two of you might spontaneously combust, the looks you were giving each other at the dinner table last night were so hot. I reckon you could be in there if you wanted. You should give it a go, man.' He clapped a hand on Dan's shoulder and grinned. 'Love's great, you know?'

'If you say so,' Dan said, non-committal.

He knew how great it could be. Could sense even now how phenomenal he and Laurel could be together. But that only told him how much more it would hurt to lose it.

'Come on. We need to get you married.'

Then he could get back to his regularly scheduled life. Without love, without Laurel, and without all these feelings that made his chest too tight.

The wedding was perfect.

Laurel strode into Morwen Hall ahead of Melissa and their father, ready to stage-manage the wedding of the year and make sure absolutely nothing stopped Melissa and Riley from getting married—as long as they both still wanted to.

With all that determination she'd built up, it was actually kind of an anti-climax when nothing went wrong.

Riley was waiting at the front of the aisle when she checked, and even Eloise was waiting with the other two bridesmaids. She looked kind of detached—as if she wasn't going to let anything about the day affect her.

Laurel couldn't blame her for that.

She sidled up to Eloise as they stood outside the ceremony room, waiting for the signal to start the procession. Caitlin and Iona were fussing with Melissa's train, while the bride checked her reflection one last time and straightened the tiara on her veil-less head.

'Told you she wouldn't wear the veil.'

'You were right,' Eloise said, with no emotion in her voice.

'You okay?' Laurel asked, lowering her clipboard and looking up at her, concerned. 'I heard… Well, there's been a lot of talk this morning.'

'I'm sure there has,' Eloise replied serenely.

'You seem very…calm,' Laurel said. 'Serene, even.'

Eloise gave her a small smile and raised one shoulder in a half-shrug. 'What else is there to do?'

'I suppose…'

She could be calm too, Laurel realised. She could ignore everything Dan had said, go on about her life without him and pretend the whole thing had never happened. She could act as if it didn't hurt until the pain faded away for real.

Or she could get fired up, say what she really thought, and go after everything she wanted. Even if he said no, even if he didn't listen. Even if he could never love her… Wouldn't it be best to know for sure? To face him down and tell him everything he needed to hear before he made that decision?

To take a chance at being the princess who rescued the prince from a life of never being good enough for love.

That was a starring role Laurel could really get behind.

Never mind serenity. She had something much more important to fight for.

True love.

After so many years believing she wasn't good enough, and trying so hard to be anyway, she'd broken free. She was done with trying to earn love. She was going to *demand* it instead.

The string quartet at the front of the ceremony room started a new piece and Melissa gave a little squeal. 'It's time!'

'Good luck,' Laurel whispered as they lined up in their assigned order. 'I'm going to head in and watch from the front.'

Where she could keep an eye on everything. And grab Dan the moment this was over and give him a piece of her mind.

From his seat in the front row Dan watched Riley's face light up as he saw Melissa walking down the aisle towards him and hoped that his brother had made the right decision. As much as being married to Melissa would drive *him* insane, for Riley it was a different story. Anyone who made his face light up like that, as if his heart was beaming out happiness from within…well, he had to give his brother kudos for taking a chance on that, right?

Then he glanced across the hall and spotted dark brown hair above a blue dress and felt his own heart start to contract.

Laurel.

She'd slipped in to take a seat in the front row on the other side of the aisle, a few chairs down from her stepmother. Her cheeks were flushed, and even at a distance he could see the brightness in her eyes.

That was not a broken woman. Whatever she might have hoped for, his turning her down hadn't caused her any pause at all. She'd stormed inside, dealt with Melissa, put on the wedding of the year—and kept every ounce of her composure while doing it.

He was so proud of her he could barely breathe.

It was good that he was leaving, he reminded himself as Melissa and Riley took their vows. Good that she'd be free to seek out all the things she wanted from life, away from Melissa's shadow. Away from the distraction of their affair.

Laurel had the strength now to go out and find her prince, her happy-ever-after—he could feel it and he was *glad* about that. Really he was.

So…why did it feel so wrong?

Almost before he knew it the ceremony was over, and Riley and Melissa were walking back up the aisle, arm in arm, ready for what was sure to be the longest wedding photography session in history. Sighing, Dan got to his feet, hoping he could grab a drink at least before he had to loiter around waiting to see if they actually wanted the non-famous brother of the groom in any of the shots.

But before he could start to follow them out of the hall he felt a small hand on his arm and looked down into Laurel's blazing brown eyes.

'Don't *you* say a word,' she snapped, with all the fire and determination he'd seen in her earlier barely contained. 'Because I have a lot of things to say to you. And you are going to listen, and then I am going to go and organise the wedding breakfast. Okay?'

'Okay.' Dan blinked. 'Wait, I mean—'

'Too late. Now listen.'

She took a deep breath, and Dan braced himself for a list of all his faults—probably organised alphabetically, knowing Laurel.

'I know you think you can't have this. That love isn't something that stays for you. But you're wrong. Maybe you haven't found the right woman yet, or maybe you don't let any of them in enough to love you in the first place. But whatever it is you have to give it a chance, Dan. You have to be the hero of *your* story too, you know. You can't always be the stand-in, the fall guy, the one who gets beaten up and edited out. You don't have to be a star to chase your own happy-ever-after, okay? And this week…this week you showed me all that about myself. You gave me the confidence to stand up to Melissa—not to go behind her back and ruin her day, but to tell her the truth, to explain how I feel and to move on. To stop trying to earn her love because I thought I wasn't good enough. I *am* good enough—for me. And that's all that matters. You showed me that there's life beyond Melissa's shadow—and, trust me, I'm going out there looking for it. And I think it'll be a crying shame if you don't do the same.'

She let go of his sleeve and took a step back, staring up into his face as he tried to get his scrambled thoughts in order.

'I get it if you don't want to look for that happy-ever-after with me. You're right—we only agreed to a fake relationship and I'm not going to try and hold you to anything more. But if you don't want to try because you're too scared—because you think you can't be good enough, that you can't live up to expectations—you're an idiot. Because I'd rather have the real you than some mythical prince any day.'

He opened his mouth to respond, still unsure of the words he was looking for, but she reached up and put a finger to his lips.

'One more thing,' she said. 'You also taught me that we each need to be true to ourselves and our own dreams—not try to be the people our families or friends think we are. We have to be our own people. And I wouldn't be doing that if I didn't tell you that my own person is in love with yours.'

Love. *Love?* Dan started to shake his head, but Laurel was already walking away.

'Can't stop. I've got a wedding reception to pull off, before I can go and start my own life. Goodbye, Dan.'

No. Not goodbye.

She was leaving him…walking away…and it was all his own fault.

The reality of his own culpability came crashing down so hard that he practically fell into the seat next to him. It was Cassie all over again—a woman he cared for walking away, seeking her own happiness because he couldn't share it with her. No, not couldn't—*wouldn't*. He wouldn't take that chance, that risk of not being enough for her. And that meant he'd always be alone. Always be left behind and put aside—not because there was someone better, but because he wouldn't give enough of himself to find a true partnership.

He'd spent so long expecting people to leave, to be disappointed in him, he'd built up walls to stop them even coming in in the first place.

The question was, did he even know how to knock them down again? And if he did…could he risk it?

Laurel leant back against a pillar in the ballroom, wishing she could take off her stupid shoes, and watched Melissa and Riley take their first dance together as husband and wife.

She'd done it. She'd got through Melissa's wedding without any major disasters—if you didn't count the state of her heart. But even taking that into account she felt stronger, more certain about the future than she had in years.

The credits were about to roll on Melissa's big day, and Laurel was still standing.

She raised her champagne flute just a little, toasting herself, and took a sip as Noah and Eloise took to the dance floor too, for the planned 'best man and maid of honour' dance. Laurel winced at the distant look on her friend's face and hoped that the desperate way Noah was talking to her meant that he was apologising.

Somebody should, she felt. And, as she'd said to Eloise earlier, they couldn't let the men they loved break them.

She wanted Eloise and Noah to work things out— find their happy ending. Even if she couldn't just yet.

She would one day—that she was certain of. She had the tools and the knowledge she needed to be happy now. She knew she was enough just as she was—and she knew she needed a man who believed that too.

After that everything would be easy. She hoped.

'Laurel.'

She spun on her heel at the sound of Dan's voice, almost overbalancing until he caught her by the elbow.

'I've said everything I need to say to you.' She looked up into his eyes and swallowed, trying to keep any fledgling hope buried deep, where it couldn't disappoint her again.

'Then maybe it's my turn to talk,' Dan replied.

Laurel waited.

And waited.

'Well?' she said impatiently. 'Are you going to? Because if not I really do have some more work I should be getting on with.'

'I… This is hard for me, okay?' Dan said. 'I'm trying to find the right words.'

Laurel blew out a long breath. 'Maybe they don't have to be the *right* words. Maybe you just have to talk to me.'

'I love you,' Dan said suddenly, and all that hope in her belly bloomed bright and strong.

'That's… What?'

'I love you. And it's crazy because I've only known you four days. And it's stupid because I've given you no reason to believe me. And it's terrifying because you could walk away right now and I wouldn't even blame you. But I love you. And the thing is, I'm starting to think that I always will.'

'I don't… What changed?' Laurel asked, shaking her head in confusion. 'You said it was just an act. A game. You said it wasn't real.'

'I lied.' He sighed and took her champagne flute from her. After taking a long gulp, he placed it on the table behind them and wrapped his hands around her waist, pulling her closer. 'I was scared. Scared of what I felt and how I knew it would end. I… I always disappoint, Laurel. I've never once been enough for someone. And I couldn't bear for that to happen with you. You deserve everything—every happiness you ever dream of. And I wanted to be the man to give that to you… I just didn't believe I could.'

'And now?'

'Now… I'm willing to try.'

He swallowed so hard she could see his throat move, and she knew how difficult this must be for him, and loved him more for it.

'Because you were right—I was so certain that everyone would leave me, choose someone else over me, that I never gave anyone the chance to stay. I never let anyone choose *me*.'

'I would,' Laurel whispered. 'I'd choose you every time.'

His eyes fluttered shut and he kissed her forehead. 'I hope so. Because I realised today...when I saw you across the aisle... I've already chosen. It's you for me, Laurel. Whether you stay or go—whether it lasts or it doesn't. It's not even a choice. You're the one I love—the one I'll always love. The one I'm meant to be with.'

'So what is there to be scared about?'

He gave a shaky laugh. 'Are you kidding? *Everything*.' He gazed down into her eyes. 'But if you're with me...it's worth being scared.'

Stretching up, Laurel kissed him, long and deep and with every bit of the love she felt for him. Smiling against her lips, Dan pulled her behind the column, away from the watching eyes of the wedding guests. She liked that. This wasn't for them. They didn't matter to her at all.

All that mattered was that Dan was here and he was hers.

'So, what happens now?' she asked when they finally broke apart.

Dan shrugged. 'We start our own story. Here... there...wherever you want. I have faith that we can make it work.'

'We can,' Laurel agreed, nodding. '*Our* story. You know, I like that even better than *my* story.'

'Good. Because I've heard it's going to be an epic. One of those that just goes on and on and on...'

'And does it have a happy ending?' Laurel asked, smiling up at him.

Dan smiled back and kissed her lightly once more. 'The happiest,' he promised. 'For ever and after.'

New Year's Day dawned bright and blue and breezy. Most of the wedding guests were still in bed—probably sleeping off the prodigious bar bill, Dan assumed. But not him. With one arm around Laurel's waist he stood beside Eloise and Noah on the front steps of Morwen Hall and watched as Melissa and Riley climbed into the car that would take them to the airport and their honeymoon.

'We're really just here to make sure they're actually going, aren't we?' Eloise said, raising her hand to wave.

'Basically,' Laurel agreed. 'Are you looking forward to getting your hotel back?'

'I don't know,' Eloise said. 'I'm starting to think I might have other ambitions beyond Morwen Hall.'

'What about you, Laurel?' Noah asked. 'Are you looking forward to getting your life back?'

Laurel grinned, and Dan couldn't help but smile with her. 'Actually, I'm looking forward to starting a whole new one.'

'I know how that feels,' Noah murmured, kissing Eloise's cheek.

'So, what are you going to do first?' Dan asked. 'With this brand-new life of yours.'

'Honestly? I feel like I could sleep for a week,' Laurel said, making them laugh.

'A-List celebrity weddings are hard work, I guess?' Noah said.

'Very.'

'I suppose that means you don't fancy organising another one some time?'

Eloise elbowed Noah as he spoke, and he put up his hands in self-defence.

'What? Just asking. I mean, it never hurts to have the best in the business on your side, now, does it?'

'Best in the business, huh?' Laurel echoed. 'I like the sound of that.'

'And I'm not just saying that so you'll take the job. When the time comes,' he added quickly as Eloise glared at him.

'You might have to get in line, you realise?' Dan said, staring out at the beautiful blue sky as Riley and Melissa's car disappeared around the corner into the trees. 'I might have a wedding for her to arrange first.'

'Might you, indeed?' Laurel said. 'And whose would that be?'

'Ours,' Dan said, hardly believing the word as he spoke it.

But then he kissed her, and suddenly everything felt very real.

'Was that a proposal?' Laurel asked as they broke apart. 'For real?'

Dan smiled, as his future fell into place.

'For real,' he promised.

Because reality with Laurel beat every story he'd ever heard hands-down.

* * * * *

If you enjoyed
PROPOSAL FOR THE WEDDING PLANNER,
make sure you read the first book in
Sophie Pembroke's
WEDDING OF THE YEAR duet!

SLOW DANCE WITH THE BEST MAN

MEET THE FORTUNES

Fortune of the Month: Chloe Fortune Elliott

Age: 26

Vital statistics: Five foot two, eyes of blue and a heart as big as Texas.

Claim to Fame: None—until she discovers Jerome Fortune is her biological father.

Romantic prospects: Questionable. She has loved and lost. Once you've "fallen off the horse," it can be hard to pick yourself up again.

"I've been working as a counselor at Peter's Place ranch for just a few weeks now, and it's just as challenging—and rewarding—as I thought it would be. One challenge I *didn't* expect was Chance Howell. Graham Fortune's new ranch hand makes me feel, well... he makes me feel. I thought my heart died along with my husband when Donnie got killed in Afghanistan.

I suppose any red-blooded female would respond to a cowboy as sexy as Chance. But he's a former soldier himself, and he's made it clear he doesn't "do" permanent. And I'm still trying to wrap my mind around the fact that I'm a Fortune. There are a million reasons why we shouldn't get involved. So why do they go flying out the window the minute he sidles up beside me?"

* * *

The Fortunes of Texas:
The Secret Fortunes—
A new generation of heroes and heartbreakers!

FORTUNE'S SECOND-CHANCE COWBOY

BY
MARIE FERRARELLA

First Published in Great Britain 2017
By Mills & Boon, an imprint of HarperCollins*Publishers*
1 London Bridge Street, London, SE1 9GF

© 2017 Harlequin Books S.A.

Special thanks and acknowledgement are given to Marie Ferrarella for her contribution to the Fortunes of Texas: The Secret Fortunes continuity.

ISBN: 978-0-263-92279-0

23-0317

USA TODAY bestselling and RITA® Award–winning author **Marie Ferrarella** has written more than two hundred and fifty books for Mills & Boon, some under the name Marie Nicole. Her romances are beloved by fans worldwide. Visit her website, www.marieferrarella.com.

To
Tiffany Khauo,
who is about to have her own population explosion.
Tiffany, this one's for you.

Prologue

"Hello, Chloe, are you still there?"

Chloe Elliott's hand tightened around her landline's receiver as she heard the caller's deep male voice asking her the same question again.

Was she still there?

Part of Chloe felt like answering the question by simply hanging up. She'd had enough disappointments in her twenty-six years to last a lifetime, why would she set herself up for yet another one?

But there was this other part of Chloe, the part that *needed* to believe that good things could happen, that they still *did* happen. That was the part that had been instrumental in making her get out of bed every morning even after Donnie, the husband she'd adored, had been killed while serving in Afghanistan after they had been married for only an incredibly short two years. That was also the part that had decided to make her gather her courage together and to try to get to know her father's family.

The father who had, up until just recently, been a complete mystery in her life.

Ever since she could remember—until she'd gotten married—it had been just her mother and her. There had *been* no other family members to speak of, and that had been just fine with her. Filling in the blanks for herself, Chloe assumed that her father had been her mother's high school sweetheart who'd been killed in a car accident before he could marry her nineteen-year-old mother.

Because that had been her belief since forever, Chloe hadn't been prepared to learn that her father was actually tech giant Gerald Robinson. And even more, that for years now he'd been living under an assumed name. Gerald Robinson was in fact Jerome Fortune, one of the famous Texas Fortunes, no less. Neither had she been prepared for the eight legitimate Robinson offspring, giving her half siblings she'd never known she had.

And that didn't even begin to take into account the various illegitimate offspring the man had left scattered in his wake, as well.

All in all, it had been a great deal for her to take in and process.

Realizing that the man on the other end of the line, Graham Fortune Robinson, the third of Gerald's eight children, was still waiting for a response, Chloe answered quietly, "Yes, I'm still here."

Chloe could almost hear the pleased smile in her half brother's voice as he continued. "You might not remember me, but we met at that big family dinner at Kate Fortune's ranch."

How could she not remember? Chloe thought. She remembered everything about that evening, which had come about when Keaton Fortune Whitfield had contacted her out of the blue to tell her that he was her half sibling and invited her to come. And just like that, she'd gone from having no living relatives, now that her mother was gone, to having so many of them that she needed a scorecard just to keep track of them all.

She remembered how frightened and excited she'd been, walking into that huge mansion that evening. She'd harbored such great hopes.

Hopes that had been completely dashed when she'd met Sophie Fortune Robinson, her father's youngest daughter. At least his youngest *legitimate* daughter, Chloe silently amended. Everything had gone downhill from there when she'd introduced herself to Sophie. The latter had looked utterly appalled to meet her, and if looks could've killed, Chloe definitely wouldn't be alive to take this phone call right now.

Not that she could really blame Sophie, Chloe thought. It had to be quite a shock to find out that the man she had thought of as her father all those years had a completely other identity that she knew nothing about.

"Yes, I remember you," Chloe finally responded to Graham's comment.

She recalled that Graham had been the handsome, energetic young rancher and businessman whom Kate

Fortune had tapped to run Fortune Cosmetics for her. It was obvious that the reserved woman had been quite proud of him.

"I know this must seem strange, my calling you out of the blue like this," Graham said.

"No stranger than finding out after all these years that my father was Gerald Robinson," Chloe replied, wondering where all this was going.

After that family dinner, she would have bet that that was the last time she would ever see any of those people again. And, to be quite honest, the run-in with Sophie had left a bad taste in her mouth. She'd decided to keep her distance from the Fortunes, especially since her mother had never had an interest in reuniting with her father.

"If I remember correctly, you have a degree in counseling, don't you?" Graham was saying.

She was surprised that anyone even noticed her that night—other than thinking of her as an interloper. After all, how else would anyone regard their father's bastard child? Chloe thought ruefully.

"Yes, I do," she said uncertainly, waiting for Graham to get to the point—and wondering if, once he did, she was going to regret it.

"I know this might seem unusual to you," Graham continued.

Unusual doesn't begin to cover the half of it, Chloe thought.

"—but I'm calling with a job offer."

"A job offer?" Chloe echoed, stunned. "But you run Fortune Cosmetics. And I don't know anything about cosmetics, other than what I have in my medicine cabinet."

She heard Graham laugh. "You won't have to. Have you ever heard of Peter's Place?"

"Of course I've heard of it. That's a therapeutic ranch for troubled teenaged boys."

"Right." He sounded pleased with her answer. "Currently, my wife, Sasha, is the only counselor there. Because of a recent, rather generous donation from the Fortune Foundation, we're going to be expanding Peter's Place. I've been doing double duty running the ranch as well as helming Fortune Cosmetics. Frankly, between that and taking care of a baby plus our eight-year-old daughter, I'm spread pretty thin. I—we," he amended, including his wife, "could definitely use a bigger staff. Now, I realize that you're just starting out, but I've got a good feeling about you, Chloe. I'd like you to come down to Peter's Place for an interview—it'll pretty much just be a formality. And while you're here, you can take a look around the ranch—that is, if you're interested," he tagged on. It was clear from the way he spoke that he really hoped she was.

Life had robbed her of some of her optimism, making her suspicious of things that seemed to be too good to be true—which was why Chloe didn't immediately jump at the offer, the way she might have only a few years ago.

"Like you said, I'm just starting out. Why would you be offering this to me?" she wanted to know. "It sounds like you could hire anyone you wanted to."

"I know. And that's what I thought I was doing," he

told her. "I've made inquiries about you, Chloe. According to my sources, you're talented and you have a way with people. And," he added most significantly, "because you're family."

You're family.

Chloe felt a funny little sensation in the pit of her stomach. For most of her young life, it had been only her mother and her against the world. And then she'd married Donnie, only to have him taken from her all too soon two years ago. There was a part of her that was *starving* to be part of a family, even as part of her distrusted that feeling and the invitation she was being tendered.

Still, because there was that hunger to be part of something greater than just herself, to be accepted into a family, Chloe heard herself asking, "When would you like me to come down?"

Chapter One

Dear Lord, what am I doing?

The question echoed in her brain as Chloe pulled up before the main ranch house of Peter's Place.

Yes, she really wanted to be part of a family, part of this family, but did she really *want* to leave herself wide open like this? To get this close to the Fortunes? After all, she sternly reminded herself, her encounter last month with the clan was less than successful to say the least.

It all came vividly rushing back to her now as she turned off the ignition and sat quietly in the car for a moment.

She never should have agreed to this interview. She was too intimidated by Kate Fortune, the family matriarch, who Chloe figured would be at this meeting.

And why not? She seemed to run everything associated with the Fortune family.

Kate Fortune might well be ninety-one years old, but she looked decades younger and was sharp as the proverbial tack. The woman was not exactly the warm, cuddly grandmotherly type.

Was it too late to change her mind? Chloe thought not for the first time.

Then again, it wasn't as if she was exactly hip-deep in job offers, able to pick and choose which position she was willing to accept. Given that, this job that Graham was offering her was at least worth a look. Heaven knew she wasn't getting anywhere looking for work so far and she knew that Donnie wouldn't have wanted her to give up on life just because he was gone. And who knew? Maybe she'd actually get it and things would work out for the best.

There was always a first time, Chloe told herself philosophically, doing her best to bolster up her flagging courage.

"Well, here goes nothing," Chloe murmured under her breath as she unbuckled her seat belt and opened the door.

Glancing up into the rearview mirror before she exited the vehicle, she made one futile attempt to smooth down her wayward curly blond hair. Not that it did all that much good, she thought ruefully. Her hair seemed to have a mind of its own.

"Just like me," Chloe murmured, thinking of what her mother had often said.

You just keep dancing to your own drummer, Chloe. The world'll come around eventually to join you.

Satisfied that she looked as good as she was going to look on this crisp March day—the wind had seemed determined to restyle her hair the moment she'd stepped outside—Chloe got out of her sedan and closed the door.

She didn't bother locking the vehicle because it wasn't the kind of car that anyone would think to steal. It had already gone through several owners before she'd bought it a year ago. Close to ten years old, it ran mostly on faith and used parts.

Warning herself not to expect too much, Chloe went up the three steps to the ranch house front door. Mentally counting to ten as she took a deep breath and centered herself, she knocked on the door.

The second her knuckles made contact, the door seemed to fly open. As a matter of fact, she could have sworn that the door opened a second *before* she actually knocked on it.

But that had to be her imagination—right?

"Oh, Chloe, you're here," Graham said, looking startled to see her.

He wasn't in the doorway alone. Chloe recognized the pretty blue-eyed blonde right behind her half brother. It was his wife, Sasha. The petite woman looked even more frazzled than Graham did.

"I'm sorry. Did I get the dates mixed up?" Chloe asked, looking from Graham to his wife. It was the only conclusion she could draw, given the expressions on their faces and their almost breathless manner.

"No, no, you've got the right date," Graham assured

her. "But something's just come up. There's been a sudden family emergency. I just got a call from our babysitter that Maddie—that's our eight-year-old," he explained quickly, "decided that she'd give flying off the swing a try." He frowned, shaking his head. "It didn't turn out quite the way our fearless daughter had hoped. From all the screaming and crying, the sitter thinks that Maddie broke her arm. We're just on our way out to meet them at the hospital."

"Oh, I'm sorry," Chloe cried, genuinely concerned. She could just imagine what was going through their minds. But at least they had each other to lean on. "Is there anything I can do?"

It took him only a second to answer Chloe. "As a matter of fact, there is."

"What do you need?" she asked, ready to pitch in and help.

Chloe thought he was going to ask her to accompany him and his wife to whatever hospital their little girl had been taken. Maybe they were too rattled to drive safely. But that wasn't what he needed her to do.

"Would you mind sticking around for a while?" Graham asked her. "I've got someone else coming in for an interview and I couldn't reach him on the phone. I was going to call you as soon as we were on the road," Graham quickly explained. "When he gets here, tell him that as soon as I make sure that Maddie's all right, I'll be back. I know this is a huge imposition on you and I wouldn't ask if—"

"That's okay," Chloe said, cutting him off. She could tell just by his tone of voice that if he remained, the man's mind wouldn't be on the interview. "Go. See to your daughter." She all but shooed the couple out. "I'll stay."

"We won't forget this," Sasha promised, tossing the words over her shoulder as she and her husband rushed out of the house.

Chloe offered the couple an encouraging smile. "Glad to help," she called after them.

After all, it wasn't as if she was exactly pressed for time, Chloe thought, watching the duo get into their car and drive quickly away.

Besides, Chloe reasoned, walking back into the ranch house and closing the door behind her, this way she could get a look at whoever it was that she would be competing against for this job.

Chloe looked around. She liked the looks of the ranch from what she'd seen of it, driving up here. Maybe she was reading things into it, she thought, but it had a good feel about it.

Chloe sat down on the sofa, prepared to wait. She remained sitting for all of five minutes before she began to feel restless. On her feet again, she started to prowl around the large living room with its comfortable masculine furnishings.

Definitely a good feel to the place, she thought as she moved about, touching things and envisioning herself working here.

She looked at an old-fashioned clock with gold numbers on the fireplace mantel, and she could almost feel the minute hand dragging itself in slow motion, going from one number to the next.

How long was she expected to wait? If she'd had some sort of a handle on that, then she could put things into perspective—or at least know when it would be all right for her to leave.

The sound of a back door slamming made her jump. As did the sound of a wailing baby.

The next second, a rather beleaguered-looking older man came in, holding the crying baby in his arms and looking as if he was at his wit's end.

Without bothering to ask her who she was or to introduce himself, the man complained, "I can't get her to stop crying. I've tried everything and she just keeps right on bawling. Do you know how to make her stop?" he asked pathetically, holding the baby out to her like an offering. "Please?"

Chloe stared at the stranger, stunned. She didn't know the first thing about babies, and for all this man knew, she could have been some random thief who had just broken in to the house.

But he looked so distraught, she decided to skip pointing that out. Feeling sorry for the man, she said, "Give her to me," although, for the life of her, she had no idea what she was going to do.

"Thank you, thank you," the man cried. "This is Sydney. I'm Sasha's uncle Roger, by the way," he said as he placed the baby into her arms. "Graham and Sasha had an emergency and asked me to watch the baby while they were gone." He flushed, embarrassed. "I said yes before I knew what I was getting myself into. I thought the kid would stay asleep. But the second they were gone, she started crying." And then Roger stared at the infant, relieved and awestruck at the same time. "Hey, will you look at that," he marveled, looking from Sydney to the woman holding her. "She's really taken to you."

To Chloe's absolute amazement, the baby had stopped crying. She would have said there was some sort of magic involved, except it was obvious that Sydney appeared to be fascinated with the way the light was hitting the sterling silver pendant she was wearing around her neck.

The pendant that Donnie had given her just before he'd shipped out, she thought sadly.

Even now, you're still finding ways to help me out, Donnie.

"More like she's taken with my necklace," Chloe told Sasha's uncle.

To prove her point, she grasped the pendant and moved it around ever so slowly. Sunlight gleamed and shimmied along its surface. Sydney followed the sunbeam with her eyes, mesmerized.

"Hey, whatever it takes." Roger laughed. "I'm just really relieved that Sydney's finally stopped crying. I was afraid she was going to rip something loose inside that little body...or that I was going to start to lose my hearing. For a little thing, she's sure got a mighty big set of lungs on her."

For the first time, Roger turned his attention to Chloe. Apparently realizing that he didn't know who she was, he asked, "You a friend of Graham's and Sasha's?"

"Not exactly," Chloe replied.

She wasn't really sure how to introduce herself. Yes,

she was Graham's half sister, but she was still getting used to that title herself. She didn't know if she was comfortable enough to spring it on anyone else yet, not to mention that Graham might not welcome their connection becoming public knowledge.

Sitting down on the sofa as she continued to cradle and entertain the baby, Chloe evasively explained, "I'm here to interview for a job that's opened up at Peter's Place."

"Ah."

Roger nodded his head as he sat down, too. "Great place," he told her. "Sasha and Graham do a lot of good here. And they could certainly do with a few more willing hands to help them out with the work. You got a job in mind?" he asked.

"I'm applying for the counseling job," Chloe explained. Now that he was no longer distraught because he couldn't get the baby to stop crying, the older man seemed very easy to talk to.

"Counseling, huh? Like my niece."

She nodded. "Do you work at Peter's Place, too?" she wanted to know.

Roger's face registered surprise. "Me?" he cried, obviously stunned that she would think that. "No, I actually own the spread that Peter's Place sits on. The Galloping G Ranch," he told her proudly. "My house is down aways. I just came by when Graham and Sasha called, saying that they needed someone to watch Sydney here for a while. They forgot to tell me that I needed to bring my earplugs," he added with a laugh. "You don't mind my asking, how many kids have you got?"

"None," she replied, sincerely hoping that the pang she felt making that admission wasn't evident on her face.

She and Donnie had really wanted to start a family, but they had held off because Donnie was going overseas. He'd said that he wanted to be around while she was carrying his baby. Besides, he had told her, they had time. They had their whole lives in front of them.

Until they didn't, she thought sadly. She really wished he had gotten her pregnant before he left. At least she would have had a part of him to help her ease the pain of loss.

"I'm sorry. Did I say something to upset you?" Roger asked, clearly concerned.

Chloe shook her head. "No, I was just thinking of something."

"Oh, well, good. I wouldn't have wanted to upset you, especially since you've been such a help with Sydney here and all." He glanced at his watch, then looked up at her almost sheepishly. "Um, listen, I really need to make a phone call. Since Sydney here seems to really like you, would you mind holding her a bit longer while I make my call? Shouldn't be too long," he added.

The man was already edging his way toward the back of the house as he spoke. It was obvious that he was hoping she'd agree.

Chloe really wanted to hand the baby back to this man, but she couldn't very well turn down his request. Besides, she *had* promised Graham to wait until whoever he hadn't been able to reach on the phone turned up for his interview, so what was one more thing added to that?

"Sure, I can watch her," she told Roger.

The heavyset man beamed at her. "Thanks," he cried. "You're going to love working here. They're both really great people," Roger told her, giving her a quick fatherly pat on the shoulder just before he turned on his heel and quickly disappeared, leaving the same way he had entered.

"Looks like it's just you and me now, Sydney. I'm Chloe, by the way," she told the baby, who was staring up at her with enormous blue eyes, looking as if she was hanging on every word. "Your dad's half sister," she explained. "What's that?" Chloe pretended to lean in toward the baby to hear the "question" that Sydney had "asked."

"You didn't know he had a half sibling? Well, he does. Several of them from what I hear," she added with a laugh.

"Your grandfather really took that 'Be fruitful and multiply' passage in the Bible to heart, I guess. I've got a feeling that there's going to be lots of us popping up around here from now on. I hope when you start talking, Sydney, you're going to be good with names," she told the baby.

And then she smiled down at the sweet, innocent face that seemed to be listening to every word she said.

"You don't have a clue what I'm saying, do you?" Chloe asked and then laughed. "Know what? Maybe it's better that way. Maybe it'll all sort itself out by the time you're old enough to know what's going on. Until then—"

Chloe stopped talking abruptly when she heard someone knocking on the door.

Knowing it wouldn't be Graham and his wife, she figured it was the other candidate. *The one who's after my job.* She set her shoulders to do battle. "Let's go see if we can scare him off or talk him out of it, okay?"

Sydney made a little noise, and then the next moment Chloe saw that there were bubbles being formed around the infant's rosebud lips.

Chloe laughed, delighted. She shifted the baby, holding Sydney a little closer to her as she rose and began to head for the door.

"I'll take that as a yes," Chloe told the baby.

Sydney responded by making even more bubbles.

Chloe opened the door, but whatever greeting she had come up with to offer the person on the other side temporarily vanished.

This was *not* the type of person she had expected to see when she opened the door. Given the position that she assumed they were both competing for, Chloe had unconsciously thought that he'd be a rather scholarly-looking man. The kind who seemed to fade into the woodwork without anyone taking notice of him.

Instead, what she found herself looking at was a cowboy, most definitely an adrenaline-stirring cowboy. The kind whom women were given to fantasizing about whenever the word *cowboy* came up.

The man standing before her had to be about six foot three with shoulders wide enough to give him trouble getting through narrow doorways. He had somewhat unruly, dirty-blond hair and eyes so blue they looked as if they'd been cut right out of the sky. He was wearing tight jeans, a long-sleeved denim shirt, boots and a Stetson—set at what could only be described as a sexy angle. In summation, he looked picture-perfect.

If she had to guess, she would have said that the cowboy was somewhere in his late twenties.

What she didn't have to guess at was that the man was utterly gorgeous.

The second the thought occurred to her, it hit her with the force of a thunderbolt.

Gorgeous?

She hadn't even so much as *noticed* another man since Donnie had died, much less labeled that man as "gorgeous." What was happening here? she upbraided herself. Had she just lost her mind?

Chapter Two

Chance Howell realized that he wasn't just looking at the petite blonde holding the baby, he was actually staring at her. That couldn't be viewed as exactly getting off to a good start with who he assumed was the potential boss's wife. He'd gathered some background on Graham Fortune Robinson and knew the man had two kids, one of whom was an infant. Hence the logical leap.

"Um, excuse me," he began, feeling rather tongue-tied as he took off his hat and held it in his hands. "I'm Chance Howell. I've got an appointment with Graham."

"He's not here right now," the woman told him. "He was called away because of an emergency, but he wanted me to tell you that he'll be back soon."

"You must be Sasha. His wife," Chance added when the woman who was looking at him with large cornflower-blue eyes gave no indication that he had guessed her name correctly.

"What? Oh, no, no, I'm not. I'm Graham's half sister."

"Well, it's nice to meet you, 'Graham's half sister,'" Chance acknowledged, putting his hand out to her.

The woman shifted the baby to her other side so that she could shake hands with him.

"Chloe," she told him. "My name is Chloe. Chloe Elliott. And I guess we'll be interviewing for the same job once Graham gets back."

Chance could only stare at her. What was she, five-one, five-two? Did she say they were going to be competing for the same job? She didn't look like a rancher, and she certainly didn't look like any former military person he'd ever met. The ad he was answering was for a rancher, and it had said that preference would be given to any veterans who applied.

But then, what did he know? The world had been doing a lot of changing in these last few years. Black was white and white was black, and he'd heard that with proper drilling, tiny little ladies like her could mop the floor with guys like him.

That might even turn out to be an interesting experience, Chance caught himself thinking. The one thing he was certain of was that he was glad that the petite blonde wasn't married to the man who he hoped would be hiring him.

He glanced down at her hand, which she had tucked around the baby. It was still clearly visible for his purposes.

There was no wedding ring.

Maybe things were looking up, Chance mused. He could use a little good luck right about now.

"What branch of the service were you in?" he asked her, curious.

Chloe looked at him quizzically. "Service?" she repeated.

"Yeah, you know, navy, army, marines, air force. Service," he repeated. Had she been in some sort of secret branch? he wondered. Was that why she looked so reluctant to say anything?

"I wasn't in any branch," Chloe told him, looking bewildered. "What makes you think I was in the service?"

Aware he might have made a mistake, Chance backtracked. He didn't want to get off on the wrong foot by insulting the woman.

"Well, the ad said that preference would be given to veterans," he began, feeling as if he was on really shaky ground here.

"I didn't see the ad," she told Chance. "Graham just called to tell me about the position and he asked me to come out to the ranch to interview for it. And then he got called away because of that emergency."

He nodded. "Right. The emergency," he repeated. "So you said. Um, do you have any idea when he might be coming back?" He wasn't much for small talk, but this had to be a new low, even for him.

Chloe shrugged. "Not a clue. He just said he'd be back as soon as he could." She paused for a moment, as if searching for something to say in order to fill the stillness. "So, you served?" she asked.

Chance nodded. "Special Forces in Afghanistan—

until that IED sent me straight to the hospital, and eventually, stateside."

"Recently?" she asked, trying but failing to covertly scan his appearance.

The cowboy looked perfect, but she knew that there were some injuries and scars that weren't visible.

But in her opinion, the worst ones were the ones that didn't allow you to come home at all, other than in a coffin.

"No, I've been home for a few years now," Chance told her.

"Where's home?"

"Here and there," he answered vaguely. "I go wherever the work is." He didn't want it to sound as if the reason for his nomadic existence was because he didn't do a good job and was let go. "I don't stick around long in any one place," he confessed.

"Why? Are you looking for something?" Chloe asked.

"Not particularly."

It wasn't that Chance felt he was actually searching for something specific, he just stayed in one place until he began feeling restless. It was as if something inside him would suddenly tell him that it was time to go.

"I already know that the only place I ever feel like I'm at peace is on the back of a horse. I guess you could say that's my haven, my church," he explained.

She smiled at him, and it seemed to make its way to her eyes. "Lucky for you, you can keep your church close by so it's there whenever you need it."

He smiled back at her. "Something like that."

It wasn't really like that, but he wasn't about to

correct the blonde right off the bat. They hadn't even known each other for a total of five minutes yet. Correcting her wasn't exactly the way to get to know her any better.

He did, however, appreciate the fact that she wasn't grilling him, trying to make him explain his thinking. Some of the women he'd encountered would try to do just that—especially the ones who made it clear that they wanted him to stay with them.

Just as Chance was searching his mind for something to say, an older man burst into the living room.

Chloe looked at the older man in surprise. She'd completely forgotten he was in the house, making a call. "Did you finish making your call?"

He looked at her a little sheepishly. "It took longer than I thought," he apologized.

Obviously realizing that Chance had no idea who this man was, Chloe made the necessary introductions.

"Chance, this is Sasha's uncle Roger. Roger, this is Chance Howell. He's the other person Graham was going to interview today."

"The one he couldn't reach," Roger acknowledged, nodding his head as he shook hands with Chance. "Matter of fact, that's why I came back. Graham just called me to say that he and Sasha will be home soon. Looks like Maddie just broke her wrist, not her whole arm, but she's still got a big cast and from what I could tell, that is one unhappy eight-year-old," he added sympathetically.

"Anyway," Roger continued, addressing Chance, "Graham told me to tell you that you can reschedule your interview if you don't want to wait around until he gets in." He turned to Chloe. "Same goes for you if you're getting a mite antsy, waiting for him. Course, since you're so good with the baby and all, I'm hoping you'll stay."

"Sure, that's okay," Chloe told Sasha's uncle. "I'll stay until he gets here. No point in my going back and forth."

"Same here," Chance chimed in. His eyes met Chloe's and just for a moment, the job he had come out to apply for slipped into the background for him. "I'll be happy to stay."

What he really meant was that he was happy spending a little more time talking to the petite blonde with the sunbeam smile—even if talking didn't exactly come easy for him.

Chloe felt a quickening in the pit of her stomach. It was identical to the one she'd experienced when she'd first opened the door and caught sight of the tall, rangy-looking cowboy.

Careful, Chloe. Remember, been there, done that. You really don't want to go down that road again, do you? You know exactly where that road leads.

Donnie had been her first love. She'd fallen really hard for Donnie and had felt like jumping out of an airplane without strapping a parachute to her back. The feeling was nothing short of exhilarating, but in the end, leaping out of an airplane without a parachute was just asking for trouble, and that was the very last thing she wanted in her life: the kind of trouble that led directly to heartache.

But on the other hand, Chloe reasoned, she didn't

want to come across as rude, either, and being nice—
cautiously nice—to Chance didn't hurt anything, she
silently insisted.

The trick was that she had to remember not to get
carried away.

Before she could say anything to him, Sasha's uncle
stepped up.

"While you're waiting for Graham to get back,"
Roger offered, "I could give you two a tour of the place
if you're interested."

"You mean of the house?" Chloe asked, looking
down at the baby in her arms.

Sydney, to her surprise, had fallen asleep. Chloe had
been so taken with the handsome cowboy, she hadn't
even realized. Nor did she realize the pain in her shoulder till now. She didn't want to take a chance on waking
the baby up, but on the other hand, she would really welcome the opportunity to set Sydney down in her crib.

"Well, the house to start with," Roger said, answering her question. "And then the rest of the ranch. I could
take you two on a quick tour in my truck," he added in
case they were worried about missing Graham when
he and his wife returned.

Chloe looked down at the baby. "I don't want to risk
waking Sydney up."

Roger looked as if he suddenly realized the position
that Chloe was in.

"I guess I completely forgot about making you hold
that little one," he confessed, embarrassed. He looked
at Chance.

"It's up to you, Chloe," he said. "If you don't feel

comfortable about waking that little baby, we can stay right here and wait for Graham and his missus. I don't need special entertaining," he went on to tell her as he smiled. "I'm just fine the way I am."

You certainly are, Chloe thought.

The next minute, ashamed of herself, feeling guilty at being so flippant about Donnie's memory, she admonished herself for thinking that way. She really had to get hold of herself. What was wrong with her? This wasn't like her at all.

"I don't want to keep you from seeing the ranch," she protested, ready to wave Chance and Roger off on their way.

"If I get the job, I'll be seeing it soon enough," Chance told her. "And if I don't get the job, well then, there's really no point in taking a tour around the place, now is there?"

Roger looked a little perplexed as he listened to the exchange between the two younger people. Lifting his somewhat sloping shoulders, he shrugged and then let them fall again.

"Suit yourselves," he told them. "But meanwhile, I can show you where Sydney's room is so you can at least put her down in her crib. That way you can see if you can still move your arms." Turning, Roger beckoned for her to follow. "It's this way, Chloe."

She saw no reason not to do that, as long as she could hear the baby if she started crying again. She was fairly confident that there had to be a baby monitor in Sydney's room.

Feeling a sense of relief that she'd at least be away

from Chance for a minute or two—enough time to
break whatever spell he'd seemed to cast over her—
Chloe happily fell into step behind Sasha's uncle.

"Guess I might as well come, too," Chance said to
them. "No sense in standing around, talking to myself."

Oh, joy. Just what she needed. More of the handsome cowboy.

Chapter Three

Chloe eased the baby ever so slowly into the crib. She held her breath the entire time until she was able to successfully withdraw her hands from around the baby's little body.

Sydney made a little noise, then sighed before settling back to sleep.

Success! Chloe silently congratulated herself.

She took a step back and almost gasped as she bumped up right against Chance.

"Oh, sorry," he whispered, immediately moving aside. He wasn't sure if he was apologizing for being in her way or for feeling that sudden zip of electricity surging through his body when it made contact with hers. Granted the contact wasn't of the intimate variety that he was normally accustomed to, but there was still just enough to get him going.

Chloe instantly turned around and nearly caused another, far more dead-on collision between them. At the very last minute, because Chance had moved back so quickly, the one-on-one collision between their two bodies was avoided.

She wasn't really sure if she was relieved—or perhaps just a little disappointed.

Again? What is the matter with you? she silently demanded.

Yes, the man was attractive, she acknowledged, but lots of men were attractive and she hadn't been drawn to them. So why was this man, this *cowboy,* different from the others?

He's not. Get a grip, Chloe, she ordered herself angrily.

"Um, that's okay." She flushed, absolving him of any guilt in what had just transpired. "I shouldn't have moved so suddenly." She looked down at the sleeping infant. "I just didn't want to take a chance on saying something too loud and waking up the baby."

Since the room was relatively small, Roger had kept back, standing almost out in the hallway. He peered in now at the sleeping infant.

"She sure is a pretty little thing, ain't she?" The whispered rhetorical question was steeped in complete admiration. And then he looked from Chance to Chloe. "You got any kids?" he asked Chance.

The cowboy looked surprised by the question. "No."

"You already told me that you don't have any," Roger

said to Chloe. And then he laughed to himself, as if he knew something they weren't privy to yet. "Well, you two are young yet. You've got time."

Time—that was what Donnie had thought. They had time. Time to be together, time to enjoy one another before they took that step to become parents. Again she wished with all her heart she had insisted on getting pregnant before he had left for overseas. At least she would have had Donnie's child to hold in her arms instead of all that emptiness that he left behind.

"But once you've got 'em," Roger was saying, "there's just nothing like it in the world. Makes you realize just what you were put down here on earth for, what makes everything else all worthwhile." Rousing himself, he beckoned them out into the hallway. "C'mon, we'd better slip out before I forget myself and start talking loud again."

Roger put a hand on each of their shoulders—he had to stretch in order to reach Chance's—and he guided them both out ahead of him.

The hallway was too narrow to accommodate all three of them. Roger fell behind them again.

As she and Chance fell in step beside each other, he glanced her way. "You want kids?" he asked her out of the blue as they made their way back down the stairs ahead of their unofficial escort.

"Right now, I just want a job," she told him honestly. The next second, she realized that he might think she was trying to guilt him out of competing for the position he was here for. "I mean, if I turn out to be more qualified for it. But if it turns out that you are, well then, I'll just have to keep on looking for something," she concluded.

Chance caught himself studying her. Something just wasn't adding up for him.

"Just how much do you know about ranching?" he finally asked her.

Reaching the bottom of the stairs, she stared at him, confused. Why would he ask her such a strange question? "Not much. Why?"

Something's really *not adding up*, Chance told himself. "Well, because that's the job I'm here about. The one I'm interviewing for. Graham wanted someone to run the ranch. Someone who was good with horses," he finally said when she just kept looking at him.

"Run the ranch?" Chloe repeated, confused. She'd gotten the impression from Graham that she and Chance were here about the same job. She looked at him now. "You're here about ranching?"

"Funny, I thought I just said that," Chance answered. Judging by the expression on her face, she *wasn't* here to apply for that job the way she'd made it sound earlier. "What are you here about?"

"Why, counseling, of course," Chloe replied in no uncertain terms.

"Counseling what?" Chance asked, clearly surprised by her answer. And then it suddenly occurred to him what the sexy-looking blonde was saying. He had to admit that what he'd just asked made him feel like an idiot. "You mean the boys?"

Her smile was a natural reflex. "I kind of have to. Horses don't listen to me."

Chloe's sense of humor tickled him and he laughed. Now it all made sense. They were here about two different positions. "I could teach you how to make them listen to you."

"You're talking about the horses, right?" she asked, a hint of mischief dancing in her eyes.

He found himself being pulled in and mesmerized by those deep pools of blue. It took effort to tear his gaze away. "Right," he finally replied. "I've got no trouble getting horses to listen to me. Most people, though, just ignore me like I wasn't there."

"I don't believe that for a minute," she told him with feeling. How could *anyone*, male or female—especially female—not notice this man? His presence seemed to just fill up the very space around him. Heaven knew he certainly did that for her.

The way he was looking at her right now made her feel like nervously shifting from foot to foot. The butterflies in her stomach were multiplying at a phenomenal rate. It was hard to gather her thoughts together to answer him.

"For one thing, you're really tall." She knew that wasn't much of an answer, so she searched for a better one. "And you have this commanding air about you. If you *were* a counselor, I'm sure that the boys here would listen to whatever you had to say."

"Good thing we won't have to put that to the test," Chance answered, then confessed, "I'm not much when it comes to giving orders. I had enough of that when I was over in Afghanistan."

The mention of the place that had seen Donnie die had her quietly saying, "At least you got to come back."

The words slipped out before she could think to stop them. Any hope that Chance might not have heard her died the second she looked up into his eyes. He'd heard. There was curiosity mingled with a touch of pity in his blue orbs.

The moment grew more uncomfortable for her.

"Did you lose someone?" Chance asked kindly.

Her first impulse was to deny his assumption. But that would be like denying Donnie had ever existed, and she couldn't bring herself to do that.

So after a couple of beats had gone by, she answered him. "Yes."

"Brother? Father? Husband?" Chance kept guessing when she made no acknowledgment that he had guessed correctly. By the time he'd reached the word *husband*, with no visible response from her, Chance shook his head. "No, never mind. Don't tell me. It's none of my business. Sorry I asked," he apologized. "It's just that sometimes it feels like some kind of exclusive veterans club—the kind you really don't want membership to," he added ruefully.

"Does that mean you wish you hadn't gone?" she asked, curious.

How many times had she lain awake at night, wondering if Donnie ever regretted enlisting before the war had taken him from her. Even now, after all this time, she hadn't really come to any sort of a satisfactory conclusion.

"No," he told her honestly. "I went to fight for my

country, and I'm proud of that part. I just wish I hadn't seen what I'd seen. Nobody should see that kind of thing," he said quietly. "Nobody should have to live through it, either."

Then, as if he replayed his own words in his head, Chance blew out a breath, mystified. "How'd I get started on that?" he asked. The question was meant more for him than for her. Clearing his throat, he abruptly changed the subject. "Anyway, at least now we know that we're not out for the same job."

Roger, who had been hanging back quietly this whole time, finally spoke up.

"Well, glad that's been cleared up—and just in time, too." His attention was immediately redirected to the sound of the front door being opened. "Looks like your future bosses are back," he told Chloe and Chance with a broad wink.

They turned toward the front door in time to see Graham and Sasha walking in, along with a little girl. With her straight blond hair and her delicate features, she looked like a miniature version of her mother. All except for the arm that was in a cast and held by a sling around her neck.

Chloe winced in sympathy. That had to be Maddie, she thought, her heart immediately going out to the little girl. She hoped that Maddie wasn't in too much pain.

"Well, we made it back," Sasha announced. "Sorry for the wait." She looked around. "Uncle Roger, where's the baby?"

Roger pointed to Chloe. "This one got her to go to sleep just like that." He snapped his fingers to illustrate just how fast Chloe had performed what was clearly a magic trick to him.

Sasha smiled warmly at Chloe.

"Well, I'm won over. You've got the job," Sasha quipped.

"You're not serious, are you?" Chloe asked uncertainly.

"No, she's not," Graham agreed. "But almost," he told Chloe. "Sasha goes on gut instincts, same as me," he told her.

"Hey, kiddo, you want to go upstairs and lie down?" Roger asked his grandniece, who had momentarily gotten lost in this verbal exchange between the adults.

"No," Maddie cried, protesting the very idea. "They had me lying down forever when I was in the hospital, getting all those pictures took of my arm." She looked at her cast. "What I want is you to sign my cast," she declared, pointing to the newly applied cast with her other hand. Barely an hour old, the cast already had a handful of autographs and well-wishes written on it. "I got these from the nurses. And that's from that doctor who put it on," she told her granduncle, pointing out the different signatures. "Isn't it neat?"

"It sure is," Roger agreed with the kind of enthusiasm that appealed to young children. "Neatest thing I've ever seen. What do you say you and me go get us a sandwich in the kitchen and I'll see if I can come up with something real good to put on that cast?"

Maddie perked up visibly. "Can I have anything I want to eat?" she asked eagerly.

"You can have anything that's in the refrigerator," Roger qualified with a wink.

Maddie's grin all but split her face. "Cool!"

Roger pretended to misunderstand her declaration. "Cool or hot. Whatever's there, is yours."

Sasha exchanged looks with her amused husband. "I think maybe I should go supervise," Sasha said, following her uncle.

Wanting to be as accommodating as possible, Chloe called out after Sasha's departing back, "I'll just sit right here until you get back."

"You can if you want to, but feel free to move around if you like. You've already got the job," Sasha called back over her shoulder, accompanying her injured daughter to the kitchen.

Chloe looked at Graham. Sasha hadn't asked her a single question that had to do with the job she was applying for. Just what had gotten the woman to decide in her favor?

"I'm confused," Chloe confessed.

He laughed. "Sasha'll do that to you," he said in a completely understanding voice. "I feel like my head's been spinning ever since I first met her. But since she's a better judge than I am when it comes to this position, I've made up my mind. You do have the job." And then he grew more serious. "Do you mind being left alone for a few minutes?" he asked. "I'd like to ask Chance some questions in private."

Then, before she could answer him, he made a suggestion. "Feel free to look around the house, or to join Sasha, Maddie and Uncle Roger in the kitchen."

Chloe shook her head, declining both offers. Right now, she just wanted to sit exactly where she was and absorb what had just happened.

And, in her opinion, what had just happened amounted to being given a job, a rather important job in her estimation, practically sight unseen.

Well, she'd been seen, Chloe amended, but obviously a great deal had just been read into whatever Sasha Fortune Robinson *thought* she saw in her.

"I'm good, thank you," she told Graham, turning down his offer.

In response, her half brother smiled at her and nodded. "I won't be long," he promised.

Her half brother.

It was still hard to think of him that way, Chloe thought as she watched him take Chance into what appeared to be a den that was directly off the living room.

Hard to think of herself as being anyone's half sister.

Or a half sister to what amounted to practically a legion of other half siblings, she added silently. She'd grown up thinking she had no family at all beyond her mother and now she had more family than she could shake that proverbial stick at.

And one of those half siblings had just given her a job.

Not just *any* job but the kind of job she had set her heart on before she'd ever sent in her application to college. So far, she'd been stitching together a living taking anything she could get—even working at a local coffee shop on weekends to help pay her rent. She felt as if she'd finally crossed a threshold into her field.

Talk about luck.

Glancing around to make sure no one could see her, Chloe pinched herself. And then, just to make certain, she pinched herself again because she had to admit this all seemed like some sort of dream. A dream that she was going to wake up from at any minute now.

Except for the part about Donnie, she thought grimly. If this *was* a dream, he'd be right here beside her.

But he wasn't.

She was sitting in this big old living room all by herself, waiting for her half brother to come back in and tell her all the details she needed to know about this job she was going to be starting. She was convinced that she'd gotten this position strictly because she was "family" despite all of Graham's talk about instincts and gut feelings.

No matter, she was determined to prove to them that they hadn't made a mistake in hiring her. She was going to work really, really hard and be the best counselor they could have possibly hoped for. She owed it to them.

Most of all, she owed it to herself—and to the memory of her husband, who had always encouraged her and told her she could be absolutely anything she wanted to be once she set her mind to it.

She glanced toward the door that Graham had closed behind him and Chance. She wondered how the interview was going.

She really hoped that Chance was going to get the job. She'd gotten the impression that although Chance wasn't down on his luck, landing this position at Peter's Place was really important to him.

Without realizing it, Chloe crossed her fingers for him, wishing that she was one of those people who actually believed in sending good vibes. Because if she was, she'd be sending them right now.

She watched the door intently.

And when it finally opened, only a few minutes later, she popped to her feet like a newly refurbished jack-in-the-box. Fingers still crossed, her eyes immediately went to the taller of the two men emerging from the room.

Chance was smiling.

She was confident that she knew the results before he said a word.

Chapter Four

Chance's smile was as broad as his shoulders as he crossed to her.

"Looks like you turned out to be my good-luck charm," he told Chloe. "'Cause I got the job."

"Luck has nothing to do with it," Graham told him, reaching up just a little to put his hand on his newest ranch hand's shoulder. "The people you worked for all spoke very highly of you. As a matter of fact, Kyle McMasters said to tell you that if it doesn't work out for you here, he'd be more than happy to have you come back to work for him at the Double M."

Chance made no comment regarding his former boss's remark. Instead, he looked at his new boss and asked, "When can I start?"

"Bright and early tomorrow morning'll be fine." As

a rule, ranch hands were usually up around sunrise, if not before, so Graham made a suggestion. "How does seven o'clock suit you?"

The early hour didn't faze him in the slightest. He was accustomed to being up earlier, even when he wasn't working. It was just the way his inner clock worked. "I can be here earlier if you need me to be," Chance told him.

"No, seven'll do fine. You can bring your gear then and move in to the bunkhouse," Graham told him. "We've got two on the premises. One just for the ranch hands and the other one's where the boys stay."

"Sounds good to me," Chance replied. "All I really require is enough space to stretch out at the end of the day, nothing more."

Graham nodded. "We're going to get along just fine," he predicted. "Just to let you know, I've got plans for you. You're not just going to be a ranch hand. After you get the lay of the land around here, and things look like they're going well, I want to make you the coordinator for Peter's Place."

Graham smiled. "I think your being ex-military might just come in handy. The boys who are here now need a firm hand and they need to be made to respect authority. That's not to say I want you coming down hard on them. Just make sure they don't take advantage of you or anyone else here," Graham added. He looked deliberately at Chloe as he said the last part.

Chloe appreciated the thought, but she had been looking after herself for a long time now.

"You don't have to worry about me," Chloe told her

half brother. "I might not be as tall as you two, but I'm not a pushover, either. And I can definitely take care of myself."

Graham held up a hand. "I never meant to imply that I thought of you as a pushover. But knowing someone has your back certainly doesn't hurt in this kind of a situation," Graham assured her.

Then he launched into a rundown of the current residents staying at Peter's Place. "Right now, we've got four boys staying here. They're all decent kids, but for one reason or another, they've lost their way and all of them feel like they've been dealt a pretty bad hand." He spared a glance at Chloe. "Sasha can do a better job filling you in," he said to Chloe.

As if on cue, his wife came in from the kitchen. "Did I just hear my name being mentioned?" she asked, a bright smile on her face. Before Graham had an opportunity to respond to her question, Sasha told her husband, "You'll be happy to know that breaking her wrist did not affect our daughter's appetite. She's eating up a storm in there. Uncle Roger's whipping up his 'famous' corn dogs wrapped in bacon for her. I set the limit at two but I've got a feeling he's not going to stick to that. Maybe you can make him understand the wisdom of not letting Maddie stuff herself to the gills."

"I'm on it," Graham said, beginning to leave the living room.

Sasha looked at Chance and Chloe. "So, I take it that they both said yes."

"That they did," Graham said, tossing the words over his shoulder.

"Well then, welcome to Peter's Place," Sasha told the duo warmly. "I hope you like it here," she added. "We try to keep it homey. For some of these boys, this is the first actual 'home' they've had in quite a while."

The sound of a baby crying was heard coming over the monitor that Chloe had positioned on the wide coffee table.

Sasha sighed wearily as she looked at the monitor. "Looks like I'm being summoned," she told Chloe as she started to get up.

"Why don't you stay here and get Chloe up to speed on the boys who are currently here?" Graham suggested. Sasha began to point out the obvious, but never got very far. "I'll go see to Sydney," Graham told her. "I'm sure Uncle Roger knows enough not to overfeed Maddie. If he doesn't, Maddie's got enough sense to stop." Pausing for just a moment before he went up the stairs, he turned toward Chance. "And I'll see you in the morning."

"Count on it," Chance told him. Putting his Stetson on, he tipped it ever so slightly to the right, unaware that he was creating a rakish image as he did so. Chance nodded first at Graham's wife and then at Chloe. "Ladies, I'll see you tomorrow," he promised just before he headed for the door.

Chloe just stared at his retreating form. A very sexy form, she had to admit.

"He's a tall one, don't you agree?"

The comment snapped Chloe to attention. She hadn't even realized she was still staring at the closed door.

"What? Oh, you mean Chance. Yes, I guess he is at that," she murmured.

When she looked at Sasha, she thought she saw a hint of a grin on her lips. She hoped that Sasha didn't think that there was anything between her and Chance—or that there would be in the future. She'd come here strictly because she wanted work as a counselor and nothing more, she silently insisted.

"So tell me about the boys at Peter's Place," Chloe urged. She thought it best to change the subject immediately.

Sasha sat down beside her on the sofa, and then a sudden thought occurred to her. "Oh, where are my manners? Having your daughter break her wrist kind of knocks everything else out of your head," she apologized, then asked, "Can I get you anything? Something to drink perhaps?"

Chloe shook her head. She didn't want anything to distract her. Right now, all she wanted to do was focus on any information that Sasha could give her. She wanted to be as fully prepared as possible when she finally met the boys who had been sent here to atone for their misdeeds and to ultimately become better people.

"No, I'm fine. Really," she stressed when Sasha looked at her somewhat skeptically. "Just tell me about the boys I'm going to be working with. I want to learn all I can about them."

Sasha seemed to ponder her reply for a moment, no doubt wanting to cite the boys in the proper order.

Then she began. "The first teen we took in here at Peter's Place is Jonah Wright. A basically good boy,

Jonah kind of hit a rough patch when his father ran off, deserting the family. Consequently, to make ends meet, his mother had to hold down two jobs. Because she wasn't home very much, she expected Jonah to look after his three younger siblings. I don't have to tell you that that's a lot of responsibility to heap on such young shoulders. Jonah loved playing baseball after school and he had to give that up in order to be there for his siblings.

"After a while, life felt as if it was crashing in on him and Jonah just kept getting angrier and angrier. He started ditching school, vandalizing property and getting into fights almost all the time. He started shoplifting and got away with it the first couple of times.

"And then he got arrested. They were going to send him to jail, then at the last minute, the authorities decided to send him here instead. It was kind of touch and go with Jonah for a while, but he turned things around and it looks like he's on the road to getting his life back." Sasha smiled, clearly pleased to be able to relate this to Chloe. "Things look pretty promising and he's even going to be playing baseball soon, just like he always wanted to."

Sasha stopped for a moment, seeming to gather her thoughts.

"The second teen who was sent here was Ryan Maxwell. He was a lot less hostile than Jonah was when he came here, but he was also a great deal more depressed and withdrawn."

"Do you know why he was depressed?" Chloe wanted to know.

Sasha nodded. "Both of his parents died and social services sent him to live with his uncle. Family isn't always the best way to go," Sasha told her. "In Ryan's case, his uncle turned out to be a lowlife. He stole and spent all of the money that Ryan's parents had set aside to pay for his college education. Personally, I suspect that Ryan got into trouble and vandalized private property just to get away from the man."

"You're probably right," Chloe agree. "He probably felt he had nothing to lose and just maybe something to gain if he got away from his uncle."

Sasha smiled. "Since he came here, he's been doing a lot better. He's now in both a math club *and* a science club in school. If he keeps things up this way, he's on track to get a college scholarship," Sasha told her proudly. "And if that happens, he can write his own ticket. His future is a great deal more promising than his past."

"And the other boys?" Chloe asked, wondering if their stories would wind up ending this well.

"Well, the last two are newer and I'm afraid they haven't really adjusted to living here—yet," Sasha emphasized, obviously holding out a great deal of hope for the fates of both of these newer residents at Peter's Place. "Brandon Baker lost his older brother in Afghanistan, and I get the distinct feeling that he's just mad at the whole world right now."

Chloe could certainly identify with the way Brandon felt. When Donnie had been killed, there was a point when she'd been convinced that her anger was going to suffocate her. It had been touch and go for a while.

"And the last boy?" Chloe prompted.

"That would be Will Sherman. His mother is a single parent, and she has her own share of problems. The woman is an alcoholic," Sasha confided. "The Dr. Jekyll/Mr. Hyde kind who takes all of her frustrations out on Will. A social worker found him wandering the streets one night, so battered she didn't know how he was able to even stand up, much less walk." Tears shone in Sasha's eyes as she told Chloe, "When the social worker questioned him, he denied that his mother had beaten him. It was heartbreaking how protective he was of that woman. But it was obvious to everyone who came in contact with this boy that he couldn't be allowed to go back home. It was just as obvious that it would be just a matter of time before Will turned to less than acceptable ways, trying to support himself on the street.

"He's been here for a while, and I think he still feels that life has abandoned him, just like his mother has. He needs to learn how to relate to people and how to trust again."

Finished with her brief summation, Sasha paused and looked at Chloe. "Well, have I managed to scare you off yet?"

Chloe didn't have to hunt for words in order to answer her. As far as she was concerned, what Sasha had just outlined was her mission in life. Helping boys like the ones she spoke of.

"No, of course not. It's obvious that all these boys need help, and that's what I'm here for. What kind of a counselor would I be if I turned tail and ran at the first sign of a problem?"

"Possibly one who slept better at night?" Sasha suggested, a hint of a smile playing on her lips.

"The exact opposite," Chloe contradicted with feeling. "I wouldn't be able to sleep, knowing I didn't even try to help these boys. That I'd failed to reach out to them. Nobody deserves to have their dreams shattered the way these boys have, or to have their mothers beat them every time they descend into an alcoholic stupor."

Chloe knew the sort of first impression she made and the image that she projected when people first met her. She made people think of a sweet Girl Scout selling cookies door-to-door. But she wasn't interested in selling cookies.

"Believe me," she said, "I know life isn't all milk and cookies, but it shouldn't be all pain and sorrow, either."

As she spoke, Chloe could feel that she was really getting into the spirit of this new job she was about to undertake. She also felt she had a lot to offer.

"I know what it's like to grow up without a father and be raised by a single mother. I know what it's like to have to do without things other kids have, and I *definitely* know what it's like to lose someone and how that can cut right into your very soul." Her eyes met Sasha's, determination shining in them. "I think I can really help these boys," Chloe told her sister-in-law with fierce feeling.

Sasha beamed at her as she took the woman's hands in hers.

"I think you can, too," she said. "And I'm really glad Graham suggested that we hire you." She let go of Chloe, then tilted her head as if in thought for a moment. Then she said, "You know, we have an extra bedroom right here in the house. It might be easier for all of us if you lived here, on the premises."

Chloe hesitated, which prompted Sasha to quickly make another suggestion.

"We also have a small guest cottage on the property right behind the house. Now that I think of it, that might be more to your liking. You'd still be on the premises, but there wouldn't be that feeling of having Graham and me breathing down your neck," she added with an understanding smile.

"Oh, no, I wouldn't feel that," Chloe protested.

She didn't want to insult either Sasha or her half brother. They had gone out of their way to reach out to her while the others hadn't. That meant a great deal to her. She doubted that either one of them could begin to understand how much this new connection—being part of the family—meant to her. She was thrilled and excited about it and didn't want to do anything that would make them regret bringing her into the fold.

"Well, I'd feel that way in your place," Sasha said quite honestly. Her eyes met and held Chloe's. "Chloe, I have just one real hard-and-fast rule," she told the younger woman. "Always tell me the truth. No matter how you think hearing it might affect me, *always* tell me the truth. This way I won't have to wonder if you're being honest with me, or if you're just trying to spare my feelings."

Chloe took a breath. "Okay, this is me being honest. Yes, I can see how having me live here would be more beneficial so I could be on call anytime for the boys, and yes, I would rather have my own small space than live in the main house with you. That way, I won't be underfoot," she added.

Sasha laughed, looking pleased at the progress they seemed to be making. "There now, was that so hard?"

"Actually, yes," Chloe admitted. When Sasha raised her eyebrow quizzically, she explained, "I don't like worrying that I might be hurting people's feelings."

"Well, I for one would rather have my feelings hurt than find out I have been lied to—even if it involves just a little white lie," Sasha added with a wink. "All right, it's settled," she announced, rising to her feet. "You'll be moving in to the guest cottage," she told the other woman. "It hasn't been used for a while, so if there's anything you find that you need—or that needs fixing—please don't hesitate to tell either Graham or me.

"While I have to admit that we aren't exactly the handiest people in the world, we do have the connections to always find someone who is." Again, she took Chloe's hands in hers. "We want you to be happy here," she told Chloe.

"Just being given the opportunity to try to help those boys you told me about will make me happy," Chloe responded.

"Good, I'm glad." Sasha released her hands. "But don't expect miracles," she warned. "This isn't some TV drama where everything's tied up neatly with a big red bow and fixed in sixty minutes—not counting commercials," Sasha added flippantly.

"I know that," Chloe assured her. "I have a degree in counseling, not fantasy."

"As long as we're on the same page," Sasha said agreeably.

Just as Chloe rose to leave, Graham came in carrying Sydney. The baby was crying just the same way she had when Chloe had first encountered her.

"What's wrong, little one?" Sasha asked her daughter.

"I'm not sure. I changed her and I don't think she's hungry. Uncle Roger said that she was screaming her lungs out earlier, until Chloe—" he nodded at his half sister "—got her to stop."

"Chloe?" Sasha asked, looking at the other woman with interest.

"All I did was just hold her when he handed her to me," Chloe said, not about to take credit for any sort of "miracle."

The next thing she knew, Graham was handing the baby over to her.

Startled, she took the baby and after a few seconds of rocking, Sydney stopped crying again.

Sasha looked on, clearly surprised and very pleased. "Maybe we should offer you two jobs here at Peter's Place," she quipped.

Graham exchanged looks with his wife. "Works for me," he chimed in.

In response to their words, Chloe felt a warm feeling spreading out all through her. A feeling of acceptance.

She blinked several times to keep the tears back.

Chapter Five

"Looks like today's moving day for both of us," Chance observed the next day, peering into the guesthouse through the door that Chloe had left opened.

Startled, Chloe swung around, her hand pressed against her pounding heart, to find the tall cowboy standing just outside the doorway. Naturally assuming that she was alone, she had just begun arranging the furnishings in her new quarters to her liking.

The guesthouse was actually more of a large studio apartment with a small bathroom attached to it than an actual house in the traditional sense. But located about a hundred yards behind the main house, it felt like her own private little space, which was all that really mattered to Chloe right now. It made her part of the whole organization, yet just separate enough to satisfy her need to be alone at times.

Except that right now, she wasn't alone.

"Hey, I didn't mean to scare you," Chance apologized, crossing the threshold. "I guess I should make more noise when I come up behind someone."

Embarrassed at her reaction—he was probably going to think she was afraid of her own shadow—Chloe waved away the cowboy's apology.

"No, I was just really focused on trying to figure out where to put my things." She glanced around again. Somehow, with Chance inside, the space looked smaller to her than it had a few minutes ago. "I think I brought too much with me. I just wasn't sure what I was going to need."

He'd seen a sedan parked by the guesthouse. There were a number of boxes and a couple of suitcases in the backseat.

"You have a place of your own apart from here?" he asked. Sometimes he forgot that most people did. He'd moved around so much since he'd been discharged from the army that when he was in between jobs, he just lived out of his truck. It was simpler that way.

Chloe nodded. "An apartment in town." It wasn't all that big—but it was bigger than the guesthouse, she thought.

Usually one to keep to himself, Chance realized he was asking too many questions, but curiosity was spurring him on. "If you've already got a place, why aren't you staying there? Can't be that far away from the ranch," he guessed.

"Sasha thought it might be easier if I was on the premises to begin with. You know, just in case there was some kind of an emergency with one of the boys, they wouldn't have to wait for me to drive in." Replaying her words in her head, Chloe laughed. "I guess that sounds kind of dramatic, doesn't it?" She supposed she could have just told Sasha that she could make the run from her apartment to the ranch quickly enough if the need arose. "It's just that this is my first real counseling job and I don't want anything to go wrong."

She saw a look akin to sympathy enter Chance's piercing blue eyes. "Oh, it'll go wrong," he said with certainty.

This wasn't the sort of pep talk she'd expected, Chloe thought. As a matter of fact, it sounded more like some kind of prediction of doom.

She stared at him. "What?"

Maybe he should have explained what he meant when he said that, Chance thought. "No matter how perfect things are, something is always bound to go wrong. It doesn't have to be some kind of a major disaster—and it usually isn't," he said with certainty. "But it's a fact of life that things do go wrong, usually when you least expect them to. Once you make your peace with that, you can relax and get the job done," he told her. "Just remember, do the best you can. Nobody expects perfection."

Easy for you to say, she thought. *Just look at yourself.* "Do things go wrong for you?"

What he'd just said made her curious. She imagined that Chance was quite good at what he did. Practice alone probably made him perfect, and from what she'd gathered from Sasha, Chance had worked on ranches both before and after his stint in the military.

He laughed, tickled by the fact that she actually thought he might say no.

"Do you want that alphabetically, chronologically or listed in order of importance? And if it's the last one, would you like that in descending order or ascending order?"

Realizing that maybe she'd made a mistake, Chloe put her hands up as if to ward off any further questions.

"Point taken," she told Chance.

Looking at him more closely, she decided that he looked pretty relaxed. Since he'd mentioned something about it being "moving day" for both of them, she assumed that Chance had finished moving in to the bunkhouse. Men always had less baggage than women, she thought enviously. "I guess you're all settled in."

Chance moved his shoulders in a careless shrug. "A couple of changes of clothing, an extra pair of boots, razor, shaving cream and toothbrush. Not exactly much to 'settle,'" he told her, going through everything he'd brought with him.

Chance looked around the guesthouse. There was a combination stove, refrigerator and sink unit against one wall with a table for two right in front of it. Next to that was a sofa that he suspected pulled out into a bed. It was facing a small flat-screen on the wall that looked as if it was the latest piece of technology. Near the flat-screen was a chest of drawers.

It seemed like almost too much space for him, he thought.

"Need help with anything?" he asked her.

She'd already gotten started. "I just need to bring in a couple of suitcases and three boxes from my car. Oh, and I picked up two bags of groceries on my way here. But now that I see the size of the refrigerator, I'm not sure if it'll all fit in there."

"You could always stash the excess in the closet," Chance suggested with a straight face.

"I could," she allowed, taking his suggestion at face value. "If it was a walk-in. But it's not. It's barely a hang-in," she quipped.

His eyebrows drew together as he tried to make sense out of what she'd just said. "A what?"

She flushed just a little. "That was a lame joke about there not being enough room to hang more than a handful of clothes in the closet."

That had never been a problem for him. "I never really had more than a handful of clothes at any one time myself."

That fit the image she'd gotten of him. "Of course you didn't. Just your cowboy hat, your boots and your lariat should cover it," she deadpanned.

His eyes crinkled a little in amusement. "You been peeking into my closet, Chloe Elliott?"

The thought of peeking into his living space suddenly made her blush. She struggled to get that under control. "Just making an educated guess."

He wondered if he seemed that predictable to her, or if she was just kidding. Either way, she struck him as a fairly sharp lady. "Well, if that's the kind of thing a de-gree in counseling gets you, I'd say that it was money well spent."

That being said, he had to admit he was a little leery of psychologists and people who felt all problems could be tackled and solved by delving deeply into people's backgrounds and into what made them tick. That meant hours and hours of talking. He believed in action, not in talking a thing to death.

"But just so you know," he added, "I don't really enjoy having someone poking around in my head, want-ing to know if I grew up thinking there were monsters under my bed."

"I don't blame you," she agreed so readily, he found himself believing her. "Neither do I."

Chance jerked a thumb toward the car she had parked out front. "Want me to bring in those suitcases and boxes for you?"

She didn't want him feeling as if he had to do any-thing for her. And she didn't want him thinking of her as helpless, either. "You don't have to."

"I didn't say I had to. I asked if you wanted me to," he pointed out.

On the other hand, she didn't want to come off like someone who slapped away a helping hand, either.

"Yes, please. That would be very nice of you," she told him.

Chance was out the door before the last word had left her lips. He was back just as quickly, juggling both suitcases as well as the three boxes. It amazed her that he hadn't dropped anything.

"You certainly move fast," she marveled.

"It's a little something you pick up when people are shooting at you," he told her. Looking around the room for a likely spot, he asked, "Where do you want me to put these?"

"Doesn't matter, just any place," she said vaguely. "I've got to empty the suitcases and hang the things up inside that shallow closet." She waved at the small door that was off to one side.

He set the suitcases and boxes down next to the sofa. "Again, that wouldn't be a problem for me—if I had a closet," he added with a hint of a grin.

"You don't have a closet?" Chloe asked, surprised, trying to visualize his living quarters.

"Does a footlocker count?"

"Only if you're in boot camp," she said before she realized that he was being serious.

Chance grinned at the reference. It hit home. "Well, it's kind of like that," he told her.

Picking up one of the suitcases, Chloe placed it on the sofa and snapped opened the locks, then lifted the lid.

Chance caught himself looking into the suitcase. Instead of the jeans and practical shirts he'd expected, he saw that she had packed several very flowery, pastel-colored dresses. The kind, he thought, that seemed more suited to sitting on a porch swing, sipping lemonade, than following around teenage boys as they did their chores on a ranch. From what Graham had explained, Peter's Place had been founded on the idea that the chores were what taught these troubled kids discipline and doing those chores in turn brought order to their lives.

Somehow, that kind of dusty activity just didn't seem compatible with flowing, feminine dresses. At least not to him.

She saw Chance looking rather skeptically at what she'd packed. She could almost read his thoughts by the expression on his face.

He was probably right, she thought. What she'd brought with her wasn't all that sensible. It reflected who and what she was, but it fell short in the practicality department.

Still, as long as Chance didn't bring the subject up, she wasn't about to try to defend her choices.

She thought of something that Chance had said when he brought her suitcases in. Something that had made her think of Donnie. She'd understood her husband's reasons for joining up, just like she understood what Chance had said about it the other day. Fighting for your country were sentiments to be admired. But they were also idealistic and they didn't explain how Chance had dealt with the day-to-day struggle of just trying to survive.

"How did you stand it?" she asked Chance suddenly.

He looked at her, confused. She had him at a complete disadvantage. The question had come out of the blue, and since they weren't actually talking about anything, he really wasn't sure what Chloe was referring to.

"How did I stand what?" he wanted to know.

"When you brought the boxes and suitcases in, you said you learned to move fast because people were

shooting at you. How did you stand that?" she asked
in all sincerity. "Knowing that any second, no matter
what you were doing and how quiet it was, someone
could just start shooting at you? Worse, that they might
actually wind up killing you?"

"Most of the time I didn't think about it," he told her
honestly. "You really can't spend time thinking about
it, or it'll wind up paralyzing you. You just hope that
when someone does start shooting at you, the bullet
won't have your name on it. Or that you get to return
fire quickly enough and accurately enough to take out
whoever it is who wants you dead." He paused, his eyes
meeting hers. "Everyone who goes over there just wants
to get home in one piece."

Chance watched as Chloe slowly unpacked, neatly
hanging up the dresses. He could easily envision her
wearing those dresses, a soft spring breeze flirting with
the material, causing it to lightly press against her body
in ways that could make a grown man weak.

He felt his stomach muscles tightening and forced
himself to breathe.

He had no business thinking like that about her,
Chance told himself.

Just like he had no business asking her questions,
yet here he was, doing both.

He had to watch that, Chance upbraided himself.

Even so, he heard himself telling her, "You know,
whenever you're ready to talk about it, I'm here to listen."

"'Talk about it'?" she asked quizzically. Was Chance
just talking in general, or was he somehow intuitively

referring to the single loss that had ultimately broken her heart?

Chance felt as if he was getting in too deep, but now that he had opened the door, he had no choice except to continue.

"Talk about whoever it is that you lost," he explained. "I figure it has to be someone in the military. Even with all the communication we have available today, it still has to be tough, being cut off like that. Not knowing what's going on until a lot later—if at all."

He knew he wasn't great with words, but he did have a sense of empathy and he knew without putting it into words what she had to have felt. What she still might be feeling. Because he had gone through the same thing.

"Thank you," Chloe said quietly.

She sounded sincere. Awkward or not, maybe he'd pushed the right buttons after all.

"Then you do want to talk?" he asked.

"No." She'd actually thanked him for the offer, not for the opportunity. "No offense, but I can't. Not yet."

Maybe not ever, she added silently because she didn't know if she actually could. The mere thought hurt too much.

"But if and when I am ready to talk about 'it,'" she said, deliberately using his terminology, "I'll take you up on that offer."

Chance nodded. "Good enough," he told her. "I'll be around." He realized how that had to have sounded, so he amended the last sentence. "At least for now."

That last comment caught Chloe off guard. "You make it sound temporary. Is there a time limit to the job?" she asked, wondering if there was something Graham had said to Chance before they had come out of his den yesterday after the interview.

Chance answered her honestly. "Only the one I set for myself," he said. "I only stay in any one place for as long as it feels right. When it stops feeling right, that's when it's time to go."

That sounded just too nomadic for her. If things were working out, why would he want to leave? It didn't make sense.

"And what makes it time to go?" she challenged.

No one had ever questioned his actions before. But Chloe put him on the spot. Though it made him uneasy, it also had him looking at her in a different light. The woman had spunk, he had to admit.

He shrugged. "Just a feeling. Can't really put it into better words than that," he confessed.

Chloe assessed his words. Was he running from something without realizing it? she couldn't help wondering.

"Maybe that feeling is fear," she suggested. She saw that her suggestion did not please him. But she honestly believed what she was saying to him. She couldn't apologize for that; it would be a lie. Instead, she tried to explain what she meant. "Maybe what you fear is complacency. You get too comfortable, too used to something, and you start to worry that you're losing your edge, that you're getting soft. That the challenge is gone. So you have to leave to find another mountain to climb, another dragon to slay."

Chance looked at her as if she was suddenly babbling nonsense.

"I'm not climbing any mountains, and I sure as hell am not slaying any of those dragons. Anyway, dragons aren't real." He was trying his best not to sound annoyed—but he was.

"No," she agreed, "they're not."

He knew he should just go. Normally, he would have. But something was making him dig in his heels and stay. He wanted to get something straight.

"Is this the kind of stuff you're going to be feeding those boys?" he asked. "Stuff about slaying dragons?"

"No, this is the kind of 'stuff' I'm going to be using in order to try to understand the boys," she said. "To help them reconnect with the world."

He laughed drily. Still sounded like a bunch of mumbo jumbo to him.

"Well, good luck with that," he told her, shaking his head. "But if you ask me, a little hard work and a little responsibility should help those boys do all the reconnecting that they need."

"Hard work and responsibility," she repeated as if he had just quoted scripture. "Has it helped you?" Chloe asked innocently.

His scowl deepened for a moment, and then he just waved her words away. "Don't try getting inside my head, Chloe Elliott. There's nothing in it for you. I'm doing just fine just the way I am."

She suppressed a sigh. "Okay, as long as you're happy."

Happy? When was the last time he'd been happy? He couldn't remember.

"Happy's got nothing to do with it," Chance answered. "I'm my own man on my own terms, and that's all that really counts."

He felt himself losing his temper, and he didn't want to do that. Once things were said, they couldn't get "unsaid" and a lot of damage could be done. He didn't want that to happen. Not with this woman.

"I'd better go find the boss. Graham said that he wanted to take me around the spread as soon as I stashed my gear."

She didn't want to be the reason he was late. "Then I guess you'd better get going."

"Yeah, I guess I'd better." With that, he crossed back to the door.

He walked out feeling that there were things left unspoken. A great many things. But then, maybe it was better that way. He wasn't looking to have his head "shrunk" any more than it already was. Even if the lady doing the shrinking was nothing short of a knockout.

Some things, he reasoned, were just better off left alone.

Chapter Six

Chloe could feel the butterflies in her stomach. Flexing, but at present unable to fly. They were huge butterflies with wingspans that would make an eagle seriously jealous.

But as she walked to her first meeting with the boys at Peter's Place, she knew that if she gave any indication that she was even slightly nervous—never mind that she was about a minute away from having a full-on panic attack—she was certain to lose any advantage and all credibility. Putting up a calm front was all-important during this first encounter.

She was well aware that this would set the tone for the rest of the visits to come.

No pressure here, Chloe mocked herself.

But she knew that if she didn't project that she was

completely in control of the situation, word would spread to the other boys immediately, and then none of them would view her with the respect she needed in order to be of any help to them.

And helping them was why she was here, why she'd become a counselor in the first place.

And maybe, in helping others to heal, eventually she'd find a way to help and heal herself.

When she took the job, she'd assumed that she would be conducting a group session, with Sasha present, in which she'd get to meet all four of the boys at once and learn a little about each of them by the time the session was over.

But Sasha had been concerned that since this was her maiden run, so to speak, she might be a little overwhelmed meeting four teens at once. Graham's wife had suggested that she start out small, talking just to one of the ranch residents at a time.

Naturally, Chloe had agreed. She thought that a one-on-one meeting might work a little more in her favor. Besides, she didn't have a ton of experience. New on the job, she needed to abide by Sasha's wishes. After all, Sasha was the expert here.

So here she was, walking into the small, cheery room that had been set aside in the main house for counseling sessions, doing her best to try to control the squadron of butterflies in her stomach that were morphing into Boeing 747s.

At least the sun was cooperating, she noted, filling the room with warm light thanks to the full-length windows that looked out onto the corral and the stables beyond that.

The sun might be cooperating, but her first patient didn't look as if he was inclined to follow suit.

Brandon Baker eyed her suspiciously the moment he walked into the room less than a couple of seconds after she'd entered. A good-looking fifteen-year-old with dark, almost black hair and brown eyes, he was a lot thinner than he should have been. His stance and his very gait exuded defiance.

His eyes quickly swept around the room. "Where's the doc?" he wanted to know.

Chloe didn't bother asking him if he meant Sasha. That would be stalling. "She won't be joining us for the session," Chloe began.

Brandon made a 180 without missing a step and headed for the doorway he'd just entered through.

Chloe knew she had to say something quickly or he'd be gone in a flash. She called after him. "Mrs. Fortune Robinson thought we could get to know each other better if she wasn't here."

Brandon had his hand on the doorknob and didn't bother turning around. "She thought wrong," he said flatly.

"Come back and sit down, Brandon."

Chloe hadn't raised her voice and she definitely wasn't shouting, but there was no mistaking the firmness in her tone. It wasn't a request; it was an order. She surprised even herself.

Brandon still didn't turn around, but neither did he

turn the doorknob and go out. It was as if he was still waiting to be convinced.

"Now, please," she requested.

Brandon blew out a breath, turned around and then walked over to the folding chair that was set up opposite hers.

Chloe gestured toward the padded green chair. "Sit, please." Both words were given equal weight.

After a moment, during which time she had a feeling the boy was mentally going over his options, as well as wondering how far he could push her, Brandon Baker finally sat down.

"Okay, I'm sitting." He looked at her, but she couldn't read the expression on his face. All she knew was that it wasn't warm. "Now what?"

"Now we talk," Chloe told him in as bright and engaging a tone as she could summon.

"Talk?" The single word seemed to mock her, and she saw a smirk on Brandon's sullen face. "Lady, I don't even know you."

"That's where the talking part comes in," she told him in as upbeat a manner as she could project. "We talk so that we can get to know each other."

"And then what?" he challenged cynically. "Become best friends?"

"Maybe," she allowed. "Eventually. If enough time passes."

The scowl on the young face was dark and forbidding. "I don't need any more friends."

"Maybe not," Chloe said agreeably. "Maybe you're one of those people who have all the friends he needs—

although I doubt it," she couldn't help adding. A warning look rose in Brandon's eyes. Chloe pushed on. "But it's obvious that you do need a way to get rid of all that anger you're holding on to."

Brandon shifted restlessly, indicating that he had heard all that he was willing to listen to. His eyes narrowed. "Look, lady—"

"Chloe," she supplied. She knew that she should have told the boy to address her by either her surname or simply "ma'am," but somehow, using her first name just seemed friendlier and she needed to find some sort of an opening if she was going to forge a bridge between them.

Brandon looked bored. "Whatever," he said dismissively. And then, in case there were any lingering doubts about the situation, he told her in no uncertain terms, "I don't know what you thought when you came here, but I'm not some kind of a guinea pig for you to practice on so you can earn your merit badge or whatever it is you're trying to get out of this."

She realized that he was trying to get her angry, angry enough to walk out. She had no intentions of letting him.

"What I'm trying to 'get out of this' is to find a way to help you help yourself," she explained patiently. "No matter how you feel about it, Brandon, I'm not the enemy here."

"Okay, you're not the enemy," he parroted. "*Now* can I go?" he demanded.

Chloe glanced at her watch—as if she wasn't keenly

aware of every second that went by. "We've got another forty-five minutes left to the session."

Brandon slouched in his chair, crossing his arms defiantly across his chest as he glared at her. "So you're what, a shrink?" he wanted to know, his hostility almost palpable.

"I'm a counselor," she corrected, fervently wishing she had more ammunition at her disposal for this battle she suddenly found herself in.

"Uh-huh." Hostility momentarily turned to boredom, and he deliberately yawned. "Same difference."

"Not exactly," she told him. In actuality, there was a world of difference, especially in the two disciplines' approaches to the people they dealt with. But she wasn't about to bore Brandon further by explaining them. "Tell you what," she said instead, "why don't I ask you some questions and you can fill in the blanks for me. How would that be?"

He made no answer, other than to scowl and to slouch even lower in his chair, his body language telling her that he didn't care one way or another what she proposed to do.

Chloe had to concentrate not to allow the hand that was holding Brandon's file to tremble. Showing fear was the worst thing she could do, and she knew it.

"According to the information on your entrance form, you had an older brother, Blake, who was killed—"

Brandon instantly sat up, and his body became almost rigid as his eyes blazed accusingly at her. "You shut up about my brother!" he ordered.

She couldn't do that. If she hadn't thought so before,

she knew now that Blake was at the root of Brandon's anger. Chloe pressed on.

She understood what he was going through better than he knew, she thought.

"Your brother did a noble thing," she told him in a calm, even voice. "Don't you think that should be acknowledged?"

"No!" Brandon shouted at her. And then he cried, "My brother did a stupid thing! If he hadn't joined the military, he wouldn't have gotten himself killed. He'd still be alive today. He'd still be here! With me!" His voice cracked as he made the declaration.

"Brandon," Chloe continued in a quiet voice, doing her best to try to calm him, "I know that you're hurting right now—"

His temper flared again. "Don't talk like you know me!" He jumped to his feet now. "You don't know anything about me!" he insisted furiously.

Chloe refused to back down. If she retreated right now, she might as well give up. "I might not know you, but I know how you feel," she told him doggedly as she tried again.

"No, you don't! Don't say that!" The boy looked like he was fighting back tears. "Nobody knows how I feel!"

With that, Brandon dashed right past her and out the door.

He would have dashed down the hall and presumably out of the house if he hadn't run straight into Chance, blindly colliding with the towering cowboy.

The impact might have knocked Brandon to the floor

if Chance hadn't reacted quickly and caught hold of the boy by his shoulders.

"Hey, where's the fire?" Chance asked. The next moment, he saw Chloe coming up behind the fleeing boy. He saw the look of concern on her face. "Everything all right here?" he wanted to know.

Unlike his first question, this one was addressed to Chloe.

"Everything's all right," she told Chance resolutely. She caught the surprised look that Brandon slanted her way. "I just decided to end the session a little earlier than planned. Since this is our first session, I thought maybe Brandon needed a little time to digest what we talked about before we could move forward."

Chance looked at the boy he was still holding steady. He had his doubts about the validity of what Chloe was telling him.

"Is that so?" he asked, looking at the boy.

Brandon shot a look toward Chloe, and Chance could read his thoughts. The teen was calculating his next move, deciding if now was the time to play the odds or to just go along with things.

His gaze flickered as if he'd decided to run with the excuse Chloe had handed him. "Yeah, getting used to someone new takes time. The doc's giving me time."

Chance looked over the boy's head at Chloe. "Is that what you're doing, Doc?" he asked, even though he was highly skeptical about the excuse he was being given. "Are you giving Brandon time so he can get used to you?"

Chloe nodded. "This was an introductory session

only," she said, her eyes meeting Brandon's. "The next one will be longer. Right, Brandon?"

Rather than agree, Brandon merely raised and lowered his thin shoulders in a careless, disinterested shrug. "You're the doc," the boy replied.

"Well, since you're free," Chance told the boy, "there's that stall waiting for you to muck out." He saw the face that Brandon unintentionally made. He didn't pretend not to notice. "You know the rules. Chores first, then you can ride—unless of course you want to talk to the doc here some more," Chance said, offering the boy a choice.

Brandon waited, as if he was actually weighing his options for a second. And then he made his choice. "I'll be at the stable."

He walked toward the rear of the ranch house to the exit closest to the stable.

Chance turned his attention to Chloe and saw the disappointed expression on her face. "Didn't go all that well, huh?"

He was kidding, right? "Well, I just took second place to cleaning out manure in a horse stall, so no, it didn't go all that well."

Chance laughed, not at her but at the situation. "Don't take it personally. The kid's mad at the world right now." Graham had given him a quick background summary for all four of the boys. Chance felt for them, even if he wasn't prone to showing it. "He looked up to his big brother, thought of him as invincible. When it turned out that his brother wasn't bulletproof, it threw the kid for a loop. He's still trying to find a place for himself in a world that no longer has his big brother in it. That is *not* an easy adjustment to make," he told her. "Especially at Brandon's age."

"Losing someone is not an easy adjustment to make at *any* age," she told Chance in no uncertain terms. "I was trying to tell Brandon that. Trying to let him know that I understand what he's going through."

Chance was closer to the boy's situation than he cared to admit, so he tried to explain to her just what she was up against.

"He's not ready to hear that," Chance told her. "Right now, he's wrapping himself up in that pain and anger that he feels. That rage. It's the only way he has to cope. Without it, he's afraid that he'll just break down, fall to pieces and never be able to get back up. Being angry is all he has," Chance stressed, trying to make her understand. "You take that away from the boy before he's ready to let it go and, well, there's no telling what can happen."

It was a warning. He didn't want her good heart to accidentally cause her to make a really bad mistake. He had a feeling that she'd never forgive herself.

Chloe laughed shortly. He had a better handle on the situation than she did, she thought ruefully. "You know, you sound pretty wise for a cowboy."

The corners of Chance's full mouth curved just the slightest bit. "I think, on behalf of cowboys everywhere, I should be taking offense at that."

She wasn't getting anything right today, was she? "I didn't mean it that way," she told him apologetically.

He laughed and stopped her before she could launch

into a full-scale apology. He'd just been trying to tease her out of her very serious mood. "I know. I'm just having fun with you."

It was her turn to turn the tables on him. "You can do that?" she asked, pretending to be surprised. "You can have fun?"

"I've been known to," Chance deadpanned. "Every once in a while."

It suddenly occurred to her that Chance was standing much too close to her. So close, she wondered if he could hear her heart beating fast. So close that she was sure he could easily kiss her without any effort at all.

And although the thought of being kissed by Chance did instantly raise her pulse rate, Chloe knew that kissing him would be a huge mistake, especially for her. Because being kissed by and kissing Chance would mean opening a door to a place she had absolutely no desire to revisit.

A place filled with feelings.

The very idea of having feelings for someone—*those* kinds of feelings—much less falling in love with that person, scared Chloe beyond words.

And right now, she needed all her words in order to reach the four boys whose care she had been charged with. That left her no time for anything else, she silently lectured herself. No racing pulses, no pounding hearts. No sexy cowboy to cause her imagination to take flight.

"Um, I'd better get ready for my next session," she told Chance, backing away.

"Who are you seeing?" he asked.

Good. She could talk about work. There was safety

in that. "Will Sherman. Hopefully, I'll do better my first time out with him than I did with Brandon."

He'd asked her who she was seeing next for a reason. So he could offer her some help. It was obvious that she needed it.

"That one's got trust issues," he told her. "Because his mother turned on him and beat him so badly, he's closed down. But the good news is that he really doesn't want to be like that. You can make a connection if you're patient enough. Just go slow, and listen. He'll open up eventually."

"Sounds like he already has," Chloe said. "With you."

Chance didn't want her thinking that he was treading on her toes. "No, I'm just good at reading signs," he told her. And then, in an effort to make her understand, he reminded her, "I'm good with horses." It wasn't a boast, just a fact. "They don't talk, either. But if you watch them closely, you get to understand what they want, what they need. Once you know that, gaining their trust is easy and inevitable. Same goes for people, too."

She smiled at him. He'd just summarized an entire year's worth of studies in a few sentences. The man was a natural, she thought. He should probably be in her place.

But there was no sense in talking herself out of a job she both wanted and needed, Chloe thought. So she simply said, "Thank you. I'll keep that in mind. Now I'd better get ready for my next session."

He nodded. "And that's my cue to get out of here," he said—just before he did.

Chapter Seven

The 747s in her stomach were finally down to the manageable size of normal butterflies. Maybe even *small* butterflies, Chloe thought.

She'd been counseling the boys for a couple of weeks now and she was slowly getting used to it, to the routine that Sasha had instituted. After enduring rather tense initial sessions with each of the four boys, she knew what she was up against with them now. They were coming to the office for private sessions three, sometimes four times a week. More if any of them felt they needed it or if they sought a little extra guidance with something they were attempting to work out.

Although conducting a one-on-one had been admittedly scary to her at first, Chloe decided that maybe Sasha was right after all. The four boys had plenty of time to interact with one another while they did their chores and when they spent time riding under Chance's supervision, not to mention that they were always all together at mealtime.

Going with the philosophy that everyone needed their own space and the idea that the boys might be more inclined to open up about something that was bothering them if they didn't have to make a public declaration of it, Chloe continued to see each of them on an individual basis rather than meeting with them as a group.

The two boys who had been at Peter's Place longer were in a better place mentally than the two newer arrivals. Jonah and Ryan had had more time to work out their anger and the issues that had brought them here in the first place. Happily, they both seemed as if they had gotten back on track again after their emotional derailments had threatened to turn them into repeat offenders. Thanks in part to her and to Sasha's joint efforts, both boys were learning how to cope with the curves that life had thrown at them and might very well throw at them again.

None of the battles had been won yet, especially not in the individual cases of Brandon and Will, but Chloe felt that the latter two were definitely taking baby steps in the right direction. It made her proud that she could say that she was a part of their progress, slow though it might seem.

Her own life might still need some work, Chloe thought, but at least she was helping four teens with their whole lives ahead of them work toward fulfilling their destinies. That was definitely something to be proud of, she told herself.

"You look pretty happy with yourself," Chance observed the next time that their paths crossed—which unbeknownst to her was as often as Chance could make happen. Ordinarily, he would have kept to himself the way he usually did, but there was something about this woman that just seemed to burrow into him, to pull him out of the solitary state he'd learned to prefer. She made him remember another time when life hadn't been so deadly serious. When sadness hadn't been his constant companion.

"Actually, I am—kind of," she added, lest Chance think she had an ego problem, or that she was giving herself way too much credit.

Chance read between the lines. "I take it that things are going well on your end with the boys," he guessed. He leaned against the doorjamb to her office. "I don't hear any of them grumbling in the corral anymore. Oh, Brandon still has a bit of an attitude problem when it comes to doing some of his chores, but even he's toned down somewhat in the last week. So I guess whatever it is you're doing here with them, you're doing it right," he told her with an encouraging grin. Then he summed it up simply. "It's working."

He was being kind, she thought. This wasn't just her doing. She really doubted that the tall, quiet cowboy was unaware of the effect that he had on the boys.

"Thanks, but I realize that it's a team effort. What you do with them when they're with you is just as important when it comes to stabilizing their mental health and turning them into well-adjusted young men as what's being said here in this room when the door's closed."

Chloe couldn't help thinking that Chance was the epitome of the strong silent type, enduring things without complaint, and that had to make a real impression on these boys, all of whom were in need of a strong father figure they could look up to and use as a role model. Even if they didn't consciously realize it.

Chance merely nodded, not about to argue with her about it. Arguing had always seemed like a waste of time to him.

"If you say so. Say, are you free now?" he asked suddenly. "I don't know what Sasha's got you doing when you're not counseling the boys, but I'm going to have them out in the corral, exercising their horses in a few minutes, and you're welcomed to come out and watch. Maybe it'll help you with their sessions later on," he speculated. Then a rather infectious smile split his lips. "Who knows, you might even enjoy getting a little fresh air. It might get to be habit-forming," Chance teased.

"Are you hinting that I'm some kind of a hermit?" Chloe retorted. Was that how he saw her? The idea bothered her more than she was willing to admit.

Chance looked perfectly serious as he elaborated. "Not a hermit, exactly. Hermits don't interact with people. But what are those people called? You know the ones I mean," he said, as if hunting for the correct word. "The ones who don't go out in daylight?"

Her eyebrows rose up so high that they all but disappeared beneath her bangs. "Vampires?" she guessed, stunned. "Are you saying I'm a vampire?"

"Well, no, not exactly," he said, backtracking just a little. "You definitely don't suck blood or anything like that, but those vampires you mentioned, they're supposed to have a thing about not going out into the daylight, don't they?"

"I wouldn't know," she informed him a little stiffly.

"Well, I've heard talk," Chance allowed, completely deadpan. But then a smile teased the corners of his mouth, bringing out the same sexy dimples in his cheeks, the ones that made her stare at him, dream about him, even though she told herself not to. "I'm just messing with you," he admitted with a laugh that backed up his words. "But you are kind of pale," he pointed out a little more seriously.

Chloe wanted to protest, but in good conscience, she couldn't. She knew she really was pale, especially in comparison with Chance.

So instead, she inclined her head, conceding the point. "I guess I do stay indoors a lot."

"Well, there's one way to fix that," Chance said, reminding her of the invitation he'd just extended to her a couple of minutes ago. "Come outside to the corral and watch the boys put their horses through their paces. You might even find that you enjoy it. I kind of suspect that the boys will enjoy showing you what they've learned when it comes to handling horses, seeing as all of them were city kids when they came here."

Initially, she'd thought of Chance as being exceptionally closed-mouthed. She was going to have to reassess her original impression of the man.

"You know, for a man who claims not to be much of a talker, you certainly do know how to sell something," she told him with genuine admiration.

He looked at her in all innocence, as if he had no idea what she was talking about.

"I'm not selling anything," he told her. "I'm just telling you the way things are. Nothing more, nothing less. If you're interested in *really* joining in," he went on, "we've got a real gentle mare in the stable named Mirabel. Mirabel wouldn't hurt a fly. You can saddle her up and ride her along with the boys if you want."

Chloe was already vigorously shaking her head. "No, that's okay. No riding. I'll come out to watch the boys, but I'm just coming along as a spectator, not as a rider," she told Chance emphatically.

She'd succeeded in arousing his curiosity. "You ever been on a horse?"

"This is Texas," Chloe told him, as if that fact should be enough of an answer for him.

But he saw what she was trying to do. Chloe was being evasive, trying to use a diversion rather than answering his question outright.

Chance smiled at her. "I know where we are. I didn't ask you that. I asked if you've ever been on a horse. A moving horse," he specified in case she was going to pretend that she thought he meant a merry-go-round or a hobby horse of some sort.

Chloe bristled for a moment. She didn't like being cornered. She also didn't like admitting to any shortcomings, and as she'd already said, this *was* Texas, where everyone was thought to be born on the back of a horse, or at least knowing how to ride one.

For a second, she thought of bluffing her way through this, but then she decided that he was undoubtedly going to find out sooner or later. Better to tell Chance the truth, embarrassing though she felt it was, than be caught in a lie, which, when she came right down to it, was even more embarrassing to her.

"My whole childhood was a hand-to-mouth existence for my late mother and me. Horseback riding was a luxury we couldn't afford—or even have time for, actually," Chloe told him honestly, a solemn look on her face. "I grew up in a run-down section of the city. There was no 'horse next door,'" she quipped.

Chance nodded, straightening. His relaxed stance was gone as his eyes met hers and he looked at her intently. For a moment, she couldn't read his expression.

"So then you don't know how to ride a horse," he concluded.

"I thought that was what I was telling you," she said with a touch of impatience.

He nodded, as if he had just been given a problem to work with. Taking her elbow as he spoke, he carefully urged her toward the doorway, and then guided her out. "We're going to have to take care of that little oversight first chance we get."

The last thing she wanted was to have him see her being inept at something. "I think we both have a lot more pressing things to concern ourselves with than my lack of riding skills," she told him. They were being paid to work with the boys, not to broaden their own skills.

"No law that says we can't do more than just one thing," he replied. Long ago, Chance had learned when to retreat, so for now, he did. "For starters, just come with me to watch the boys. You'll see there's nothing to be afraid of." The easy smile was back as Chance told her, "Think of it as getting two birds with one stone."

She was keenly aware that he'd used the word *afraid*. Was that what he thought? That she was afraid of horses? Afraid of riding?

"I'm not afraid of riding a horse," she protested. "I told you, it's just something I never got around to."

"If you're not afraid, that's good," he pronounced. "That's one less thing for you to overcome."

She'd been so focused on what he was saying—and on trying to dispel this afraid-of-her-own-shadow image he seemed to have of her—that she didn't realize he had brought her out behind the back of the house. They'd gone past the guesthouse, where she was staying, and over to the corral.

All four boys were already there, along with the horses whose grooming and feeding they were each charged with. Five horses were saddled and ready to be ridden, even though the boys still had their feet firmly planted on the ground.

Jonah, who'd been there the longest and in everyone's estimation had come along the furthest, was standing between two horses, the one he had been caring for the last few months and the one that Chance rode when he was out riding with them.

Chance nodded at Jonah in acknowledgment, but before taking his stallion's reins from him, he turned toward Chloe first.

"You'll be all right here?"

She was surprised that he took the time to take her into consideration. "You asking me or telling me?" She couldn't tell from his tone.

That small smile she was growing so familiar with curved just the corners of his mouth. "Asking, mostly," he replied.

She didn't see why he was concerned. For the most part, she was out of the way here. "Sure—unless you suddenly decide to all ride toward me, at which point I'll probably be flattened."

Chance suppressed a wider smile as he shook his head. "Nope, no flattening. Not on the agenda today," he told her. And then he nodded toward the fence directly behind her. "If you want, you can climb up on the fence and straddle it. You'll get a better view that way," he told her.

Chloe looked over her shoulder, glancing at the fence a little uncertainly, even though she told him, "Maybe I will."

He caught the hesitancy and recognized it for what it was. Chloe wasn't one for climbing, he guessed. "Need a boost?" he asked.

Just because he asked, she was determined not to accept it. She tossed her head, sending her blond hair flying over her shoulders. "No, I can manage," she informed him.

But she actually couldn't, she discovered as she attempted to climb up the fence's slats.

Just as she realized she was in serious danger of falling backward and not just embarrassing herself but possibly hurting herself as well, she felt a very firm hand on her backside.

Sucking in her breath, she tried to look over her shoulder only to have Chance chide, "Steady or you're liable to fall. I'm not getting fresh here, I'm just trying to keep you from breaking anything fairly important," he told her. And then the next second, as he helped get her to the top, he declared with a note of triumph, "There you go. Now you've got a better view. Just don't get it into your head to leave before I get back to help you down," he warned.

And with that, Chance headed over to the cluster of boys.

He nodded at Jonah. "Thank you," he said as he took the reins from the group's oldest member. "Looks like we've got ourselves an audience today, boys. Show her what you've learned—and remember, don't embarrass me or yourselves," he reminded them as if that was one of the rules of procedure instead of something he was just now telling them.

"Is she going to be riding with us?" Ryan wanted to know.

"No, Ms. Elliott's strictly here as an observer," Chance answered. "So, no fancy stuff—and no slacking off, either," he told the boys. "Just nice and easy, like I showed you." He glanced toward Brandon, who looked as if he was ready to kick the horse's flanks and lead the others in a gallop around the corral. "Nice and easy, Brandon," he repeated with emphasis. "This isn't the preliminary trial for the Kentucky Derby. Remember, these are horses, not your personal toys," he warned them. "You push your horse too hard and you're back on stable duty—full-time. Are we clear?" he asked, looking around at the four faces before him.

"Clear," they all responded, their young voices blending together.

Chance nodded. "Okay then, let's show Ms. Elliott what you've learned."

Delighted, Chloe watched as the boys put the horses through their paces. The gaits varied from simply walking along the perimeter of the corral, to trotting to finally galloping at a moderate pace. She thought that was the end of it, but then she saw that the boys began leading their horses through several other exercises, one of which involved weaving in and out as if they were following the beat of a song that only they could hear.

When they were finally finished, the four riders lined up next to each other and then, almost in unison, turned toward her to see if she had enjoyed the show they had put on for her.

Chloe applauded enthusiastically. "That's wonderful," she told the boys.

"I wouldn't exactly say *wonderful*," Chance told her, bringing his own horse up to where she was perched on the fence. "But at least they've learned to follow the rules." He paused, looking at the four boys, who brought their mounts closer to where Chloe was sitting. "I'm talking about the boys, not the horses. The horses already knew how to follow the rules. All they needed was to have someone issue them."

Turning in his saddle, he looked at her. "So, how about it?"

His question came out of the blue and caught her completely off guard. "How about what?"

"Are you willing to give it a try now?" Chance wanted to know.

She suddenly realized that there were five sets of eyes turned in her direction, waiting for her to answer.

Chapter Eight

It took Chloe a minute before she realized that the cowboy was serious. When she did, she was quick to respond to his question.

"No, not right now," she told Chance, doing her best to avoid looking at the four boys. "I've got all that paperwork I need to catch up on," she added vaguely, coming up with the first excuse she could think of.

With care and effort, she managed to climb down off the fence.

But she found that her exit was blocked, not just by Chance, but by the boys, still on their horses, as well.

"C'mon, Ms. Elliott. Try it. It'll be fun," Ryan coaxed.

"We won't let anything happen to you," Jonah promised solemnly, adding his voice to the others. "Mirabel really *is* the gentlest horse on the ranch, honest."

"And Jonah and I will ride on either side of you, to make sure you don't fall off," Ryan added, obviously thinking she needed extra convincing.

It was clear that they thought she was inept when it came to horses, never mind that she really was. She didn't want that shortcoming to be general knowledge. That was the sort of thing that would make her stick out like a sore thumb on the ranch.

She looked accusingly at Chance. "What did you tell them?"

"Not a thing," Chance answered. "They're capable of figuring things out on their own."

"Horses aren't anything to be afraid of," Brandon told her, speaking up. Then he glanced at his bunkmate. "Right, Will?"

The latter flushed. When he opened his mouth, it became apparent why. "Hey, when I came here, I'd never been around a horse before." He gestured to the mount he was on. "But I learned how to ride."

"You rode very well," Chloe told him, impressed. She was well aware of the fact that it had taken a lot of work for the boys to be able to ride as effortlessly as they did now. "You all did," she added. And then Chloe looked around at all four of their faces. The light dawned on her. "Oh, I see what you're doing."

The face Ryan turned toward her was one of complete innocence. "What are we doing?"

Like he didn't know. "You're trying to get me so caught up in what you're telling me that I forget all about not wanting to get up on a horse and riding it.

That horse," she amended, seeing the saddled dapple gray mare that Chance was leading toward her.

"Will you?" Jonah asked.

"We meant what we said. Jonah and I won't let Mirabel run off with you—not that she ever would," Ryan quickly added. "I'm just saying what you're thinking."

"So now I've turned you all into mind readers, huh? I guess the sessions are going better than I thought they were," she told the boys with a grin. She was feeling rather proud of her accomplishments when it came to the teens. Which just reinforced her determination not to look like an inept fool around them.

"Now *you're* doing it," Ryan told her, shooting her a shrewd look.

She looked at him innocently. "Doing what?"

"You're trying to distract us," Ryan told her. "You're getting us to talk about something else so we forget about giving you that riding lesson."

It was like being faced with four tenacious pit bulls. Once they sank their teeth into her, they were holding on for dear life. Well, she could play that game, as well. "I don't need a riding lesson," she protested.

Chance brought his horse closer to her. "I thought those sessions of yours were all about always telling the truth," he said.

They were really ganging up on her, she thought. But she was determined to stand her ground. "They are."

"Well?" he asked, looking at her pointedly. She didn't have to look at the boys; she felt their stares. They were all thinking the same thing, that she wasn't owning up to her shortcoming.

And then it occurred to her how to answer them. "I don't need a riding lesson because I don't *want* to know how to ride. Now if you boys—" she deliberately looked at all of them, including Chance "—will excuse me, I really do have work to do. But good job, all of you," she told them again enthusiastically.

With that, Chloe made her way back to the main house, keenly aware that she was being watched by five sets of eyes as she walked.

She really did have work to catch up on, she thought defensively. It just wasn't as pressing as she made it sound.

What *was* pressing was her need to get away. *Now.*

Chloe wasn't sure if she imagined the knock on her door that evening until she heard it a second time. There was definitely someone at her door.

It was after dinner and rather than linger at the big house with Graham and his family the way she had done on several occasions now, Chloe had left the table early and retreated to her quarters in the guesthouse. She wanted a little time to herself to regroup.

She was still feeling somewhat uncomfortable about this afternoon and the fact that she'd had trouble owning up to not being able to ride.

She had to remember that it was okay not to be perfect, she told herself. It was just that she was trying really hard to present a strong front before these boys.

Maybe, she thought, it was one of them at the door. Perhaps one of them wanted to talk to her about this afternoon. Probably to give her more of a pep talk, she surmised.

Chloe smiled to herself. They were all rather sweet in their own way, and she appreciated that they were trying to be supportive of her.

Maybe she'd just forget about being nervous and throw herself into learning how to ride. It seemed like practically everyone in the state did it, she reasoned. How hard could it be?

It was definitely something to think about.

Tomorrow.

Psyching herself up, Chloe swung open the door. The cheery "Hi" she was about to utter never made an appearance when she saw it wasn't any of the boys standing on her doorstep.

It was Chance.

Ever since she'd lost Donnie, her first thoughts always seemed to entertain a dark explanation. "Is something wrong?" Chloe asked, her heart already lodged in her throat.

Chance's answer was annoyingly vague. "That depends on your point of view."

Damn it, for a plainspoken man he could be maddeningly unclear. "Meaning?" she demanded.

He crossed the threshold, but made no effort to come any farther into her quarters than that. "Meaning that you tried to lie to those boys."

He was referring to her initial pretense of knowing how to ride. She didn't care for his accusation, especially in light of the way things turned out. "Well, they wound up hearing the truth so it's not really lying, is it?"

His eyes pinned hers, making her want to squirm. "What would you call it?"

She could tell him exactly what she would call it. "I'd call it not wanting them to think any less of me."

That didn't make any sense to Chance. "Because you can't ride?" he asked incredulously. Why would they think any less of her for that? "Why? You never told them you traveled with the rodeo as a trick rider."

Why did she think he would understand her motivation? The cowboy had probably never known an insecure moment in his life. He was perfect at everything he did, and he knew it.

"Let's just drop it, all right?" she said shortly.

"Sure," he agreed, then added one condition. "As soon as you come out with me." Just to ensure that she would, Chance caught her hand in his and began to lead her outside.

Not wanting to cause a scene, she went along reluctantly. "Just where are we going?" she wanted to know.

"Don't look so spooked," he said with a short laugh. "I'm not kidnapping you."

Damn it, was he laughing at her? She was *not* going to be his source of amusement just because she didn't measure up to Annie Oakley in his eyes.

"I know you're not kidnapping me and I'm not spooked," she said between gritted teeth. Chloe tried to dig in her heels and found that it was a totally futile act. "But I do want to know where you're taking me."

Chance spared her a glance over his shoulder. "It's not what you think," he assured her calmly, wanting her to know that he had no intentions of getting physical with her in any way.

The problem was, it *was* the first thing that came to her mind. She instinctively knew that Chance was an honorable man, that he wouldn't just drag her off somewhere in order to have his way with her. He just wasn't that sort of person. But even so, she could feel her cheeks getting flushed, heating up and turning a deep shade of red that by no stretch of the imagination was her natural shade.

"Okay," Chloe retorted. "Then you tell me what to think."

She didn't expect him to laugh at that, but he did. "Oh, I doubt very much that there's a man alive who could do that, Chloe."

Maybe she *was* a woman who couldn't be told what to think, but if she was as independent as Chance was giving her credit for, she would have never allowed him to drag her out of her quarters in the first place.

Fueled by that thought, she demanded again, "Where are you taking me?"

"Some place where you can get rid of your inhibitions," he told her simply as he continued to pull her along behind him.

Okay, he was beginning to make her nervous. *Was* he taking her somewhere so that he could—that they could—damn it, how could she be so wrong about a person?

Nervous, incensed, she finally did manage to dig her heels into the ground, making him come to an abrupt stop. When he turned to look at her quizzically, she informed him in no uncertain terms, "I don't want to get rid of my 'inhibitions.'"

"Sure you do," he contradicted. She was about to yank her hand out of his and make a run for the main house when he went on to say, "No self-respecting Texan wants people to think that they can't ride."

"Can't ride?" she echoed. Panic and anger evaporated instantly. "This is about *riding*?" she questioned.

"Not exactly," he amended. "This is about teaching you the fundamentals of riding and ultimately getting you on the back of a horse. If that goes well," he continued, a hint of a smile curving his lips, "then we'll let Mirabel move a little with you on her back and we can call it 'riding' if anyone asks."

He led her to the stables, and when they entered, Chance let go of her hand. There was no need to continue pulling her in his wake. Turning around to face her, he told Chloe honestly, "And if you're going to ask me why I'm doing this, it's because I saw the look on your face earlier."

She didn't know what he was talking about. "What look?"

"The one that you had when you admitted to the boys that you didn't know how to ride. I figured it really bothered you more than you were willing to say. And when something winds up bothering you that much," he told her, bringing her over to Mirabel's stall, "you've got to do something about it or it'll just wind up haunting you." His eyes met hers for a moment. "I know all about things haunting a person," he told her. "Trust me, it's not a good thing."

He cleared his throat, as if that was enough to chase away the emotion that he had accidentally unearthed. He'd gotten very good at blocking out unwanted feelings—except in the middle of the night, when he had no control over them.

He forced himself to focus on Chloe. "Now, take it from me. There's no more peaceful place in the whole world than on the back of a horse, and the sooner you find that out for yourself, the better you're going to feel about the whole experience," he promised.

She was surprised to see that the mare was saddled, as if she was about to be taken out for a ride. Had Chance been that sure that he was going to get her to come here at this hour?

"And we have to do this now?" she asked him.

In response, he offered her that easygoing, sexy smile that transformed his uncompromising expression into a very compelling one. "No time like the present," he told her.

"Oh, I can think of plenty of other times," she assured Chance. She was doing her very best to hide her nervousness.

Despite her efforts, he saw right through them. Instead of making him feel sorry for her, or stopping him from continuing, it just urged him on. "Which is why this is the best time," he assured her.

The cowboy's reasoning completely mystified her. "How do you figure that?"

"The sooner you get over being afraid of riding," he explained patiently, "the sooner you'll be able to actually ride. And in no time at all, you'll find yourself wondering what the big deal was and what took you so long to get to it."

Chloe looked as if she was trying very hard not to be nervous, and he felt for her, but he also knew that what he'd just told her was true. She needed to meet this fear of hers head-on. He'd learned that firsthand. When he'd first returned to the States, all he'd wanted to do was go off into the wilderness and avoid people altogether. Separation, isolation—he realized that he just wanted to be alone to try and escape from the memories that plagued him of the death and devastation he'd seen. Loss of friends he'd served with, day in and day out had worn his soul to the breaking point—and yet he knew that logically he couldn't completely withdraw from society. He'd compromised by taking ranching jobs but never staying in any one place too long.

For his part, he couldn't see being afraid of riding, but then, except when he was stationed overseas, horses had always been a part of his life. It was like being afraid of the family dog.

"Give me your hand," he told her.

Instead of complying, she did just the opposite and pulled it behind her back.

"Why?" she wanted to know.

"Because I need a third hand," he quipped. Then his expression softened a little. "Just give it to me," he coaxed. "I promise this won't hurt."

Letting out a shaky breath, Chloe hesitantly put out her hand. He took it, covering it with his own, and guided it up to softly stroke the mare's muzzle.

"See, nothing to it," he told her, watching her expression. He was pleased to see her relax a little. Disengaging his hand from hers, Chance said, "Now you do it."

Holding her breath, Chloe did as he instructed, moving her fingertips lightly along the mare's coat. When Mirabel unexpectedly shook her head from side to side, as if tossing her mane, Chloe suppressed a gasp as she pulled her hand back.

"It's okay," Chance assured her. "Mirabel is a horse, not a statue. She's bound to make a few unexpected movements every now and then. She's not rejecting you. She's probably just inhaled something that's tickling her nose."

He paused a moment, allowing Chloe to regroup. "Now try it again," he urged.

It was meant as a suggestion, but to Chloe it sounded just like an order. Orders made her bristle. Still, she didn't want to come across like a coward in his eyes, so she put her hand on the mare's muzzle again and stroked it.

This time, the mare held still.

A smile lit up Chance's penetrating eyes. "See, that wasn't so bad, was it?"

"No," she admitted almost grudgingly, then added, "that was kind of nice."

She wasn't prepared for his question. "Think you'd like to get up on her?" he asked.

Her eyes widened. "You mean like ride her?"

Chance heard the nervousness in her voice and was quick to put her fears to rest. "No, I mean get up into her saddle and just sit still. We're not going anywhere just yet," he told her.

Standing beside the mare, Chloe looked up, judging where she would be sitting. She felt her stomach tightening.

"It's awfully high up," she said. "What if Mirabel decides to take off?"

"Her days of crashing through stable walls are definitely behind her." The second he assured her of that, he realized that Chloe thought he was being serious. "I'm kidding," he told her. "She's never crashed through a stable wall—or anything else for that matter. I'll help you up," he offered.

Chloe really didn't want to do this, but once she looked into Chance's eyes, she had the unerring feeling that he would keep her safe—even high up on a horse. So, reluctantly, she said, "Okay," and had him help.

Chance talked her through it, physically guiding her when he had to. He had her put her foot into the stirrup, then coaxed her through the steps until she swung her leg up over the mare's hind quarters, finally managing to get her other foot into the stirrup.

"You're doing fine," he told her.

"How come I don't feel fine?" Chloe challenged.

Probably because she looked stiff as a board, he thought.

"I've got an idea," he told her.

"I can get off the horse now?" Chloe asked him hopefully.

"No," he told her.

She didn't have very long to wait to see what he was up to. He took hold of the reins and in one fluid movement pulled himself up onto the horse directly behind her.

"What are you doing?" she cried, starting to turn in the saddle and then abruptly stopping because she was brushing up against Chance.

"My best to make you feel safer," he replied.

Having Chance so close that she could feel the heat from his chest against her back made her feel a whole host of sensations—but "safer" definitely wasn't one of them.

Chapter Nine

He needed some air. Right now, the scent of Chloe's shampoo was filling up his senses and making him think and feel things he shouldn't be thinking *or* feeling. If he didn't get moving, he was liable to do something one of them was going to regret.

For a moment, in an act of self-preservation, Chance had considered just going ahead and guiding the mare outside. But he had a feeling that it was in the best interests of both of them if he asked her first. He thought it would be better if Chloe was prepared rather than just springing things on her. She seemed to be jumpy enough against him as it was.

"So," he asked her, "are you game?"

For the life of her, Chloe didn't know exactly what he was asking her. She knew what she *wanted* Chance to be asking her, but that would be leaving herself wide open for all sorts of complications that she knew she just couldn't handle.

"Game for what?" she asked uneasily.

"To take a little ride."

"And do what?" she asked suspiciously.

"Ride?" It was more of a question because he didn't know what she was expecting to hear, or what she wanted him to say.

"Oh. How far?"

She felt him shrug against her back. "I thought just around the outside of the stable for tonight. Next time we'll go farther—and on separate horses," he added. She heard the amusement in his voice. And then he asked, "Ready?"

Chloe was ready, all right. To jump off the horse and run back to her cottage. But for some reason she nodded her assent. Whom was she kidding? It wasn't the horse she wasn't ready for. It was Chance.

She wasn't ready to have his arms tighten around her as he took control of the reins, to feel his warm breath on her neck as he coaxed the mare out of the stable, to feel his muscled thighs around hers as they rode the perimeter of the corral. Not at all ready.

Suddenly the evening seemed to get too warm, and she had to steel herself against this man wrapped around her.

"You all right?" he asked her. "You're as stiff as a board."

She gave him the first excuse that came into her head. "Just trying not to fall off."

"You can't fall off," he pointed out. "I have you, and besides, Mirabel isn't exactly trotting. If she were going any slower, she'd be going backward."

Up against him the way she was, she couldn't get comfortable. It would mean lowering her guard, and she couldn't afford to do that. "I had no idea the corral was this large," she commented.

"It's not really. It just seems that way because we're moving around it at a snail's pace. We can go faster," Chance offered, pretending to get ready to kick his heels into the mare's flanks to make her pick up her pace.

"No, no," Chloe protested, raising a hand as if that somehow made her plea more emphatic. "This pace is just fine. Unless you mind," she added, suddenly realizing that riding like this had to be immensely boring to someone like Chance. Given this speed, any second now he was liable to fall asleep.

Mind? Chance thought, astonished that she should phrase it that way. Why would he mind having his arms around a beautiful woman, holding her a hair's breadth away from him?

Being here like this with Chloe reminded him that it had been a long, long time since he had allowed himself to get physically close to someone without worrying about the resulting consequences.

"No, I'm just fine," he assured her. "Matter of fact," he told her as they approached the stable door, "we can go around again if you'd like."

Yes, she'd "like"—which was just the problem. With very little effort, she could just close her eyes and transport herself to another place in time, a time when everything seemed right in the world.

A time when she fantasized about the future that lay ahead of her. A future that included the husband she loved and a family. Having Chance hold her like this made it so easy for her to remember—so easy to yearn.

She had to stop doing that, she silently upbraided herself.

It was time to stop dreaming and face reality—a reality that included neither her husband nor a family.

"No, that's all right," she told him. "Once is enough for now—if you don't mind. We both have things to do," she added, being deliberately vague.

"I don't," he told her honestly. Lord, but she smelled good, even out here with the night air diluting the mind-numbing scent that was still lingering in her hair. "This is the guys' free time," he pointed out, explaining, "They're either doing homework or just kicking back. After I check in on them, the rest of my evening is wide open," he told her.

"Oh, well, mine isn't."

What was with her? Two lies in one day? But she absolved herself of the guilt over this last one. It was self-preservation. She simply couldn't be around Chance in her vulnerable state. There was just something about having him close to her like this with the dusk slipping into nightfall that made her uneasy. Not because she thought that Chance might try something but because she was afraid that *she* might.

"I have to get back," she told him.

"Sure, I understand."

He wasn't about to make things difficult for her, and he certainly wasn't about to press her for details. The last thing he wanted was to make Chloe feel as if he was encroaching on her space or trying to box her in in any sort of way.

After bringing the mare back into the stable, Chance dismounted, then turned to face Chloe and offered her his assistance to get down.

Chloe hesitated, but she knew that she wasn't in any position to attempt a graceful dismount. Not yet. Because she had absolutely no idea how. So she took the arms that were being offered to her and allowed Chance to help her down.

That maneuver involved getting very close to him for another very long moment.

A moment in which her heart seemed to stop even as her pulse accelerated to double time.

Chance picked her up off the mare and brought her down, holding her by the waist and sliding the length of her body down a hint away from his until her feet were finally touching the ground.

He was holding her close enough for her imagination to vividly take flight—and to silently lament when he finally withdrew his hands from around her waist.

When she opened her mouth to thank him, Chloe found that she couldn't speak. Her mouth had completely gone dry, and her words stuck to the roof of her mouth.

Swallowing, she gave communication another try. This time, she did something more than just croak. "Thank you for the lesson."

Chance laughed shortly. "I'd hardly call that a lesson."

"Okay, have it your way," she allowed. "Thank you for the introduction…to horseback riding," she added belatedly, realizing it might sound as if she was thanking him for something entirely different.

"My pleasure," he told her.

It was only after she'd turned from him and began to hurriedly walk away, back to the guesthouse, that she heard him call after her, saying, "This isn't over, you know. I intend to give you that riding lesson."

"When I have time," she tossed over her shoulder without even looking back.

She wasn't about to make promises. She'd had enough of that.

"*Make* time."

It wasn't a suggestion; it was clearly an order.

His order rang in her ears as she all but ran the rest of the way to the guesthouse.

Chance remained outside longer than he knew he should have, watching her and admiring Chloe's form until she was gone from sight.

Nothing wrong with that, Chance told himself as he turned away and went back into the stable. *Just admiring one of the Lord's finer creations, nothing more than that.*

And he would continue telling himself that, Chance thought, until it finally stuck.

"Something on your mind?" Sasha asked her the next day.

Graham's wife had sat in on one of Chloe's sessions with Ryan and then another session with Brandon.

Chloe knew she had to be sporadically supervised, especially since she was so new to Peter's Place. But she still couldn't help being a little nervous.

Added to that was the fact that she kept expecting Chance to come walking in at any moment, announcing that he was going to give her another lesson. Right now it felt as if the last of her nerves had been worn down to a tiny nub. She felt so tense inside that if she were a guitar string, she would have snapped in half.

But she was trying her very best not to appear that way on the surface.

Judging by Sasha's question she wasn't succeeding very well.

"No," she replied, trying to sound laid-back. "Other than doing right by these boys," Chloe qualified at the last moment.

Sasha smiled. "Nice answer but not the one I was looking for." She leaned forward in her chair. "I mean, is there anything else going on? You seem like you're waiting for something to happen."

Obviously, being an undercover spy was never going to be an option for her, Chloe thought.

"No," she denied again. And then she decided to own up a little, hoping that would be enough for Sasha. "I guess being observed puts me on edge a little. I realize that I'm not as good as you are at this, but—"

"Nobody's comparing us," Sasha told her firmly. "We all have our own individual styles. I'm just here to observe whether or not you're connecting with the boys—and I'm happy to say that you are."

The truth was, Chloe was somewhat nervous about

measuring up to the woman who had hired her. After all, these had initially been "Sasha's boys" and in a sense, they still were. She'd been rather afraid that both the boys and Sasha would view her as an interloper.

"You don't know how happy it makes me to hear you say that," Chloe told her.

"Then it's mutual," Sasha told her with a warm smile. "Because it makes me very happy to honestly be able to say that." Sasha looked at her a little more closely. "But are you sure there's nothing else? You don't need some time off, do you?"

"Time off?" Chloe echoed. "I just got here." She felt as if she was just beginning to get the hang of the routine. "I've still got a long ways to go before I make a niche at Peter's Place. Why would I want to take some time off?"

Sasha shrugged. "To acclimate yourself to the area a little more. This is different from living in the city," she said sympathetically.

"Amen to that," Chloe said with a laugh. "It's almost too quiet here at night to sleep, but I'm slowly getting used to that, too."

"So you're settling in?" Sasha asked.

"Absolutely," Chloe told her with feeling.

"I'm glad because I can't tell you how nice it is to have another woman around. I mean, I have the girls," she said, referring to her two daughters, "and I love them to pieces, but it'll be a lot of years before either one of them is anywhere near being someone I can actually talk to." She quickly amended, "I mean, Graham is a wonderful man and he's really great with the girls, but well, you know men, there's a lot they don't understand when it comes to the way we women feel."

Smiling at her, Sasha put her hand over Chloe's.

"I just want you to know that if you ever need to just talk—about nothing or about something—I'm here for you."

When Chloe couldn't help but laugh, Sasha looked at her a little uncertainly, wanting to be let in on the joke. "Did I just say something funny?"

"Not exactly." The whole thing struck her as rather ironic. "What you just said to me is what I told all four of the boys after I had my first session with each of them."

"Well, my offer was rendered from a nonprofessional position," Sasha said. "As a friend," she further qualified. And then she continued. "And as a friend, I have to say that being around you right now reminds me of that old adage, the one about being a cat on a hot tin roof."

"I make you think of that?" Chloe asked, secretly wondering if the same thing had occurred to Brandon and Ryan, the two boys she'd seen today for their sessions.

"Well, not exactly," Sasha admitted. "But certainly close to that. Tell me, are you waiting for something to happen, or for someone? Or is it just that I make you very nervous?"

"*You* don't make me nervous," Chloe quickly told her. How could she tell her boss that it was Chance who made her nervous?

It was time to be truthful with herself. To admit that she wasn't afraid of the riding lesson he intended to give her—or the horse—although she wasn't exactly confidence personified when it came to either. What had her feeling so internally jumpy was the man. And the prospect of her next interaction with him.

Her next *solo* interaction with him, she silently emphasized.

Interacting with Chance when there were others around was fine. They were just two employees at Peter's Place with the same prime focus: getting the teens assigned to the ranch to find their better inner core.

She could go on working alongside Chance all day like that.

It was the anticipation of being alone with him that had her acting like that so-called restless cat Sasha had just likened her to. Because being alone with Chance woke things up within her that were better off left dormant and sleeping.

She was certainly better off if they were left dormant and sleeping, Chloe thought.

Looking at Sasha now, she realized that the woman was still waiting for some sort of response from her as to why she was acting so unsettled.

Sasha seemed almost *hungry* for some sort of shared confidence, Chloe thought. She supposed that it was almost cruel of her not to say *something*, even though it was against the privacy she tried so desperately to maintain.

Taking a breath, Chloe made her decision. She'd confide in her half brother's wife. Maybe then they could move past this and get on with her work at Peter's Place.

"Chance wants to give me riding lessons," she told Sasha.

The other woman's face literally lit up.

Chapter Ten

"Oh, really?" Sasha asked. If possible, she sat up even a little straighter, her interest unwaveringly engaged. Delight was all but vibrating in her voice.

"Yes," Chloe replied. Her voice was as quiet as Sasha's was vibrant and enthused.

"You don't know how to ride a horse?" Sasha questioned, clearly surprised.

Chloe shrugged. Not wanting to get into a discussion about that, she just said, "The opportunity never came up."

For a second, Sasha was quiet and Chloe thought that, mercifully, that was the end of the discussion on that topic. But then Sasha looked at her, her smile even wider than it had been a moment ago, her eyes dancing.

She clapped her hands together. "This is wonderful!" the woman exclaimed.

"I wouldn't exactly go that far," Chloe protested, not really sure why her newly discovered sister-in-law would be so happy to find out that there was this definite gap in her education. "It just...*is*," she finally said.

This was what she got for trying to be completely honest, Chloe thought a second later. Rather than moving on, she had the feeling that she was about to get sucked down in the ocean by the undertow.

If the gleeful look of anticipation on Sasha's face—the origin of which was a complete mystery to her—wasn't enough, Chance picked that exact moment to walk into the room.

The man had awful timing, Chloe thought, feeling her stomach tighten at the same time that there was this sinking sensation right in the center of it. She was definitely a woman torn.

"Speak of the devil," Sasha declared, amusement as well as pleasure surrounding every syllable that she uttered.

Chance looked just a little taken aback. "Since when have I become the devil?" he asked uncertainly, not quite sure what he'd just walked in on.

Sasha rose from her chair. The binder she'd brought in with her to make notes while observing Chloe's session was in her hands and pressed up against her chest.

"We were just talking about you," she said dismissively. "Well, I'm sure I hear Maddie calling for me so I'll just leave the two of you to it," she said.

Chloe shifted self-consciously. Sasha had all but held up a sign with instructions on it as to what she thought they should do next once she left and they were alone.

One of Chance's eyebrows arched as he turned to regard the woman who was left standing in the room.

"'To it?'" he asked Chloe, torn between being bemused and confused.

"I told Sasha you offered to give me riding lessons." Chloe cleared her throat. She couldn't remember when she had ever felt more awkward. "Sasha thought it was a good idea."

"Oh." He nodded as if comprehending what he had just walked in on—except that Chloe wasn't 100 percent convinced that he wasn't reading a great deal more into Sasha's comment. "Well, it is a good idea," he told her. "Everyone should know how to ride."

"I would think it's more a matter of preference," Chloe countered. "It's not like it's a life-or-death situation, like learning to swim."

Chance wasn't about to get into an involved discussion on the subject. He had a far simpler way to resolve it.

"Wouldn't you rather know how to do something than not know how to do it?"

Chloe suppressed a sigh. She supposed that Chance did have a point. And she didn't want him to think that she was reluctant to broaden her horizons.

"Sure."

She stood up, telling herself she was making way too big a deal out of this. Chance was just giving her a simple horseback riding lesson—same as what he was hired to do with the boys. She had to stop feeling so nervous about it.

So nervous about him.

A thought suddenly occurred to her. "Are you going to be teaching me to ride in the corral?"

Chance hadn't given it much thought. "Yes. That's where I've been doing it with the boys. Why? Would you rather not have your lesson there?" he asked, sensing her reluctance.

She avoided making eye contact with him as she spoke, not wanting to see amusement or something even more demoralizing in his eyes.

"I'd rather we didn't have an audience," she confessed. "Is there any place else that we could go for these lessons?"

"Sure. It's a big ranch," he reminded her. "I just thought you'd rather get your first lessons somewhere where you felt safe."

That was when she finally looked at him. "Why wouldn't I feel safe somewhere else?" she asked him.

"The corral's contained. If I give you riding lessons out in the open, I figure you'd worry that Mirabel could get it into her head to just run off with you on her back."

"Oh." Enlightenment came to her riding a thunderbolt. He wasn't talking about her feeling safer in the corral because she felt he wouldn't try to kiss her in broad daylight in front of possible witnesses. He was talking about the mare running off with her. "You've got the faster horse, don't you?" she asked.

"No disrespect meant for Mirabel, but yes, I do. By quite a lot when you come right down to it."

This time her eyes didn't leave his when she responded. "Then if something happens, say, to spook Mirabel, you could catch up to me on your horse, couldn't you?"

"If it came to that, yes. But from what I've been told, Mirabel doesn't spook easily. That's one of the reasons why I picked her for you."

She believed him. "Then I'd rather you took me somewhere where no one else can watch and see how bad I am at this."

"You're not bad at riding," he told her. "You just need to learn the right techniques, that's all. It's not all that hard." He tried to soothe her, but he could see his words weren't working. "But if you feel that strongly about it, I know this quiet clearing not too far from the lake that'll do just fine for our purposes."

A quiet clearing by the lake sounded as if it would do fine for other purposes, too, Chloe thought. But she kept that to herself, hoping that the same idea hadn't occurred to him.

Because the lake was some distance from the corral, Chance decided to take her there on his horse. He told Chloe that right now it was safer for her if they rode double on his horse.

"What about Mirabel?" Chloe asked, wanting to be clear on the logistics. "Isn't she coming, too?"

"She'll be right behind us," he explained. "I'll just hold on to her reins so she doesn't get it into her head to hang back."

"And your horse won't mind?" she asked, looking at the black stallion that Chance had already saddled and was waiting for them in the stable. Mirabel was in the next stall, saddled, as well.

Chance unconsciously furrowed his brow. He wasn't sure he understood her question. "Mind what?"

"That we're both going to be riding on him at the same time?" She looked at the stallion doubtfully, worried about the extra weight.

Chance laughed, tickled by what she was innocently suggesting. "He's fine with it," he told her. "He's not the jealous sort."

Chloe flushed. When he said it out loud like that, she realized that she sounded like an idiot. "I didn't mean…"

He was quick to try to save her from embarrassment. "I know what you meant. C'mon, we're wasting daylight," he urged. "Or was that the idea?" he asked, pretending to look at her as if the light had suddenly dawned on him.

"No," Chloe denied quickly. She wound up sounding almost breathless.

He was going to have to tread lightly with this one, Chance thought. Most of the time, he preferred to keep to himself and not bother interacting with people. It saved time and saved him from spinning his wheels. But he had to admit there was something about this woman that had burrowed under his skin.

He liked seeing the way her eyes flashed and the way she tossed her hair when she was digging in and being stubborn. But for all that, Chloe made him think that he was dealing with a vulnerable, wounded bird.

The whole thing was a revelation to him, he thought.

He had never realized until just now that he had any desire to protect a wounded bird.

Or that he rather liked it.

Maybe his soul hadn't died on the battlefield after all.

"Then we'd better get going," he told her. "Come on. Let's get you up there."

The next moment, while Chloe was absently regarding just how much taller his stallion appeared in comparison with her mare, she felt strong hands come around her waist. Suddenly, she was airborne.

As her breath caught in her throat, Chance had her in the saddle in a matter of seconds. She barely had time to suppress the cry of surprise that had all but escaped from her lips.

And then, the next moment, there he was, right behind her. *Snuggly* right behind her, she couldn't help noticing as his body seemed to fit perfectly against hers.

A multitude of sensations went zipping through Chloe, some familiar, some brand-new, all unsettling.

A riding lesson, this is just a riding lesson, she silently insisted.

There was no need for her to react like this to *any* of this. Chance was just doing her a favor, teaching her how to ride so she could go out with the boys. She had to think of it in that light, she told herself.

And *only* in that light.

Chance brought his arms around her, picking up his horse's reins as he formed a protective circle around her.

"You all right?" he asked.

"I'm fine," she answered. *If you don't count the fact*

that my heart is just about ready to break the sound barrier.

She felt Chance leaning into her. Her heart raced a little harder.

The next moment he was whispering into her ear. "I guarantee that you'll feel a whole lot better if you breathe."

"Right. Breathing," she agreed the next second.

And then, just to prove that she had heard Chance, she went on to elaborately do just that.

Chloe really didn't remember the journey to the clearing, at least, not when she thought if it in terms of miles or scenery. All she was aware of was how the gentle back-and-forth rocking of the stallion caused Chance's body to move seductively against hers. She was concentrating so hard on not reacting to him that she didn't even realize when they'd reached their destination.

"We're here," Chance announced.

The next second, without any warning, Chance was dismounting. Abruptly deprived of his support and thinking something had gone wrong, Chloe quickly turned to look down at him and wound up nearly tumbling out of the saddle.

"Hey, no sudden trick moves until after I'm satisfied that you know how to ride. We don't want to rush you off to the nearest doctor." He looked up at her face. She'd turned almost completely pale. "Hey, are you all right?" he asked, concerned. "I was just kidding."

"I knew that," Chloe mumbled although she clearly didn't.

"Good." He didn't believe her for a second. Chance extended his arms up to her and said, "Let's get you down from there." Taking hold of her waist, he eased her down until her feet were back on the ground. "This is the last time I'm going to help you dismount," he told her. "I'll teach you and then you're on your own."

He saw the apprehensive look that crept over her face. Rather than being off-putting, he thought she looked even more adorable.

"Don't worry," he assured her. "You'll do fine."

"I wasn't worried," she informed him perhaps a little too quickly.

He graciously accepted her protest, even though he felt he knew otherwise. "My mistake."

Bringing Mirabel closer to Chloe, he announced, "Okay. This is lesson number one."

And so it began.

Chance patiently kept at it for the next four hours, verbally diagramming every move he wanted her to make so precisely that after a little while, Chloe forgot to be nervous.

Progress came by tiny inches—but it came.

At the end of the session Chloe had a good handle on the basics. He'd taught her how to fluidly mount her horse and how to dismount, as well. He'd taught her how to give the most basic commands to the animal so that the mare knew when she was expected to go and when to stop.

Through it all Chance didn't raise his voice or lose his temper, nor did he easily dispense praise, either.

He did, however, let her know if she was doing something wrong so that she wouldn't repeat it. On the few occasions that she did repeat her mistake, he patiently reviewed the steps again, and had her go through the paces over and over until she got it right.

And then, finally, when she thought she was never going to see it again, it happened.

Chance smiled.

"I think that's it for today," he told her.

She was exhausted and so ready to go home, but even so, she had to ask him. "That bad?"

"That good," Chance corrected.

Her eyes fairly danced as she asked, "Really?"

"Really," he echoed. "And our next session is going to be in the corral," he informed her, "because you have nothing to be ashamed of. Now, for your reward, I want to take you to see something that a lot of people live out their whole lives without ever being able to see or appreciate."

"Oh? What?"

The nervousness was back in her voice, Chance thought. But he knew just how to put it to rest. Taking her hand, he led her over to the lake.

"Look," he said, pointing out what he wanted her to see.

Once again, Chloe's breath caught in her throat.

Chapter Eleven

Chance was right. It was glorious.

Chloe had seen sunsets before. They were, after all, a part of everyday life. But she'd never seen one like this.

Standing there with him, at the edge of the lake, she looked up at the sky.

And promptly had her breath stolen away.

There was a multitude of muted colors reaching out to the heavens, as if the sun was having one last hurrah before finally retreating into the dusk and then the darkness, where it would wait for dawn and a rebirth.

"I never get tired of seeing this," Chance told her. "Makes me realize how really beautiful nature is. It also makes me feel that no matter how bad things might seem, in the scheme of things, everything is going to be all right."

Listening to him, Chloe could appreciate the noble sentiment—as well as the man who uttered it. "It is magnificent."

Maybe it *was* the sunset that did it. Or maybe it was standing here so close to Chance, being infused with a sense of peace she hadn't felt in a long time.

Maybe it was all of the above.

Chloe couldn't honestly pinpoint the reason. All she knew was that when she turned toward Chance, she felt this undeniable, incredible pull within her. Pulling her toward him.

It kept her transfixed so that when Chance lowered his head, bringing his lips close to hers, she didn't move. Didn't breathe.

Didn't do anything—except will the moment to go on forever.

Her wish increased tenfold when he finally kissed her.

The moment their lips met, she could feel something explode within her. Something gleeful and joyous, as if she had been holding her breath, waiting for this to happen from the first moment she'd met him.

Hoping this would happen, she realized.

And yet, it surprised her.

Surprised her that Chance kissed her. What surprised her even more was that she actually *felt* something rather than just the deadness that had existed within her ever since she'd first found out that Donnie was never coming back to her.

Chloe could sense her heart slip into a wild double-time beat when Chance deepened the kiss, when his arms went around her waist and pulled her flush against him.

Almost breathless, she laced her arms around his neck, leaning into Chance as well as into his kiss. The sun might have been setting over the lake, but right now, it felt as if it was bursting out from within her, sending out long sunbeams to every single part of her.

She was certain that if Chance opened his eyes, he would see her glowing in the dark.

Chance wasn't sure just what had come over him. Yes, it was a beautiful sunset, and yes, he was here sharing it with a beautiful woman, but that alone wasn't enough for him to do what he was doing. They worked together, and he firmly believed that it was never a good idea to mix work with pleasure.

Since he'd come back from the service, he'd been a loner and the first to admit that things ultimately had a habit of not working out in these sorts of situations. When that happened, they wound up turning awkward. He made it a point to never stay in any one place for long, moving on when he grew restless, and he knew that he could do that here, too.

But there was something about this place, about the work that was being done, that appealed to him. That *spoke* to him. Peter's Place was a place he could believe in and for the first time in a long time, he found himself wanting to be a part of it, not just in a cursory way but in a way that actually mattered. That made a difference.

He wanted to make a difference.

That was all the more reason for not getting involved with a woman who worked here, he argued with himself. But again, there was just something about Chloe that reached right into his gut and grabbed him. Something that made him want to protect her, want to be her hero and want to make her smile.

Heaven knew that right now, *she* was making him smile. Not only that, but it had been a very long time since kissing a girl had actually rocked his world, and she was certainly doing that right now for him.

So much so that he shed his common sense like a snake shed its skin and continued doing exactly what he had been doing.

Chance tightened his arms around her, getting lost in the kiss he had initiated. Getting lost in the sweet, heady fragrance he always detected whenever he was standing anywhere close to Chloe.

He could feel himself wanting her.

If she were any other woman who had crossed his path for the evening, he might have gone on to see where this would lead. But he instinctively knew that Chloe wasn't someone meant for a casual coupling—or even a torrid one. Chloe was the kind of woman a guy brought home to his mother—if he had a mother.

But for him that hadn't been the case for a long time now, he thought. His mother had died six months after he'd graduated high school. His father had died in a hunting accident years before that. Being on his own and alone had been a way of life for him and he'd made his peace with that.

Until now.

He didn't have to be told that Chloe could be easily hurt, and he already sensed that she *had* been hurt—

badly—by something or someone. There was pain in her eyes when he looked into them, even when she was laughing at something. He wasn't about to add to that pain. He didn't need that on his conscience.

But he knew that if he continued kissing her like this, he was definitely going to want more, and he also knew that if he pushed, even just a little, he could convince her to make love with him.

But that's not how he wanted it to happen.

And that wouldn't be fair to her. So, hard though it was for him, Chance forced himself to draw his mouth away from hers.

His heart still hammering wildly, he made himself take a step back, although he still kept his arms around her waist, wanting to take comfort in that contact for just a moment longer.

Chloe's eyes sought his, and he saw the question in them. Why had he stopped? He also felt her shudder as she tried to catch her breath.

Chance was coping with a few struggles of his own. He wasn't accustomed to abruptly stopping like this once he'd started kissing a woman. But he knew he had to.

"I think we should be getting back before Graham sends out a search party to come looking for us."

The sun had all but set, taking almost all of the available light with it. But there was still just enough left for him to see that her cheeks had grown appealingly pink.

Had he embarrassed her by kissing her? Or embarrassed her by stopping? He couldn't tell.

"We wouldn't want that," she agreed. She kept her

face averted as they walked back to their tree-tethered horses. "Thanks for the riding lesson," she told him, trying to sound casual. "And for sharing the sunset."

Chance laughed softly. "Not exactly mine to keep," he told her. "The sunset," he explained when he saw her looking at him quizzically. "As for the riding lesson, that was my pleasure." Mindful of her still-limited experience, he helped her mount, then swung onto his own horse. "But remember, you're not off the hook yet. I still have a little more to teach you."

As they headed back to the ranch, Chloe felt her thoughts—and her pulse—race. Maybe she was just reading things into what Chance had said, or maybe that kiss they'd shared had changed her focus. Whatever the reason, Chloe caught herself thinking that Chance had a great deal to teach her and riding was only a small part of it.

What's the matter with you? she upbraided herself as they continued riding to the main house. *One kiss and you're ready to forget about Donnie? Forget about what you had with Donnie?*

A shaft of guilt at her disloyalty to her husband's memory shot through her. How could she let herself get carried away like that?

Besides, that kiss probably didn't mean anything to Chance, she told herself. He was just taking advantage of an opportune moment, nothing more.

Just look at him, she thought, slanting a quick glance at him. The man was gorgeous, every woman's idea of the perfect cowboy. He undoubtedly had his pick of women, and that meant he had no need for a permanent relationship. Or any sort of a commitment.

Even if she was, by some wild chance, ready to allow herself to get carried away and start being serious about Chance, she knew she was bound to be hurt.

And the very last thing her heart needed was to be bruised. She already had gone through enough pain to last her a lifetime. There was absolutely no way she was going to set herself up to be hurt ever again—even if Chance was inclined to get involved with her, which she was willing to bet he wasn't.

She had a strong feeling that relationships weren't for him. The man was a loner. He'd all but told her so the first time they'd met.

No, she argued as they rode back, what happened at the lake was an aberration. A lovely aberration, but still just an aberration. And there wasn't going to be a sequel—ever—she told herself.

By now they had reached the ranch and were nearing the stable. Chloe was more than ready to call it a night.

But Chance had other ideas.

"You're not done yet," he told her.

She had no idea what to expect as she finally forced herself to look in his direction. "Oh?"

"I might have saddled Mirabel for you, but now it's time for you to learn how to take care of her. There's more to working with a horse than just riding it," Chance told her as he led the way into the stable. "So, since you're through riding her for the day, you have to unsaddle her. It's like when you were little and had to put away your toys when you were finished playing with them," he added, hoping the metaphor would help her get the idea.

There was just one thing wrong with his analogy, she thought, and she told him so. "I didn't have any toys when I was little."

That piece of information caught him by surprise. Just how poor had she been? At that moment it occurred to Chance that he really knew very little about this woman whom he found himself attracted to.

"No toys? None? Really?" he asked. After all, he knew that she was Graham's half sister. He'd just assumed that all the Fortunes were well cared for. But since there was no reason for her to lie, maybe she'd had it rougher than he'd thought. His heart—a heart he'd thought he'd forfeited on the battlefields of a foreign land—went out to her as he listened.

"Well, I did have one," she admitted. "I had a stuffed bear—Theodore," she told him, recalling the bear's name. "And I took Theodore everywhere, so I guess you might say that I never stopped playing with him. And since I didn't, I never put him away."

"What happened to Theodore?" he asked, curious.

He watched, fascinated, as a fond, faraway smile curved her lips. "I loved him to death and eventually, he just fell apart."

He dismounted before putting his horse in his stall. Chloe followed suit, and he came to join her.

"I guess then being loved by you comes with a price," he said.

She knew Chance just meant it as a joke, but the

comment had her thinking of Donnie. And aching—
on two counts.

"I guess so," she said quietly.

Her tone made him realize that he'd blundered.
Chance quickly changed the subject to something more
neutral.

"Because you're new at this, I'm going to walk you
through it this time. But from now on, when we go riding, you'll have to saddle and unsaddle Mirabel—or
any other horse if you decide to go on to a more lively
one," he added.

There was no chance of that happening, Chloe
thought. "Mirabel is lively enough for me, thank you,"
she told him. She was grateful to Chance for switching
subjects. "And I'll be happy to saddle her the next time
we go out—although I have to say that I'm not too sure
how happy Mirabel will be about it."

"You do it right and she'll be fine," he told her. "It's
not that complicated." And then he unconsciously went
into teaching mode. "Okay, you'll need to loosen the
cinch in order to get the saddle off."

"Loosen the cinch," Chloe repeated gamely, looking
at the saddle. She had no idea what the cinch looked like
or where it was located. Moreover, she was afraid if she
did the wrong thing, the mare was going to get skittish.
Biting the bullet, she asked, "And how do I do that?"

Chance laughed. "The cinch is right here."

Lifting the stirrup on Chloe's side, he pointed it out.
And then he walked her through the entire process,
narrating every move he made until he had the horse
standing in her stall, sans saddle, blanket and bridle.

He saw that Chloe looked as if she was ready to leave.

"Not yet," he warned her. "You're not finished."

Everything had been taken off the mare except for her horseshoes, Chloe thought. She couldn't see what else needed to be done.

"You going to put a nightgown on her?" she joked.

"No, but you're going to wipe her down—just in case she's wet." He saw that Chloe looked a little bemused. "You're familiar with the phrase 'Ridden hard and put away wet?'" he asked. Then, not waiting for a response, he told her, "Well, we don't do that around here.

"Just in case the horse is wet and the temperature drops at night, your horse might get a chill. No matter what you might have seen in the movies or on TV, horses are a lot more delicate than you might think. They come down with a lot of the same ailments that people do in addition to having their own set of diseases.

"You take care of your horse, and your horse will take care of you," Chance concluded, then stopped abruptly, catching himself. "Sorry, I was giving you the exact same lecture that I usually give the boys," he apologized.

He didn't want her thinking he was talking down to her. It was just that he really cared about the way the horses were treated. Though they were powerful animals, he thought of them as defenseless when it came to being on the receiving end of bad treatment. Any horse in his care had to be treated well.

"That's okay. I like it," she told him truthfully. "And I did learn something," she added.

He looked at her doubtfully. "Don't kiss up to me, Chloe," he told her.

She thought that was an odd phrase for him to use, given what had happened a while ago at the lake, but she let it go, other than to protest, "But I wasn't."

"Oh, in that case, good to hear." And then he handed her a brush with coarse dark bristles.

She looked at it, confused. "Are you telling me that my hair's a mess?"

Chance laughed. "No, I'm telling you to brush the horse."

"Is that part of the ritual?" There were certainly a lot of steps to remember when it came to taking care of a horse, she thought.

"No, but Mirabel likes it, and I thought having you brush her might help build a bond between you two." Since Chloe still looked just a bit perplexed as she contemplated the brush in her hand, he asked, "May I?"

Chloe was quick to surrender the brush. "Sure."

"You don't want to brush her too hard," he told her. "Just long, even strokes. Think of it like getting a massage."

That didn't help. She shook her head. "Never got one," Chloe told him. Then she looked at him curiously. "Have you?"

The very thought of it made him laugh. "I'm not exactly the beauty spa type," he told her. "I was just trying to find a way for you to be able to relate to the brushing."

Chloe took the brush from him and began to brush Mirabel's flanks. "Like this?"

"Almost." Chance covered her hand with his own and then slowly guided her through the first few strokes. "Like this," he told her, then continued to move her hand beneath his and along the horse.

She knew that technically all they were doing was brushing the horse's coat, but they were doing it in one joint motion, and somehow, it felt rather intimate that way.

She could feel her body heating up, the way it had at the lake when he'd kissed her.

She needed to maintain better control over herself than this, she silently lectured. And part of maintaining that control was not having him get so close to her.

She needed space.

Shrugging his hand off her own, she told him, "I think that I can take it from here now, Chance."

"Go for it," he told her, stepping back. He watched her for a few moments, and then he abruptly turned away and went into the next stall to take care of his own horse.

And to think about something else other than Chloe. Or try to.

Chapter Twelve

Chloe finally felt as if her life was slowly falling into place.

She was making decent headway with the four boys who were currently staying at the ranch, albeit at a different pace with each one. Initially, she'd felt as if all of the teens regarded her warily and were keeping up their defenses, but mercifully, that was all changing.

Jonah and Ryan had taken less time to come around than the other two. Since they had already made a bit of progress under Sasha's counseling, it didn't take them all that long to lower their guard and trust her. She was here a few weeks and they had begun to talk to her about things that were troubling them, as well as some things that they were trying to work out.

She found it rougher going with Brandon and Will.

Brandon didn't want to risk getting close to anyone because he was afraid of ultimately losing that contact, the way he had lost his brother. As for Will, although he clearly yearned for his mother, because of what she had done, he didn't trust any woman who entered his life.

Although their progress was at slower pace, seeing all four of the teens come around because of her efforts proved to be exceedingly gratifying for Chloe. She felt as if she was actually making a difference in their lives, which in turn added a great deal of significance to her own life. She felt it gave her a real purpose.

And then there were the riding lessons with Chance. She would have never thought, not in a million years, that she'd be proud of the headway she was making with that, but she was.

Chance turned out to be the consummate teacher, which really surprised her. She would have said at the outset of their association that teaching someone to ride wouldn't have made a difference to Chance one way or another. He had struck her as being the poster boy for the quintessential loner. But it turned out that Chance was nothing if not patient with her.

He was patient with the boys, too, she noted whenever she had the chance to observe them together. And she could see that they began to regard him as the father figure they'd lacked in their childhoods.

For that matter, she thought as she finished working on that day's notes and looked out the window at the corral where Chance worked with Will, in a way he was the father *she* had never known, as well.

Except, she reminded herself, she would have definitely never reacted to her father the way she was re-acting to Chance.

Chloe sighed.

She was still rather uncertain about all that. Uncertain how she felt about having feelings for him.

She felt as if she was going around in circles.

"You think too much," she murmured to herself under her breath.

But she couldn't help herself, couldn't help analyzing, comparing—remembering. Remembering how it felt to be in love with Donnie—and how that had all ended so heartbreakingly.

Stop it, she upbraided herself. *Just enjoy whatever happens as it happens. For heaven's sake, for once in your life just float, don't plot.*

Chloe shook her head. Easier said than done.

She turned away from the window and went back to her work.

Like a delayed reaction, it slowly dawned on Chance that for the first time since he'd gotten back from serving overseas that he finally, *finally* had a renewed sense of purpose. That was something that had eluded him while he'd been in the military and certainly afterward, when he'd returned stateside.

He supposed that was why he had subconsciously drifted from ranch to ranch and job to job. He'd blamed it on restlessness, but he now realized that he'd been searching for a meaning to his life, some sort of a purpose. Working here, at Peter's Place, with its rescued horses and its rescued kids, was giving him that sense of purpose.

And it felt damn good, Chance thought. The troubled teens he had been put in charge of had essentially come a long way in a short time. He knew in part that was because of Chloe and her sessions with them, but in part it was because of him, as well. And their noticeable evolution gave him a reason for getting up in the morning.

He never thought he'd ever feel that way again. For the longest time he'd believed that opening his eyes each morning, feeling as if his soul had been sucked out by forces he couldn't grapple with, couldn't untangle, was going to be his fate until the day he died.

Now he saw firsthand that it didn't have to be that way. That it *wasn't* that way.

That started him thinking.

If being here, working with both teens and horses that the world had all but given up on, could ultimately rescue his soul, maybe it could do the same for other returning soldiers who were trying—and failing—to find a place for themselves in society.

The thought fired him up.

So much so that he decided to bring it to Graham's attention and see what the man thought of it.

And there was no time like the present.

So, hat in hand—literally as well as figuratively—Chance knocked on Graham's door.

"Door's not locked," Graham called out.

Opening the door to the small bedroom that Graham had converted into his office, Chance made no move to enter. "Mind if I talk to you?" he asked, standing just on the other side of the threshold.

Graham beckoned him forward. "Come on in," he invited warmly, turning away from his computer. "What's on your mind? Everything going all right with the boys?"

"Everything's fine," Chance told him. Then he fell silent. The words he had rehearsed in his head on the way over all seemed to disappear. He mentally shook himself, getting back on track. "That's kind of why I'm here."

But he still stood there like a supplicant before his boss's desk, looking no doubt very uncomfortable.

"Why don't you sit down?" Graham suggested, gesturing to the chair before his desk. "Maybe if you take a load off, you'll find it easier to share whatever's on your mind."

Chance took a seat, but he remained ramrod straight. Graham probably thought he looked like an action figure that had been bent into an uncompromising position.

When Chance didn't start talking, Graham's face took on a serious look.

Other than at the dinner table or by the horses, Chance wasn't used to talking to Graham, and he couldn't read the man's expression. He just had a feeling his boss was about to say something bad.

"You're not leaving us, are you?" Graham finally asked him.

It took a second for Chance to replay the question in his mind. "What? Oh, no, no I'm not—unless you're not satisfied with my work," Chance qualified, wondering if perhaps the man was looking for a way to break the news to him.

"Trust me, I am *more* than satisfied with the caliber of your work," Graham told him. "But something must have brought you in here."

Chance cleared his throat. While he was used to going his own way, he wasn't used to being part of a team, and yet that was what he was right now. Part of a team, and making a suggestion that would in turn affect that team.

Chance began to stumble through a response. "Yes, it did."

"I'm listening," Graham encouraged.

In order to make his point, Chance realized that he was going to have to do something he absolutely hated—he was going to have to talk about himself. But there was no way around it because in order to sell his suggestion, he could use only himself as an example.

"When I was first discharged from the military, because of what I had seen, I kind of came apart at the seams and was pretty much at loose ends." Because the story felt too personal to him, Chance kept the details vague and general. "After having seen combat, after watching more than one person's life wiped out in the blink of an eye, nothing seemed all that important anymore. I certainly didn't feel like I fit in to the world I came back to." He moved closer to the edge of his seat, his eyes intently on Graham to see if he was getting his thought across to the man. "There was no place that felt right to me."

"Go on," Graham urged when he paused.

"But when I came here, when I started working with the boys you had on the ranch, with kids who were caught between two worlds, and working with the rescued horses that you stocked the place with, things began to fall into place for me. They started to make sense." His voice took on volume as he warmed to his subject. "I knew why I came back when so many of the other soldiers I shipped out with either didn't come back at all, or came back with their bodies and spirits maimed and damaged. I found my purpose here."

"I'm really glad to hear that," Graham said, and Chance could hear the man's sincerity.

Then Graham leaned forward in his desk chair. Chance had the feeling he knew that Chance wasn't finished, that there was more to the reason why he'd come into his office this afternoon.

Chance ran his tongue along his dried lips, stalling. "So I was thinking…"

Graham was the soul of encouragement. Nodding, he said, "Yes?"

Chance took a deep breath. "I was thinking that if I could feel this way, working with kids who needed help and horses that needed their own form of rehabilitation, maybe in the long run this could work for other soldiers, as well."

Graham kept his gaze even. "Go on."

He'd come this far; he couldn't just let his courage flag now, Chance thought. "What would you think of the idea of opening up a Peter's Place for returning vets?" he asked. Then the next moment, not wanting to put pressure on the man who had given him a second chance to live his life, Chance shrugged evasively and murmured, "It's a dumb idea, huh?"

"No," Graham told him with feeling, "I think it's a great idea."

Chance was as close to being dumbfound as he'd ever been in his life. He felt his excitement growing. "Really?"

"Absolutely." Graham nodded. "In all honesty I always thought that the work we did here could have other uses. Not just for troubled teens. Give me a while to see if I can either find funding for a separate place, or if there's a way to build on to Peter's Place. You know, incorporate the vets and the teens."

This was more than Chance had hoped for. He'd come in expecting Graham to at least listen to his idea, but not to jump on it like this. He was more than delighted.

Apparently so was Graham, as he went on enthusiastically. "The Fortune Foundation's already given us funding to expand the original Peter's Place—that's why you and Chloe are here. Maybe I can talk to the people who hold the foundation's purse strings while they're still feeling generous and see if I can get them to part with a little more money for this added venture. I certainly think it's worth a try—and definitely worthy of consideration."

Graham took a deep breath as he leaned back in his chair. "You have any other suggestions?"

"No, fresh out," Chance told him, spreading his hands out in front of him, a pleased expression on his face. "That was it." So saying, he rose, ready to leave.

"Well, what you came up with was damn good," Graham assured him. "But like I said, let me see what I can do on my end and whose cage I can rattle. And, Chance—?"

Chance stopped on his way out the door, half turned and looked at his boss over his shoulder. "Yes?"

"If you have any other ideas, be sure to come see me with them. I'd be more than happy to hear you out."

Chance grinned broadly, really pleased with how well this had gone. He'd had bosses who had looked upon him as nothing more than a big dumb cowboy. Muscle on horseback. Any minor suggestions he'd tried to make regarding running the ranch had been quickly disregarded. It was nice to be working for someone who regarded him as a person. "Yes, sir, I will. Thank you, sir."

"It's Graham," Graham said, calling after him. "Graham, not 'sir.'"

"Got it," Chance called back, although he had to admit, if only to himself, that it was hard to think of his boss in terms personal enough to refer to him by his first name.

That just wasn't the way he operated.

"Well, you certainly look happy," Chloe observed when Chance walked into the stable a little later that day.

She had arrived a few minutes ago and was saddling her horse. When she hadn't seen Chance here, she'd begun to wonder if maybe he was tired of mentoring her and spending his late afternoon riding with her.

For her, these riding lessons had become the highlight of her day, but she could well understand if Chance was viewing them as time-consuming nuisances.

Then again maybe she was worried about nothing, Chloe thought, because he was here now and he was smiling.

"I am happy," Chance declared, still running on the energy generated by what he felt had been an extremely successful pitch. It amounted to his first small victory in a long, long time.

He was still flying so high on his earlier exchange with Graham that he completely forgot all about being on his good behavior with Chloe—something he'd instituted for himself after that long kiss at the lake. Instead, he took hold of her shoulders and kissed her before he could think to stop himself.

He kissed her hard and with enthusiasm that melted into something more, something meaningful and soul searing. It was only after Chance unlocked his brain and began to think that he realized he'd done it again. He'd gotten carried away.

Chloe made it all too easy to do that.

Releasing her shoulders, Chance still didn't step back immediately. Instead, he forced himself to look into Chloe's eyes, half afraid he would see condemnation there, but nonetheless hoping against hope that what he would find there would be acceptance.

Having been soundly kissed by this handsome cowboy, Chloe found that, just like the first time, she had to struggle to get air in, struggle not to sound as if she were some addled-brained, incoherent groupie who had just been kissed for the first time.

It took her more than a second to find her mind, which had temporarily gone MIA. When she and her mind were reunited, she was finally able to question him. "Mind if I ask what's made you so happy?"

"I just talked to Graham about the possibility of establishing another center like this one, to help returning veterans. You know, the ones who feel like they're caught between two worlds and don't really belong to either."

It sounded like a noble suggestion to her, and she was proud of him for making it. "What did Graham say?" she wanted to know.

"That he'd look into it." The paltry sentence didn't begin to cover the hope he had attached to the proposed venture.

Chloe felt torn. Torn between being happy for Chance and being unhappy for herself. Because if this suggestion of his worked out and Graham went ahead with establishing a new companion facility to Peter's Place, this one strictly for veterans, she knew that she'd lose Chance. He'd move on, just as she had been afraid he would.

She admonished herself for being selfish. This would help a lot of servicemen if it came to fruition. But she couldn't quite help her emotions.

Feeling almost disloyal, she still had to ask, "Does that mean that you'll be leaving here?"

He honestly hadn't even considered that possibility. He just assumed that if the center he'd suggested turned out to be a separate one, it would still be built somewhere within the area. It had to be, he silently insisted.

"What? No," he told her. "I don't want to leave here."

"But if you wind up running this new center for Graham," she began, "wouldn't you have to?"

But there was so much up in the air that Chance didn't want to talk about it right now. And he silenced Chloe the only way he knew how.

By kissing her.

Chapter Thirteen

That kiss by the lake hadn't been a fluke, Chloe realized. It hadn't been just a one-time exhibition of fireworks going off within her and somehow managing to light the darkening skies. Because whatever she'd felt that evening when Chance had kissed her, right now she was feeling that and more.

So much more.

She was feeling almost too much, Chloe realized, a sliver of panic burrowing its way through to her consciousness.

Because of that, *she* was the one who called a halt to the kiss by drawing her head back. Pulling in air, she put her hands up against his chest to serve as a wedge between them.

When Chance looked at her quizzically, undoubtedly wondering why she'd stopped him, Chloe grasped at the first excuse that she could think of.

It was also true.

"Someone might walk in and see us," she warned him breathlessly.

Chance blew out a breath. She was right. What had come over him? They were both in positions of authority when it came to the boys at the ranch. If one of the boys accidentally saw them behaving like hormone-driven teenagers, that wouldn't exactly be the best kind of example for them.

"Right," he murmured, striving to regain control over himself. He flashed her an apologetic look. "Don't know what I was thinking."

Actually, he knew *exactly* what he had been thinking. What he was *still* thinking. That more than anything, he wanted to take Chloe to his bed and make love with her.

But he wasn't about to force his will on her, and if Chloe wasn't interested in making love with him for one reason or another, then that was that.

End of story.

But was it? He couldn't help thinking about that sunset on the lake—and the kiss they'd just shared now. He was certain that he wasn't imagining things. Chloe had kissed him back—with as much feeling as he had experienced himself.

He was just going to have to be patient, he told himself.

"You were probably thinking that we're both human," Chloe said, answering his rhetorical question. "But right now we have to be more than that—for the sake of the boys," she added emphatically. "They look at you as a father figure, you know," she told him.

Since both horses were saddled and ready to ride, Chloe swung onto Mirabel's back and pointed the mare toward the open stable doors.

"Father figure? I wouldn't go that far," Chance told her, easily mounting his stallion and following her out through the doors.

"I would." She knew what it was like to desperately want a father figure in her life and was acquainted with the signs. She saw them in the four teens at Peter's Place, in the way they interacted with Chance. "Because it's true. I think it's a good thing," Chloe went on, seeing she needed to convince him. "All of them need a father figure in their lives. It's an awful thing for a kid when that space is left empty."

He was only vaguely aware of her backstory, her connection to the Fortunes. None of it was his business, he knew that, but he had the feeling that she wanted to talk, so he asked, "You lose your dad early?"

She laughed and he thought the sound was a bit hollow. It made him wonder about what she'd gone through, growing up.

"Yeah, *really* early," she emphasized. "My father was gone before I was born."

"Sorry for your loss," Chance told her, echoing the phrase that people somehow thought was supposed to make up for the pain and cover every sentiment in between mourning and anger. He knew her father wasn't dead, but if he'd been an absentee father, in a way, that was even worse.

Chance sounded genuinely sincere, Chloe thought, and she appreciated it. But the whole tale was just too sordid to get into right now. She was trying to find her purpose here, feeling better about herself because she was reaching out to these boys. For the most part, until just now, she'd managed to focus on the present and not the past.

"It wasn't my loss, it was his." Chloe said. "The man just ran for the hills when he found out my mom was pregnant with me, and he was never heard from again."

She saw that Chance was struggling to find something appropriate to say to her—as if there was such a thing. Which there wasn't.

"It's okay," she assured him. "I got over it. For a while there, I harbored hopes that he'd just come walking back into my life someday, like a scene in one of those 'feel good' movies—you know, the kind that never really happen in real life. But to be honest, I did miss having a father," she admitted. "Until I turned about twelve."

"What happened when you turned twelve?" he asked before he could stop himself.

He realized that perhaps this was going to get way too personal and she was going to tell him about some traumatic event that was better left unsaid. He didn't feel he was equipped to offer her the kind of comfort she might deserve.

She tossed her head almost defiantly, sending her

hair flying over her shoulder. "I decided that it was his loss if he wasn't there, not mine."

There was admiration in Chance's laugh. "You know, you turned out to be a lot feistier than I first thought you were."

"That's what happens when you've got only one parent and you have to half raise yourself," she told him. "Don't get me wrong," she quickly added. "I didn't have the kind of childhood that Will had. I adored my mother and she was my best friend until the day she died. Heaven knew she tried her best to be both mother *and* father to me. But there were times, more than a few," she admitted, "when I was acutely aware that I could have used having a father around, the way a lot of the other girls did."

"So, does it feel any better now?" Chance wanted to know.

"Now?" she questioned, not sure what he was asking her.

He would have thought it was the first thing that came to her mind.

"Well, you're part of the Fortune family now," he reminded her. "That has got to feel different to you, doesn't it?"

"It does," she agreed. "In a way." Chloe searched for the right words to make him understand what was happening and how she felt about it. "But to be honest, I'm not exactly being embraced by one and all and pressed to the bosom of my family."

"Graham hired you." He'd just assumed that was a sign that she'd been accepted.

"Yes," she allowed. "And being a Fortune no doubt had something to do with that. But some of the others—the ones I met at a family dinner at Kate Fortune's last month—they regard me as an outsider, an interloper they made clear they were on their guard against. I got the feeling they thought I wanted more from them than just their acceptance." She was thinking of Sophie Fortune Robinson. The woman had been especially accusatory and downright unkind. Chloe was still trying to get over that ill-fated meeting because it had hurt so much.

And then it dawned on Chloe that she was talking too much, admitting too much. She didn't ordinarily open up like this. Attempting to cover up her feelings, she shrugged.

"That's okay," she said, affecting a careless attitude. "I've been on my own for the most part for so long, I'm pretty used to it. It's nice to have a family, but at this point, if for some reason that changes, I'm okay with that, too."

Chance wasn't buying the nonchalant act. There was a look in her eyes, a distant, wary, hurt look that he didn't know if she was even aware of. But he was. And what it told him was that she had her guard up.

What it didn't tell him was why. He had a feeling that it had something to do with whoever it was whom she had lost—he remembered the one time that she'd let that slip—but until she trusted him enough to really open up, he wouldn't know anything for sure.

"Well, this still looks like a good spot," he said when they came to a stop by the lake—the same exact place he had brought her to that day he'd first kissed her. "Feel like stopping here for a while?"

"Sure, why not?" Chloe thought it looked as perfect now as it had the first time, and it was quickly becoming her favorite place. Dismounting, she saw that Chance had already gotten off his horse and held a blanket in his hands.

"I thought we could just sit here and enjoy the sunset," Chance told her, spreading the blanket on the ground.

"I guess we think alike," she told him. When he stopped to look at her, a question in his eyes, she told him, "I packed a couple of sandwiches for us." She took them out of her saddlebag, along with bottles of water.

They sat down on the blanket. Facing the lake, they watched the sun going progressively lower in the sky as they ate.

When they were finished, Chloe rolled the sandwich wrappers into a transparent ball. "It almost looks like the sun is sinking into the lake, doesn't it?" she observed in hushed awe as she looked on.

"Just gets better every time I see it," Chance admitted.

His words seemed to linger in the air as he turned to look at her.

She told herself that she was imagining things, but it almost sounded as if Chance was applying the words to her as well as to the sunset.

She couldn't help the flash of excitement that went through her veins.

"Does it?" she asked in a hushed whisper.

Chance started to answer.

Or thought he did.

But what he wound up doing was framing Chloe's face with his hands and turning it up to his.

The next moment, he was kissing her again. Kissing her and losing himself in the taste of her mouth, the scent of her breath as she exhaled. Losing himself in the very essence of her.

The sun continued dipping down lower in the sky until it looked as if it was gracefully dancing along the lake's edge, savoring one last moment before it finally vanished completely into the water.

Despite being in the presence of a magnificent display by nature, Chance was aware only of the woman in his arms. How she felt, how soft her lips were, how inviting the press of her body was against his.

And how much he wanted her.

The kisses grew longer.

And deeper.

As did his desire.

His body urged him to go faster, to take what was right there in front of him. But with effort, Chance forced himself to go slow, to not just enjoy her, but to give Chloe the opportunity to consider what was happening between them—and to say no at any point if it came to that for her.

Although he fervently hoped that she wouldn't.

It was inevitable. The more he caressed her, familiarizing himself with every soft, inviting curve of her body, the more he wanted her.

His heart was hammering wildly as he drew Chloe

beneath him on the blanket, slowly exploring every inch of her, finding pleasure in every inch of her and giving her the same pleasure.

And she loved every second of it.

Still, Chloe tried very hard to resist the allure of what Chance promised. Not because she didn't want this to happen, but because she did.

And because she wanted it, guilt hovered on the edges of her consciousness, threatening to break in and shatter everything. That guilt reminded her that she'd already given herself to a man. A man who was no longer able to claim her.

But this feeling that was traveling through her—the desire, the heat, the passion—was exquisite, and she had missed this feeling oh, so much. For the very first time in two years, Chloe felt like she was alive, and she'd missed that feeling.

Missed making love and being made love to.

Her heart was racing like a car at the Indianapolis 500 as her desire for more of Chance's kisses, his touches, just kept increasing at a stunning rate.

She didn't remember tugging off his clothes, didn't remember him pulling hers off, either. But somehow, it had happened because they were on the blanket, naked, their limbs tangled around one another as they lay beneath the full moon, each trying to get their fill of the other.

Each deeply involved in pleasuring the other.

She bit her lip to keep from sighing with delight as she felt his sensual mouth almost artfully glide along her skin, silently claiming everywhere he touched, everywhere he kissed.

Chloe let herself absorb each and every sensation that went spiraling through her body in response to the almost magical things this cowboy was doing to her.

Till her very core felt like an inferno.

She had trouble catching her breath. Her mind scattered in a thousand different directions—which was just as well. She didn't want to think because thinking was bad. Thinking brought guilt, and all she wanted to do was feel. Because in feeling, there was freedom, and what she was feeling had her soaring above the clouds, above everything. As free as a bird.

Finally pulling in a deep breath, she turned and rose above Chance, doing her best to give him back a little of the intense pleasure he was giving her. She'd had only one other partner her whole life, while she was certain that Chance had had many, but she did her best to show him her gratitude for this timeless gift that he was bestowing on her.

After a few moments of reciprocation had passed, he pulled her beneath him again.

He slid his body along hers, sending electric currents of anticipation surging all through her.

Her heart raced faster, all but stealing her breath away.

His eyes met and held hers, communing with her even though not a single word was exchanged. And she answered his unspoken question in kind.

Chance kissed her, then kissed her again. She could feel her body priming.

Waiting.

For him.

When his knee parted her legs, she was ready for him. And then they were joined together, one heart, one mind and one desire overseeing them both.

His body rocked against hers, and then began to move in the timeless rhythm she'd been waiting for.

She moved with Chance, her hips all but sealed to his. The movements grew quicker, stronger as each seemed to anticipate the other, and suddenly they were racing to the end goal, to the explosion that was waiting for both of them.

It seemed to take forever and yet was only as long as a blink of an eye. When it came, rocking them both with its explosion, they clung to one another as if letting go meant extinction.

She could feel her body shuddering, could feel the fireworks receding, ushering in an aftermath awash with a feeling of well-being. She lay there, cradled in the crook of his arm, wondering just how things had come to this moment in time.

She was too tired to come up with an answer, even if it was just for herself.

The sounds of nature were soothing, and she found herself relaxing.

If only for the moment.

Chapter Fourteen

Chloe felt a hand on her shoulder, gently shaking her. Startled, she opened her eyes. Until that moment, she hadn't realized that her eyes had closed or that she'd wound up falling asleep.

"Chloe?" She detected concern in Chance's voice. "Are you all right?"

Embarrassed, flustered, for a second Chloe was at a complete loss for words. They'd made love, and then she'd fallen asleep. What had to be going through his head about her right now?

"I'm okay," she mumbled.

The smile she saw on his lips was totally unexpected. "You're a lot better than 'okay,'" he told her, his smile widening. "But I thought maybe you were upset, you know, now that everything kind of settled down." It was obvious that he must have thought she was only pretending to be asleep.

Chance had never been much for small talk, or really any sort of talk at all. He was a man who believed in doing rather than talking, and as far as he was concerned, his actions—and hers—had done all the talking that was necessary this evening.

But he wasn't so naive or obtuse to believe that men and women thought alike when faced with the same situation. That meant that what was "fine" with him most likely wasn't that way for a woman. Specifically, for Chloe.

So he pressed the matter a little further. "You're not upset or anything, are you?"

"Because we just made love?"

He would have said "had sex," but Chance left it her way and nodded. "Yes."

Chloe took a breath, stalling as she tried to gather her thoughts into a coherent whole. She didn't know what she felt.

Falling asleep beside Chance had to mean that she trusted him, right?

She could see that he was still waiting for an answer. "Well, it wasn't exactly something I'd planned to have happen, especially out in the open like this, but no," she told him honestly after considering the matter, "I'm not upset."

That was a relief, he thought. Out loud, he said, "That's good, because I wouldn't want you to be upset." Replaying his own words in his head, Chance flushed a little. Talking was definitely *not* his strong suit. "Guess that sounds kind of lame to you."

That more than anything else—except for perhaps the way she'd seen him interacting with a couple of the boys—really touched her. Instead of feeling awkward or embarrassed, she felt her heart swelling.

"No," Chloe said, reaching up and lightly caressing his cheek. "As a matter of fact, I think it sounds rather sweet."

"'Sweet,'" Chance repeated, bemused. He laughed shortly. "I don't think anyone's ever called me that before."

"Maybe nobody's ever taken the time to get to know you before," Chloe said. The next second, she realized how that had to sound to him. "Not that I think I know you all that well. I mean—" She was floundering and she knew it. "This isn't coming out right."

Damn, there was just something about her, about the way she talked, even about the way she made mistakes that kept drawing him in.

"I think it came out just fine," he told her right before he kissed her.

He was doing it again, Chloe thought. He was making her head spin. Making her body heat.

It took Chloe several moments before she could finally force herself to draw her mouth back, away from his. It definitely wasn't easy.

"We start doing that again and we're never going to get back to the ranch. Graham's liable to send a search party out for us come morning."

"Wouldn't want to be found like this," Chance agreed. Even to his own ears he didn't exactly sound as if he really meant what he was saying.

She looked beautiful in the moonlight, he thought.

So beautiful that everything he'd felt earlier just before he made love to her was coming back in spades. You'd think that having consumed the forbidden fruit would have negated the overpowering desire for it. But in Chloe's case, it seemed to have just the opposite effect.

Having made love with her had just whetted his appetite for her, because Chance now knew just what was waiting for him.

Rather than let her start getting dressed, the way he knew he should have, Chance lightly brushed his lips against her bare shoulder, sending shock waves through himself—as well as through her.

"One more for the road?" he asked, a very sensual look in his eyes.

The question, so guilelessly asked, had laughter bubbling up in her throat.

"I guess it can't do any harm," she replied, her heart already revving up.

"None whatsoever," he agreed as he pulled her back into his arms.

It began all over again, the thunder and lightning, the excitement, all culminating in a breathtaking shower of stars.

Chloe thought it might prove awkward, running into Chance, having their paths cross half a dozen times a day, not to mention at the dining room table for meals, but it was just the opposite.

It was nice. Very, very nice.

Neither one of them took any liberties with the other or resorted to private jokes or secretive looks that left the others on the ranch guessing. But there was still something enormously comforting about just being around one another.

She wouldn't have given that feeling up for the world.

For one thing, Chloe felt a great deal less alone now. She was still Graham's half sister and Gerald Robinson's offspring, for whatever that was worth, but neither of those two things made her feel as if she was actually part of anything, as if she was connected to anything, despite the implications and despite what Graham had told her when he'd first called her.

But being around Chance and catching glimpses of him during the day *did* make her feel as if she was part of something larger than herself. Something larger and oh, so emotionally comforting.

Chloe knew she was letting herself get carried away and that all this was just temporary, but for now, for this tiny space of time, it didn't matter. She was determined to enjoy this for however long it lasted.

"A family picnic?" Chloe repeated, looking at Graham after he had called her into his small office.

A couple more days had passed and things had been going very well at work as well as during her free hours, but admittedly, in that same time she had barely socialized with her half brother and his family. Despite the fact that they shared some of the same DNA, she still tended to think of Graham more as her boss than as her kin.

And now, out of the blue, Graham had sought her

out to invite her to a family picnic he was planning for that Sunday.

Recalling her last venture into a family function, Chloe had some grave doubts about the invitation. "Are you sure you want me to attend?"

"It *is* a family picnic," he pointed out. "That means it's for both the Fortune family and my work family," Graham explained. "And you actually qualify as both, so yes, I want you to come. Sasha and I both want you to come. Besides," he added, "you're good with Sydney and Maddie."

Now it was starting to make sense to Chloe. "If you need a babysitter—"

Graham was quick to cut her off. "If I wanted a babysitter, I would have said so," he told her. "I was just trying to tell you that the girls would love to see you there, not that we require your services in any other capacity than as an attendee," he said pointedly. Then he added what he felt would cinch the deal for Chloe. "Oh, and Chance should be there."

Chloe looked at him in surprise. "He already agreed to come?"

Graham paused a moment. "He will if he knows that you're going to be there," he admitted. "So what do you say? I'd really like you to come. I'm inviting the boys, too," he added, hoping that would convince her to attend.

Chloe surrendered. She really didn't want to drag her feet about this. "Can't say no to my boss—or to my half brother."

"How about you just call me 'brother'?" Graham suggested. "'Half' brother makes me feel like I've been sliced in two and you get to pick which half you want to deal with. It's not exactly a flattering image," he added.

Chloe grinned. "Well, that's easy enough…"

Graham raised his hand to stop her right there. "I think I'll quit while I'm ahead—provided you did just agree to come to the picnic."

She laughed, knowing that she'd been set up. "How can I say no now?"

"Good, then my plan worked." He picked up the land-line receiver and pulled over a list of phone numbers he'd written down. "Now I have to corral the rest of the people for this picnic."

That caught her by surprise. "I'm the first one you asked?"

"Not exactly," Graham admitted. "I did ask Sasha first. Actually, it was more of a discussion as to what day would be the best to have the picnic. So, in a way, I guess you are the first one." He saw the surprised look on her face. "Why?"

Chloe thought of waving the whole exchange away, but decided, in light of everything, she owed her new-found brother the truth. "I'm used to being the last one asked—to everything—so thank you for that."

"No thanks necessary, Chloe," he responded, already tapping a phone number into the keypad.

Chloe walked out of the office smiling.

When Chance was invited, Graham asked him to extend the invitation to the boys. Like him, they were surprised to be included and at first, all four seemed hesitant to attend what was going to be, after all, a family gathering.

"Why? You need us to act as servers when the food's brought out?" Brandon wanted to know, reverting to his old chip-on-his-shoulder attitude as he posed the question to Chance.

"If you want to help out, that's fine," Chance told the teen, then looked at the other boys who were gathered around him in the stable. "But nobody expects you to. You're just welcome to join in—as guests, just like everyone else."

"Is it mandatory?" Will wanted to know, shifting restlessly from one foot to the other as he eyed Chance.

"It's an invitation, not an order."

"Don't be a jerk," Jonah told the two younger residents. "It's a chance to eat some really good barbecue and be around regular people. Relax. Nobody wants anything from you."

Color crept up Will's shallow cheeks. "I guess you're right," he conceded.

Chance knew the comment from their peer would carry some weight, but he was still grateful when he saw Chloe stepping out of Mirabel's stall, no doubt having heard the entire conversation. He knew she'd add her two cents to the persuasive argument—but only if she felt that he might need backup.

Evidently, she decided he did.

"Old habits are hard to break, aren't they?" Chloe asked knowingly.

The boys turned, almost in unison, to the sound of

her voice. From the looks on their faces, she judged that they hadn't realized that she was anywhere in earshot.

"Sometimes people do things just because they want to be nice without expecting anything in return," she told Brandon and Will. "Get used to it. You'll find that it happens a lot more frequently than you thought— once you put your guard down.

"So," she concluded, looking around at all four of the teens. "Are you guys in?"

Will raised and lowered his thin shoulders in an indifferent shrug. "I guess so."

"Sure," Ryan chimed in with a ready grin.

"I'll be there," Jonah assured them.

"How about you?" Chloe asked Brandon when he kept his silence.

After several beats, Brandon, like Will, shrugged, Unlike Will he avoided looking at either Chloe or Chance when he answered.

"Yeah, I guess so," he mumbled.

"Enthusiasm," Chloe teased, putting her arm around Brandon's shoulders and giving him a quick hug.

Brandon's shoulders were stiff, but she noted with pleasure that he was forcing himself to relax them a little.

Progress!

"I love it," she added.

"Yeah, whatever," Brandon mumbled. For the moment, he let her keep her arm where it was.

"Baby steps, Brandon," Chloe whispered into his ear. "Take baby steps."

"Uh-huh." He shrugged her off, but the moment had

lasted longer than Chloe'd expected. "Well, I got chores to do," he announced to no one in particular.

"Then you'd better get to them," Chance told the boy. He looked at the other three. "How about the rest of you? Stalls cleaned?" he wanted to know.

"Cleaner than our bunks," Ryan volunteered, speaking for the others.

"Then maybe you'd better see about those bunks," Chance suggested pointedly.

The quartet dispersed immediately, one going deeper into the stable, while the other three went to the bunkhouse where they stayed.

"I think that they're coming along pretty well," she said to Chance once the boys were well out of hearing range. She turned toward him for an answer. "What do you think?"

"There's still a lot of work left to do," Chance replied.

He had never been one to allow himself to be overly enthusiastic about something, especially when it was still a work in progress. And that was exactly what he considered the evolution of the four teens to be—a work in progress.

He saw that Chloe was still looking at him, obviously waiting for a positive response.

He sighed, giving in. "But yeah, I think they're coming along. I have to admit that I'm kind of surprised that they're willing to go to this picnic," he told her, lowering his voice in case Brandon could pick up on their conversation.

"Well, I think that it's a hopeful sign," she told him in all sincerity.

He wished he could be as optimistic as she was about this. But life had knocked him around too much. Because of that, he always anticipated the worst.

"Maybe you should keep an eye on them just in case," he suggested.

She wanted to ask in case of what, but there was a bigger question in her mind than that at the moment. "Why? Aren't you going to be there?"

She couldn't think of any other reason for him to say that. Had he changed his mind about going? She was sure that Graham had convinced him to attend. What happened?

"It's a family picnic," he told her, as if that explained everything.

"Not *strictly* family," she reminded him. "Besides, as Graham pointed out, he considers the people at Peter's Place family, too. That means the boys. *And* you," she said pointedly. "Why don't you want to come?"

He frowned slightly, wishing she hadn't put him on the spot like this. "I don't do well in crowd scenes."

That was a lot of nonsense, she thought. "You were in the military. That was a crowd."

"Yeah, and I did my time," Chance pointed out, as if that ended the argument.

Refusing to give up, Chloe tried another tactic. "You can't insult your boss by not showing up. Remember, you're still waiting for his decision on that expansion for a center to help returning vets." She pinned him with a look. "You have to come."

Chance laughed quietly as he shook his head. The woman just didn't give up. There was a time, not all that long ago, when he would have found that to be annoying. But for some reason, not when it came to her.

"You do know how to present a convincing argument," he commented, surrendering.

Chloe's eyes were shining as she replied, "I do whatever I have to do." Then, patting his cheek, she walked out of the stable humming to herself.

Chapter Fifteen

He had told Chloe the truth. He had never really been all that fond of crowds. Wide-open country where a man could travel all day without running into anyone else held far more appeal for him, which was why he preferred spending most of his time on the back of a horse rather than at a table, talking to people he didn't know.

But he had to admit that lately, he had begun to broaden his horizons just a little more. The work he'd been doing with the boys, taking sullen, angry-at-the-world teens who felt that they had been cheated by society and helping them turn their lives around—both by working with them and by his example—had made him reevaluate his take on the world at large.

And then, of course, there was Chloe, Chance thought. He couldn't very well do what he'd done with her on the back of a horse. Not without one of them hurting themselves, he tactfully amended.

Still there was a world of difference between being around Chloe or the boys and these wall-to-wall—or more accurately, he thought, tree-to-tree—people he was looking at today. People who seemed to come in all sizes and shapes, united only by their last name—or at least the DNA that ran in their veins.

Apparently, Gerald Robinson had been extremely generous with his seed, if at times not so generous with his name, Chance thought. The former Jerome Fortune had fathered eight children with his wife, Charlotte. Apparently, that hadn't been enough to satisfy the man. He also snuck around procreating more children—Chloe being one of them—with unsuspecting, easily infatuated young women, leaving them high and dry—and pregnant—as soon as the time seemed right to him.

Chance had to admit that he was surprised to see just how well-adjusted a lot of these people seemed to be, given their background and their father's less than Boy Scout–like history.

But well-adjusted or not, this gathering of Fortune Robinsons and their extended family was just no place for him, Chance decided.

After less than half an hour into it, he began searching for the best time to make his unobserved getaway.

As he moved about, trying his best to look unobtrusive and blend in with the background, Chance suddenly felt someone slip their arm through his. Caught entirely off guard, he turned his head to find that Chloe had quietly walked up behind him.

Chloe returned his rather startled look with a smile. "I know what you're thinking," she told him.

"Oh? And what is it that I'm thinking?" Chance wanted to know, rather impressed by the confidence he heard in her voice.

She knew because in his place, she would have thought the same thing. "You're thinking that it's so crowded here, you could just easily slip away and nobody would notice that you're gone."

She was good, he thought.

"The thought did cross my mind," Chance admitted in a conversational tone.

"Well, they would notice. *I* would notice," she told him, looking at Chance pointedly.

That look in her eyes had him remembering the way she'd been at the lake the other night. And the memories had him fervently wishing they were there alone again right now, instead of milling around in a crowd of people.

"You're just saying that," he told her.

"No, I'm just meaning that," Chloe insisted. "You forget, aside from Graham and Sasha and their kids—" she pointed at the small quartet out in the center of a larger circle of people "—you and the boys are the only other people here I really know."

Something wasn't quite making sense to him. "I thought you said you met these people at a big dinner party at Kate Fortune's ranch last month ago."

"I *saw* them at a big dinner party a couple of months ago," she corrected. "There's a big difference between seeing and knowing. I just recognize some of these people by sight. That's not the same thing," she stressed, wanting him not to feel as if he was the only outsider here.

Still, Chance looked unconvinced by her argument. "Recognizing some of these people by sight is a start," he pointed out.

Chloe laughed as she picked up a paper cup filled with diet soda from one of the smaller tables that had been set up. "Don't try to snow me with rhetoric, Chance. By your own admission, you're not all that good with words."

"No," he agreed, then spared her a meaningful look. A look that instantly made her feel warm and wanted. "I have other talents."

She blushed, unable to stop the surge of color that raced to her cheeks.

"Yes, you do," she quietly admitted. "And I'd really like it if you and your 'talents' stayed awhile longer. And the boys would like it, too."

She pointed them out for his benefit.

He was surprised to see that all four were not that far away from them, caught up in a conversation with one of the other Fortune Robinson family members.

"They're finally beginning to learn how to adapt to people," Chloe told him. "This is very good for them."

He saw her point about how being here was good for the teens, but he didn't see the dots connecting in his case the same way that she did. "Don't see what my leaving or not leaving has to do with them."

Some people needed to be hit by a two-by-four before they understood things, she thought. Chloe tried her best to get her point across. "Don't you see? You're their leader. They look to you to set an example. You leave, it won't be long before they leave."

It was a hell of a burden she was putting on his shoulders, Chance thought. "What about you?"

"I'm not leaving," Chloe answered, deliberately tightening her arm around his.

"No, I mean, you interact with them. They come to you for advice on top of those counseling sessions you have. Why can't *you* be their leader here?" he wanted to know. That made sense to him.

But Chloe had no intention of giving an inch in this matter. "Sorry, the role of leader's already been cast, and it's you," she told Chance, patting his arm with her free hand. She smiled up into his face. "Deal with it." Chloe gestured toward the barbecue grills that had been set up. "Have a burger, have a beer. *Smile.*" The last seemed almost like an order.

He moved his lips spasmodically in response to the last word.

Chloe laughed. "That'll do for now."

"Who *are* all these people, anyway?" he asked her, looking around at the sea of people, both pint-size and adult.

Chloe looked around, trying to see them through his eyes. She could understand how all this might be kind of overwhelming to a loner like him. Being a part of this family was still overwhelming to her, too.

She took a breath, wanting to get the names and faces straight in her mind before answering him.

"Well, I don't know all of them," she qualified. "But

over there, next to Graham and Sasha and the girls, are Ben and Ella Fortune Robinson and their newborn, Lacey. Well, she's not a newborn anymore, she's two months old—"

"Practically old enough to go to work," Chance joked.

Relieved that he seemed to be in a better mood, Chloe pointed to another couple.

"That's Ben's brother, Wes, and his new wife, Vivian. Over there—"

She stopped as she suddenly recognized the young woman who had made her feel so unwelcome at the last gathering. For a split second, Chloe thought of turning around and leaving herself—but after what she'd just said to Chance, she knew she couldn't do that. So instead, she mentally regrouped and tried again.

"Over there," she told Chance, "is Sophie Fortune Robinson, and her fiancé, Mason Montgomery."

As covertly as possible, Chloe turned the other way so that Sophie wouldn't see her face if she looked in this direction. All Sophie would see would be the back of her head. One blonde was more or less like any other, Chloe reasoned.

"Now, right over by the lake is Zoe Fortune Robinson. Except she's married now. That's her husband, Joaquin Mendoza, with her."

Because she'd started this, Chloe continued to systematically identify the next cluster of people she recognized even though she suspected that Chance would be perfectly happy if she just stopped right here.

She pointed to the next four people. "That's Olivia

and Kieran, two more of Gerald Robinson's legitimate children. And that guy with the British accent is Keaton Fortune Whitfield. He's one of the…" She hesitated, then added, "…well, illegitimate offspring, like me. And that's his fiancée, Francesca Harriman."

She looked around but didn't find the last Robinson daughter. "Seems the only one missing is Rachel. Graham told me she lives in Horseback Hollow with her husband."

Chance nodded. They were nothing but names to him, but because it meant so much to her, he mentally reviewed the people she'd pointed out. He noticed the expression on the man she called Kieran. "Now, there's a man who looks as unhappy about being here as I am."

Because she'd named so many for him in quick succession, she wasn't sure whom Chance was referring to. "Which one?"

He didn't want to come right out and actually point to the man. That seemed kind of rude. But he had been paying more attention than Chloe probably thought he was.

"That guy you called Kieran," he told her.

She had to admit that Chance had surprised her. She looked over to the man he'd singled out and saw that Chance was right. Kieran did look exceedingly unhappy. Pausing, she recalled what Sasha had told her about his situation.

Things fell into place.

"He's not unhappy because he's here," Chloe told him. "He's worried about Zach."

"Zach," Chance repeated. Another new name. This was getting really complicated. "Maybe I should be taking notes here," he said sarcastically.

She could understand Chance's confusion. There were a lot of names, a lot of details to keep straight. She gave him a quick summary. "Zach is Kieran's best friend, and Zach's been in a coma for a week now, ever since he was thrown by a horse. He suffered a skull fracture. Obviously, not everyone can become one with a horse the way you can," she couldn't help adding.

Chance's immediate response was one of sympathy. "Poor guy." And then he asked, "Is he going to be all right? The guy who got thrown, I mean. Zach," he finally remembered.

"Nobody knows," she told Chance. "But we can ask for an update on his condition."

Taking his hand, she urged Chance to come with her as she drew closer to Kieran.

Chance was reluctant at first. After all, this wasn't any business of his. He didn't know either of the two men involved. But he did know what it was like to be worried about a friend, worried about that friend not making it. That memory would always be very vivid for him, he thought ruefully.

That got the better of him, and he came along with Chloe.

As they drew closer to Kieran, she overheard one of the other people at the gathering asking him about Zach's condition before she had a chance.

"It's the same," Kieran answered. He was toying with the glass of lemonade in his hand, but he had yet to drink any of it. "He hasn't opened his eyes in a week. I've been in the hospital with him every day, and I keep waiting for Zach to sit up and laugh, 'Gotcha!' but he just goes on lying there."

"What about his three-year-old?" someone else spoke up, wanting to know about the man's daughter. "Rosa-belle, right? He's the only one she has."

That only added to the sad scenario, Chloe thought.

"Zach's parents have been taking care of her while they've been praying for a miracle. We've all been pray-ing for a miracle," Kieran murmured more to himself than to anyone around him.

"What if there is no miracle?" This question came from Francesca, who looked deeply moved by what she was listening to. "What happens to Rosabelle then?"

Kieran took a deep breath, as if that would give him the strength he was looking for in order to reply. But it wasn't enough. His voice came out quiet, dis-tant. It was obvious that this was not an outcome that he welcomed.

"Then Rosabelle comes and lives with me. Zach asked me to be her guardian." Kieran shook his head. "He must have been out of his mind," he said sadly.

"Or maybe just very intuitive," Chloe told him, speaking up.

Kieran flashed her a grateful, albeit sad smile. "I doubt it," he replied.

"That was a nice thing to say," Chance told her as they moved away from the cluster of people who were around Kieran.

She shrugged off his compliment a bit self-consciously.

"That would be what I'd like someone to say to me under those circumstances," she confided. "Maybe it would even make me feel better."

To Chloe's relief, as the afternoon wore on, Chance no longer looked as if he needed to be tethered in place to keep him from fleeing the premises. And once he relaxed, that in turn had an effect on her, and Chloe felt herself relaxing, as well.

The picnic seemed to go on forever, but it was the good kind of forever, the kind that wound up being one of those memories people looked back on fondly over the passage of years.

Consequently, she and Chance were still at the picnic as the day tiptoed toward twilight.

The conversation, which had revolved around a whole host of different topics, turned to Ariana Lamonte, a reporter, Chloe discovered, who was systematically interviewing various members of the family for a piece the woman was writing entitled "Becoming a Fortune."

From what she was picking up from various family members, it sounded to Chloe like a huge invasion of privacy.

"I don't particularly like her angle on this," Sophie was saying. "She's been doing a lot of hinting that our mother—well, the mother of some of us," Sophie amended, trying to be as tactful as possible given the situation. Taking a breath, the young woman started again. "She's broadly hinting that Charlotte," she said, referring to her mother by her given name, "knew quite a bit more about Dad's cheating on her than she admits to."

"Well, that's because your mother's a smart woman," Sophie's fiancé said. "Let's face it, unless he kept her drugged or locked in a closet, she had to know something."

Chloe caught the indignant look that Sophie shot at Mason, but then she noticed Sophie's face soften. Perhaps because she felt Mason was right, Chloe thought. What Gerald Robinson had done was nothing short of terrible. He had willfully broken his vows and slept with every woman who apparently wasn't smart enough to run for the hills when she met him. Including her own mother.

"Guess we're kind of a sorry bunch," Sophie said to the others.

"Hey, I'm not sorry," Keaton told her. "Because no matter how I got here, I *did* get here," he said with emphasis. "And it doesn't matter who sired you or how. You're here, you're breathing and the rest is up to you from here on in. You've got your own future in your hands," Keaton maintained. "That's not to say that you can't look to family for a little backup," he added with a grin. "And there sure is a lot of family to look to around here."

"I still feel bad about Mother," Sophie told the others.

"Don't," Zoe said. "I'm sure she feels more than compensated for her 'pain and suffering' whenever she takes a look at the bank account balances, or goes shopping in one of those high-end department stores she loves so well."

"That's terrible," Sasha said to Graham, apparently not quietly enough because she was overheard.

"That's life," someone else countered. "Not everyone's a romantic at heart like Sophie."

Appalled at the criticism of a woman she'd never met, Chloe spoke up. "But money doesn't keep you warm at night no matter how much there is of it."

"But it can certainly pay for a really good heating system," one of the other people pointed out, laughing at their own joke.

This was a conversation Chance felt he had no right to be part of, as well as no interest. No doubt it had to be disturbing Chloe, too.

Feeling protective of her, he took Chloe's hand and guided her away.

"C'mon, let's see if we can find something sweet to take the bitter taste out of my mouth," Chance urged, nodding toward some of the tables that were set up beyond the grills. Sasha had several different desserts arranged there, and there were still some left.

Chloe looked around at the picnic gathering. Despite some of the differences of opinion that had been thrown out over the course of the last few hours, she was beginning to believe that maybe, just maybe, she could have it all. A career, a family that numbered more than just one other person and, most important of all, love.

She slanted a look toward Chance, her heart swelling with hope. "Sounds like a good idea to me," she agreed.

Chapter Sixteen

"Chloe, could I speak to you for a minute?"

About to go with Chance to get some dessert, Chloe was stopped dead in her tracks by a familiar voice. The last time she had heard that voice, she was being reviled for having the nerve to crash a family celebration, pretending to be Gerald Robinson's daughter. More things had been said, but Chloe had tuned them out, leaving the party soon after that.

With effort, Chloe forced herself to turn around and face Sophie Fortune Robinson. Although she was doing her best to hide it, an awkward feeling immediately wrapped itself around her. The exact same feeling that she'd experienced at the dinner party when Sophie had cornered her only to give her a complete dressing-down.

Gerald Robinson's youngest legitimate daughter had been furious with her.

Bracing herself for the worst, Chloe said, "All right, I'm listening." *Which was more than you did*, she added silently.

Looking rather uncomfortable herself, Sophie glanced in Chance's direction. "Alone?" she requested.

Chance took his ground. "I can stay with you if you want me to," he told Chloe, deliberately not looking at Sophie. "Or I can wait for you over there." He nodded toward the dessert tables. "Your call."

The fact that he had volunteered to remain with her and was willing to do whatever she wanted heartened Chloe. It also gave her the strength to face whatever it was that Sophie had to say.

Chloe squared her shoulders. "It's okay. Just don't leave," she added as a coda, afraid he might take this opportunity to walk away from the picnic and go back to the bunkhouse.

"I'll be by the dessert table," Chance promised. And then he slanted a glance at Sophie before adding, "Within earshot if you need me."

With that, he walked away.

Stepping over to an area that was temporarily devoid of any picnickers for the moment, Chloe told Sophie, "All right, we're alone—or as alone as we can be at a family picnic." She pressed her lips together, centering herself before asking, "What is it that you want to tell me?"

It took Sophie several moments before she finally said the words Chloe never figured she'd hear.

"I'm sorry."

Chloe didn't know if she was being set up, or if she'd missed something. Sophie had looked almost hostile when their eyes had met that night at the dinner party. She assumed that nothing had changed. Or had it?

"Excuse me?"

"What I said to you the night at Kate Fortune's ranch… Well, I was out of line and I'm sorry. But you have to understand, it was a huge shock to me."

"Finding out that Gerald Robinson was my father?" Chloe asked. "Think how I felt," she pointed out.

Sophie nodded. "All I could think of was how *I* felt. And it wasn't just about finding out about you. It was finding out that the father I grew up adoring was nothing like what I thought he was. That the man I thought was so honorable couldn't seem to remain faithful or true to anyone." Her voice trembled as she spoke. "I was angry, I was hurt and I felt betrayed. And I'm afraid that I took it out on you." She looked at her, clearly embarrassed. "And for that I'm very sorry. I shouldn't have been angry with you. We were both in the same boat."

"Actually, we weren't in the same boat," Chloe politely corrected her. "Yours was a luxury liner. Mine was a leaky rowboat," she said, referring to the fact that while Sophie's childhood was spent in the lap of luxury, hers had been more of a hand-to-mouth existence because her father had deserted her mother.

Sophie's discomfort seemed to increase. "And that makes me feel twice as bad," Sophie told her.

"That wasn't your fault," Chloe pointed out. "That was your father's fault. When my mother finally told me who my father was—that he wasn't her high school sweetheart who was killed in a car accident before he could marry her, which was the story she'd told me all along—she admitted that she'd loved him a great deal. And she told me how devastated she was when he just up and left her."

Chloe felt emotion choke her, and she cleared it from her throat before she continued. "Anyway, that practically destroyed my mother—but she realized that she had to go on living because I needed her, so she pulled herself together and created a life for the two of us.

"Because of the strength she displayed, my mother made me see that we each have the ability to be the masters of our own destinies. That means we can't put the blame on some outside forces that might or might not come swooping in."

As Chloe spoke she saw the shift of emotion on Sophie's face. Her expression went from sorrowful to hesitant and now hopeful. "So does that mean you forgive me?"

"There's nothing to forgive," Chloe told her, wanting to put the matter to rest.

But Sophie wasn't finished atoning for what she'd done. "Still, it took a lot of courage for you to come meet us the way you did, and then having me jump down your throat like that had to have made you feel just awful."

"Well, it didn't make mè feel good," Chloe admitted. Since Sophie had apologized, she didn't want the other woman to continue feeling badly. "But if I were in your place, maybe I would have said the same thing."

Sophie shook her head. "No, you wouldn't have—but thank you for saying that," she told Chloe as she hugged her.

A smile bloomed on Chloe's lips. It looked like she was finally being accepted, not just by one or two members, but by the whole family in general.

It felt wonderful, Chloe thought.

Disengaging herself from Sophie, she pointed behind the young woman. "I think someone's waiting for you to get back to him," she told her half sister.

Sophie turned around to see that Mason was standing off to the side, patiently waiting for things to be resolved.

"He's been my rock through this whole thing," she told Chloe. Releasing her, Sophie lingered a moment longer. "We need to get together again—soon," she emphasized sincerely.

"It's a deal," Chloe told her, relieved that Sophie no longer looked upon her as some sort of a troublemaking agitator.

Chloe breathed a sigh of relief as she turned around to look for Chance.

He was waiting for her exactly where he said he would be—at the dessert table.

As she joined him there, Chloe had the impression that he had been watching her the entire time she'd been interacting with Sophie.

When she approached, he said, "I guess you didn't need rescuing after all."

"No, it turns out that I didn't," she told him. "Sophie came to me to apologize."

Ordinarily, he never asked for more information than was offered. But this time, he made an exception. Since he was in the dark about the whole incident at the previous dinner party, Chance asked, "What was she apologizing for?"

Chloe filled him in on the details.

"And she just apologized to you now for having a bad attitude?" he asked.

"I think, in part, she was apologizing for accusing me of lying about the whole thing. I get the impression that until the man's numerous partners came to light, Sophie thought her father walked on water." Chloe shook her head. "I guess it kind of goes along with the way my mother felt about him.

"When she finally told me the truth about who my father was, my mother admitted that she'd literally worshipped him—right up to when he walked out on her and broke her heart." Chloe frowned, thinking back over the years. So much made sense now. "I guess that's why she never got married or even had a relationship. She couldn't bring herself to trust another man enough to let her guard down."

Chance shook his head. He didn't say what he was thinking. That in his opinion, after what Chloe's father had done and all the people he had hurt with his behavior, Chloe's father should have been horsewhipped—at the very least.

"How many illegitimate kids did you say this man has?" Chance asked her.

Chloe sighed. She honestly had no idea how many

there were. It was an odd thing to admit about her own father.

"The final count isn't in yet," she told him when she saw that he was waiting for an answer. "A couple of my half brothers are still trying to track down other potential siblings."

"Damn, that's really one for the books, all right," Chance commented.

It certainly was, Chloe thought, growing quiet. Gerald or Jerome or whatever he chose to call himself now was still her father, but she felt no affection for the man, no desire to be protective of him. She did, however, feel protective of her late mother, and she felt that to criticize the man her mother fell in love with, even temporarily, was to criticize her, and Chloe wouldn't allow that.

When Chance commented on the fact that she had grown very quiet, she deliberately changed the subject by suggesting they find the boys to see how they were faring at the picnic.

It took some looking, but when they did find all four of them, the teens were apparently having a good time, mingling with the younger people who had been brought to the picnic. They were also getting along with one another rather well.

When she saw that, Chloe felt warm all over. She'd been right to talk the boys into coming.

The way she saw it, the picnic, by almost all accounts, was a success.

There was only one downside to the picnic, and it was only a minor by-product, affecting no one but her.

She'd been riding high for almost the entire duration

of the picnic. First because Chance had stayed, as she'd asked him to, and then because he had acted like the perfect hero, offering to stand by her. But now Chloe began to examine her feelings for Chance as well as what she'd hoped was her developing relationship with him.

The conclusion she came to was that any way she looked at it, Chance was too good to be true.

The phrase stunned her, echoing in her brain.

She realized that these were the exact same words her mother had used to describe the man who was her father. The man who had ultimately just run out on her, disappointing her so badly that he had crushed her young heart and prevented her from ever venturing to love anyone again.

That had to have been so emotionally crushing for her mother, Chloe thought. Even so, her mother had refused to crumble. Instead, she became a strong woman who had gone on to make a life for the two of them.

Admittedly, Chloe didn't know what she would have done if she'd been in her mother's place. What she did know was that she never *wanted* to be in her mother's place.

Too good to be true.

The phrase continued to echo in her head each time she looked at Chance. How could she expect a man like him to remain with her? To love her?

She knew the inevitable answer to that.

There was something she needed to do, Chloe decided, if she didn't want to be hurt the way her mother had been. She needed to make a preemptive strike in order to save herself.

* * *

The thought haunted her for the next few days, growing progressively larger and larger in her mind until it felt as if there was nothing else on her mind except for that.

"Miss Elliott? Are you okay?"

Chloe realized that she'd allowed her thoughts to get the better of her—again. It had been happening to her for days. In this case, instead of listening to Will and responding, she'd drifted off.

She looked at the boy apologetically. She couldn't afford to jeopardize the progress he and the others had made by allowing herself to become obsessed with her personal life. That wasn't fair to the boys, and it just wasn't right.

"I'm sorry, Will. I'm afraid I was just thinking about something."

"Yeah, I can tell." A shy smile curved the boy's mouth. "I asked you a question three times and you didn't answer."

Chloe looked at him, appalled. "Three times? That's unforgivable," she told the teen.

"Well, maybe it was two," he admitted, shrugging his thin shoulders. "But you did look like you were really far away. Anything I can help with?"

How far the teen had come, she thought. She was proud of having had a hand in his progress. She didn't want to be the cause of its undoing. "No, but you're a doll for asking."

Will flushed. "You're not going to call me that in

front of the other guys, are you?" he asked, clearly horrified at the possibility.

She struggled not to laugh at the look on his face. "Your secret's safe with me, Will," she assured him, then, in case there was a question, she added, "*All* of your secrets are safe with me. You know that."

Will nodded. Their session was over and he had homework waiting for him, so he needed to go.

"Yeah, that's what you said when we started these things," he said, referring to the sessions as he got up. And then he stopped to look at her. "Um, Miss Elliott, you know that goes both ways, right?"

"I'm not sure I understand, Will," Chloe admitted.

Rather than just retreat, the way he would have a few short weeks ago, Will tried to explain. "What I'm trying to say is that if you've got something you want to talk about to someone, you can talk to me. I'm a good listener," he told her. "And I won't tell anyone anything. I promise."

She was tempted to hug him, but she knew how fragile teen egos were. She didn't want him thinking she regarded him as a child. He was a budding adult. So she kept her arms at her sides and simply told him, "I appreciate that, Will."

Even so, she wasn't about to tell him or any of the boys what was on her mind, especially since it involved Chance.

"But there's nothing I need to talk about," Chloe said.

There was something, though, she thought, that she needed to *do*. And soon.

But it wasn't going to be easy.

* * *

She'd agonized over it the entire day, until it was finally time for what had become a minor ritual: going out riding with Chance at the end of the day. She knew she couldn't put this off any longer. Because the longer she did, the harder it was going to be for her.

When Chance walked into the stable, expecting to go riding with Chloe as he did every late afternoon, he was surprised to see that although she was there, her horse wasn't saddled yet.

"You just get here?" he wanted to know. Even that was unusual for her. Punctuality was a thing for Chloe. She didn't like being late.

As he looked at her, he sensed the tension in the air and couldn't help wondering what was wrong. Rather than push, he waited for her to answer.

"Actually, I've been here for a while, waiting for you." Every word felt as if she was dragging it out of her mouth from the very depths of her soul. And every word tasted bitter on her tongue.

Her answer didn't make any sense to him. He frowned. "But your horse isn't saddled. Something wrong?" he asked, subconsciously trying to brace himself.

She didn't answer his question directly. Instead, Chloe went on to say the hardest words that she had ever had to say. "I don't think that we should go out riding together anymore."

"Okay." He regarded her warily as he spoke. Still, he had to go on as if everything was all right. Because he really wanted it to be. "You want to do something else instead?" Almost every time they went out, they returned to end their day in the guesthouse, enjoying each other's company to the fullest.

He had a feeling that wasn't going to be the case today, but he still had to ask.

She shook her head. "No, you don't understand. I don't think we should do anything together—including what we do after we go riding," she added, deliberately being vague because she didn't think she could say anything more specific without breaking down. As it was, she was fighting back tears. Her throat felt as if it was closing up.

She was looking away. Gently taking her face between his hands, Chance forced her to look up at him. "Have I done something to offend you?"

"No, you've been perfect," she cried, pulling back. Needing to put distance between them. "You've always been perfect."

It almost sounded like an accusation, he thought. One that just didn't make any sense at all. "I don't understand."

Tears were welling up in her eyes, and she looked away, not wanting him to see her cry.

"Please, don't make this any harder than it already is. I just can't see you anymore."

"Did Graham say something?" he asked, trying to make sense out of what was happening. Was there some sort of nonfraternizing rule in place that he didn't know about? If there was, then he'd quit. She meant that much to him.

For the first time in years, he'd been able to get beyond himself, and it was all because of her. And now she was pulling back. It didn't make sense to him, and he needed to know why this was happening.

"No, nobody said anything, and it's not anything you did." Her voice cracked and she tried again. "Please, Chance, don't ask me any more questions."

He felt as if he had been sliced in half, and he had no idea why or even what had gone wrong. All he knew was that he needed to get out of there now, while he could still function.

Before he couldn't move.

"All right," he told her stiffly, "I won't."

It was the last thing he said to her before he walked out.

His voice echoed in the stable long after he left. Just as long as she went on crying.

Chapter Seventeen

It's better this way. It's better this way, you know that. Better to stop this now, before you give away your heart. You know what happens after that.

Chloe kept telling herself that over and over again, and while she believed she had done the right thing, that still didn't make it any easier for her to live with. She tried to keep as busy as possible, but a sadness saturated her every waking moment.

Especially the evenings, which now seemed to last twice as long as they used to.

But the hardest part was running into Chance. Their paths seemed to cross a lot less than they used to, but when they did, she felt an unbearable pain, as if she'd been stabbed by a sword with rusty, jagged edges every time she realized that he was there, somewhere near her space.

When was it going to get better? When was the pain going to go away? She had broken things off with Chance to avoid being hurt and yet, that was exactly what was happening. Pain, raw and devastating, was eating her up from the inside out.

In its own way, this was every bit as difficult to endure as when she'd found that Donnie was no longer going to be part of her life, that he'd never be coming back to her.

Chloe began to second-guess herself. Had she acted too rashly? In trying to avoid heartache, had she unwittingly opened the door and allowed heartache to come into her life?

Chloe had no answers, only more questions.

"How come you don't go riding with Ms. Elliott anymore?" Brandon asked out of the blue one afternoon as he and Chance were in the corral, working on taming a new addition to the herd that Graham had just bought.

Chance had picked Brandon to help him because the teen showed the most promise when it came to working with the horses. His hostility finally under control, Brandon was usually on the quiet side. But that obviously wasn't the case today.

"That's not a question you should be asking me," Chance told him.

"I thought you told me that I could ask you anything," Brandon said innocently.

The horse was fighting the bit he was trying to put

into its mouth. For the moment, Chance stopped to look at Brandon. "About your own life, not mine."

"Well, since I've been here, you've become part of my life," Brandon pointed out. "You and Miss Elliott." Determined to get an answer, he tried again. "So how come you don't go riding together anymore?"

"It's just better this way," Chance told the teen dismissively, hoping that would be the end of it.

It wasn't.

"Doesn't seem better," Brandon observed after several minutes. He stroked the stallion's muzzle, doing what he could to keep the animal calm as Chance made another attempt to put the bit into the stallion's mouth. "Seems like both of you look real unhappy. If things were better, you two wouldn't look like that."

Chance sighed. *No arguing with that*, he thought. "It's complicated."

"That's what people say when they don't want to talk about something—or admit that they're wrong about something," Brandon added. "From where I'm sitting," he continued when Chance made no comment, "it doesn't look complicated at all. You were happy riding together, and now you're not riding together and you're not happy. Seems to me like you were both better off riding."

The third attempt to get the horse to accept the bit succeeded. Chance paused, not wanting to rush things with the stallion.

"Yeah, well, that's not going to happen," he told Brandon as he fed the horse a lump of sugar. "Get the blanket."

Brandon did as he was told, hurrying to the fence where the blanket hung and then back again. He held it out to Chance, along with more advice. "You could tell her you're sorry."

Chance handed the reins to the teen and spread the blanket on the horse's back. The stallion remained relatively still. "What?"

There was a warning note in Chance's voice, but Brandon pushed on anyway.

"If you made her angry," Brandon explained, "you could tell her you're sorry. Women like it when you tell them you're sorry."

The assertion by one so young made Chance laugh. "And how would you know that?"

"That's what my brother told me," Brandon said matter-of-factly. "You know what else he told me?"

Chance paused. He realized that this was a breakthrough for Brandon. Up until now, the teen hadn't talked about the brother he'd lost. He'd acted on the anger he felt because of the loss, but he had never mentioned Blake in a day-to-day context, never even referred to him.

There was a momentary tug-of-war within him, and then Chance decided to set aside his need for privacy, putting Brandon's need to heal and progress ahead of his own. "No, what else did he tell you?"

A distant, wistful look came over the teen's face as he no doubt thought of his brother. "That if you want something, sometimes you've got to fight for it. That if something just falls into your lap, it doesn't mean nearly as much as it does if you have to go out and fight for it."

Brandon grew very solemn as he recalled his brother's words. "That's what Blake told me when I asked him why he enlisted instead of going to college like he was supposed to. He said he had to fight for what he believed in. Maybe that's what you need to do," Brandon concluded, looking at him. "Maybe you need to fight for Miss Elliott."

Chance shook his head. "I don't think Miss Elliott wants me to fight for—"

"I think she's looking pretty sad lately," Brandon stressed. "And Will said she keeps losing her train of thought during his sessions. Ryan says the same thing," he added. "Maybe like she's always saying, you need to talk about it. About whatever it is that made the two of you stop doing what you both liked doing." The teen gave Chance an encouraging smile. "Might make you both feel better about things if you clear the air."

Chance looked at the boy he had been trying to reach for weeks now. The boy who had just now tried to reach him instead.

"It just might at that," he agreed. "But right now, we've got a horse to work with."

"I don't think he'd mind waiting," Brandon speculated.

"Get the saddle." He indicated where he'd placed it on the top rung of the corral. "Always finish a job you start."

"That's a good one," Brandon said, nodding with approval as he went to fetch the saddle. "You might want to remember that one when you go talk to Miss Elliott later," he suggested.

Chance grinned as he took the saddle from Brandon and placed it carefully on the stallion's back. The horse tried to pull away, but Brandon was holding firmly on to the bit, keeping the animal in place. Chance slowly tightened the cinch, watching the horse intently.

"I might at that," Chance agreed.

For the first time since he'd arrived at Peter's Place, he saw Brandon grin.

"Come in," Chloe said in response to the knock on the door of her small office.

When she looked up from her work, she was surprised. Expecting to see one of the boys coming in for what she assumed was an extra session, she found herself looking up at Chance instead.

Her heart leaped, and she felt the definite rush of adrenaline surge through her veins before she managed to tuck it away and get it under control. She wasn't supposed to be reacting to Chance like this anymore, she upbraided herself. Especially since in the days that followed her breaking it off with him, Chance hadn't attempted to approach her, not even once. That convinced her that her so-called preemptive strike in pushing Chance out of her life before he walked out on her had been the right move. Because if he'd actually cared about her—even a little—he would have at least *tried* to get back into her life, tried to get her to give him a second chance.

But he hadn't.

Instead, he'd kept his distance. Even at the table,

when they took their meals, he didn't say even two words to her. A man who cared didn't behave that way.

A man who was glad things were over, however, did.

Not waiting for Chance to say anything that she might not want to hear, she took the lead. Doing her best to sound cheerful, she said, "I hear congratulations are in order."

For a moment, because he was still trying to sort his thoughts out and find the right words to say to her, Chance didn't know what she was referring to. He looked at her, puzzled. "For what?"

"For getting Graham to approve your idea. He seemed very enthusiastic about it," she added, recalling the look on her brother's face when he told her the news.

Because of what he'd been going through, Chance had almost forgotten that his proposal had been approved. Graham had gotten the funding, and plans were under way for expanding Peter's Place to include a military equine therapy center for returning vets. "Oh. Right. Thanks."

She would have thought that he would be happy about his victory. Why wasn't he? "Well, you don't sound like you're nearly as excited about it as Graham is," Chloe observed.

"Right now, that's not the main thing on my mind," Chance admitted, his eyes meeting hers.

She wished he wouldn't look at her like that. It made her remember. And yearn. She had to keep herself from squirming.

"Is there something I can help you with?" Chloe asked stiffly.

She sounded like a robot, Chance thought. Was it because he was here? He began having second thoughts about the whole thing. Maybe this wasn't such a good idea.

But he *was* here now, so he might as well say what he'd come to say. He knew Brandon would ask him about it. Just as he knew that he had to give this one final try so that he knew he had done all he could before giving up on the situation.

On her.

On them.

Here goes nothing. "You can help me understand why you suddenly decided to pull back. I thought things were going pretty well," he told her, forcing himself to be honest about his feelings. "I realize that I don't measure up to your late husband, but—"

She stared at him, stunned. "Wait, what? Who told you about Donnie?" she wanted to know. She had never said anything about her late husband to Chance, never mentioned how distraught she'd felt about losing him. How had he found out?

Chance didn't see how that was the point, but he answered her question. "Sasha told me. Don't blame her, I made her tell me. I asked if you were involved with anyone. I thought maybe that was why you didn't want to go riding with me anymore. Or anything else for that matter," he added meaningfully.

He'd missed being with her more than he could possibly say, but it was hard for him to actually admit that. "She told me that you were devastated by your husband's death."

He'd done his homework, contacted people he knew, people he hadn't spoken to in years and asked questions about the man.

"I know I don't measure up to him in your eyes, but I don't want to take his place. I just want to be with you." She was seated at her desk, and he stood over her now, looking down into her face as he searched for an answer. "Why can't I be with you?"

"Because you're perfect," she blurted out, "and before long, you'll realize that you can do a lot better than me and you'll move on. I just can't take dealing with loss again," she informed him, sadly adding, "This way is better."

His thoughts had come to a grinding halt several sentences ago. "Hold it. You think I'm *perfect*?" he questioned incredulously. "You're pulling my leg, right? I mean, you can't be serious." He was as far from perfect as a man could be, Chance thought.

"Of course I'm serious," she told him. "Why wouldn't I be?"

"Well, for one thing, because I'm not perfect," he told her with a disparaging laugh. Thinking back on the image he'd portrayed to her, he realized how he might have misled her. "I just wanted you to see the best in me because a really classy lady like you isn't going to want to be with any ol' cowboy, especially one that's got his own set of demons."

Despite everything, she couldn't help the smile that rose to her lips. Couldn't keep it from curving the corners of her mouth.

"Haven't you heard?" she asked him. "That's what

I do. I exorcise demons." Her smile faded a little as she grew more serious. "But you never indicated that you were anything but a tall, silent cowboy, the kind that used to be in all those old Westerns that they made in the fifties and sixties."

"A cowboy, yeah," he scoffed. "A cowboy who fought overseas."

Why would he think that changed anything in the way she saw him? "At least you got to come back."

He didn't see that as a plus. It was more like his cross to bear. "At times, I really feel that I shouldn't have."

That made absolutely no sense to her. "Why?" she cried.

He told her what weighed most heavily on his conscience, something he hadn't shared with anyone since he'd returned stateside.

"Because I couldn't save my best friend," he confessed. "Evan and I had been friends since grammar school. We enlisted together, did everything together." His mouth felt dry as he relived his friend's final moments. "Evan got between me and enemy fire. He died in my place, in my arms. And I haven't been able to find a place for myself since." Chance took a breath, and then he looked down at her. She had made the difference in his life. "Until I met you."

"But when I said that we shouldn't be together, you just accepted it," she pointed out. "If I meant that much to you, why did you just back off and not even *try* to get me to change my mind?"

He wasn't the type to push himself on anyone. "Because that's what I thought you wanted, and I wanted you to be happy even if I wasn't."

That sounded like him, she realized. "What changed your mind?"

He laughed softly to himself before answering. "Brandon."

"Brandon?" she repeated. Brandon hardly talked now that he had stopped being angry at the world. "What could he have possibly said to change your mind?"

"He noticed how unhappy I looked. How unhappy we both looked," Chance emphasized. "Then he told me something his brother told him."

"His brother? He opened up about Blake?" Chloe asked, stunned and excited at this breakthrough. Brandon had been her last holdout.

"Yes, he did. He told me that his brother told him very simply that if he wanted something, really wanted it, he should go for it. Fight for it." Chance paused, looking at her pointedly. "So this is me, 'fighting for it.'" He took her hands in his and brought her up to her feet. "Fighting for you." He drew her into his arms and bent his head, kissing her.

Chance's kiss felt as if the sun had suddenly come out after days of being hidden behind a dreary rain cloud. This was what she'd missed, what she'd longed for.

What she'd *needed*.

She kissed Chance with all the bottled-up passion she'd been trying to convince herself she no longer felt. Wrapping her arms around his neck, she clung to him for a moment, her lips sealed to his.

When he finally drew back, he smiled into her eyes.

"Does this mean you'll go riding with me again?" he asked. There was a trace of mischief in his eyes.

"It does," she told him.

Maybe he was pushing his luck, but he still wanted to ask. "Does this also mean that you'll—"

Her eyes danced as she cried, "Yes."

He laughed. She was getting ahead of herself. "I haven't finished asking you the question."

The smile that lit up her features was warm, sunny. And oh, so relieved. "I have an idea I know what's coming."

"I have an idea that you don't," he told her. He knew he had to get this out before his courage deserted him, and he really wished he had something to give her to seal this moment. "Chloe Elliott, I don't have much to offer you—"

How could he even think that? "You're wrong," she told him. "You have a great deal to offer."

"Don't interrupt," he said. "I have to get this out before I lose my nerve."

"All right," she told him, her heart pounding madly. It wasn't easy for her to keep quiet, but she did her best. "Go on."

He started again. "I don't have much to offer you, but I love you and I'll do everything in my power to make you happy—and to never regret marrying me." He stumbled a little, his thoughts getting in the way of his tongue. "That is, if you *want* to marry me." He blew out a breath. "This isn't coming out the way I want it to. Talking isn't what I do best."

She was nothing if not encouraging. "You're doing great so far."

He took a long breath. If he talked any more, he'd mess it up. "I'm finished," he told her. "You can answer now if you'd like."

"I like," Chloe told him with all sincerity. "I like very much."

Maybe this wasn't a total disaster after all. "So will you marry me?" he wanted to know.

Her eyes crinkled as she laughed. "What do you think?"

She was drawing this out, and he couldn't stand the tension pulsating through him. "I think I'm going to have heart failure if you don't answer me in the next couple of seconds."

She kept as straight a face as she could. "I don't know CPR, so I guess I'd better say yes." And then every single part of her being grinned. "Yes, I'll marry you. Yes, yes, yes," she cried, throwing her arms around his neck again.

"I heard you the first time," he answered, gathering her in his arms.

"I wanted to be sure you did."

"I did," he answered, then added, "I do," before he kissed her again.

And, just to be sure that she wasn't going to change her mind, he went on kissing her for a long time.

Epilogue

"So, how did it feel to find out that your father is one of the famous Fortunes?"

The question came from Ariana Lamonte, the magazine writer and blogger who had already interviewed several of Gerald Robinson's children.

They were sitting in the living room of the guesthouse where Chloe was presently living, and the vivacious reporter had already asked her a number of probing questions.

At first, Chloe had thought she was just going to avoid the woman, but after the reporter had called her a number of times in the last few days, Ariana didn't give her the impression that she was about to give up until she got what she wanted. And besides, submitting to the interview seemed almost like an initiation into the family. Others had done it, and if her responses and feelings were put down on record, then by all rights that made her a part of the family, as well.

"It felt strange," Chloe admitted, answering Ariana's last question.

The woman's fingers flew over her small laptop, making notes as thoughts occurred to her.

She looked up at Chloe, giving her a sympathetic smile. "That's right, he was AWOL for most of your life, wasn't he?"

"Not most," Chloe corrected. *"All."*

Ariana nodded, her keyboard clicking rhythmically as she made more notes. "So what did you think of him when you two finally met?"

"We haven't." When Ariana looked at her sharply, she added, "Yet."

"But you're going to, right?" the woman with the long brown hair and the animated, deep brown eyes pressed. "Now that you know who he is, you can't just *not* meet the man," Ariana insisted.

"There's been talk about setting something up, yes," Chloe replied vaguely.

And there was. Gerald Robinson had actually reached out to her. But, still harboring anger over the way the man had treated her mother, Chloe was in no hurry to meet her father face-to-face. She had stalled.

"Aren't you at least curious what he's like?" Ariana wanted to know.

She supposed she was somewhat curious. She wouldn't be human if she wasn't. "Maybe a little," she admitted.

Ariana laughed. She paused and reached over to

lightly touch Chloe's hand. "Well, if it were me and my absentee daddy had all that money—"

"I don't care about the money," Chloe told her, cutting the woman off.

Ariana could only shake her head. "Well, you're a better person than most," she confided.

Chloe set her jaw. "There are some things that money can't pay for. But I will give him a chance to explain why he did what he did—if he actually has a reason."

Ariana smiled warmly at the young woman sitting across from her. "You're a good person, Chloe Elliott. Or would you rather I called you Chloe Fortune? Some of your siblings have taken on the name," the reporter said.

"I'd rather you just called me Chloe," she told the reporter.

"I think I'd like that," Ariana replied. She closed her laptop. "Well, I think I have everything I need," she said, concluding the interview as she rose to her feet. "If I think of any further questions, I'll give you a call. And after you meet your father face-to-face, I'd appreciate it if you give *me* a call," she requested.

Chloe accompanied her to the door.

"Thanks for your time," Ariana told her. "I'll email you a copy of the interview when it's finished."

As she began to walk out, the woman nearly collided with Chance, who was just about to knock on Chloe's door.

"I can see why you were in a hurry to wrap this interview up," Ariana said, looking appreciatively at the tall cowboy, then gave Chloe a grin. "Maybe I'll see you again."

The moment the reporter crossed the threshold and left the house, Chance closed the door behind her. He flipped the lock in place.

"So, how was it?" he asked Chloe, turning to face her.

"Not as bad as I thought," Chloe confessed. "She was nice. She asked a lot of questions, but I think that I managed to hold my own."

"I knew you would," Chance told her. He pressed a kiss to her temple as he gave Chloe a quick, warm embrace.

"Well, that puts you one up on me." She looked away from the door and turned her face up to Chance. She knew he had just come from a meeting with Graham about the planned expansion. "So, tell me," she urged, waiting for him to share his news.

"Everything's in motion," he told her happily. "With any luck, the military *equine*—" he deliberately drew the word out to emphasize it "—therapy center will be opening ahead of schedule. I can't tell you how good that makes me feel."

"Oh, I think I can guess," she told him, amusement dancing in her eyes.

He knew he needed to put this in perspective for her. He wanted her to understand just what she meant to him. "Almost as good as knowing that you're actually going to be marrying me. You still are, aren't you?" he asked, closing his arms around her.

Chloe's smile was wide and warm. "Try to stop me," she told him with a laugh.

"Now, why would I want to do that?" he questioned as if she had just suggested something completely absurd. "My mamma didn't raise any stupid children."

"Good. Neither did mine. Wanna go for a ride?" she asked him.

"Why don't we skip going for a ride today?" he suggested. "And just go straight to the good part."

"I thought you once told me that riding was the good part," she reminded him.

"I did and it was—until I met you and found a whole other way to feel good." He pulled her tighter. "No more talking," he said as he lowered his mouth to hers.

One touch of his lips had desire streaking through her. "No more talking," she agreed.

So they didn't.

* * * * *

0317/23

MILLS & BOON®

EXCLUSIVE EXTRACT

Griffin Fletcher never imagined he'd see his
childhood sweetheart Eva Hennessey again,
but now he's eager to discover her secret—
one that will change their worlds forever!

Read on for a sneak preview of
REUNITED BY A BABY BOMBSHELL

A baby. A daughter, given up for adoption.

The stark pain in Eva's face when she'd seen their
child. His own huge feelings of isolation and loss.

If only he'd known. If only Eva had told him. He'd
deserved to know.

And what would you have done? his conscience whispered.

It was a fair enough question.

Realistically, what would he have done at the age of
eighteen? He and Eva had both been so young, scarcely
out of school, both ambitious, with all their lives ahead
of them. He hadn't been remotely ready to think about
settling down, or facing parenthood, let alone lasting
love or matrimony.

And yet he'd been hopelessly crazy about Eva, so
chances were…

Dragging in a deep breath of sea air, Griff shook his
head. It was way too late to trawl through what might
have been. There was no point in harbouring regrets.

But what about now?

How was he going to handle this new situation? Laine, a lovely daughter, living in his city, studying law. The thought that she'd been living there all this time, without his knowledge, did his head in.

And Eva, as lovely and hauntingly bewitching as ever, sent his head spinning too, sent his heart taking flight.

He'd never felt so side-swiped. So torn. One minute he wanted to turn on his heel and head straight back to Eva's motel room, to pull her into his arms and taste those enticing lips of hers. To trace the shape of her lithe, tempting body with his hands. To unleash the longing that was raging inside him, driving him crazy.

Next minute he came to his senses and knew that he should just keep on walking. Now. Walk out of the Bay. All the way back to Brisbane.

And then, heaven help him, he was wanting Eva again. Wanting her desperately.

Damn it. He was in for a very long night.

Don't miss
REUNITED BY A BABY BOMBSHELL
by Barbara Hannay

Available April 2017
www.millsandboon.co.uk

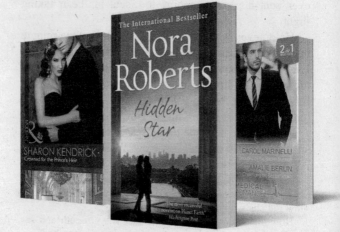

MILLS & BOON®

Congratulations
Carol Marinelli
on your 100th Mills & Boon book!

Read on for an exclusive extract

How did she walk away? Lydia wondered.

How did she go over and kiss that sulky mouth and say goodbye when really she wanted to climb back into bed?

But rather than reveal her thoughts she flicked that internal default switch which had been permanently set to 'polite'.

'Thank you so much for last night.'

'I haven't finished being your tour guide yet.'

He stretched out his arm and held out his hand but Lydia didn't go over. She did not want to let in hope, so she just stood there as Raul spoke.

'It would be remiss of me to let you go home without seeing Venice as it should be seen.'

'Venice?'

'I'm heading there today. Why don't you come with me? Fly home tomorrow instead.'

There was another night between now and then, and Lydia knew that even while he offered her an extension he made it clear there was a cut-off.

Time added on for good behaviour.

And Raul's version of 'good behaviour' was that there would

be no tears or drama as she walked away. Lydia knew that. If she were to accept his offer then she had to remember that.

'I'd like that.' The calm of her voice belied the trembling she felt inside. 'It sounds wonderful.'

'Only if you're sure?' Raul added.

'Of course.'

But how could she be sure of anything now she had set foot in Raul's world?

He made her dizzy.

Disorientated.

Not just her head, but every cell in her body seemed to be spinning as he hauled himself from the bed and unlike Lydia, with her sheet-covered dash to the bathroom, his body was hers to view.

And that blasted default switch was stuck, because Lydia did the right thing and averted her eyes.

Yet he didn't walk past. Instead Raul walked right over to her and stood in front of her.

She could feel the heat—not just from his naked body but her own—and it felt as if her dress might disintegrate.

He put his fingers on her chin, tilted her head so that she met his eyes, and it killed that he did not kiss her, nor drag her back to his bed. Instead he checked again. 'Are you sure?'

'Of course,' Lydia said, and tried to make light of it. 'I never say no to a free trip.'

It was a joke but it put her in an unflattering light. She was about to correct herself, to say that it hadn't come out as she had meant, but then she saw his slight smile and it spelt approval.

A gold-digger he could handle, Lydia realised.

Her emerging feelings for him—perhaps not.

At every turn her world changed, and she fought for a semblance of control. Fought to convince not just Raul but herself that she could handle this.

Join Britain's BIGGEST Romance Book Club

- **EXCLUSIVE offers every month**
- **FREE delivery direct to your door**
- **NEVER MISS a title**
- **EARN Bonus Book points**

Call Customer Services
0844 844 1358*

or visit
millsandboon.co.uk/subscriptions

* This call will cost you 7 pence per minute plus your phone company's price per minute access charge.